The
PRESIDENT'S
WIFE

BOOKS BY ANNA STUART

The Berlin Zookeeper
The Secret Diary
A Letter from Pearl Harbor
The English Wife

WOMEN OF WAR
The Midwife of Auschwitz
The Midwife of Berlin
The War Orphan
The Secret Message

THE BLETCHLEY PARK GIRLS
The Bletchley Girls
Code Name Elodie

The PRESIDENT'S WIFE

ANNA STUART

bookouture

Published by Bookouture in 2025

An imprint of Storyfire Ltd.
Carmelite House
50 Victoria Embankment
London EC4Y 0DZ

www.bookouture.com

The authorised representative in the EEA is Hachette Ireland
8 Castlecourt Centre
Dublin 15 D15 XTP3
Ireland
(email: info@hbgi.ie)

Copyright © Anna Stuart, 2025

Anna Stuart has asserted her right to be identified
as the author of this work.

All rights reserved. No part of this publication may be reproduced, stored in any retrieval system, or transmitted, in any form or by any means, electronic, mechanical, photocopying, recording or otherwise, without the prior written permission of the publishers.

ISBN: 978-1-83618-233-7
eBook ISBN: 978-1-83618-232-0

This book is a work of fiction. Whilst some characters and circumstances portrayed by the author are based on real people and historical fact, references to real people, events, establishments, organizations or locales are intended only to provide a sense of authenticity and are used fictitiously. All other characters and all incidents and dialogue are drawn from the author's imagination and are not to be construed as real.

*In loving memory of Grandma—Courtney Swiggett Gibb
I wish we'd had more of you.*

PROLOGUE
WASHINGTON, MARCH 4, 1933

Eleanor stands at the window of her new bedroom, in her new home, and looks out at her new view. She's been imagining this for years, picturing it to guide her through the tough times, but now she's here, it feels unreal. She knows the house is not hers. It's on loan. In trust.

She lifts a sheet of writing paper from her new desk and runs a finger over the embossed address:

THE WHITE HOUSE

1600 PENNSYLVANIA AVENUE

WASHINGTON DC

Tomorrow, her secretary, Malvina Thompson, will report at 8 a.m., as always, and together they will start to reply to the many, many letters of congratulations. Perhaps then it will feel real. Perhaps then she will comfortably sign her name: Eleanor Roosevelt, First Lady of America.

Or perhaps not.

This was always her husband's dream. Franklin was the one with his eye on the White House. She would never have dared to presume such a lofty address for herself, though she'd been here often enough as a youngster, when her Uncle Ted had held the presidency. She'd seen, first-hand, what hard work it was, though she's never been afraid of hard work so perhaps it was more the responsibility of it that struck her—the sense that, by entering this hallowed residence, you took the nation in your hands.

Eleanor puts her fingers to the glass. It's cold to her touch, solid—real. She is truly here, at the end of a path that has been long and winding and thick with thorns. The first time she heard Franklin mention his ambitions for the White House was on their wedding day. They giggled over it together, not quite believing their own daring, but giddy enough with love to believe themselves capable of anything. Well, marriage has proved rockier than she could ever have imagined but she is still here, so maybe the presidency will be the same. Perhaps persistence is all it really takes. Persistence, belief and courage. Plenty of courage.

They'll need it. There is the Depression to mend, and she hopes Franklin's "New Deal," creating jobs for the masses, will do so. Over in Europe, a man called Adolf Hitler has propelled himself into power in embittered Germany and is dealing with their Depression in a very different way, loudly promising "restitution" via a series of harsh, militant methods, in total opposition to all they want to do in America. Which way will be right? Love, or fear? Eleanor knows which she would back every day of the week, but the world doesn't always see things the same way she does.

Now, at least, Franklin might be able to do something about it. And she—well, she can help. It might be his dream, but she is in it with him. Beyond the window, across the lawns, she can make out the Washington Monument, tall and proud against the milky sky, and, as she lets her eyes accustom themselves to the dark, she sees a small red light twinkling on the top, as if saying hello.

"Hello," she whispers back. "Hello. I'm here. I'm really here."

The White House might not be her house, but at the moment she is lucky enough to make it her home. The American people have entrusted the country to Franklin and herself and she intends to repay that trust with every attempt to bring light to the current darkness. It will require hard work, and it will require teamwork. The former she has never been afraid of; the latter... Her personal 'team' with Franklin took a hard knock a long time ago and whilst they've held it together to get this far, she can only pray that the strains of the Presidency do not break them apart once more.

PART ONE

ONE

HYDE PARK, UPSTATE NEW YORK, SEPTEMBER 2, 1939

The urgent buzzing penetrated Eleanor's sleep like a nightmarish insect and she put out a hand to ward it off.

"Mrs. R! Mrs. R, wake up, it's Mr. R calling from Washington."

Summoning up willpower from the depths of her consciousness, Eleanor forced her eyes open to find Malvina Thompson holding out the phone receiver. She blinked, amused to see "Tommy," her sturdy, middle-aged secretary, in pretty pink pajamas, then realized this could only be bad news.

Rubbing a hand over her face, she took the phone. "Franklin?"

"Babs!" The familiar nickname (a shortening of the fond "baby" he had called her once upon a time) rattled at her heart.

"Are you all right, Franklin?"

"Me? Fine, yes. Except that I thought you were never going to answer."

"But it's..." She squinted at the clock on her bedside table, faintly lit by the thin threads of dawn shining through the windows of her sleeping porch. "5 a.m."

"Not in Europe," Franklin said.

Instantly Eleanor was awake. She pushed herself up, glancing out across the familiar landscape of her corner of the Hyde Park estate in upstate New York. The Roosevelts' land stretched over a thousand acres from the Hudson River, incorporating Springwood, the fine family mansion, Top Cottage, Franklin's retreat on the peak of the hill, and her own Val Kill residence at its foot, named for the prettily babbling stream that flowed past it. She'd come here for a much-needed rest, but leaving the White House was always a worry.

"What's happened?" she demanded. "Has Hitler declared himself?"

"In the worst possible way, yes. He's invaded Poland."

"Poland? The country Britain and France have sworn to defend?"

"Exactly. You always put your finger on the nub of the matter, my dear. Chamberlain has given them until 11 a.m. on the third to retreat or he'll declare war."

War: the word seemed to boom around her cottage and she shivered at it.

"Hitler won't retreat, Franklin."

"No. Hitler will only advance, wherever his damned Panzer tanks can crush a way."

Outside the windows, the top of the sun showed itself over the trees to the east and peach-warm rays slid along the stream. Beyond, a deer looked up as a rabbit stirred the long grass. Eleanor watched the peaceful scene, battling to imagine the carnage that must be ensuing on the other side of the world.

She remembered Hitler coming to power in Germany at much the same time as Franklin had taken the reins here in America. In the six years since, Eleanor had traveled as much of America as she could and met a great variety of people. Some of them had such different lives to her own that it could feel a little scary, but the moment you got stuck in and talked to them— *listened* to them—you found out they were folk like any other, with their own sets of hopes and worries. Segregation on the basis of race, gender, or any other damn man-made distinction, seemed to Eleanor to be the lowest form of bullying. And Hitler was most definitely the lowest form of bully.

Eleanor tutted at herself. It was easy to dismiss him as a madman from this side of the Atlantic, but he was dangerous. He was closing down Jewish businesses, forcing the poor people into ghettos, and he was systematically killing the disabled, saying they weakened society. Good God above, if he had power over here, he'd be wiping out Franklin and his polio-withered legs, and then where would they all be?

Her heart clenched and she threw back the covers; this was no time to be idling in bed. Downstairs, she could hear Tommy making coffee, so she grabbed her dressing gown and followed the long telephone cord down to the living room.

"Have you got a radio there?" Franklin was asking.

"Of course I have a radio. You know that."

"I know that," he agreed. "Sorry. I'm dopey. Missy woke me with a call from our ambassador in Paris half an hour ago. He's in a state. Says the French are panicking."

"The French have the best army in the world."

"I'm not sure it's feeling that way right now."

"And the Maginot Line," she said. "They have still got the Maginot Line, Franklin?"

"For the moment."

Tommy came into the living room with two steaming mugs of coffee and Eleanor gratefully accepted one as she switched on the radio.

"What channel am I looking for?"

"Any German channel. Hitler's addressing the Reichstag. It'll be on all of them."

Hand shaking annoyingly, Eleanor turned the dial, feeling her way through the static until she located the wavelength of a station in Berlin and Hitler's brash voice boomed from the set in staccato German. She spoke the language well from her three years in international boarding school, but she had to concentrate hard to cope with the poor sound quality of the Nazi dictator spitting hate in his cavernous parliament. Franklin, too, could speak German well, but she translated it in snippets for Tommy, hating the words that came from her lips.

Hitler blamed the "intolerable" taking of Danzig from the Germans after the Great War, putting the blame squarely on Poland for stealing this precious piece of coastline, then he announced an alliance with Russia. She heard Franklin moan, but had to stay focused: "I am, from now on, the first soldier of the German Reich," she translated. "I have once more put on the uniform that was the most sacred and dear to me. I will not take it off again until victory is secured, or I will not survive the outcome."

"Hopefully someone shoots the son-of-a-bitch right now," Tommy commented.

"Fat chance," Franklin said mournfully.

Eleanor shushed them. Hitler was promising not to attack women and children, although swiftly added that, "if the enemy should decide he might get away with waging war in a different manner he will be knocked out of his wits." It was fighting talk from a man preparing for vicious warfare. "Whoever fights with poison gas will be fought with poison gas, whoever disregards the rules of human warfare can expect us to do the same."

"He's lining up his excuses," Tommy said indignantly.

It was hard to argue. Hitler was building himself into a frenzied climax that chilled Eleanor's bones. "I want to tell the whole world: never again will there be a November 1918 in German history. One word I have never known: capitulation."

"He's saying he won't stop," Franklin said, as cheers rang out across the Reichstag and down the line to America. "He won't stop ever. That means until he's taken Europe—until he's taken the whole world."

Eleanor, sullied by speaking Hitler's hate-filled words, looked slowly around her cozy living room. Franklin had built this cottage for her back in the 1920s when… well, when Eleanor had been finding herself some much-needed independence. He'd given her the land, in the far corner of the Hyde Park estate, and designed the buildings himself. A "gift" he'd called it, though "peace offering" might have been a fairer designation. Not that she wanted to dwell on that. There were far more important concerns. While she sat in her happy home, others, on the borders of a land not so very different, were being chased from theirs in the most brutal of ways.

"It's hard to imagine war," she said, turning off the radio and blinking at the merry birdsong flooding incongruously into the room.

"That's because we've never experienced it," Franklin said. "Even when I went over in 1918, I was safe on a ship."

"Not so safe—you caught Spanish flu."

Franklin's breath hitched and Eleanor knew he was remembering, as she was, the awful time of his illness and all it had brought. Coming home from the Great War, twenty-one years ago, he had almost died in the brutal epidemic. For three days and nights he had battled a terrible fever but it had not, in the end, been the worst thing about those dark days. The worst thing had been the letters she'd discovered—scented with violets and bound with ribbon and bringing a painful, crashing end to their intimacy.

But not, she reminded herself sternly, their partnership. They had battled to save that and it had carried them through two successful terms. There was a year until the next elections, when Franklin would surely be ousted from the White House, but he was there right now and it seemed there was still vital work to be done.

"Never again will there be a November 1918 in German history." Eleanor repeated Hitler's vow in a dark voice. It was a clever bid from the self-proclaimed Führer, appealing to the wounded pride of his beleaguered nation as he had done again and again over the last six years.

"We said, didn't we, Franklin, that the terms of the peace were too harsh on Germany? We said she would need to recoup, to rebuild."

"No one was listening to us back then, Babs."

"But they are now."

"They are now."

Eleanor closed her eyes and pictured her husband in his bedroom in the White House. Soon his valet would help him up and dress him to head into the Oval Office, the hub of world politics. Later, he would have to address a Congress determined to stay out of the war. As if war worked that way! Eleanor hated fighting as much as anyone, but that didn't mean she couldn't see it coming. The isolationists were like children, believing that if they put their hands over their eyes, their enemies would not be there. But this was Hitler—he would take their candy from them while they sat, innocently believing themselves safe. And then he would take their liberty, their precious constitution and, most likely, their lives. Not yet, perhaps, but one day, when his neighbors had all fallen.

"The poor King," Eleanor gasped out. Last summer, she and Franklin had hosted King George V of Great Britain, a shy man with a quiet charm and a clear sense of duty who had clearly been worried for his country. Eleanor pictured him sitting at the barbecue they'd held for him and his lovely wife, Queen Elizabeth, right here in Hyde Park. He'd been chatty and entertaining, gamely eating the hot dog Franklin had embarrassingly pressed upon him; now he was facing war.

"We should invite them over here," she suggested.

"They wouldn't come."

"How do you know?"

"We talked about it. King George said Parliament would

not let him fight, but they could not make him leave. He's a brave man, my dear."

"He's going to have to be."

"Yes."

They sat there, the line buzzing between them. Eleanor could hear bustle around Franklin and knew the country was calling on him. She didn't have long.

"What about the princesses—Elizabeth and Margaret? They're still young, aren't they? Perhaps Queen Elizabeth would like us to look after them?"

"We could offer. Europe is going to be a terrible place to live. Thank God Mama is out."

"She is?" Eleanor asked weakly, trying to avoid Tommy's knowing smirk. Sara Roosevelt had been visiting her sister in Paris for the summer and, although Eleanor obviously didn't want her mother-in-law in danger, it might have been nice if she'd been detained a while.

"I heard from her yesterday that her ship was sailing, so that's a relief, isn't it?"

He sounded so happy that she felt mean—a not unfamiliar emotion when it came to her formidable mother-in-law.

"That's excellent news," she agreed firmly, turning away from Tommy who was making comic gestures. Her dear, down-to-earth secretary found Sara every bit as patronizing and controlling as Eleanor, and felt herself far freer to express her dislike. Not that Eleanor disliked Sara. Her mother-in-law had embraced her as a daughter—a nuisance of a daughter, perhaps, and one trying to treacherously steal away her treasured only son, but a daughter all the same—and for years Eleanor had felt pathetically grateful for it. She was over that now. "I look forward to seeing her here safe," she said smoothly.

Luckily Franklin was distracted. Word was out around the White House and Eleanor could hear his staff arriving. Franklin was shifting from her husband to the President as smoothly as he moved from bed to wheelchair.

"I'll come back to Washington," she said.

"Yes please, Babs."

It was a rare admission of need, but then male voices filled the room and Missy came on to say goodbye.

"Make sure he gets some rest," Eleanor instructed her.

"Of course," Missy said, and Eleanor knew she would, for his secretary cared for him as a man, not as a politician.

With Eleanor, it wasn't so simple. Her world had once revolved around Franklin D. Roosevelt but then he had blown it apart. Now, she focused more on helping everyone else and, really, that was a far, far better thing to do. When the fate of the world was hanging in the balance, what did one woman's trembling heart matter?

TWO

NEW YORK, DECEMBER 1902

Eleanor pulled at the overblown flounces of her dress with hands that were unpleasantly sweaty in the silly long gloves that were "de rigueur" at society balls. She was used to dressing discreetly to mask her over-tall body and felt very uncomfortable in this attention-seeking gown. This time last year, she thought longingly, she'd been at Allenswood school in England, deep in suppertime debate with their inspirational headmistress, Marie Souvestre, who believed girls should "learn to form opinions and speak them with confidence."

Eleanor had never felt more alive than at Allenswood and had blessed her grandmother—in charge of her upbringing after the loss of both parents years before—for sending her to such a liberal establishment. But now here she was, ordered by the same grandmother to stay in America and "come out" in society, as if her education counted for nothing. No one in this room cared about her opinions, only about her looks and her dance skills—neither of which were up to much. The whole evening was going to be a terrible waste of her time.

Eleanor edged toward a wall, the only thing in this crowded ballroom that might hide a girl who topped six foot when shoehorned into uncomfortable heels. Roosevelts were meant to be "belles." Her mother had been celebrated for her beauty and the four cousins Eleanor had come out with were simperingly pretty enough to attract a hundred males to their dance cards within moments of arriving. Not that she wanted to dance, or to drink cocktails, or to gossip with the other young ladies.

She looked longingly to a group of men talking earnestly on the balcony and caught a few drifting words of their conversation —Bloemfontein, Kitchener, Pretoria. They were discussing the ongoing Boer War and, having followed it avidly at school, she took a few steps toward them. But then she was stopped by a skinny young man she vaguely recognized from children's parties. Timothy, was it? Tristan? Something insipid like that.

"Eleanor, you look lovely."

"I look like a child's doll," she shot back crossly.

Timothy/Tristan looked taken aback, but rallied. No doubt he'd heard that she and her brother, Hall, were sole heirs to the Tivoli estate. Her dowry, she knew, was very much the most attractive thing about her and it seemed it was going to doom her to a fumbled foxtrot. How tedious. Still, Grandmother was nodding urgent encouragement from the sidelines so no doubt Timothy/Tristan had a fair-sized estate himself.

"Would you like to dance?" he asked.

"I'd love to," she lied obediently.

The foxtrot was as unbearable as she'd imagined, though, to be fair to her partner, as much because of her clumsiness as his simpering attentions, and she was glad to escape at its conclusion. Feigning a need to visit the ladies' room, she sought the safety of the wall once more but was stopped by a laughing young man who she recognized as Franklin Roosevelt, young scion of another branch of her extended family.

"Saw you getting your feet trodden on by Toby Astor, lucky girl."

"Toby!" she cried. "I knew it was something like that. He was nearly as bad a dancer as me."

"You'd have been fine if you hadn't had to bend down to him."

Eleanor laughed, then looked around guiltily. But no one seemed to be listening and Franklin was leaning attentively toward her, his subtle cologne filling her senses, his blue eyes fixed on hers.

"At least I got on the dance floor," she challenged. "I didn't see you out there."

"I couldn't find a girl to ask. I expect their brothers have warned them off old 'Feather Duster.'"

"Feather Duster?"

"My initials—F.D. Roosevelt. They think I'm a bit of a Mummy's boy."

"Are you?"

"Mama would like to think so," he quipped, then flushed. "I probably am a bit. My father died when I was eighteen and she's looked after me ever since. Other guys my age find me a little dry. I talk politics too much, or so I'm told."

Eleanor snatched at this. "I like politics. What do you think of the Boer War?"

"A nasty waste of everyone's time and resources," he said promptly.

"Quite!" Eleanor agreed, delighted. "Why are men so quick to turn to guns? If they got around the table and had proper, open discussions, they could solve their issues so much more easily."

"They could! Do you know how much the Spanish-America war cost us?" She shook her head. "Two hundred and eighty-three million dollars! Think how far that could go if we invested it in decent housing for the poor."

Eleanor gaped at him.

"You don't agree?" he asked, looking embarrassed. "I know a lot of people think the poor should—"

She caught at his arm. "No! No, I do agree, Franklin."

He stopped and trained his eyes on her once more, not on the flounces on her dress, or the sparkles in her hair, or the size of her dowry, just on her. "Why?" he asked.

"Because if the poor have a decent home, they will have decent health and then they'll be able to get a decent job to keep that home, and the loved ones within it, decent."

Franklin's eyes shone. "You're right, Eleanor. And the same goes at an international level. Everyone would benefit economically if we helped the poor countries to raise themselves up—"

"Instead of invading them and swiping the little they do have."

"And telling them how to behave."

"It's so arrogant, is it not? And so foolish. We need to unite nations, not divide them."

"Yes!" Franklin took her hand. "Yes, exactly! Come and sit down, Eleanor. Let's talk more."

She needed no second urging and, as she slid onto a bench seat with Franklin, the rest of the ballroom foxtrotted into the background where it belonged. Dancing was nice enough, but it didn't matter, did it? The state of the world mattered and in Franklin, it seemed, she had found someone who agreed and, better yet, wanted to discuss it with her.

Perhaps this evening would not be quite as much of a waste of time as she'd feared.

THREE

THE POTOMAC RIVER, MAY 12, 1940

Eleanor tried not to look down at the gangplank as she boarded the USS *Potomac*. This was a luxury yacht, she reminded herself, not an ocean liner, and they were going to chug up the lazy Potomac River, not head onto the high seas. Even so, she couldn't help the churn in her stomach every time she had to go on a boat.

It came from when she'd been three years old and sailing to England with her parents. Everyone said she'd been too young to remember their grand liner colliding with another ship and taking on water, but they were wrong. It was seared into her memory with such clear lines that she could see it now: the rising waves, the churn of the spume, the roll of the boat and then the bells clanging out the alarm. She could smell panic, hear fear and, worst of all, see the lifeboat, as tiny as a toy far below as some burly sailor dangled her over the edge. She could hear her father from below: "You're quite safe, my little Nell. I'll catch you. Daddy will catch you." And he *had* caught her, but only after a terrifying fall through wild, cold, salty air. How would she not remember that?

She'd refused to go on another boat that summer. Her

mother had been furious, calling her a spoiled brat. Father had been kinder, as he always was, and she'd been allowed to stay behind with Grandmother for the summer while her parents had gone to England alone. She'd been sad to be left behind, but, even at three, not prepared to put herself through that hell again. Surely only a fool would have done so?

She reached for the deck-rail to steady herself and heard Polly Delano, Franklin's spiteful cousin, cackling behind her.

"Eleanor, are you seasick?"

"I don't much like boats," Eleanor said stiffly.

"Then why come cruising?"

"Franklin wanted me to."

That wasn't strictly true but Polly was always looking for wedges between her and Franklin and she didn't like to make it easy for her. At fifty-four, Polly was only a year younger than Eleanor, but with her purple-dyed hair and outlandish clothing she carried herself with the panache of a thirty-year-old. It was perhaps because she'd never had children to age her. She'd fallen in love with a Japanese diplomat in her youth but been forbidden to marry him and had so loudly declared all Western men "dull" in comparison that not one had dared to propose. Family rumor held that she was having an affair with her chauffeur but Eleanor suspected the rumor had been put about by Polly herself, who had a dread of being thought boring.

"I'd better go and say hello to my husband," Eleanor said pointedly, stepping around Polly and heading into the grand interior.

Tommy was boarding, typewriter in her arms, and Eleanor longed to turn into her cabin-office to get on with some work. She had an article to write for United Features, and a lecture to plan for later today, but there was someone on this jolly day-trip she very much wanted to talk to, so she must stay focused.

Franklin's floating office was a small room at the back of the dining lounge. She gave a light tap on the wooden door before opening it. Franklin was sitting at his desk with Missy, elegant in green silk, perched on the edge, so close as to be almost on his knee. He was looking up at her as she brushed a stray strand of hair back from his face and Eleanor felt a small barb enter her heart. Or, rather, a barb that had been lodged there since the terrible letters pricked her anew.

She sucked in her breath and Franklin looked over.

"Eleanor!"

He smiled easily, as if all was normal, which of course it was. Normal for them. Since polio had taken away the use of his legs, Franklin needed someone to look after him day in, day out, and Missy was perfect for that. Marguerite LeHand, nicknamed Missy, was the sassy daughter of New York Irish immigrants who'd climbed her way out of her working-class background with charm, style and a real talent for organization. Employed as a secretary by Franklin in the early twenties, when Eleanor had taken on Tommy, she'd become indispensable to him once polio had taken his mobility. Naturally that meant they'd got close, intimate even. How intimate Eleanor did not like to dwell on, but she'd had her own friends. Her own intimates.

And her freedom.

As Franklin was less mobile than most presidents, it was often Eleanor who went to conventions, spoke at dinners, opened factories and christened ships. She was the one on the board of the many Democratic clubs and unions they both believed to be important. She was key to the New York League of Women Voters, the Democratic Party Women's Division, and the Democratic Women's Advisory Committee, and also worked with wider groups like the Women's Trade Union League. It wasn't only women, though. She did what she could with young people as well, especially via the American Youth Congress, and quietly tried to promote the rights of African-Americans with the

National Association for the Advancement of Colored People.

There seemed, to Eleanor, to be so many injustices in the world, and she urgently wanted to right as many of them as possible while she had the chance. Being in the White House helped her to do that and she had a freedom to speak and act that was denied Franklin as President. He was ever-hampered by the need to appease the different elements of the Democratic Party—notably the rigidly conservative southern congressmen—and, as a consummate politician, he did it beautifully.

Such pandering to views other than hers was anathema to Eleanor and luckily she could be more outspoken on the issues that mattered to them both. That way, even if Franklin did nothing, the public knew, through Eleanor, that he was on their side. It was a finely balanced game, and if Eleanor's part in it meant that another woman stroked her husband's hair from his brow, then so be it. Her hair-stroking days had ended with the violet-scented letters and, although she'd mourned them at the time, she was a better woman for it.

She just had to remind herself of that sometimes.

Twisting her wedding band around on her finger, she asked, "Is Mr. Davies on board, Franklin?"

"He is. He's taking tea on the foredeck to watch us cast off."

Eleanor glanced out the windows and saw the deckhands uncoiling the large ropes that bound them to dry land. The boat rocked and she put a hand to the desk to steady herself.

"Seasick?" Franklin asked, but kindly.

"The queasiness is in my head," she assured him. "I'll conquer it."

"Of course you will, my dear, as you conquer everything."

She waved his extravagance away, embarrassed. "All I need to conquer today is Mr. Davies, right?"

"Right," he agreed, but as she turned to the door he grabbed her hand. "Are you sure about this, Eleanor?"

She looked down at him. "Very sure. We've talked about it, Franklin. Someone has to do something, however small. Europe is on its knees and America is just sitting back and watching."

Franklin winced. Germany, to no one's surprise, had not retreated from Poland and two weeks later Russia had invaded her from the other side in a fascist-communist coalition that surely could not last. Over the winter, little more had happened. Children had been evacuated from London and then returned to their parents as no bombs fell. Europe's borders had been quietly patrolled but no German tanks had approached—until two days ago, when the Wehrmacht had exploded into Norway, Denmark, Belgium and Luxembourg. Now Hitler was turning his greedy eyes to France and, if that fell, to Great Britain.

There was panic in London. Parliament had cast out Neville Chamberlain and elected Winston Churchill as the new Prime Minister. By all accounts, the man was sharp, determined and downright bullish, all qualities no doubt needed in a wartime leader, and he had already written a long letter of "friendship" to Franklin. The pressure would be increasing on America to weigh in to the fight but polls suggested the public were opposed and Congress most certainly were. Plus, of course, U.S. forces, neglected during the very domestic battle against the Depression, were small and poorly trained. Whatever Mr. Churchill might think, America did not have the resources for a fight at the moment. Franklin was looking for ways to change that, but it was an uphill climb and they'd agreed that a gesture from the First Lady—a big gesture—could help.

"It might be dangerous, Babs," Franklin said.

"So might sitting here doing nothing."

"That's true."

"You're needed here, but me..."

"You're needed too."

"I'm wanted—by some—which is nice. But I'm not needed." She patted his hand. "Enough talking, Franklin. Let me go and find Mr. Davies."

He grabbed her hand, kissing it extravagantly. "Good luck!"

Eleanor smiled and escaped the office, holding down her navy-and-white dress against the river breezes as the grand presidential boat moved away from Washington. Various VIP guests were taking tea on the foredeck and Eleanor gratefully accepted a cup from an immaculately uniformed server and sipped it. An English drink; how apt. She smiled and moved forward.

"Mr. Davies, lovely to see you."

Norman Davies, chairman of the International Red Cross, looked startled at her effusive greeting, but shook her proffered hand and offered her a seat.

"No thank you, I prefer to stand. I like to see the banks."

He laughed. "You don't like boats?"

"Not terribly much."

"Ironic for the wife of a navy man."

"Isn't it? Still, the key to a good marriage is enjoying each other's differences, is it not?"

"Is it?"

"It is." Eleanor finished her tea and put the cup firmly down. No one could conduct serious business balancing a saucer. "How is the situation in Europe, Mr. Davies?"

He shook his head sorrowfully. "Dire, Mrs. Roosevelt. Truly dire. The Germans are practicing what they call Blitzkrieg—lightning strikes where their tanks go crunching in, covered by Luftwaffe planes. They destroy everything in their path, leaving the infantry to march behind more or less unopposed. They must have been planning it for years."

"Is that not what Mr. Churchill has been saying?"

"It is. Some colonel called De Gaulle in France too. Should have listened to them sooner, hey? But hindsight is a wonderful thing."

"As is foresight—which is what we need here in America."

"You wish us to join the war, Mrs. Roosevelt?"

"No!" She put up a hand. "I do *not* wish us to join the war. I would never wish that. I, with my husband, have long campaigned for men to settle their differences around the negotiating table, but it seems that shooting each other is far more satisfying."

Mr. Davies sighed. "Too true. And shooting every poor civilian caught in the endless crossfire as well. There are so many injuries, Mrs. Roosevelt. Whole villages have been burned down. Whole groups of innocent people have been shot and left to rot. Many are homeless and without supplies, and with the weather getting hotter we're seeing outbreaks of typhus. We need all the doctors and nurses we can get."

Eleanor permitted herself a small smile. "Which is where I might come in."

"You?" He flushed and put a hand to his mouth to stifle his rudeness.

But this was no time to worry about manners.

"I would like to go to Europe to help coordinate relief efforts," Eleanor told him. "The American Red Cross are raising all they can but supplies are no use without someone to coordinate their distribution. I can do that, Mr. Davies."

"You?" he spluttered again.

"You do not think I'm up to it?"

"No. That is, yes. Of course I do. Of course you would be. It's just... it's dangerous out there."

"I am well aware of that. If it were not, there would be little need for relief. I am prepared to take the risk. I worked for the Red Cross in the Great War, you know, though only here in America. I wanted to go to Europe but"—she swallowed the memory—"events conspired against me."

Franklin had come out on deck, his two cousins providing a willing entourage. Purple-haired Polly was pushing his chair and Daisy, another of Franklin's hanger-on cousins, was trotting behind with a little dog on a lead. Eleanor glanced awkwardly his way, then reminded herself that she was not on this damned boat to dwell on the past, but to fight for the future. She drew herself up to her full height—several inches above the chairman.

"I am already a member of the Red Cross, Mr. Davies, I have much experience of organizing groups, and I speak fluent French and decent German. I believe I could be an asset to your organization."

Mr. Davies looked to Franklin. It was annoying, given she was the one offering her services, but to be expected.

"My husband supports me in this," she said.

"I do," Franklin agreed, wheeling himself forward.

"You're going to Europe?" Daisy asked, eyes wide.

"Someone has to," Eleanor said.

"And you think you'll make up for the U.S. Army and Navy, do you?" Polly sniped.

Eleanor sought for a smart reply but Polly was right. One over-eager First Lady was hardly going to do much for the poor people of Europe. "Of course not. But it's all I can think of."

"And it's marvelous," Franklin said, putting an arm around her waist. "Is it not, Mr. Davies?"

"Marvelous," he agreed. "Truly. I shall get on to the Secretary of State the moment we've finished our cruise."

"Thank you," Eleanor said.

"Cocktails!" Franklin cried.

The others greeted this with effusive joy but Eleanor was no keener on cocktails than she was on boats and as soon as she could politely do so, she excused herself to seek out Tommy in her cabin and get on with some work. She had seen Mr. Davies and could now only hope the Secretary of State approved her appointment.

. . .

He did not.

Two days later, Cordell Hull came to see her and Franklin together. She was summoned to the Oval Office, set in the West Wing where the President's vast administrative machinery had its home. Her team worked from the East Wing and she wasn't happy Cordell couldn't do her the courtesy of visiting her there, but perhaps he was afraid of a hysterical female reaction. Honestly! She would never be hysterical. But she *was* angry.

"What do you mean 'the situation is too bad out there'?" she demanded. She liked Cordell normally. He was a liberal-minded man who got things done—just not, apparently, this particular thing.

"What I said, Eleanor. The Nazis are already making inroads into the French border and we can only anticipate capitulation."

"By the French? They have the best army in the world."

"I'm afraid that's no longer true. The Germans are better equipped, better trained and more highly motivated. Our men in the field anticipate the Maginot Line crumbling within a month. Already British forces are drawing back toward the coast. We cannot send the First Lady over the Atlantic to be cannon fodder—we'd look like fools."

"God forbid!" Eleanor snapped.

"What Cordell means," Franklin said in the controlled voice he always used to pour oil on troubled waters, "is that you are too precious to lose at this critical juncture."

"Exactly," Cordell agreed. Clearly they'd talked this all over before she'd arrived and Franklin had smoothly switched sides. "That's what I mean, Eleanor, even if I didn't put it as well as your silver-tongued husband. The American people love you, and if you were murdered on a European battlefield they'd be devastated."

Eleanor sighed. "But it's fine for ordinary people to be murdered there?"

"No! It's not fine for anyone to be murdered, but there's a difference between having your home in the path of the damned Blitzkrieg and willingly putting yourself there. Besides, you're the President's wife."

"For now. There's an election later this year, remember, and no one has ever served three terms."

"No one *yet*," Cordell said quietly.

Eleanor looked to Franklin but his face betrayed nothing and Cordell carried on.

"The likelihood is that you'd be kidnapped and held to ransom for God knows what evil ends. We can't risk it, Eleanor, I'm sorry."

Eleanor dropped into a chair. She heard Franklin saying goodbye to Cordell and knew she should get up and see him out but for once politeness was beyond her. Putting her head in her hands, she fought not to cry.

"I'm sorry, Babs," Franklin said softly when he returned.

"I can't go because I'm married to you?"

"No. But you can do so much here, as you always do. There are good things about being the President's wife, surely?"

She looked up and saw him offering her a cheeky smile. He was trying to pour oil again; Franklin did not like troubled waters. Usually she gave in, but today she was hurting.

"I'm not truly your wife though, am I?" she said, looking into his blue eyes. "Just your First Lady."

He drew in a shocked breath but she was already up and gone, heading out of his office and through the opulence of the main residence to the safety of her East Wing.

There were many times when she loved being married to President Roosevelt; today was not one of them.

FOUR

BOSTON, THANKSGIVING 1903

Eleanor did not normally think of herself as stupid but however hard she stared at Franklin, she could not understand. He'd only spoken four words, and they were positioned perfectly logically. But they still didn't make sense. Or, at least, it didn't make sense that he was saying them to her.

Franklin laughed nervously. "Will you, Eleanor? Will you marry me?"

"Marry you?" she repeated stupidly. "Be your wife? Live together? Till death do us part and all that?"

"And all that," he said, laughing again. He took her hands. "I think you're amazing, Eleanor. I've never met a girl like you. Hell, I've never met a person like you. You see the world with such... such big eyes."

"Big eyes?" Unconsciously she widened hers.

He leaned in close. "Big, blue eyes. I think you're beautiful."

She flushed. "Then your judgment is clearly not to be trusted. I'm not beautiful, Franklin."

"You are to me," he said simply. "You are statuesque and magnificent and beautiful and I... I love you."

More words that did not make sense, and only three of them this time.

"You love me?" she whispered. "Truly?"

"Truly! Oh, darling girl, why would you not believe it?"

It was a good question. They'd spent a lot of time together over the last few months, always seeking each other out at society dos, and meeting regularly for walks, drives, or luncheons. Eleanor liked Franklin. He was so full of ideas, so curious about the world, and he talked to her about everything. Listened to her too. Hours in his company shot past. He made her feel interesting, engaging, alive. She just couldn't quite believe she did the same for him.

He was looking curiously at her, waiting for an answer.

"I don't know," she admitted shyly. "I guess I'm not used to it."

"To being loved?"

"Well, yes. My mother died when I was eight and my father when I was ten. My brother, Elliott, only made it to three, so that left Hall and me to be brought up by my grandmother and aunts. They were very kind, really they were, but, well... it's not quite the same, is it?"

He shook his head. "Not the same at all. My mother loves me unconditionally. Dotingly even." He gave a self-conscious little laugh.

Eleanor felt a squirm of unease. She knew of the formidable Sara Roosevelt, of course, but had not yet been formally introduced.

"I hope she likes me."

"She'll adore you."

He was staring at her most disconcertingly, then suddenly stepped up and put his arms around her, drawing her against him so she could feel the warmth of his strong body and smell the soap on his skin. It was delicious.

"You are never going to feel unloved again, Eleanor, baby."

Baby! The romantic term thrilled through her. She'd never been anyone's baby. Never thought she would. That was a term for the pretty, flirty belles. She dared to pull back and found her face up against his, their lips almost touching.

"I love you too, Franklin." The words felt strange coming up her throat but once they were out they seemed to swell and grow and fill her heart. "I love you," she said again and then his lips were upon hers and she was kissing him and it felt like the sweetest, most exciting, most natural thing in the world.

"So then, Miss Roosevelt," he said when he finally pulled away, "I will ask you again—will you marry me?"

This time the words made total sense; in fact, everything suddenly made total sense.

Eleanor let out a delighted laugh. "I will, Franklin. I will!"

"Then, baby, you'd better meet my mother."

"Marriage?"

It seemed the concept was not making any more sense to Sara Roosevelt than it had to Eleanor. She'd welcomed her most graciously for Thanksgiving dinner but when Franklin had shared his marriage plans over coffee, she'd gone quite pale.

"You're so young, darling."

"I'm twenty-one, Mama. I'll graduate next year and get a job, so why not a wife?"

"I can work too," Eleanor said.

At that Sara gave a dramatic shudder. "You? Good heavens, no! You clearly haven't thought this out, either of you. Eleanor is nineteen; a child still."

Eleanor opened her mouth to protest but felt Franklin's hand on her knee beneath the table and the sheer thrill of his touch kept her silent.

"Eleanor is very mature, Mama, and we are both very certain about this. We want to be together. We love each other."

Sara Roosevelt put her hand dramatically to her chest. It was horribly clear to Eleanor that she was used to having Franklin to herself. She'd even rented an apartment in Boston to be near him at Harvard, so she wasn't going to surrender him easily.

Eleanor shifted but Franklin's grip tightened on her knee and she understood he was already hers. She cleared her throat. "Think of it less as losing a son, and more as gaining a daughter. I would love to get to know you better and I do not, as you know, have a mother of my own, or a father for that matter, so there will be no other family call on Franklin."

Sara looked at her as the implications of this registered in her brain. She might lose Franklin to Eleanor as a wife, but she would be the all-encompassing mother.

"Hmmm," she said, but then the imposing grandfather clock in the corner chimed out the hour and she shook her head. "I still think you're both too young. Let's keep this 'engagement' to ourselves, shall we, until we are certain you both mean it."

Eleanor put her hand over Franklin's. She was certain. She'd never been more certain about anything. Being with Franklin, being his baby, had made her happier than she'd known it was possible to be and she was not going to give that up. Not ever.

Franklin opened his mouth to protest but Sara got there first.

"Especially with us going on our winter cruise, darling."

"Winter cruise?" Franklin stuttered.

"To the Caribbean. Over New Year. I found it the other day. You must remember me telling you?"

Franklin's eyes narrowed. "You didn't tell me, Mama. I was intending to spend New Year with Eleanor."

"You want me to cancel the booking?"

"Yes. That is... the Caribbean?"

"You should go," Eleanor told him, unsure whether to hate or admire Sara for her bold play in what was clearly going to become a game of Franklin-chess. "I can see you when you get back." She regretted the words almost the moment she'd uttered *them, but she wasn't used to fighting for love and the orphan inside her still thought she didn't fully deserve it.*

"Lovely," Sara said triumphantly.

It was with a heavy heart that Eleanor saw Franklin off a month later. He would forget her, she was sure. There would be prettier girls on board, ones who could dance and flirt and giggle in ways that Eleanor simply could not. The few weeks of her secret engagement to Franklin had been the happiest of her life, but they could not last. She'd been a fool to even think it.

The first telegram came barely hours later: Missing you madly.

The second was at dawn the next day: Everyone here is so dull. Can't wait to get back to my baby.

The third was swift on its tail: I love you. *And the fourth barely hours later*: We will marry, Eleanor baby. We will marry and be happy forever.

Twenty-five telegrams later, Eleanor started to believe that maybe, just maybe, that was true.

FIVE

VAL KILL, JULY 1940

At last! Eleanor sank gratefully into the comfortable couch in her Val Kill living room, glad to have made it to her favorite retreat after a hectic few months. She stretched out her long legs and drew in a deep breath, though even here it was hard to truly relax. The news from Europe was relentlessly dire and in America everyone was on edge about whether to intervene. Last month, Paris had fallen to the Nazis, leaving Great Britain quivering before Hitler's wrath. Churchill had miraculously rescued thousands of men from Dunkirk in an everyman-armada of small boats but they were stuck on their island now. Colonel De Gaulle, made a general for his brave combat against the invading forces, had also escaped over the Channel and was attempting to muster what he called "the Free French" in London but it was a paltry force.

Even worse than the military news were the horrific stories of the treatment of innocent civilians. The Nazis were persecuting the Jews with relentless fury, banning them from running businesses, forcing them to wear degrading yellow stars on their arms, and driving them into ghettos. Thousands were hiding across the occupied territories, or battling to escape, and

Eleanor had been delighted to meet an ardent young man called Joe Lash who was setting up an "Emergency Rescue Committee" to try to get as many as people as possible over to the USA. It seemed such an obvious thing to do to Eleanor. Who, seeing their neighbor being kicked and beaten, would not try to bring them to safety on their side of the fence? And yet Americans were fiercely resistant to rescuing these poor fellow humans, all in the ugly name of "immigration."

A lot of German children had been brought over in 1938 after the hideous "Kristallnacht" in which Jewish businesses had been smashed apart. Families, both Jewish and Gentile, had gladly offered the little ones homes but they balked at welcoming their parents. Several ships of adult refugees had bravely made it to American shores only to be turned away in port. The SS *St. Louis* had lingered off Florida as a paltry nine hundred people, mainly women and children, had pleaded to be allowed to disembark. Eleanor had done her best to step in but been told by everyone, even Franklin, to back off.

"Immigration is a State Department matter," he'd said firmly. "Every case must be considered on individual merit. Breckinridge Long insists we are vigilant for fifth columnists."

Eleanor thought that Breckinridge Long, Franklin's Head of Immigration, was a pompous ass. She understood that security was important but surely there was room for a little common sense? The ERC had composed a list of people "worth saving" —artists and academics and philosophers—and a young man had gone to Marseilles, in unoccupied southern France, to expedite their departure. Eleanor thought everyone was worth saving, but it was a start and she would do her best to help him from Washington. Right now, however, all anyone cared about was internal politics. Europe was hanging by a thread called Churchill, but in America it was election season.

For the last two months, Franklin had been determinedly coy about whether he would stand as President for an unprecedented third term. Eleanor had tried many times to talk to him about it, but all he would say was that he was torn between a personal desire to retire and a deep sense of duty to America.

"The problem is, I'm the best man to lead the country at the moment, Babs," he'd say.

It wasn't arrogance, simply truth. In the thirties he'd been the one with the vision to rescue America from the Depression with his "New Deal," using government mechanisms to create jobs for the 25 percent unemployed and bringing the economy back from the brink of disaster. Now they were into the forties, his vision was of America as part of the wider world—a world at war. If the Republicans won, they would hunker down, believing themselves safest in isolation but their rescued economy was going global, their security with it, and there would be no avoiding Hitler in the long run. Only Franklin, like Winston Churchill, truly understood that.

"So you'll stand?" she'd ask.

"Yes. That is, no... I'm not sure," he'd reply.

She'd lost her temper with him recently. "The party needs to know, Franklin."

"They'll have to wait a little longer. It's my life."

"And mine too."

He'd looked at her as if he hadn't thought of that before. "Sorry, Babs." He'd waved his hand around the White House. "Do you want to stay?"

It was the question she'd been wanting him to ask, but once it was out there, it had been so hard to answer. The world was in crisis and looking to America for help.

"I think I would rather feel I was abandoning the ship," she'd said eventually.

He'd nodded and given her a weak smile. "You've hit the nail on the head, my dear—as always."

But still he hadn't made up his mind.

The Democratic Convention was meeting in Chicago to

nominate their candidate so presumably his hand would be forced. It wasn't the done thing for potential nominees to attend so Franklin was on his boat, and Eleanor had escaped to Val Kill for some precious time with her close friends.

She watched Tommy bustling around the kitchen with Henry Osthagen, the man coyly referred to at official functions as her "companion." The big bear of an ex-colonel currently stirring a delicious-smelling tomato sauce would like to marry Tommy, but, divorced by a selfish man for wanting to keep working for Eleanor, she refused to "subjugate" herself. She insisted she did not want a "slave-ring" on her finger, so Henry was kept to the not unenjoyable status of "boyfriend."

"Smells delicious, Henry," said Joe Lash, clapping Henry on the back as he came through from the kitchen with a beer for himself and a glass of fresh lemonade for Eleanor.

Joe was another person prepared to fight against convention. A stalwart of the American Youth Congress, he'd matured into a caring young man, passionate about fighting for those on the margins of society and had swiftly become one of Eleanor's great friends. He was utterly unlike her sons, who she loved dearly but who were sometimes so busy with sports and parties that they could find little time to ponder the world's problems. Joe, in contrast, pondered them constantly and, looking at him now, Eleanor thought she had perhaps found in him the son she had lost. She shivered and pushed the thought away, focusing on the happiness ahead, not the sadness behind.

"Henry's sauce looks amazing," Joe said, dropping onto the couch at her side. "He learned how to make it when he was in Italy apparently. I'd love to go to Italy."

"Not at the moment, Joe!" said a pretty girl arriving on his heels with a glass of wine.

Trude Pratt was a brilliant German academic who'd openly rebelled against the rise of fascism and had to flee permanently to the States. She'd met Joe through the International Student

Service and often joined their little get-togethers. Eleanor suspected the pair were something closer than friends but where did the boundaries of friendship tip over?

She herself had trodden those boundaries with Lorena Hickok, to whom she'd been so very close when they'd first moved into the White House. Her dear "Hick," a hard-boiled journalist, had taught her to see the press as friends and, even more astonishingly, had taught her to see the worth in herself again, after it had taken a crashing knock from the one man who'd built it up in the first place. Hick had gifted her a beautiful sapphire ring that Eleanor still treasured, and shown her what it was to be loved once more. They were still close, but not in the intimate way they'd once been. These days there was too much to do for Eleanor to be truly close to anyone. But that didn't stop her wanting it for others.

"Almost ready," Henry called from the kitchen.

Eleanor smiled contentedly, loving being among friends.

Then the phone rang.

The noise blared into the cozy room, brash and insistent. She pushed herself reluctantly to her feet and picked it up.

"Eleanor," a clipped voice said down the line. "It's Frances."

Eleanor suppressed a groan. Frances Perkins was Franklin's Secretary of Labor and the only woman in the cabinet. Eleanor admired her greatly but if she was calling from the convention, it could not be good news.

Whatever good news was...

"All well, Frances?" she asked cautiously.

"Franklin has agreed to stand," came the answer.

"I see," Eleanor said carefully, though inside she felt a small thrill that they might stay in the White House and maybe, just maybe, help poor Europe to defeat Hitler. "Isn't that good?" she asked.

"It's very good," Frances said crisply, "but he wants Wallace as his running mate."

"A wise choice." Henry Wallace, currently Secretary for Agriculture, was a plain-speaking, hard-acting New Dealer, working his guts off to ameliorate rural poverty.

"I like Wallace," Frances agreed. "He's solid. But the old guard are saying he doesn't understand the world."

"Idiots," Eleanor snapped. "Anyone who can bring the farming community into modern practices understands more than any of those lot and their fancy economics degrees."

"Well quite," Frances sighed, adding, "I don't suppose you fancy telling them that yourself?"

"What?"

"It's getting brutal, Eleanor. They need someone to tell them some home truths and I can't think of anyone better than you."

"Franklin?" Eleanor suggested drily.

"Franklin insists he's staying out of it and I think he's right. It'll get too personal if he tries to speak for Wallace."

"And we'll be accused of petticoat government if *I* do."

"I don't think so," Frances said. "Any other wife, maybe, but not you, Eleanor. You're a voice in your own right. The party respect you."

"I don't think that's true, Frances. They—"

"Please, Eleanor. Franklin said to ask you not to abandon ship."

Eleanor sucked in a breath; how could she ignore that appeal? She looked longingly over her shoulder into her kitchen. Joe and Trude had joined Tommy and Henry around the table and she could hear the clink of plates and the rich glug of wine into glasses.

"Let me talk to him," she said, stalling. Surely her husband wouldn't want her riding in like the Lone Ranger.

"Good idea," Frances agreed, far too quickly for Eleanor's liking.

She put the phone down. In the kitchen, Tommy told a

joke, doubtless one of her usual coarse ones, and the others laughed. Eleanor ached to forget the call and go join them, drink wine, eat spaghetti and talk hooey, as if the problems of the world were none of her concern. But she didn't really like wine and the problems of the world were far too noisy to ignore.

Sighing, she lifted the receiver. "Get me the President please."

"I thought you might call," Franklin said once the connection was made.

"Frances wants me to go to Chicago."

"Yes. Will you?"

"Do you want me to?"

The silence seemed to stretch out forever and then, unusually quietly, he said, "Yes. Please."

Eleanor twisted the cord around her fingers. "You think they'll listen to me?"

"Why not? I always do."

"Not true!"

"It *is* true. I can't do as much about it as either of us would like, but I always listen. I always have. You're the most interesting woman I know."

Her heart ached. "Even now?"

"Even now. I could happily sit at the side of a ballroom with you all night."

Eleanor pressed a hand to her chest to stop her foolish heart pumping tears out of her eyes. Franklin used to say these things to her a lot but life in the White House left little time or space for endearments—from either of them.

"I'll go," she said. "But I can't promise I'll be any use."

"Just be you," he said. "That's all we need."

Twenty-four hours later, Eleanor stood in the wings of the stage at a ridiculously noisy convention, feeling constricted in the tight suit with which she'd had to replace her comfy slacks. In the giant auditorium, thousands of Democratic Party members were arguing, bickering and baying like hooligans at a baseball match, watched on by equally rowdy journalists. Eleanor was exhausted. She'd stayed up far too late last night, unwilling to sacrifice her friends for petty politics, and had snatched barely four hours' sleep before the car had come to take her to the airport for the eight-hour flight to Chicago. Tommy had offered to accompany her but this was private party business so she'd reluctantly come alone.

Frances had spirited her into the hotel where she'd met an embarrassed Wallace and his small but determined team. They seemed so sure she could help and she'd grown more and more nervous as the clock had ticked toward her 6 p.m. speech. Standing waiting, however, she could hear the men—and a few women—gathered to determine the future of their country muttering about rural reform and wanted to grab them by the scruff of their over-priced shirts and remind them that there was a war on. People in Poland or Norway or France weren't fretting about the efficiency of their farms, but trying to stay alive to run them in peace. Stuffing her rough notes into her pocket, she pulled herself up to her full six foot, strode onto the stage and banged on the podium. The sound echoed down the microphone and fifty thousand faces turned, in surprise, to face her.

"Seats please, ladies and gentlemen. I would like to say a few words."

The delegates looked at each other. A few seemed as if they might protest but Eleanor wasn't about to wait and spoke on regardless. She thanked the convention for welcoming her and got straight to the meat of what she wanted to say.

"I know, and you know, that any man who is in office today faces a heavier responsibility, perhaps, than any man has ever faced before in this country." She drew in a breath, but this was no time for pauses or hesitation and she pushed on, encouraging them to unity and asking them to trust the judgment of their chosen nominee on his running mate. The room fell quiet. The last people took their seats. No one looked at each other. All eyes were on Eleanor. Well, good. It was time someone talked sense into them.

"This year, the candidate who is the President of the United States cannot make a campaign in the usual sense of the word. He must be on his job. So each and every one of you assume for yourselves a very grave responsibility, because you will make the campaign. You will have to rise above considerations which are narrow and partisan."

A few small protests rose from somewhere near the back but Eleanor ignored them. Leaning closer into the microphone, she looked along the lines of people as if she were chatting to them over a coffee, keen to impress the urgency of the situation upon them.

"No man can carry this situation alone. This is only carried by a united people who love their country and who will live for it to the fullest of their ability, with the highest ideals, with a determination that their party shall be absolutely devoted to the good of the nation as a whole and to doing what this country can to bring the world to a safer and happier condition."

Silence. Then someone called, "hear, hear" and more voices joined in. It was hardly a resounding ovation but it was a ripple of positivity and, more importantly, it was met with no jeering putdowns. The convention was silenced.

"Thank you," Eleanor said quietly, then turned and walked from the stage.

The convention leader leaped to propose a move to nominations and Eleanor took the chance to slip from the room and return to her car. She'd done all she could and she had to admit it had been invigorating. But it would be a long flight home and she still had her column to write.

Six days a week for the last four years she'd written a short diary, entitled "My Day," for the newspapers. She wasn't sure she was interesting enough to command the number of readers she apparently did, but it was useful for explaining her thoughts to the nation alongside the snippets of her routines as a First Lady that they seemed to enjoy. She set up the typewriter as the little plane bumped down the runway, but suddenly the pilot stamped on the brakes and it almost went flying. Clinging to the precious machine with her fingertips, Eleanor looked out of the window to see a black car chasing them down.

"What is it?" she asked, trying not to panic.

"I've been asked to wait, madam," the pilot said. "Your husband is on the phone."

"Now?"

Eleanor set the typewriter back in place as the plane pulled aside and was escorted off the runway. The car drove her back to the terminal and into a hastily tidied office.

The phone line crackled into action. "Eleanor?"

"Franklin! I was on my way home."

"Glad I caught you." He was unabashed. "You've worked wonders, my dear. Wallace is nominated and harmony is restored within the party. Thank you so much. I'm going to make my acceptance speech shortly but didn't want to do it without speaking to you first."

"I'm glad I could help," Eleanor said. His gratitude was going to cost her a precious hour's sleep but it was lovely to hear from him. "You'll have a wonderful third term, my dear."

"We haven't won yet!" he countered, but his voice was bubbly with enthusiasm.

Eleanor knew that, having committed to elongating his presidency, he would throw himself into the fight with his usual vigor. The thrill rippled through her belly again. She wouldn't have to leave the White House, wouldn't have to go back to obscurity. Dearly as she loved Val Kill, it was better as a retreat from a busy life, than a life itself. There was still so much to do.

"I'd better go," she told Franklin. "Can't keep the pilot waiting."

"You're worth waiting for, Babs. Thank you, truly. I couldn't do this—any of it—without you."

Eleanor felt faintly tearful; it must be the exhaustion. "You don't have to, Franklin."

"You're the best. See you soon?"

"See you soon, my dear."

Eleanor replaced the receiver and leaned back, closing her eyes and drawing in a deep breath. Today had been most peculiar but it seemed to have worked out well. Franklin was undoubtedly the right man to lead America for the next four, critical years and, his nomination settled, she would throw herself into the fight against the reactionary, inward-looking Republicans. His vision for the conduct of this terrible war and, more to the point, his vision for how to create a lasting peace, were everything she could hope for and, if given the chance by the people, she would be proud to stand alongside him and fight for them.

It was the path they had been on since the very start of their marriage and she had to admit that, exhausting as White House life might be, she was glad it was not yet at an end. She had sworn to work for the American people's trust and, even if those people didn't realize it yet, with Hitler pulling the dark cloud of war over the world, that work felt more vital than ever.

SIX

NEW YORK, MARCH 17, 1905

"He's coming! There, look, in the fancy car! Isn't he handsome?! Ooh, and he's wearing a shamrock in his lapel. How swanky is that? Can you see, Eleanor? Can you see him?"

Eleanor, forced to stand still for the adjustments to the Brussels lace of her wedding gown, was unable to make it to the window to see the star of her special day. Not herself, the bride, nor even Franklin, the groom, but the man who was giving her away—her uncle, Theodore Roosevelt, newly inaugurated as President of the United States. It had been very kind of Uncle Ted to offer, in the absence of her dear father, to walk her up the aisle, but it did come with certain... accommodations.

The wedding had been scheduled for today, St. Patrick's Day, so that the President could take two hours out from the usual New York parade to attend the ceremony. Loudly played renditions of "The Wearin' of the Green" from the streets were competing with the calming bridal music in the house and excitement was high. Eleanor didn't mind. She'd hated the thought of all eyes being on her, so it was nice everyone had a distraction.

"Are you ready?" Cousin Susie asked, peeking her head

around the door. She was hosting the event in her grand house on 37th Street and was pink with the responsibility.

"Five more minutes," the seamstress pleaded.

"Three," Susie said sternly. "We can't keep the President waiting."

"But it's the bride's prerogative to—"

Susie was gone.

"Don't worry," Eleanor said to the poor woman. "I'm sure it looks lovely. Shall we go?"

The bridesmaids gathered around, six of them, in cream taffeta with silver roses embroidered on their sleeves and three silver-tipped ostrich feathers in their hair. They were too ostentatious for Eleanor's taste, and the poor girls kept plucking nervously at them, but they were the symbol of the Roosevelt family so Sara had insisted. And when Sara insisted, there was little to be done.

Eleanor's soon-to-be mother-in-law had finally embraced their engagement two years after the proposal and allowed Eleanor to wear the large, princess-cut diamond ring Franklin had bought her for her twentieth birthday. Today it would be joined by a golden marriage band and Eleanor could not wait. The dresses, the feathers and the fuss could go hang as far as she was concerned, she just wanted to be Franklin's wife. She wanted to move into a house with him and make babies to create a family of their own, one not tainted by deaths or power struggles, just ruled by love.

She was hazy on the exact details of the baby-making. Cousin Alice had tried to tell her some nonsensically lurid details at a sleepover when they were sixteen, but Eleanor had refused to believe her. She knew only that there was kissing involved, which was fine by her as she very much enjoyed Franklin's kisses, and that they had to be naked, which felt embarrassing but surely if everyone did it, it would work out fine? Anyway, there was no time to worry, for the music was sounding out, loud enough to *silence the street drums, and the bridesmaids were processing down the stairs and here was Uncle Ted, smiling and offering her his arm.*

"You look beautiful," he said, dropping a kiss on her forehead. "Franklin is a very lucky man."

Briefly, Eleanor wondered why it was her, frankly spurious, beauty that made him so lucky but the doors were opening and there Franklin was, smiling fit to burst as she moved toward him, and it didn't matter what Uncle Ted or anyone else thought, only that Franklin was there and she was marrying him. Finally, she was marrying him.

The ceremony was brief. Eleanor spoke her responses loudly and clearly so there could be no doubt of her happy acceptance, and Franklin did the same. Then they were signing the register and the guests were clapping and, just like that, they were pronounced man and wife.

"If you'd like to stand here, by the mantelpiece," the priest suggested, "then people can come up and congratulate you in an orderly manner."

They did as instructed. Franklin twined his hand in her beringed one and snuck a kiss, then another. It was so delicious that it took her a moment to remember they were meant to be receiving guests, but when they pulled apart, they were almost alone. The President had strode through to the next room for refreshments and all the guests, bar a handful of the elderly who were still in their seats, had followed.

Eleanor looked at Franklin and they both burst out laughing.

"Upstaged at our own wedding!" he said.

"But by the President of the USA, at least," said Eleanor.

Franklin watched the guests milling excitedly around Uncle Ted's imposing figure and Eleanor saw his eyes sharpen.

She tugged on his hand. "What is it?"

He looked at her. "Would you think it very arrogant of me, Eleanor, if I said I'd like to be President one day?"

"Would that make me the President's wife?"

"It would."

"Then that would be fine and dandy."

"You think the White House would suit you, my love?"

She giggled. "Is that very arrogant of me?"

"Not at all." He kissed her. "Our secret, yes?"

She kissed him back. "Our secret."

"Shall we go? It seems we're not needed here."

"Now?" she asked, shocked.

"Why not? You're the only person here who interests me."

"Franklin!" she admonished, embarrassed. "These are our friends and family. What would your mother say?"

"Oh yes!" He rolled his eyes. "Fine, we'll stay an hour or so—but no more!"

Well who was she, a brand-new wife, to argue?

Their exit was, predictably, obscured by the hysterically greeted departure of the President. A fine car drove them out of Manhattan and up the familiar road along the Hudson to Hyde Park. Franklin had wanted their first night to be in his family home and Eleanor had not known how to say no. At least Sara would not be there, but as Franklin led her into the dark entrance hall, the myriad talismans of his idyllic childhood seemed to loom in on her. A specially made glass case in the corner contained a collection of birds he had stuffed as a child. The portraits around the walls were all of Franklin or his parents, and there was even a bust of him as a boy inside the door.

"Does it not make you feel odd, looking at yourself every time you come in?" she asked.

Franklin glanced at the bust. "That old thing? I barely notice it. I'm not that child any more."

"Part of you must be."

He shrugged, untroubled. "Perhaps, but I'm a man now, and

a groom to boot, with a gorgeous bride in my arms who I do not want to waste on discussing sculpture! Shall we to bed, my lady?"

"So soon?"

"Why not?"

She glanced to the servants ranged around to greet them.

"Oh, don't mind them. It's our wedding night. I've asked for supper upstairs, so we'll be utterly private. Come on!"

Eleanor let herself be tugged up the stairs, past Sara's vast bedroom to Franklin's equally large one. A silver tray loaded with champagne and all manner of snacks sat incongruously in front of a shelf of childhood toys.

"Franklin." She grabbed his hand to stop him bouncing around the room. "I'm nervous."

He stopped and came over to her. "Of course. Me too. It's probably why I'm being a bit... bumptious. Shall we open this champagne and, maybe, get into bed?"

"Together?"

"I think that's usual, yes."

She giggled. "Sorry. I. Yes. Where shall I undress?"

He smiled. "How about I undress you?"

"You? But..."

"It'll be fun."

It wasn't. They tried hard but the wedding dress was a complicated affair, made worse by the stitches the seamstress had sewn into it at the last minute. Franklin fumbled for ages with the little pearl buttons and then the corset ribbons got pulled into a tight knot so that, in the end, it was simpler for her to spin it around and work it free herself. He poured champagne and said it would be "even nicer to watch" but taking off her undergarments in the glare of his gaze felt mortifying to Eleanor and, despite his gasps of admiration, she was mightily relieved when she could jump under the covers. Franklin was far quicker to undress—men's garments were wonderfully simple—and then he was next to her and his bare leg was against her bare leg and his hands were reaching out to caress her shoulders and down to her breasts and it was all rather mortifying again.

"Come here," he said, pulling her into his arms and kissing her. "It'll come quite naturally when we get going."

It didn't, at least not for Eleanor. Cousin Alice's details had not, it seemed, been as nonsensical as they'd sounded, and when Franklin parted her legs and raised himself above her, she was only able to grip at his shoulders and bite down on her lips to keep her cries of pain inside as he thrust and thrust like a pig or a dog. Eleanor was not sure what she'd imagined but it had been nothing as undignified as this. Still, his cries came loud and ecstatic, so that was something.

"Oh my goodness, Babs," he said, throwing himself onto his back and pulling her close. "That was amazing."

"Amazing," she agreed weakly.

"And it will be even better next time."

"Next time?" she squeaked.

He laughed. "Give a man time to rest! Champagne? Here. What a day, hey? The people seem to love Uncle Ted."

"He's not bad, I suppose, for the opposition."

Franklin roared with laughter and leaped up to fetch the tray of snacks. Eleanor averted her eyes from the sight of his buttocks though, actually, they were rather nicely rounded and his legs were very finely muscled.

He caught her looking and grinned. "Satisfied with your husband, my love?"

"Very," she said, blushing, and then hurriedly changed the subject. "Now, tell me, what do you think Uncle Ted's first policies are going to be?"

"There's a question!"

Franklin leaped back into bed, offering her the tray, and she took a pastry, suddenly starving, as he began to outline what he thought Theodore Roosevelt would do first and, more excitingly, what he, Franklin Roosevelt, would do in his place. So passionate were his ideas and so keen his interest in hers that she soon forgot that she was naked, or that there were crumbs all over the bed, or even that she would have to have him on top of her again at some point. There was so much to discuss and it was almost dawn before, finally, Eleanor slid into a happy slumber in his arms, excited for their life ahead.

SEVEN

WASHINGTON, OCTOBER 29, 1940

Eleanor shifted on her seat, very glad the lights were low in the Departmental Auditorium for she didn't want any attention on herself at this tense event. Not that it was likely. All eyes were glued to the giant, bucket-shaped fishbowl sitting on a sturdy table on the stage as, with a horrific clatter, thousands of capsules were poured into it. Each one contained a number and each number had been allocated to a call-up batch of around six thousand young men across America. Everyone aged twenty-one to thirty-five had been registering for the draft for the last two weeks and now the order in which the numbers were drawn out would determine when their batch was called into the forces for training. The first intake would be in a fortnight, so it paid to be at the bottom of the bowl.

"This is barbaric," Anna whispered at her side, and Eleanor nodded and reached for her hand.

Her daughter was visiting from Seattle with her three children, and it was wonderful to have their cheery voices ringing around the White House. Today, though, was no place for children. A uniformed officer stepped up with a long wooden spoon and dipped it into the fishbowl to stir the balls. The master of ceremonies declared it to be the spoon used for the Great War draft, as if that made it better, and the randomly selected members of the public in the audience leaned forward, mesmerized by the turning of the balls that held the fate of their husbands and sons.

"I don't know why we have to make such a spectacle of it," Eleanor whispered to Anna.

"It's how it's 'always done,'" Anna replied, her tone making it very clear what she thought of such traditions.

Eleanor looked to Franklin standing, stony-faced, at a lectern beside the bowl and knew he hated this as much as she did, but they had no choice. Last month Germany and Italy had signed a tripartite pact with Japan. The three dictators had declared that in the "new order" of the world, Japan would hold sway in the East and the West would be run along a Berlin–Rome axis. People were already referring to them as the Axis powers. "Axis of evil," Tommy had said caustically and she wasn't wrong. Hence, the draft. But it did not feel good. The election was only a week away and Franklin had stuck his neck out ordering it.

"I must, Babs," he'd said to her after he'd finally signed the order. "America needs to be ready to face her foes and if this is the last major thing I do as President, then so be it."

It had been her first indication that he was worried he would not be re-elected and, moved, she'd sat at his side and taken his hand.

"It won't be, Franklin. The people will choose you. They have to."

He'd smiled wanly. "Come, my dear, you know they don't *have* to. That's the whole point of democracy, though right now it feels as if we and Britain are the only ones standing up to fight for it. If we fail, democracy fails."

It had been a stark statement but horribly true. The dictators were winning and it could not be allowed to happen. She just prayed that democracy, precious as it was, did not throw Franklin out of the White House.

She watched her husband clutching the wood to support himself. Standing was agony for him, possible only with painful steel leg-braces and a great deal of willpower, and she was glad the bank of microphones along the front of the lectern was offering him a small amount of privacy. They were broadcasting the lottery results to the nation via every radio station on the airwaves and it would be his job, as President, to read them out, like a hooded bingo-caller. All around the country, families would be hunched over their radios, clutching their numbered slips in sweaty hands as they waited to see how soon their young men would be called.

The choice of capsules fell to Secretary of War, Henry Stimson, who was standing behind the bowl, discreetly mopping his face with a crisp white handkerchief. Neither he nor Franklin wanted to be here but the need was urgent. Congress were determined to ignore the war, refusing to even allow the supply of arms to Great Britain. Franklin was sneaking them in via the back door by asking the Army to declare them "surplus," but the Army and Navy chiefs were panicking. They could see that war was coming—be it from the Japanese forcing their way down China to threaten American bases in the Pacific islands, or from Germany, possibly via Mexico, as had been threatened in the Great War—and were clamoring for more supplies and men. Franklin was upping production, trying to push the car manufacturers to move over to tanks and planes, but with the borders still intact, it was hard to enforce any sense of urgency.

It drove Eleanor insane. She'd lie awake at night picturing the marvelous European destinations she'd visited on honeymoon, or with Madame Souvestre in school holidays, and hate the thought of them being torn apart by guns and bombs. Most Americans, she knew, couldn't imagine it, even when desperate refugees were on ships in their own harbors. Last month, another one had arrived from Hamburg, the SS *Quanza*. Eleanor had been made aware of it as they were about to be turned back to Lisbon with eighty-six poor passengers still on board. Furious, she'd swung into action, urgently pulling every string she could until all the refugees had been granted entry. She'd celebrated with her friends—though only briefly.

Breckinridge Long had been furious, fiercely protecting his role as Head of Immigration and swearing every fleeing refugee was either a Nazi or a communist. He'd demanded sole authority to grant visas be placed in the hands of the relevant American consulates, which sounded reasonable, but, as they fell within his department, meant that, in practice, he had full control. Red tape, as Eleanor knew all too well after seven years in the White House, was one of the most effective weapons of all.

For now, though, she must focus on those who would be called to bear actual arms. Henry Stimson was being blindfolded with a strip of dirty-looking linen that, they were told, had been taken from the cover of one of the seats on which the Declaration of Independence had been signed. How men loved their symbolism. If this had been up to Eleanor she would have drawn it far more discreetly but Franklin had said it had to be seen to be fair and she supposed that was true.

Their own sons were not in the draft, but only because they had already signed up. The youngest two, Frank and John, had followed their father's footsteps into the Navy. Elliott, always the rebel, had signed to the Army air force to train as a pilot, and Jimmy had chosen, of all things, the Marines.

"That's so dangerous," she'd protested when he'd proudly told her.

"Exciting too though, Ma."

This is why they had wars, she'd said to Franklin later, because men thought they were exciting. He'd somberly agreed that was a problem, but she'd seen the way he'd clapped Jimmy on the back and said "good man, good man" over and over, and feared that if even decent men like her husband, set on securing international peace, were seduced by the glamor of battle then the world was doomed.

"Your John is still safe?" she asked Anna. Her son-in-law, also a John, ran a big Seattle newspaper, so was currently protected from call-up.

"He is," Anna confirmed as, above them, Stimson was guided to the bowl, fumbling for the edge like a fool. "But he's already saying he 'feels bad' about it. If we actually go to war, I think he might volunteer to serve."

"Serve?!" Eleanor spat. "Why do we use that word so reverently? You can serve the country just as well as a politician, or doctor, or teacher. Or trash collector!"

"True," Anna agreed, "but you'll never get to be a 'hero' that way, right?"

Eleanor sighed. "Perhaps we should give out medals for civil service."

"We do—the congressional medals. I'm not sure they're viewed the same though."

She was right. Putting your life on the line would always be considered the highest service, and maybe correctly, but while it was so revered there would surely always be wars?

Eleanor shook herself. This was no time for philosophizing. In front of her, men's fates were about to be drawn from a fishbowl and she must pay attention. Her boys might not have a number in there, but Joe Lash did and he was not a man made for fighting. Trude had suggested he consider putting in a conscientious objection but he'd stuck his slim chest out and said that, although he most definitely *did* conscientiously object, he would do his bit. Eleanor had thought that a worthy attitude, but still found herself praying his number was a long way down the draw.

On stage, Henry reached into the bowl. His fingers closed around a ball and the crowd leaned forward as he drew it out and handed it to Franklin's aide, who discreetly opened it up for him and smoothed out the scrap of paper on the lectern. Franklin cleared his throat and the microphones let out a static cackle. To one side, Eleanor saw the technicians scrambling to adjust the volumes, but all other eyes were on the President.

"The first number," he said, his voice icily calm and his pace even, "is 158."

In the auditorium, someone screamed. The lights came up and Eleanor spun around to see a middle-aged woman, about four rows behind her, clutching her hair and keening like a banshee. A medic rushed to her side, a reporter with a microphone two steps behind.

"Harry," she moaned, her misery echoing around the cavernous hall. "That's my Harry. My Harry is 158. He's only twenty-one and he... he..." She broke down in sobs.

Eleanor glanced to the stage to see Franklin putting a hand out to the still blindfolded Henry. He was poised to reach for the second capsule but it would be heartless to push past this woman's grief, especially with everyone in the room hanging on it.

"He's getting married next week!" the woman forced out. Then she was sobbing again and the medic, thank God, was helping her from the room. Everyone watched her go, then, with much shuffling and muttering, turned back to Henry. Swallowing visibly, he plunged his hand into the fishbowl for the next poor buggers in line.

"How long do they serve?" Anna asked as the second number was read out with, thankfully, no dramatic response in the room.

"A year, in theory, but if we go to war that will be extended."

"And we will go to war?"

Eleanor smiled sadly at her daughter. "We will go to war. I'm not sure when, or how, but we will."

"Then Pa will have to decide the fate of all the boys represented by those numbers?"

"If he's elected," Eleanor shot back.

She remembered herself standing at the convention, convincing the party to support Franklin and his chosen team so that he could stand for a third term. Why had she done that? She could, even now, be packing up their things and moving them to the peace and quiet of the Hudson River with nothing more to do for the nation than pray.

But that, she knew, would have been unbearable.

This dark lottery would go on until every last number was drawn and recorded. Then it would be time to turn their attention to the next lottery—the national elections, and her and Franklin's continued place in the White House. There were more ways to fight a war than in a uniform and this morning had cemented Eleanor's desire to stand up and do her bit to stop the brutally bigoted Nazis before they destroyed all that was still good in the world. Now she just had to see if the people still wanted her to do so.

EIGHT

SPRINGWOOD, NOVEMBER 1940

A week later, it was not looking good. The Republicans had made huge gains in the lead-up to election day and now those were turning into solid votes. The Roosevelt family and their political team were gathered in the drawing room at Springwood to await the count and mark it up on a large chart tacked to the wood paneling. All were in their finest evening wear but the cordiality of the early evening was wearing thin. Throughout dinner they'd covered their nerves in chatter and the clink of cutlery, but now the clock was ticking toward 10 p.m. and the results were starting to come in—most of them on the wrong side of the chart.

"This can't be happening," Anna cried as Maine went to the opposition.

"It must be wrong," Sara agreed.

"It'll change," Jimmy insisted.

"They probably don't approve of me," Wallace said, wringing his hands in one corner. "I'm going to lose it for you, Franklin. I—"

"Enough!" Franklin roared.

A shocked silence fell.

"Thank you," he snapped. "And now, if you don't mind, I'm going to listen alone."

They watched, stunned, as Franklin wheeled himself imperiously between his anxious supporters and up the exit ramp. Eleanor took a step after him but he put up a warning hand to stop her and shot at speed into his study. Missy ran after him and the door slammed behind them.

Eleanor dug her fingers into her silk skirts, reminding herself that she had chosen not to be intimate with her husband. But that "choice" had been forced by the horrible, violet-scented letters and tonight it felt like a very public slight.

"Someone's a bit tense," Tommy said drily.

"Is it any wonder?" Sara snapped. "The country's going mad."

Eleanor drew in a deep breath, forcing herself to calm. "Or we are. An election is a free choice—that's the whole point."

Sara glared at her and Eleanor reached for her knitting to distract herself as the counts came in one by doom-laden one. Over in Britain, Hitler had, thankfully, withdrawn his invasion plans but had instead set the Luftwaffe to bombing London, killing many innocent civilians and destroying their homes. A New York socialite had set up an initiative called Bundles for Britain, urging American women to knit socks and jumpers to send to the homeless. Jenny Miller, a CBS broadcaster in London, had agreed to run the distribution end and America had gone "woollies" mad. Eleanor felt it important to do her bit. Plus, it was an excellent way to keep nervous hands busy.

She reached the end of her row and turned her needle for the next. Tonight was a far cry from four years ago, when Franklin had romped into his second term with a landslide majority. That had been in the middle of the New Deal measures, when he'd been giving the people back employment, dignity, and pride. This time he was threatening them with war. What would they do?

"Michigan's gone to them," one of the many senior aides said, marking it off on the chart. The room sucked in a collective breath.

"Republican states always come in first," Eleanor said stoutly.

Sure enough someone called, "That's New York for us!" and a young aide leaped enthusiastically to the chart to mark up a Democratic victory. New York might have been expected, with it being Franklin's home state, but it had been traditionally Republican before him so was never guaranteed.

"See," Eleanor said.

"And that's California."

Was the tide turning? Or were these just outlying waves? With Franklin gone, the room settled into studied calm, only the ticking of the clock and the ringing of the telephone marking out the momentous minutes in their lives. Eleanor thought she might be sick.

"Colorado's gone to them."

She focused on her knitting. She was dropping stitches, she knew, but it was impossible to concentrate properly.

"Think of all the time you'll have if you don't have to flit around being First Lady," Tommy said, nudging her gently, and Eleanor tried to laugh.

It was true. If they were kicked out of the White House, she'd be able to retire to Val Kill, to walk and ride every day, to devote herself to the articles and books that were backing up in her packed schedule. United Features had signed her for five more years of "My Day" saying, "You'd be interesting to our readers even if you weren't the President's wife," which had been so nice of them it had nearly made her cry.

"Would you stay with me if I was a nobody?" she asked Tommy.

"I'll stay with you forever," came back the instant reply. "But you'll never be a nobody."

Eleanor thought she might cry again. Maybe leaving the White House wouldn't be so bad after all.

"Pennsylvania to us."

Jimmy handed Eleanor a brandy and she smiled her thanks to her eldest son. He had leave for the election, and was looking breathtakingly smart in his Marine uniform and taking quiet command of the room. She was grateful; grown-up children were the best! She lifted the drink to her mouth, but the sharp tang of the alcohol—not something she'd ever really enjoyed—made her feel even sicker. She set it aside and knitted on.

Suddenly someone called, "Texas for us! That's huge. That might tip it."

The aides rushed to the chart, making frantic calculations. A near-hysterical euphoria filled the room and they all looked to Franklin's study door.

"Oh dear," Eleanor said to Tommy, "for a moment there, being a nobody sounded quite pleasant."

"And Georgia! That's it! That has to be it! Willkie has to concede!"

Franklin's door swung slowly open. He wheeled himself down the corridor and into the room as everyone stood, clapping and cheering. He was looking rather bewildered, Eleanor thought. Had he decided being a nobody would be fun too?

His eyes met hers and he cut through the people to sit before her, handsome in his dinner jacket. "Well, Babs—baby—looks like it's four more years. Can you stand it?"

He held out his hand and she took it, feeling his fingers clasp, vice-like, around hers. Missy hovered behind, but he was with her now and she nodded keenly.

"I can stand it if you can."

He smiled. "Grand."

. . .

A vast crowd was waiting on the lawns, torches held high against the freezing darkness, and they roared with delight as Franklin stepped onto the porch, leaning heavily on Jimmy's strong arm. He beamed around and, as quiet eventually fell, waved to the young lads who'd swarmed up their trees for a better view.

"I used to love to climb," he said, with just the tiniest glance to his braced legs. "I used to love to climb here and all over Hyde Park. I love this place and am so grateful to all who voted for me to represent it." The cheers rolled around the cold air and he raised one arm, Jimmy hastily bracing him. "I say to you now that, however much time I spend in Washington, I will always come home to here, to the River!"

More cheers. Franklin looked to his mother, who beamed with proprietorial pride. The night felt hazy, with the smoke from the torches hanging almost mystically over the gathered people as they roared their approval. Eleanor put a hand to her heart, feeling their love and almost reeling with gratitude. There'd been a time, as a young orphan, when she'd felt as if nobody in the world loved her; tonight it felt as if the whole world did.

She tutted at her foolish fancy and when Franklin headed inside, she followed gratefully, exhilaration giving way to exhaustion. The crowd were calling for him to return, as if he were a cabaret act, and she turned to laugh about it with him but then heard a new chant: "Eleanor! Eleanor!" She froze. "Eleanor!" It came again. And then, "We want Eleanor!"

Tommy, ahead of her on Henry's arm, turned. "They're calling for you, Mrs. R."

"They know a star when they see one," Franklin said with a smile.

"Are you going to go out to them, Ma?" Anna asked.

Eleanor shook her head. "Goodness no. It's very kind of them, but tonight isn't about me. I'm just the First Lady."

"No 'just' about it," Tommy said. "That was mighty tight and only one thing swung it."

"Texas?" Eleanor asked.

Tommy let out a rough laugh. "No, idiot—you. Franklin wouldn't be half the President he is without you and I hope he knows it."

They both glanced to Franklin, but his valet was whisking him away to bed. Very wise, Eleanor thought, he'd need all the rest he could get. Giving the kind people outside a shy wave from the window, she turned back to the drawing room and began clearing glasses. Best to have it clean for the morning if they were heading back to Washington. There was much to be done and it seemed the American people, despite the draft, had chosen them to do it.

Tomorrow night she would sleep in the White House once more and the next day... the next day the real work would begin. Good. She might not excel at being the pretty, waving wife, but she could put her nose to the grindstone And she *would*. She could hardly wait to get started.

NINE

THE DOLOMITES, SUMMER 1905

Eleanor stepped onto the balcony and gratefully sucked in the gloriously fresh mountain air. She'd been feeling queasy—perhaps the sweet pastries served at breakfast—and her lungs welcomed the rush of oxygen. Steadying herself against the balustrade, she looked around, admiring the view from every angle. She was in the heart of the Dolomites and thought it quite the most beautiful place they had been to yet—which was saying something. She'd been delighted when Franklin had proposed a three-month tour of Europe for their belated honeymoon and it had fulfilled all her dreams.

They'd started in Paris, a city Eleanor had last been in with her amazing headmistress Marie Souvestre. She'd been terrified that approaching it as an old married woman, it would have lost some of its romance, but the reverse had been true. Franklin had swept her across the city, insisting on buying her dresses and furs in the finest shops, then taking her around a maze of antiquated bookshops and stationers to feed what had emerged as a voracious collecting habit. He loved stamps, she'd discovered, and spent many happy hours poring over his large collection, or perusing auctioneers' catalogs for unusual finds.

"Why stamps?" she'd asked, intrigued.

"Because they speak of journeys," he'd replied straight away. "Of foreign lands and the stories winging their way between them. Because they show us how connected the world is—or can be."

She'd loved that idea. "Maybe one day, when the nations join each other around the table, there will be a single stamp—common to all."

Franklin had frowned. "You know how to confound a man, Babs. Politically that would be a dream for me; practically it would ruin my favorite hobby."

They'd both laughed and she'd lain down on the bed next to him to be taken through his rarer prizes and told their provenance and history until she'd kissed him quiet, for once the first to initiate the intimate side of their union. He'd been delighted and gladly cast his albums (very carefully) aside to take her in his arms.

She'd got used to "making love." She couldn't say much more than that. It still seemed to her an awkward, messy business, not nearly as stimulating as a lively debate, but it made Franklin happy so she tried to look enthusiastic. And she did like the cuddles afterwards. They'd had a very full schedule of places to visit and people to meet on their honeymoon so that they'd often gone to bed far too worn out for anything other than a quick kiss and a sleepy conversation, which was perfect as far as she was concerned. Especially the last few days, when she'd been feeling unconscionably worn out.

"There you are!"

Eleanor laughed as Franklin's arms went around her waist and his lips brushed her neck.

"Isn't it beautiful here?" she said, indicating the majestic Alps before them.

"Not as beautiful as you." He kissed her. "But, yes, it's glorious and will be even more so from the top."

"The top?"

Franklin pointed to a particularly craggy-looking peak. "That group of fellas we met in the dining room last night are planning to hike up there tomorrow. Fancy it?"

"Me? Franklin, I don't think I have the gear to climb a mountain."

"Oh, that's fine, you can hire boots and sticks from reception. And two of them have done it before—say it's not too vigorous."

Eleanor tried to smile but the queasiness was back. She usually liked the musky notes of Franklin's aftershave but today it churned in her stomach and made her knees feel weak.

"I'm a little tired, darling."

"You are?" He swung her around. "You look it. My poor baby, you must rest. Come on, I'll tuck you up right this moment. Might jump in with you and—" He broke off as her stomach rebelled and she had to dash for the bathroom. "Perhaps not," he said, peering cautiously around the door. "Are you all right?"

"I will be," Eleanor said. "But I think you should go hiking without me."

"Leave you alone?"

She laughed. "I'll be fine, Franklin. I'll have a lovely restful day on the balcony admiring the view and recovering from whatever this is, and you can wave to me when you reach the top."

"Yes!" He was smiling again. "Splendid idea. I'll do that."

They set off the next morning, all chatter and excitement—Franklin, three lively young men, and, to Eleanor's surprise, a woman, brazenly dressed in men's jodhpurs, her dark hair in two Swiss-style plaits beneath a broad-brimmed sunhat.

"Who's that?" she asked Franklin.

"That's Miss Kitty Gandy. She dined with us last night when you were resting. She's traveling on her own. How daring is that?"

"Dangerously daring?" Eleanor suggested.

Franklin waved this away. "She has a maid with her, but she's a timid type and Kitty says she loves an adventure. You don't mind, do you? It's only a hike with the fellas."

"Of course I don't mind," Eleanor said, the lie slipping as easily from her lips as when she told him she enjoyed making love. But her heart turned over as she watched pretty Kitty stride out in a jaunty way that made the lines of her fine form far too clear in the pale jodhpurs.

"Don't forget to wave from the top," she called after Franklin, but he was already gone and, really, it was far too far away to see even if he thought to do it.

Eleanor spent a miserable day on her balcony. The view was magnificent, and the air fresh, but she still felt queasy, especially when she thought about Franklin scaling the mountain behind Miss Kitty Gandy.

The party finally came in as the sun was starting to set behind their precious mountain and she rushed to join them, wearing her prettiest new Parisian dress. Franklin swept her into his arms, which was gratifying, and led her to join the others but the champagne was flowing and the chatter was all of loose boulders and eagles and some "hilarious" anecdote about "Kit" getting her foot stuck mid-stream and having to be carried to safety by Franklin. Eleanor listened with a smile plastered on her face and thought, perhaps, she might be sick again. The Dolomites no longer seemed such a perfect location and she was very glad when it was time to move on.

The last days of the honeymoon were subdued. They had to go via England to visit some of Sara's friends in a place called Sherwood Forest. It was apparently the romantic fairytale home of a folk hero called Robin Hood, but the weather had turned swiftly to autumn and the forest had been dank and miserable—Sara's friends much the same. Eleanor had sailed for home feeling as if she'd failed in her honeymooning skills and got back *just in time for her twenty-first birthday, more tired and sickly than ever.*

As a birthday treat, Franklin called the doctor. He hovered with gratifying concern at the edge of the room as the physician examined her, then beckoned him forward.

"Well, sir," he said, talking right over the top of Eleanor. "I can confirm that there is nothing wrong with your lovely young wife, save the natural by-product of marriage."

Jealousy? Eleanor thought woozily.

"She's pregnant!" the doctor proclaimed. "Congratulations!"

"Pregnant?" Franklin said wonderingly.

"Pregnant?" Eleanor repeated. It seemed that, however uncomfortable, the lovemaking had been worth it. "I'm going to have a baby?"

"You're going to have our baby," Franklin said. "Oh my Eleanor, my baby, you're a marvel."

He took her in his arms, holding her as if she were precious china, and suddenly the sickness was explained, and the tiredness was explained, and Kitty Gandy could go hang. Eleanor might not have forded any streams or spotted any eagles, but she was carrying Franklin's baby and that was worth more than any mountain peak in the world.

TEN

POUGHKEEPSIE, EARLY SEPTEMBER 1941

Eleanor put down her knitting to look at the banks of the Hudson from the train window and felt the peace of the river flow through her veins. She, like Franklin, had grown up in this pretty corner of upstate New York, her grandmother's beautiful country house, Tivoli, being located barely half an hour's drive north of Hyde Park. Unlike Franklin, however, her visits here had been sporadic, interspersed with periods in her unstable parents' Long Island house—manically named Half-Way Nirvana—a couple of crazy years in France, and a succession of visits to various aunts in Manhattan as her mother got ill and her father drank himself out of custody of his children.

He'd been sent away to run a mine in Virginia, living with some other family who'd had children he'd written about in his many loving letters to Eleanor and of whom she'd been fiercely jealous. Her fantasy for years, even after he'd died drunkenly falling out of a window, had been to run his Virginia ranch for him, just the two of them living there in perfect peace and stability. It had never happened, and she'd been orphaned by ten and dependent on grandmothers and aunts to see her into adulthood.

The contrast between her chaotic upbringing and Franklin's dotingly peaceful one was stark. She was not as fond of "the River" as he, and in the early years of her marriage had resented coming to his childhood home. She'd hated dark Springwood, with grand chairs at either end of the dining table for Franklin and Sara. She'd hated the tiny bedroom they'd made for her out of what had once been a storeroom, between their two far grander ones. She'd hated the silly bust of Franklin, turning the house into a shrine to his glory.

The change, of course, had come when Franklin had built Val Kill for her in the twenties and she'd finally had a home she could call her own. It was a shame it had been in exchange for a marriage she could call her own—a "guilt present" for a betrayal that had hurt far more than any pretty house could ever mend. But compromise, Eleanor had learned from an early age, was life.

Still, today she was truly looking forward to the peace of Hyde Park for it had been a hectic year in Washington so far. Franklin, fed up with Congress blocking support for Britain, had dreamed up the idea of Lend-Lease—not selling arms to their Allies, not giving them, but lending them on the promise of payment at some unspecified time in the future. He had taken to the airwaves to explain it to the people in one of his rare but justly famous "fireside chats," suggesting they should think about it as lending their garden hose to a neighbor whose house was on fire—a kindly act, with the added benefit of keeping your own house safe from the flames. The people had responded enthusiastically and Congress had been left with little choice but to pass the bill.

Since then, America had gone manufacturing mad. Franklin had banned the sale of new cars and the car manufacturers, not surprisingly, had embraced the production of tanks and planes. They were currently producing them at the phenomenal rate of fifty per day and every man in America was employed by either the forces or the factories, plus quite a few women besides. Franklin's "New Deal" back in the thirties had created jobs to get the people back on their feet, but, ironically, it was the war that was providing the mass employment to set them running and jumping into prosperity.

Washington was alive with generals, admirals and business chiefs, and life in the White House was a non-stop round of meetings and dinners. Add to that Eleanor's own groups, lecture tours, and daily column, and life had been hectic. There had barely been time to get through her many letters. Tommy, bless her, started every day filtering them into those that could be adequately answered by her small pool of secretaries, and those that needed the First Lady's personal attention. Around fifty a day reached Eleanor of which she answered maybe twenty in her own hand, but it took time. She liked it on the whole—it was far better than the boredom of indolence—but a few days' rest would be welcome, for war must be close.

America had stayed out of it so far, but the news was relentlessly bad. The Japanese were conquering more and more of China. America had placed an embargo on fuel supplies to the empire to protect their key naval bases in the Philippines, the Solomon Islands and Hawaii, and the Japanese were becoming increasingly belligerent in their communiqués. Over in Europe, meanwhile, the Nazis had shocked everyone by invading Russia. The Soviets had joined the Allies and the political map of Europe was being redrawn.

The Nazi grip on southern France was tightening and the Emergency Rescue Committee had been forced to give up their rescue mission and return home with barely half of the paltry 567 chosen refugees rescued. They'd got many to Marseilles but even when they'd secured American entry visas, they'd found French exit visas impossible. Breckinridge Long's red tape reached far, and paranoia, it seemed, had defeated basic humanity. Eleanor frequently railed to Franklin about it, but he would always insist it was not his department.

"You're the President, Franklin," she'd shouted the other day. "Everything is your department."

"I have to trust my staff."

"Why? They don't trust anyone else!"

He'd told her she was being hysterical—every man's last resort when bested by a woman in an argument—and taken her resultant fury as proof.

"People are dying, Franklin," she'd shot at him as she'd left.

"I know! And the sooner we end this war, the sooner we can stop it."

That was his focus, Churchill's too—pour all resources into weapons to end the fighting for everyone. Eleanor could see the argument, she just didn't see how they bore the suffering going on in the meantime.

Polls showed that the American public was finally beginning to favor intervention. An Office of Civilian Defense had been established to shore up coastlines, with the irrepressible Mayor La Guardia in charge. Eleanor, certain that defense was as much about stable social order as it was about anti-aircraft guns, had pushed to include community projects, and two weeks ago La Guardia had suggested she join him as his co-director. She'd resisted. It would be a full government position, unpaid of course, but more official than the catchall title of First Lady. Franklin, however, had talked her into it, saying they needed "all hands to the pump," and that sort of appeal had been impossible for her to refuse. She was to start at the end of the month and had to admit she was looking forward to her first proper job—one where she might actually be able to *act*, instead of perpetually nagging others to do so.

For the next few days, though, it was time to gather strength. Eleanor tucked away her knitting in her traveling bag as the train pulled into Poughkeepsie station, and reached for her fur, glad of the warmth over her light traveling suit, for the days were drawing in. The Roosevelts' driver, William, was waiting in the car park and she pictured Val Kill—the cozy living room filled with her own furniture, her simple bedroom and blissfully fresh sleeping porch with a view of the eponymous stream—and her heart ached to get there. Why did the last part of a journey always seem the longest?

She thought guiltily of Franklin, back in stuffy Washington. He loved being President but it was taking its toll. Last June, Missy, aged just forty-five, had suffered a terrible stroke that had crippled her elegant body. She'd been sent to Warm Springs, Franklin's treasured spa resort down in Georgia, to recuperate, and Grace Tully had taken over as his secretary. Grace was an efficient, able young woman but did not offer him the same pandering care as Missy, and Eleanor suspected her husband was lonely in the White House.

Still, she reminded herself firmly, he had chosen his path and she'd had to choose hers to fit. A picture flashed, unbidden, into her brain—a ribbon untangling, letters falling free, violet-scented poison wafting into her life—and she had to put out a hand to steady herself against the memory. That terrible day had broken the conventional limits of her marriage and, although she would always be Franklin's greatest supporter, she was no longer the woman tasked with tending to his every need. She must look to herself. Sara was at Springwood, the eighty-six-year-old back from the family home on Campobello, a Canadian island just north of Maine, where she'd been recuperating from a small stroke she'd had in June. Eleanor would go and see her very soon. First thing tomorrow. For now, though, she craved her own space.

"Straight to Val Kill please, William," she said to the driver, getting into the front seat. She didn't hold with sitting grandly in the back—how on earth were you meant to talk to people that way?

"Yes, Mrs. Roosevelt," he said, though his enthusiasm did not match hers and his shoulders were tight.

"Is that a problem?"

"No, no, of course not. It's simply that... well... you might like to go to the Big House first."

"I might not!" Eleanor said, then caught herself. William looked nervous, upset even. "What is it? What's wrong?"

"It's Mrs. Roosevelt senior, is all. She seems a little... frail."

"Frail?" Eleanor had never before heard her mother-in-law described that way. Her heart lurched. She might resent the endless control Sara tried to exert over her and Franklin's lives, despite the fact they were far into their fifties and running several houses of their own—one of them the White House!—but Sara had been good to her, in her own way. And she was an institution.

"The Big House," she agreed heavily and was rewarded with seeing William's shoulders relax.

"Thank you, Mrs. Roosevelt," he said. "Thank you so much."

Now she was really worried.

Sara sat in her usual high-backed chair in the drawing room but she was slumped low within it and had pulled a rug up to her chin. Her skin was gray and saggy and her eyes, when she looked up at Eleanor, were milky white and unfocused.

"Mama!" Eleanor ran to her. "You should be in bed."

"Fiddlesticks," Sara attempted, but so weakly that the word ran out halfway.

Eleanor summoned the staff and had her carried, protesting, up to her room. She ordered the fire lit and a hot-water bottle brought and asked Chef to make a light broth. Sara barely took three pitiful sips before she pushed it away. That was when

Eleanor knew it was bad; her mother-in-law had always had the appetite of an ox.

"Call the doctor," she instructed the maid. "And get me Franklin on the line."

"Yes, ma'am."

The girl scuttled away and Eleanor paced, trying to work out how to find the words to tell her husband how unwell Sara was. In the end, hearing his voice, she choked up and only managed, "It's your mother, Franklin. I think you'd better come."

It was all he needed. "I'll get the overnight train," he said immediately. "I'll be there at first light."

She could only hope that Sara would still be there too.

It was touch and go. Eleanor dozed at the bedside, waking periodically to check her mother-in-law's butterfly light pulse and administer the morphine the doctor had left to "ease her." He had not talked of cures, not suggested anything more than making her comfortable, and promised to return in the morning "if needed."

Dawn finally threw rays of pink light across the Hudson and in on Sara, rallying her briefly, though not half as well as when Franklin—her true sun—wheeled himself into the room.

"Darling boy, you came. How silly of you! You must have far more important things to do than visit little old me."

Franklin took his cue in style. "There is nothing more important than seeing you, Mama."

She smiled weakly. "Well, I'm sorry Eleanor bothered you all the same. It's only a silly bit of influenza. I'll be right as rain in a day or two."

What was right about rain? Eleanor wondered idly. If you were a young shoot, she supposed it was welcome, but Sara was no shoot and she looked as if even a small shower would knock her over.

"It's wonderful to see you, Mama," Franklin said smoothly. "How was your summer?"

"Oh, you know, restful. I didn't do much."

Eleanor felt instantly guilty. They'd been too busy to get to Campobello this summer and evidently Sara had been unwell for far longer than they'd realized. Why had no one said before?

Franklin, however, smiled easily and said, "Glad to hear it. That's what summer's for. And Campobello is the perfect place for it."

Sara's face turned dark. "It used to be," she said. "Before it stole your legs."

"Mama!" Franklin looked shocked, as well he might, for Sara never spoke about his paralysis.

Today though, it seemed they could not stop her.

"Your lovely legs," she moaned on. "You were so strong, son, so agile, so full of life."

"I still am, Mama. I simply have to put my energies into other things these days."

"And what wonderful things, too. President of the United States of America. I'm so proud of you, so very, very proud." Sara, briefly enlivened by her beloved son, was sinking back into her pillows.

Eleanor saw a tear sparkle in the corner of Franklin's eye and tiptoed out to let him sorrow with his mother in private.

The old lady battled her way through another night, the breaths rasping increasingly faintly out of her collapsing lungs. Eleanor sat at Franklin's side, holding his left hand while his right clutched his mother's. There was nothing he could do to hold on to her, however, and finally, just before the strike of noon, she opened her eyes, looked straight at him, gave a broad smile, and died.

Franklin dropped his head onto her hand, his body horribly

still. Eleanor, feeling curiously numb, stood slowly to call for the doctor but just then the ground seemed to shake and a strange ripping noise tore up the air outside the open window. She ran to it in time to see a great oak toppling to the ground with a wrenching of roots and a wild clatter of branches, setting loose a flock of furious birds who flew up into the air, filling it with a dark cloud. Eleanor stared. Below her, servants came running out, pointing and exclaiming. They looked questioningly up to her and she could only nod that, yes, the mistress was gone. The air filled with awestruck wails.

"What happened?" Franklin asked, looking up.

"I think your mother took an oak tree with her," Eleanor said shakily.

"Sounds like Mama," he said drily, then tears sprang to his eyes and he held out his arms, childlike.

Eleanor rushed to him, holding him close as he wept into the folds of her dress. First Missy and now his mother; 1941 was not being kind to Franklin and Eleanor's heart ached for him.

"Don't leave me," he sobbed. "Don't leave me too. You won't, will you, Eleanor? You won't leave me?"

She stroked his hair. She might have done, once, but that time was long past.

"I won't leave you, Franklin," she assured him. "We're in this together. Always."

Then the door was opening, and the staff were rushing in, the doctor with them. The room was filled with talk of funerals and memorials and their brief time alone was, as always, snatched ruthlessly away by the demands of public life. Eleanor put a quiet hand on Franklin's shoulder so he would know she was there for him, and finally felt tears sparkle in her eyes as his hand closed over hers and held on tight.

ELEVEN

NEW YORK, JANUARY 1908

Eleanor shifted in bed, trying to get comfortable. She'd been dreading the aftermath of childbirth after a miserable first experience, but her second baby had not been so bad. Sure, she felt as if she'd been turned inside out and most of her ached most of the time, but baby James—Jimmy—was three weeks old and she was already mending. With her firstborn, Anna, she'd developed an excruciating case of hemorrhoids that had ended in a terrifying operation and an infuriatingly long convalescence. Day after day she'd lain in bed, hating how little she could get done and how detached she'd felt from her precious daughter. Then she'd barely been up and about before Franklin had been cuddling up to her and she'd been pregnant once more. Her body was a glutton for punishment.

Still, she felt much better this time and there was no sign of the wretched hemorrhoids. She'd even managed to breastfeed, something that had been very tricky for Anna with all the fuss. Nurse Spring was now supplementing that with bottles so that Eleanor could get a few more things done, but it had been pleasant to tuck up in bed against the winter cold and snuggle with her baby. Of course, eighteen-month-old Anna had been forever tottering in and out, demanding attention, but Franklin was always up for a bit of rough and tumble with his daughter. And he was delighted to have a son. Theirs was a happy home—if crowded. That, however, was going to be sorted too.

On their wedding day, Sara had promised them a house of their own and at Christmas had announced the time had come to get on with it. Normally, Eleanor hated the control her mother-in-law had on the purse strings. Franklin had a reasonable trust fund from his father, plus his wage now he was in full-time employment as a lawyer, but those did not quite keep the family in the manner to which either of them was accustomed. Eleanor was happy to economize. She cared little what she ate, did not like alcoholic drinks, and was content with her surroundings as long as they were comfortable and clean. Franklin, however, was used to the best of everything and would not, she feared, know how to economize if his life depended on it.

Early in their courtship, she'd taken him to see the settlement house where she'd been working—a downtown project providing day care for poor children whose parents either couldn't or wouldn't feed, clothe or educate them. One ten-year-old girl had fallen ill and Eleanor had offered to take her home. Franklin had come with them and stared in open-mouthed shock at the cramped, filthy space in which the destitute family battled to hang on to life.

"I didn't know people could live like that," he'd said when they'd emerged.

"What did you think poverty was?" she'd challenged, tugging him away before anyone could hear him.

"I'm not sure. Just not having enough money for restaurants and horses, that sort of thing." He'd looked embarrassed then. "I've got a lot to learn, haven't I, baby?"

She'd dared to drop a kiss on his cheek. "The fact you know that is a very good start."

He'd tried since then. He'd read articles and visited charities and lamented, with her, the fact that the government could apparently do nothing to help.

"All the government do is shore up business," he'd complained after he'd started at his law firm.

"Which keeps the economy going. Men need jobs."

"They do, but we must be able to provide relief for those who cannot work."

"Maybe when you're President you will," she'd teased.

"Not maybe," he'd shot back. "Definitely."

He didn't like law and was quietly eyeing up a pathway into politics with Uncle Ted as his role model. Teddy Roosevelt had gone from Assistant Secretary of the Navy, to Governor of New York, to the White House, and Franklin wanted to do the same. Eleanor was keen to support him but if he was going to keep getting her pregnant, it would be hard to find the energy.

Still, a new house was exciting and she'd spent the days since Christmas looking at the listings in the paper and wondering how they might broach what sort of price Sara was prepared to pay. She would want it in a decent area, Eleanor knew, for their "standing," and it had to be big enough for the many grandchildren she was hoping to have. (It was fine for her to say that; she'd only given birth once!) But Eleanor was keen for some specific guidelines so she could start the thrilling business of shopping for the first true home of her own.

"Mrs. Roosevelt?" Nurse Spring came into the room, looking strangely reticent. The bustling woman was usually firmly in charge, so to see her shy was amusing.

"Is something wrong, Blanche?"

"Not wrong but... Your mother-in-law has sent an... invitation."

"Invitation? I'm hardly up to parties."

"It's not a party." Blanche Spring cleared her throat. "It's an invitation to visit a house."

"A house?"

"Well... a plot."

Eleanor felt her eyes widen. A plot! They were going to be able to build a home from scratch? Her mind spun and she looked down at baby Jimmy, asleep in her arms. She'd be able to choose her own style, her own layout. Something modern perhaps —light and airy, with clean lines and plenty of space. If that was possible.

"Where is it?" she asked nervously.

Blanche consulted the note in her hand. "East Sixty-fifth street."

That must be on the Upper East Side, near Central Park, which would be perfect for the children, and close to Park Avenue for the shops.

"When?" she asked excitedly.

Blanche grimaced. "In an hour's time."

Eleanor had no idea how she made it. She'd not been out of the house since the birthing and, with Blanche firmly forbidding any sort of corset, was wearing one of her maternity smocks. Thankfully it was a cold day so her fur coat was covering up most of her battered body. Franklin, also summoned—as if his work was of little matter in the face of his mother's plans—joined them at the end of 65th Street and Eleanor took his arm, feeling shaky.

"This is so kind of you, Mama," Franklin was saying, tugging her after Sara, who was moving far too fast for a woman fresh out of childbed.

"Can we slow down—" Eleanor started but, thank heavens, Sara had stopped.

She waved proudly to a gaping hole in the street. "Here! Isn't it a marvelous spot?! I knew the moment I heard it was on the market that we had to have it."

"You've bought it?"

"I have."

"For us?"

"For us," she agreed.

Eleanor frowned, praying the collective pronoun was a slip of the tongue. She turned to Franklin. "We shall have to find an architect, darling. Think about what sort of—"

"Already done." Sara gave an imperious wave and a slim man came forward and introduced himself as Charles Platt.

Eleanor clutched at Franklin, feeling rather faint. And not because of childbirth.

"Charles has a marvelous reputation," Sara announced. "And he's designed a divine house. Neo-Georgian. Lots of classical features."

"Classical...?" Eleanor said faintly. Not modern and light then...

"Take a look." Charles proffered a sheaf of papers.

Eleanor stared. The building was imposing, she supposed, and very elegant but... She looked closer. "There are two drawing rooms on the second floor. Do we need two drawing rooms?"

"Of course," Sara said gaily. "One for you and one for me."

"You?" Eleanor clung even tighter to Franklin's arm. He pressed his hand over hers and when she glanced over, she could see this was a shock to him too.

"That's right. See." Sara pointed to the door and there, written very small, were not one but two numbers. "I will have Number 47 on this side and you will have Number 49 on the other."

"Franklin," Eleanor said urgently.

"There will be interconnecting doors of course," Sara sailed on. "But I didn't think you'd want me on top of you all the time." She gave a merry laugh, as if she was being the most considerate mother-in-law ever.

"Franklin!" Eleanor said again.

He patted her hand and shot her an apologetic look. "Lovely, Mama," he said. "We can't wait."

TWELVE

THE WHITE HOUSE, DECEMBER 7, 1941

With Christmas fast approaching, Eleanor had thought they'd be able to finally see the back of 1941, but it seemed the year was not done with them yet. To her departing luncheon guests, the White House might appear its usual self, but after nine years Eleanor knew every nuance of the building and could sense trouble. There were too many hurried footsteps, too many slamming doors, too many ringing phones. It was always busy but this—this was a crisis.

"It's been so lovely to see you," she said, ultra-calm as she shook the hands of Franklin's cousin, Mr. Frederick Adams and his wife. They looked flustered at how swiftly the staff had ushered them to the door, but they would find out why soon enough. As would Eleanor.

It had to be the Pacific. For a fortnight, the Japanese empire had been mustering their navy in a way that suggested they were going to launch an attack on key bases in the Pacific islands. Poor Franklin was meant to be in Warm Springs, but had been forced to return after only three days' rest when Premier Tojo had broadcast a speech calling for his country to wipe out U.S. and British exploitation. Eleanor was worried about him, but now she was worried about America more.

For the last week, Cordell Hull had been in frantic negotiation with Japan, trying to persuade them to draw back from coastal China in exchange for lifting the fuel embargo. Things had seemed to be going well but last night Intelligence—who'd cracked the Japanese code months ago—had intercepted thirteen points of a fourteen-point document rejecting all of Hull's suggestions. Admiral Nomura, the Japanese Ambassador in Washington, had requested a meeting with Hull at 1 p.m. American time and everyone was concerned.

Last night, General Marshall had sent an urgent dispatch to American commanders in the Pacific, putting them on high alert, but the airwaves were clogged so he'd sent it in order of where they believed Japan were most likely to strike—Manila in the Philippines, the base protecting the Panama canal, and then Pearl Harbor in Hawaii.

It was shortly after 1 p.m. now and it sounded as if their fears had been justified. Eleanor's mind raced around the possibilities as she smiled at the Adamses' two children, happily accepting toffees from Moses, the head doorman. It had to be the Philippines, she concluded. All the forces chiefs had been saying so. It was closest to the mainland and the Japanese had coveted it for years. Those poor people!

At last, the Adamses were heading down the drive. Eleanor thought they must surely notice the bank of secret service cars parked along the front, or the dark-uniformed staff patrolling the grounds, but of course this would not necessarily look unusual to them. Only Eleanor, who knew how hard she and Franklin had fought to keep family life in the White House to something like normal, would see the bristling fear. Overhead, two military planes flew past, leaving white trails behind them, innocent markings of what she feared was a very dark day.

Turning on her low heel, she headed inside, making

straight for the Oval Office. The door was shut and a gaggle of people, most in heavily braided uniforms, were milling around outside.

She spotted Cordell Hull and grabbed his arm. "What's happened?"

He grimaced. "Attack."

"Where? Manila?"

He shook his head grimly.

"Panama?"

"No, Eleanor. It's Pearl Harbor."

She gaped at him. Hawaii had been put on alert more for form's sake than out of any real thought of trouble. The islands were thousands of miles from anywhere.

"How?" she asked, her voice husky with shock.

"Seems the Japanese snuck a load of aircraft carriers into range. Hit us at dawn—nearly two hundred bombers. Our ships were moored up like sitting ducks. It's Sunday morning, Eleanor. The men were grabbing a lie-in, or lounging on deck, or going to church. They took to battle stations immediately but the planes were already on them. Almost every ship's been hit and the waters are boiling with men on fire. From what we can gather from the poor bastards who've managed to radio in, it's hell out there."

Eleanor looked around. Suddenly the White House, so bright and strong and sure of itself, felt vulnerable and for once she was glad of the ugly guns standing guard.

"Frank!" she gasped. Her third son was on a destroyer somewhere. What if that was…?

"Your son is safe, Eleanor. They all are."

"How do you know?"

Cordell permitted himself a small smile. "This is the presidential office, my dear—we have a few privileges."

Eleanor nodded gratefully. She wasn't normally keen on living above those they were here to serve, but for this she was grateful. Though the fact that her boys were safe right now did not mean they would stay that way.

"Will Japan strike again?"

"It's certainly possible. So far, they've sent two waves into Pearl Harbor, hit five bases in the Philippines and one in Guam. Small fly-bys in those cases, nothing like Hawaii, but it shows intent. And it's not only us. There've been strikes on the British territories—Hong Kong, Singapore, Malaya. Oh, and they've invaded Thailand."

Eleanor was not given to cursing, but several sailors' words fell from her lips at this dark news. "What about America?" she dared to ask.

"All clear, but we've put the West Coast on alert. God knows how they'd get to us, but we thought that about Hawaii so this is no time to be complacent. Mayor La Guardia will fly to Los Angeles tomorrow to check defenses."

Eleanor jumped. "I should go too," she asserted. After all, she'd been working with Fiorello for three months in the Office of Civilian Defense, so she should stand by him now it was critical.

"Perhaps. Let's assess the danger level first."

"Forget the danger level," Eleanor shot back. "They wouldn't let me go to Europe, which I sort of understood, but this is America, our own country. If the people can face it, so can I."

"I'll look into it," Cordell said.

"Good." Eleanor cast around her again. For years she and Franklin had been trying to tell Americans that the war might be closer than they thought, but they hadn't meant like this. They hadn't imagined enemy planes bombing their boys out of bed. "What else can I do, Cordell?"

"Let's ask Franklin." He pushed through the crowd, shouting, "First Lady coming through!"

The men parted reluctantly and she made it to her husband.

"Franklin!"

"Eleanor, my dear. A terrible day."

He looked calm—icily calm. He'd always been this way in a crisis. As a teenager his father had suffered a terrible stroke and Sara had put her son under strict instruction to assure the invalid all was good, whatever might have happened. Franklin had learned to mask his feelings, and he had learned it well. As everyone ran around him with wild eyes and panicked chatter, he sat, calmly stroking Fala, the Scottie pup Daisy had given him last Christmas, asking sensible questions and giving straightforward orders. Eleanor looked at him with pride. There had been times when his mask had brought her pain, but today it was exactly what was needed.

"What can I do, Franklin?"

"Hoped you'd ask that," he said. "I'm going to be a bit snowed under, so could you talk to the public?"

"Me?"

"You've got your radio show tonight, yes?"

"Yes, at six forty-five." It was a weekly slot, a cozy chat with listeners along the same lines as her daily column; though it wouldn't be cozy tonight.

"Perfect," Franklin said. "The rumors will have had plenty of time to rile everyone up by then and you can sweep in at teatime and calm them down. Tell them we've got it in control but that we are going to have to go to war."

"You'll declare it?"

He smiled tightly. "Only Congress can declare war. But I will most certainly urge them to do so, and I don't think they'll resist. We've been attacked on our own shores. Americans will not stand for that."

"No," Eleanor agreed. "It threatens our freedom."

"Exactly. There'll be no fascist boots on U.S. soil, not while

I'm in the White House." A shadow passed over his brow, so swiftly that only she, standing up close, would have noticed it. He took her hand. "Will you do it, Babs? Will you talk to them?"

"Of course," she agreed because, really, what choice was there?

The NBC radio studio was a snug place and one in which she had long since learned to be comfortable. She'd been broadcasting to the public since Franklin had been elected nine years ago and, after a few initial nerves, had learned to enjoy the intimacy of speaking direct to the people via the perkily inviting microphone. Tonight, though, for the first time since her debut, she felt a shudder of fear. She had to get this right. She'd worked hard on what she would say with Tommy and it had been approved by Franklin's team, but the delivery was all hers. The American people would be scared, especially the women and children, and she had to reassure them.

The microphone light went on and the technician counted her down. She drew in a deep breath.

"Good evening, ladies and gentlemen." Her voice caught and she cleared her throat and pictured Franklin, super-calm at the heart of the storm. That's what the people needed from her, so putting her chin up, she gripped her notes and went on. "I am speaking to you tonight at a very serious moment in our history."

They'd agreed that she had to be straight, had to make the people feel included as Franklin always did in his radio "fireside chats." She told them how many important people had been in and out of the White House all afternoon and how hard they were working for America. She talked about how uncertain the situation had been for so long and that at least now they knew what they had to face and were ready. She sent out her particular thoughts to the women and children, and said that she had a son on a destroyer, possibly on his way to what had just become a war zone.

"You cannot escape anxiety," she told them, for what point was there in pretending otherwise? "You cannot escape a clutch of fear at your heart, and yet I hope that the certainty of what we have to meet will make you rise above these fears."

She hoped that for herself as well. She'd lost a child before and the pain had been so intense that she still sometimes awoke feeling it clawing at her breast. She hated that women across America might be feeling that too and drew in a deep breath as she prepared for the climactic line. The speech writers had added it and, sitting in her White House office she'd thought it too hyperbolic, but now, imagining the millions of frightened families glued to their radios, it felt right. She went for it.

"We are the free and unconquerable people of the United States of America."

A small cheer went up from the technicians beyond the booth and she smiled. Perhaps everyone needed a little hyperbole from time to time.

"And now," she said with relief, "we will go back to our planned program."

She was to interview a young soldier about his experiences in training camp but, as she turned to him, she was all too aware that their conversation had become super-charged. What had been exercises for this young man might soon be real warfare. Those daring Japanese pilots had swooped in on America and brought fear and unhappiness to more than the poor unfortunates dying in the Pacific. The sky over every state felt dark with their menace.

Back at the White House, Eleanor took comfort in her favorite ritual of the week. Every Sunday she would set her gas cruet on the table of her East Wing drawing room and cook up an intimate supper for whoever was around. Scrambling eggs was her only culinary talent but she'd perfected it over the years, favoring a long, slow stir to keep them soft and moist. Everyone would sit around the table buttering toast and Franklin would mix martinis and for a short hour her life would feel almost normal. Tonight, however, was about the least normal night she'd ever known. She'd had to move through to Franklin's West Wing to be near the fiercely buzzing Oval Office, but she was determined to keep cooking.

She looked gratefully around the people gathering at the table. There was Tommy, of course, and Henry, taking quiet charge of the toaster. Joe and Trude were here, unusually somber, and two young journalists had joined them, providing a welcome boost. Jenny Miller was running Bundles for Britain in London, and Eleanor had been keen to meet her while she was home for Christmas. Her husband, Ned, was making a name for himself broadcasting the Battle of Britain and the Blitz live into U.S. living rooms, and it was largely thanks to his vivid radio programs that Americans had understood the gravity of what was going on in Europe.

Jenny had rung earlier, assuming their invitation was canceled, but Eleanor had seen little reason for that. She'd had to fetch the pair from the clutches of the paranoid security services when they'd first arrived, but now they were settled in like part of the family. A place was set for Franklin but Eleanor had no idea if he'd make it out of his office and she had put Joe on martini-making duties.

The mood was strained, however hard they tried. Tommy had got hold of tomorrow's papers and they made somber reading. Most of them had only screaming headlines and witness reports wired in from the tiny island in the Pacific, but the few rich enough to carry the technology to wire full pictures were displaying them in Dantesque glory.

"Will they strike again?" Joe asked.

"We can only assume so," Eleanor agreed, stirring eggs. "Mayor La Guardia and I will be traveling to the West Coast to check their defenses tomorrow."

Cordell had confirmed she was authorized to fly when she'd come in from the studio, and she'd been mulling over what to pack as she stirred the eggs.

Jenny gasped. "You think they'll attack the mainland?"

"I think we have to be prepared for it. If they can get to Hawaii, what stops them reaching San Francisco?"

Jenny swallowed. "Would they dare?"

"It seems so."

"And you're going to travel toward that?"

Eleanor laughed. "I'm co-director of the Office of Civilian Defense, dear. It's my job. Now, how do you like your eggs?"

"They look perfect," Jenny stuttered, adding, "You seem very calm."

Did she? Thoughtfully, Eleanor turned off the gas flame under the cruet.

"As you know," she said to the eager young woman, "Franklin and I have been saying for some time – like both of you – that this is not a war America can ignore. Now, perhaps, the people will see the truth of it."

"But it's an appalling way for that to happen."

She nodded sadly. "It was always going to be. There are men out there who want to impose themselves and their hateful brand of elitism on the world and we have to stand up and stop them. That's always hard. Bullies are notoriously unpleasant and these ones come with guns and tanks and fighter planes." She put a hand on the hellish newspaper pictures. "They still have to be stopped, though."

There was a clatter in the corridor and they all glanced up to see the Chiefs of Staff marching into the president's office, jostling for position as they went.

"The problem is," Jenny said, staring after them, "if those trying to stop them are bullies too."

"Jenny!" Ned protested.

But Eleanor admired her perception. "Quite right, my dear. Power is an intoxicating liquor and we must be very sure to temper our desire for it. America will enter this war as defenders of freedom, not as a counterforce to the Nazis or the Japanese, and we must be sure to keep it that way."

"Is that possible?"

"I truly hope so. A genuine League of Nations would help but even without that working fully I believe, perhaps naively, that most people are inherently decent."

"Even Nazis?"

Eleanor thought about this as she dished scrambled egg onto everyone's toast. "Not real Nazis, no. Anyone who thinks they have the right to call other human beings lesser is functioning on a fundamentally skewed world view and must be stopped. But they'll drag many impressionable people in their all-encompassing wake and we must stand up and show them the errors of their leaders."

Jenny sighed. "It sounds like we must stand up and do a lot."

Eleanor nodded solemnly. "That's true. Eat your eggs, dear. You'll need the strength."

Suddenly, the door burst open and Franklin came in, propelling himself in his wheelchair and smiling around, as calm as ever. "Smells like the eggs are ready."

"They sure are," Eleanor agreed, jumping up and making space. The Millers hung on Franklin's every word and looked most put out when, barely five minutes later, he scraped his plate clean and apologized that he would have to go again.

"Of course, sir." Ned jumped to his feet, Jenny with him.

Franklin waved them back down. "Stay. Enjoy your supper.

I shall be late, I expect but, Mr Miller, if you care to wait I can fill you in more fully when these meetings are over."

"Of course, sir," Ned agreed again. "I'll be here."

"Thank you. I think I'd better go and call Mr Churchill."

"He'll be glad to hear from you," Jenny said.

"You know him?" Franklin asked.

"I know his wife, Clementine, better, sir."

Eleanor looked at the young woman. Clementine? It was an unusual name and she wondered what her British counterpart was like.

"But, yes, I know him and he will be *very* glad to hear from you."

Franklin nodded. "He's a good man. Eccentric, but good. I'm only sorry that it must be on such a sad day. This is a friendship that will have to be forged of the strongest—and darkest—steel."

"But a friendship all the same," Jenny suggested.

Franklin smiled. "A friendship all the same." And then he was gone, patting Eleanor's hand and wheeling from the room as the door to his office opened and the noise of a country in crisis roared in on the supposedly cozy supper. "Get me London on the phone," they heard him demand.

Eleanor looked at Jenny curiously. "What's Winston Churchill like?"

"A force of nature," Jenny said. "As you'll probably find out."

Eleanor supposed that was true. If they were to be active allies, might she get to visit Great Britain? Meet the prettily named Clementine? She had such fond memories of England from her schooldays and hated to think of the poor people there suffering. But for now, it was their own people she had to worry about. She must finish her supper, then she must pack and head west and pray the Japanese were not on their way to meet her.

THIRTEEN

SOMEWHERE OVER AMERICA, DECEMBER 8, 1941

Eleanor pressed her nose against the cold glass of the airplane window and peered at America laid out in the moonlight below her. They were heading west, toward the site of possible attack on their beloved country, and she felt a deep tenderness for the myriad pinprick houses she was passing over. In every one, families would be tucking up tonight, afraid for their future, and it was up to Eleanor to help calm those fears and lead them into a safer tomorrow. It was both daunting and motivating.

Last night, she'd looked out her window, as she always did, just in time to see the floodlights on the Capitol snapping off. It had felt unnervingly symbolic, but at least the tiny red light on the top of the Washington Monument had still been winking away. It was there, of course, to stop any low-flying aircraft from crashing into it, but to Eleanor it always felt like her personal protector—a benign eye, telling her all was well with the world.

Now, all was very far from well.

This morning Franklin, standing tall on Jimmy's arm, had spoken to Congress to urge them to declare war on Japan. They had done so. Eleanor had sat in the balcony and watched them vote almost unanimously and now the country was at war. With a heavy sigh, she turned back to her typewriter and tomorrow's column, seeking the right words to reassure Americans while also urging them to new efforts against Hitler.

"Must you clatter like that?"

Eleanor jumped and looked over to Mayor La Guardia. He was squished into his airplane seat, a padded mask over his eyes, a rug across his knees, and his pudgy hands clasped around a glass of whiskey.

"Do you know how I might type more quietly?" she asked.

He lifted his mask and peered at her. "No. But why do you have to type at all?"

"My column won't write itself, Fiorello, and I suspect we're going to be rather busy once we land."

"Which is precisely why it would be a good idea to get some sleep."

"Oh I will," she promised. "As soon as I've finished this. Tell me what to write and we can both have some peace."

"Isn't it obvious?" He drained his whiskey. "Write about civilian defense." Then, putting his glass down, he tugged his mask into place, pulled up his blanket and turned his back.

Eleanor looked at the typewriter. He was absolutely right. Of course she should write about civilian defense. She thought for a moment and then typed furiously: "We must build up the best possible community services, so that all of our people may feel secure because they know we are standing together and that whatever problems have to be met, will be met by the community and not one lone individual. There is no weakness and insecurity when once this is understood."

She nodded. Some people would think it wishy-washy, but if they didn't like it, they didn't have to read her column, did they? Across the aisle, Fiorello was tossing and turning, making a ridiculous fuss about the simple act of going to sleep. Eleanor never understood it. She had long become adept at switching off, perhaps because she had so little time to do so that it was a necessity. Either way, she was glad of it now. Putting the typewriter carefully back into its case, she sat back, closed her eyes, and was soon fast asleep.

Her awakening was not so peaceful.

"Mrs. Roosevelt, Mrs. Roosevelt!"

A hand shook at her shoulder and she forced her eyes open to see the assistant pilot looking down at her.

"Are we here already?"

"I'm afraid not, ma'am. We're still a long way off, but that might be a good thing."

"Why?" Eleanor stretched herself out. "What on earth are you talking about?" The man shuffled and Eleanor rolled her eyes. She had no patience with pussyfooting. "Spit it out."

"There's been report of an attack, ma'am. On San Francisco."

"What sort of an attack?"

"An airborne one."

"Bombers?"

"We don't know, ma'am. It's been radioed in from the White House."

"With any instruction about what we should do?"

"No, ma'am."

"I see." Eleanor looked out the window again, straining to see evidence of fighting in the darkness ahead, but of course they were too far away. Her heart ached for any American people being bombed and she longed to get to them. "Radio for more info," she told the assistant pilot.

"Do we turn back?" he asked.

"No. We're the Office of Civilian Defense, for heaven's sake. If there's an attack, we should rush to help, not run away."

The assistant pilot did not look as if he agreed. He skittered back to the cockpit and Eleanor heard him mumbling behind the thick curtain, then the static whine of the radio. Fiorello was still snoring gently but she would have to deprive him of the luxury of rest. There were decisions to be made.

"Fiorello!"

He jumped awake and looked wildly around but his mask was still in place, blocking his view. Eleanor reached over and lifted it off and he stared at her in confusion.

"You're in a plane, remember?" she said crisply. "On the way to Los Angeles."

"Ah! Yes. All well?"

"No." She relayed the information, such as it was.

Fiorella drank down the remnants of his whiskey and squared his shoulders like a medieval knight. "They're attacking San Francisco?"

"So it seems."

"Then we should change course."

Eleanor stared at him, disappointed. She'd thought the perky mayor had more guts. "You think?"

"Of course. Pilot!" he called through the curtain. "Call in for permission to adjust course—we will fly direct to San Fran." He looked to Eleanor. "Into the breach, hey?"

Eleanor clapped. "My thoughts exactly," she said, but he was staring at her most disconcertingly. "What's wrong?"

"Nothing. That is—I just remembered you're a lady. The *First Lady*. I shouldn't lead you into—"

Eleanor put up a hand. "Let me stop you right there. I am not on this plane as a lady, first or second or any other rank. I am on this plane as co-director of the Office of Civilian Defense and, in that role, I agree that we must fly to where we are needed. My husband would do the same, my sons too—what difference is it for me?"

"Surely a civilized country protects its women and children?"

"And there are thousands of them in San Fran, who matter more than one me."

La Guardia did not look so sure, but in the shady rankings of the political world, she was above him so there was little he could do.

"If there's shooting, we don't leave the airport," he said darkly.

"I agree." Eleanor sat back down and closed her eyes, but images of San Francisco airport overrun with fascist sharpshooters ready to bring down their plane kept creeping into her usually blissfully unimaginative mind and, for once, sleep was hard to find.

They landed cautiously. The San Fran tower operators were cheerily oblivious of any disruption and it was with relief that Eleanor poked her head out of the airplane door to find a bright West Coast morning greeting her.

"The attacks?" she asked the security staff who zoomed up in dark cars to meet them.

They looked sheepish. "A simple error, ma'am. The planes were our own, out on maneuvers."

"Don't they have to inform us if they're doing that?"

"Yes, ma'am. Normally, ma'am. It's been a little chaotic, with Pearl Harbor and all."

"Surely even more reason to radio in any airborne activity?"

"You would have thought so. You can take it up with the military if you'd like?"

"I *would* like," Fiorello said, puffing out his chest. "Why did no one update us?"

"Our radio waves had been jammed because of, of..."

"The supposed attack?"

"Exactly, ma'am."

Eleanor groaned. "I very much hope, sir, that the rest of your defenses are rather more up to scratch."

They were not.

After a brief stop at the hotel to freshen up and change into a suitably somber brown dress and coat, Eleanor spent the day with Fiorello touring the coast. They found little in the way of defense, either military or civilian. Hasty notices were in abundance, inviting people to town halls and scout huts to discuss the "home front" but they were clearly a knee-jerk to Pearl Harbor and not part of the sustained program Eleanor and Fiorello had been trying to instigate.

"We sent so much information to the county legislatures," Eleanor said to the group of San Francisco officials hastily convened to meet them for lunch. "Why has nothing been done?"

"It seemed slightly... over the top," one of the officials admitted, head low.

She fixed him with a furious stare. "And does it seem that way now?"

"No, ma'am."

"No." Eleanor stood up; she'd had enough of this. The lunch was magnificent but the attitudes of her fellow diners less so. Grabbing a crab sandwich, she made for the door. "I'm going out to talk to the people."

"The people?" the mayor said.

"Yes. Do you know them? They're the ones that vote that pretty gold chain around your neck. Good day."

It was petty of her, she knew, and they would doubtless be rolling their eyes and muttering "women!" to each other, but let them. They weren't important. She made for the car and asked the driver to take her to where the real folk hung out.

He drove her to Baker Beach, a glistening stretch of sand running out from the arches of the Golden Gate Bridge. It was a cool day but bright and there were plenty of folk meeting friends, walking dogs and enjoying their lunch in the sunshine. Many of them had binoculars trained to sea, as if they might spot a Japanese plane as they would a rare gull, but then someone cried, "There's Eleanor!" and all eyes turned instantly her way.

Her guards leaped to attention as people began to crowd around but this was exactly who she'd come to see and she happily sat on a kindly offered deckchair and asked how people felt about defense.

"Isn't that what the military should do?" one old man muttered.

"It is," Eleanor agreed. "But the military can only do so much and it's *your* homes that will be lost if there's an attack."

"My son would keep me safe," a woman said. "Only they got him in the damned draft, didn't they? Want to send him to Europe. What use is that to me?"

"It's a conundrum," Eleanor agreed. Almost two million youngsters had been conscripted as the draft rolled out and now they would be called on. "But there are many men still here. Everyone over thirty-five for a start. And women too. We're more capable than men think, right, ladies?"

"Sure are," a large-armed matron said. "I'm twice as strong as my old man. And not pickled in bourbon neither."

The crowd laughed.

"So," Eleanor said, "let's prove it. If the men are going to be away, it's up to us to make our homes safe. That means working together, building networks, preparing supplies—food and medicine and places for people to meet and support one another."

"We should have guns," a burly older man said.

Eleanor sighed. It always came down to guns.

"You *will* have guns, in time, but for now you have each other."

The people looked skeptically at their fellows.

"I still say we should have our sons back," the first woman said. "Have you got your sons, Mrs. Roosevelt?"

Eleanor shook her head. "Jimmy is off with the Marines, Elliott is in England with his squadron, Frank Jnr is on a destroyer, and John is, I believe, stationed at a naval base somewhere near to here. So, you see, they are doing their best to keep us safe, as I'm sure all your sons are doing. Now, we have to do our bit too."

"Fair point," the woman said gruffly. "They sound like good sons, Mrs. Roosevelt, and I pray to God you never know what it is to lose one."

Eleanor's heart turned over. "Too late for that," she said softly.

Then, thanking the people for their help, she traced her way up the sand and back to official duty. They had avoided attack today, but who knew what tomorrow would bring. One thing she did know: she would do whatever it took to protect both her country and her family from harm.

FOURTEEN

HYDE PARK, UPSTATE NEW YORK, OCTOBER 1909

"Can't you go faster?"

"Only if you want us to kill ourselves before we get there."

Eleanor glared at Franklin and he put out a hand to pat her knee before taking the corner at a stately pace. He was icy calm. She knew that meant he was holding himself in, keeping a tight rein on the emotions raging inside him, but for once she wished he'd go ahead and rage.

"I want to get to him," she moaned.

"I know, baby, I know. It won't be long. Look—there's the river!"

Eleanor didn't want to look. The Hudson was usually a signal for rest and peace but not today. They'd got the call early. Baby Franklin Junior, born at the start of the year, was not well.

"Not well at all," Sara had said, and she was not a woman given to hysterics.

They'd got in the car as fast as they could. The two of them had returned to New York in the working week about a month ago, but the weather had stayed so warm and fine that they'd left the children in Hyde Park with their nannies to enjoy it. How Eleanor was regretting that now.

Being brutally honest with herself, she'd been relieved to give the care of the little ones to the staff and spend weekdays in town. It wasn't so much Frankie, a sunny, happy child from the start, as the boisterous older two—Anna, aged three, and Jimmy a year younger. They'd had an idyllic family summer in Campobello but that had been in part because marvelous Nurse Spring had been with them. When she'd left to attend another woman, Eleanor had felt the strain of mothering her three youngsters and been guiltily glad to escape to adult life in Manhattan for the week and return reinvigorated to enjoy the children at the weekends. Now, she was being punished.

"Kids are often ill," Franklin was saying, more to himself than her. "We'll get the best doctors. We'll sort him out."

That's how it was with Franklin. Throw money at something to solve it. And maybe he was right in this case. She prayed so.

At last, they were pulling up to Springwood. She was out of the car before it had slowed to a full stop and stumbling into the house. Taking the stairs two at a time, she reached the third-floor nursery to a terrible sight. Her seven-month-old baby was lying in nothing more than his diaper, his arms and legs flung wide and breath coming from his tiny lungs in terrifying rasps.

Eleanor ran to him, clutching him into her arms. "Mama's here, baby, Mama's here. I'll keep you safe. I'll make you well."

She kissed his damp hair, but he woke and cried pitifully, wriggling in her arms as if she were paining him.

"The doctors say he needs air," Sara said gently.

Eleanor looked to her, sitting in a rocking chair in the window, keeping vigil over the baby. She wanted to hate her for this but how could she when Sara had been here and she, Frankie's mother, had been gadding about Manhattan?

Frankie was still squirming so she laid him back on the bed and sank to the floor, holding his tiny hand and muttering her love. He was still the cheerily chubby baby she'd kissed goodbye on Monday morning but his young skin had taken on a sickly *pallor, his eyes were as glazed as a drunkard's, and his breath came in those terrible rasps.*

Franklin went to the other side of the bed, bending to kiss his son's forehead and stroke his wispy hair. "There, there, lad," he murmured. "Don't fight it so hard."

The boy stilled and his eyes focused on Franklin. Eleanor held her breath but then he thrashed out his arms and began wheezing pitifully once more.

"What did the doctor say?" Franklin asked his mother.

"They think it's his heart."

"Right." Franklin stood up. "We need to get him to New York so he can see the best doctors."

The journey back was even harder. Eleanor held Frankie in her lap, trying to keep his airways clear as they made for the hospital where a specialist would be waiting. Within minutes of arrival, their poor baby was put in an incubator and wired up to machines. All they had was a small hole in the side through which to touch his little hands.

"His heart is very weak," the consultant said. "I fear you need to prepare yourselves."

"Thank you," Franklin said.

God knew why.

"How are we meant to prepare ourselves?" Eleanor asked Franklin as night fell and the hospital emptied of visitors.

The lights dimmed and they were left in the endless twilight hush of beeps and moans and nurses' whispers. She wanted to go back to their summer in Campobello, where all was light and happiness. She wanted to go back to Franklin Junior's birth, with Nurse Spring fussing around and everything about him new and untainted. She wanted to go even further back and have him inside her again, where he was forever safe.

But what was the use in that? Life wasn't life without risk. The fragility of it was what made it so precious.

So very precious.

Their baby lasted forty-eight hours, fading with every click of the clock. In the end, they took him out and put him in Eleanor's arms and she sat, helpless, holding him against her heart as his own took its last tiny beats and he was gone.

"I'm so sorry," the nurse said, as she prized him away, limp and lifeless.

"I'm so sorry," Franklin said, as if the loss were all hers, as if he wanted her to hold it as she'd held their baby into death.

"I'm so sorry," the consultant said. "There was nothing we could do." He made for the door, then turned back and asked, "Did you breastfeed him?"

Eleanor blinked, confused. "No. That is, I did for a time, but he wasn't keen. He preferred the bottle."

"And you preferred your freedom?"

"No!" She had struggled with breastfeeding every time. Nurse Spring had said not to worry, it wasn't uncommon, and bottles were just as good. Plus, that way, Daddy could feed Baby too. And Daddy had, every so often. But mainly it had been the nannies. "Why do you ask?" she demanded.

"Curiosity," he said, tapping his pen against his notebook. "There's a lot of research that suggests breastfeeding gives Baby all sorts of marvelous antibodies against... this sort of thing. I'll make a note." Then he did, right there in front of them, as if they were part of an experiment and not a mother and father who had just lost their son.

"I didn't know," Eleanor wailed to Franklin. "I would have tried harder if I'd known. How was I meant to know?"

"You weren't," he soothed. "Ignore him. He's a stuffy old doctor. Nurse Spring is far better versed in that stuff. Come on, let's get you home."

"He was your baby too," she snapped, infuriated. "We have to get you home too."

He looked at her and she saw a tear sparkle in his eye. "My heart is breaking, Babs," he said, his voice hoarse with tightly tamed emotion. "I'd just rather it did it away from here."

Her own tears fell and she threaded her fingers through his and let him lead her out and away to nurse their sorrow alone.

"We'll make another," he said, over and over, as they tried to eat supper back at home that evening.

"How can we make another Frankie?"

"Not another Frankie. He'll always be him. But another baby."

"Maybe." She felt too raw with grief, too weighed down with the thought of how they'd tell Anna and Jimmy that their baby brother was gone, too ripped apart with guilt that she'd not breastfed him, not stayed with him, not kept him safe from the ravages of the world. "I'm not sure I dare be a mother again," she said, pushing her food aside untouched.

"Of course you dare, darling. You're the strongest, bravest, brightest woman I know. And you're an excellent mother."

"I'm not sure I am. I find them... hard work."

"Because they are hard work. But they're wonderful too." He was up and around the table, pulling her into his arms. "You're wonderful, Babs." He kissed her and she folded gratefully against him. Then his kiss deepened and his grip on her waist became more insistent. "Let's go to bed."

"Franklin, I'm sad, I'm so, so—"

"Let me love you, Eleanor. Let me heal you."

"It's not that simple. I—"

But he was pulling her up the stairs and into his room and she was so tired, so hollowed out and pained, that it was easier to go with him than to resist. And maybe he was right. Maybe what was needed was love, if that's what the sweaty bedroom tangle could truly be called. She wanted to be held, certainly, and lying *down was such a relief, but she longed to pull the covers over her head and weep her misery into the pillow, not be pawed and prized apart.*

"Let me love you," Franklin said again.

His voice was tender, his lips soft on hers. Perhaps she was the unnatural one? She couldn't breastfeed; she didn't like the marriage bed. She must be doing something wrong and had to try harder.

"Love me," she murmured. And then he was on top of her, covering her hollowed-out body with his big, strong one, and she tried to like it, she really did, but she could find no pleasure to ease her pain and as he moved, un-noticing above, she could not stop the tears from running endlessly down her cheeks.

FIFTEEN

THE WHITE HOUSE, DECEMBER 22, 1941

"Do you have a minute to run over the Christmas arrangements?" Eleanor asked Franklin, peering around the door of his bedroom. It felt a foolish question for a man who was running a world at war, but sometimes there were things a wife needed to check with her husband.

"Of course, dear," he said easily. "Come in."

He was sitting up in bed, as was his custom every morning, breakfast tray over his knees and the papers ranged around him. He was fresh from sleep, his graying hair rumpled, his cheeks pink, and his paralyzed legs hidden beneath the bedsheet so that, for once, he looked younger than his fifty-nine years. He liked to read the news reports before calling in his key advisers to run through the day's agenda. His valet would get him up and dressed around ten and then he'd be in meetings and conferences through to the early evening. Around 6 p.m. he would call a halt for cocktail hour, when he'd mix manhattans for anyone who'd take one and insist on "no business talk" until dinner.

It was a well-honed routine and gave Eleanor the freedom to attend to her own business, which was equally packed. Every day in Washington she had at least three groups to meet, guests of some sort or another for luncheon, and often a speech to give at a meeting or charity event. In between, she had to write her column, work on her articles and books, and answer the correspondence Tommy deemed needed her personal touch. And when she went away, touring factories, charities and hospitals for Franklin, giving lectures or attending conferences, it all backed up. Still, it was better to be busy than bored.

"What are the plans, then?" Franklin asked, waving her into the chair at his side.

She sank into it gratefully. "Tedious," she said.

He laughed. "Tedious? You love Christmas, Babs!"

That much was true. She looked forward eagerly to having all her children and grandchildren together and loved buying them presents. She started her Christmas shopping on Boxing Day, buying trinkets she thought her many family members might like throughout the year and keeping them in her specially labeled and locked "Christmas Cupboard" in Val Kill. She had happily wrapped its contents in a brief visit there before Pearl Harbor had ripped everyone's lives apart, but it felt rather pointless now.

She smoothed down the dark-red skirt she'd chosen to try to get herself in a festive mood; it wasn't working.

"This year will be very tedious, Franklin. None of the children can be with us. Anna says the paper is far too busy for her and John to leave Seattle, and not one of the boys can get leave."

"There's no leave on offer, Babs, you know that."

"I do." There had, thankfully, been no further attacks on either American bases or the mainland, but, only two weeks after Pearl Harbor, everyone was still on high alert. "But that doesn't mean it isn't tedious."

"I know. It's very sad. Let's pray next year is better, but for now I might have something to liven the White House up for you."

"You might?" She regarded Franklin suspiciously. He had that bright-eyed look that usually meant trouble.

"We have a guest. I thought he'd be arriving tomorrow but it seems his travel has gone more smoothly than we could have hoped, considering it was across the Atlantic in winter."

"The Atlantic?!" Her heart leaped. Elliott was stationed in England. Had he somehow got passage home?

"Is it—?"

"Winston Churchill."

Her heart plummeted. "Winston Churchill? The Prime Minister? Coming here for Christmas?"

"Coming here for high-level political talks," Franklin corrected. "But, yes, it does mean he'll be with us for Christmas. Tell Mrs. Nesbitt to sharpen up her menus. I hear he's very fond of his food. And make sure we source plenty of champagne and brandy. Finest quality. Winston's not a man for manhattans."

Eleanor gaped at him. "This is meant to make up for not having my children at Christmas?"

"No, my dear, but it will certainly keep things interesting."

Eleanor left the room fuming. It would not just be Winston arriving, but his entourage, who would have to be found bedrooms, and servants to tend them, and places at the table. More food would have to be ordered with barely days to go, and more drink besides—much more, it seemed. The White House would not only be empty of her loved ones but filled with politicians, determined to carouse away the festive period in the name of diplomacy.

She stomped back to her office to pour out her woes to Tommy.

"Typical of a man," her secretary said sharply. "They think we conjure up beds and meals out of thin air. Makes me glad I'm not married."

Eleanor smiled at her, amused. Tommy had a suite of rooms

in Val Kill, including a second bedroom for Henry, but whether he slept in it or not was no business of Eleanor's. There were, she had learned, many ways of conducting human relationships, and as long as everyone was open, honest and fair, she couldn't see what was wrong with that. Besides, depending on one person for all your emotional needs was stupid. Eleanor's release from that had been painful but since then she'd opened up her life to amazing friends like Hick and Joe, and her life was the richer for it.

Tommy, for example, was a perfect companion. The gruff Bronx-woman was caring but caustic, and always ready to make sure Eleanor did not take herself too seriously. Growing up among kind but detached adults had not led Eleanor to a life of play, and she sometimes regretted her inability to giggle and flirt and surrender to the merry silliness of entertainment in the way others seemed able to do. But she did like Christmas—or, rather, she had.

"Ah well," she said wearily. "Best get on. No one else is going to sort this out."

It was already 9 a.m. She was due at the Office of Civilian Defense at ten, with her usual press conference at midday, the Salvation Army Christmas celebration at two, and an appointment with the American Committee for British Catholic Relief at four. How on earth she was going to rearrange the entire household among all that she had no idea—but little choice.

She would write about this in her column later, she vowed. Let the ordinary housewives of America see that the President could be every bit as inconsiderate as their husbands. But, for now, there was much to be done. Winston Churchill had been bravely leading Britain's lone resistance against Hitler for a long time and deserved their best hospitality. She just hoped he wasn't too demanding a guest, for her Christmas already felt horribly fragile.

. . .

By the end of Christmas Day, Eleanor had no idea whether she liked Winston Churchill. The man was brash and boorish. He drank slowly but flamboyantly throughout the day and in the evening his pace seemed to increase. He had extraordinary stamina, helped by retiring for a two-hour nap in the late afternoon which left him refreshed to talk well into the night. Franklin was enraptured and staying up far too late over the brandy bottle, which was not good for him at all. Churchill, at sixty-seven, might be eight years older than Franklin, but he did not have polio, a condition that had withered not just Franklin's legs but his whole immune system.

It wasn't only the drinking that Franklin was following Winston on. The British Prime Minister had arrived with a plethora of maps and a small gang of assistants to update them on a regular basis. He had commandeered the ladies' cloakroom as his "map room" and it was a hive of activity. On one wall, Army units, air bases and naval vessels across Europe and northern Africa were marked up with pins, and on another the same for the Atlantic. Franklin, fascinated by the way the pins were adjusted as troop movements were radioed in to the staff, had asked for a third covering the Pacific and set his own team to monitoring the Japanese. It made sense, Eleanor supposed, but did it have to happen right here, in the heart of her home?

"Mine is slap bang in Downing Street," Winston assured her when she questioned him. "That is, it's in our underground den beneath it."

"Den?" Eleanor queried, thinking it made the Prime Minister sound like a badger.

He grimaced. "I'm trying to make it sound cozy. It's a frightful place, all blank corridors and pipes, but my ministers insist. Can't have the PM being blown up, can we? Terrible for morale."

Eleanor tried to imagine the conditions Londoners were living in and failed. She'd seen the newsreels of what they were calling "The Blitz"—the terrible pictures of homes ripped asunder and people on the street. She'd seen the ambulances bumping through the rubble and the brave medics, most of them women, lifting the injured onto stretchers. She'd seen the anti-aircraft crews, also mainly women, and the air-raid wardens and the people crowding into the underground stations to sleep in long, communal lines. The films had been vivid, as had Ned Miller's radio reports. Eleanor had frantically knitted jumpers and socks for those whose wardrobes were buried beneath rubble, but it was hard to feel what it must be like to be the people wearing them.

The Blitz had thankfully stopped when the Germans had turned on Russia in the summer but everyone knew that the moment Hitler took Moscow, his ratty little eyes would return to Great Britain. In the face of that, it was weak of Eleanor to not want the war in her home, but when she saw Winston and Franklin poring enthusiastically over the giant maps she couldn't help thinking how like little boys with toy soldiers they seemed. To her knowledge, Franklin had been more interested in birds and stamps than battle figurines but he was keen enough now. Something about the strategy of war seemed to entrance men. Perhaps that's why the world was so often sucked into it.

Winston was not a simple house guest. He loved to talk, thought little of cutting across others, and had made it quite apparent he did not think the White House food up to much. Eleanor was used to that. Her housekeeper, Mrs. Nesbitt, was more talented in economy than cuisine, but she ran a tight ship and took no nonsense, and Eleanor treasured her for that. For herself, she cared little what food tasted like as long as it was nourishing and gave her energy for the work ahead, so she found Churchill's mutterings over his dinner infuriating.

On the other hand, the man was entertaining. He could tell a story at least as well as Franklin, who was a fine raconteur, and he had a prodigious memory for history and literature, quoting reams of the classics at will. He could be very funny when the mood took him, and surprisingly tender.

Eleanor was most moved when she found him sitting quietly in the corner after Christmas dinner and asked if he was well.

"Missing home," he said with disarming honesty, a tear sparkling unashamedly in his eye. "I do love Christmas with Clemmie and the kittens."

Again Eleanor wondered what Clementine Churchill must be like—a saint, for sure, to put up with Winston all the time. And kittens?! As far as she was aware, the Churchills' children were as grown up as hers so it had surprised her to hear him using such a pet term. Nonetheless, the unaffected openness was very sweet.

"I'm sure they're missing you too," she said and offered to fix up a line for him to talk to them.

He seized on this with alacrity and later, refreshed by his conversation and most of a bottle of champagne, he toasted her kindness to the whole room. Oh, he was a confusing man!

"Should we discuss the peace?" Eleanor suggested as Christmas Day finally wound to an end.

"How to achieve it?" Winston asked. "Absolutely. I think we need to go in via North Africa and—"

"No," Eleanor interrupted him. "I mean the nature of the peace. The terms of it, if you will. How we stop anything like this from happening ever again."

"Ah," Winston said. "Yes." He gave her a curious little bow. "A timely reminder, madam. I am so caught up in the fight that I am apt to forget the end goal."

It was gallantly done and he went on to talk about the possibility of renewing and modernizing the League of Nations. This attempt to bring everyone together after the Great War had stumbled, not the least because, to Franklin and Eleanor's shame, Congress had refused to let America join.

"I think we need something new," Franklin said. "The league is tainted—not the idea, you understand, but the way it's presented and run."

"New?" Winston queried.

He was not, Eleanor had noticed, a man keen on novelty. He was rooted in the traditions of English life and wedded to their precious—and utterly outdated—empire. She assumed he'd reject Franklin's ideas out of hand but he returned to them later in the evening and, when Eleanor left the men at midnight to finish her correspondence, they were deep in discussion about how to bring the disparate nations of the world together.

"We need a name for it," was the last thing she heard them say as she climbed the stairs.

The next morning she was startled by a splash and a curious squeal from the corridor. Darting out of her room, she saw Franklin in his wheelchair staring into the bathroom, wide-eyed, and heard a laughing Churchill shouting that "the Prime Minster of Great Britain has nothing to hide from the President of the United States." He appeared a moment later, dripping wet but, thankfully, with his modesty covered by a silk dressing gown.

"Did you have something to say to me, Franklin?" Winston asked.

"The United Nations," Franklin pronounced. "That's what we should call our new organization—the United Nations."

"Perfect!" Winston cried, throwing his arms wide so that Eleanor had to hastily divert her eyes in case the dressing-gown cord was insecure. But she liked him then. She liked his enthusiasm, his positivity, his childish delight in the world and what he could do for it. And the "United Nations" *was* a perfect title, something to fight for that was not just defeating enemies or defending borders but also finding a new way forward.

. . .

Two hours later, however, Winston was infuriating her once more. He was due to speak to the crowd gathered on the White House lawn, but was lingering in his room. Eleanor sent an aide to chivvy him along and the man reported that Winston had suffered a small "episode" leaning out to close his bedroom window.

"Does he need a doctor?" Eleanor asked.

"He assures me not. He has his own physician, Dr Moran, as you know..." Eleanor did know; she'd had to make two of her staff share a bedroom to create one for him. "And he's content for Winston to carry on. He just needs a minute or two."

Twenty minutes later and the crowd were growing restless. Franklin had been ready in his heavy leg braces for some time and Eleanor was worried about him. She was about to head to Winston's room to check on him herself, when there was a noise at the top of the stairs and she saw him descending, very slowly, gripping the banister as tightly as Franklin gripped his son's arm when he insisted on walking in public.

She rushed to him. "Are you well, Winston? There's no need to speak if you don't feel up to it."

"I'll be fine," he said gruffly. "Nothing a small whiskey won't sort out."

Eleanor was pretty sure a small whiskey would only make things worse, but who was she to say? She sent a server to fetch the decanter and certainly the spirit brought color to Winston's cheeks. Even so, his hand shook and sweat glistened on his baby-smooth brow as he went over to Franklin.

"Into the breach, my dear man?"

"Ready when you are, Winston."

Eleanor watched the two men head onto the porch together, one on withered legs, the other with his hand to a clearly racing heart. Would this war kill them? she found herself wondering.

And yet, as they reached the podium and began to speak, they both seemed to visibly grow. Their voices rang out, loud and confident, assuring the people—and all those listening on radios across the country—that they would stand together and lead their joined nations to victory against the fascist evil.

Winston was an eccentric old thing, that much was undeniable, but he had courage, as Franklin had courage, and that counted for a very great deal. He had not been Eleanor's preferred Christmas guest, but he might turn out to be one of her most important. If this man could work with her husband, not just to defeat the fascists, but to build a world with truly united nations, then she would put up with all the brandy, the silk dressing gowns and even the map rooms until that vital goal was, pray God, achieved.

SIXTEEN

NEW YORK, APRIL 1942

"Here are your keys, ma'am."

Eleanor took the small bunch from the realtor and turned them over and over in her hands as if they were treasure. Maybe they were. These shiny bits of metal would let her into her new apartment at 29 Washington Square West. 15A was on the sixteenth floor and was a modest, seven-room apartment, but would provide the perfect New York base now that Sara had passed away and the grand house they'd reluctantly shared with her had been sold. Franklin had co-signed the lease but they both knew he would have little time to come here while he was President. It would be Eleanor's space and she couldn't wait to make it hers.

It wasn't her first apartment in Greenwich Village. For years after life had got... difficult, she'd rented an apartment here as a refuge, an escape, a way of asserting who she was—a driven, political woman who preferred the quirky atmosphere of the Village to the snobbish one around Park Lane. She didn't need the escape so much these days, but it felt good to have a place of her own in the city again.

Thanking the realtor, she waved away his offer to "show her

around." If she couldn't figure out how to unlatch a few windows and run a basic boiler, then she didn't deserve this place. Spotting the concierge, she went over to introduce herself, then wished she hadn't as he obsequiously bowed.

"We are honored, Mrs. President. Honored!"

She flushed furiously. This was the last thing she needed! Washington Square was to be somewhere she could relax and be herself, rather than the First Lady.

"It's plain old Mrs. Roosevelt here, please."

"Of course, ma'am. Absolutely, ma'am."

"I'm just a resident, same as any other."

"Hardly, ma'am," he said with a kind smile. "But if that's how you want it, that how it will be. I'm Walter, here for all your daily needs. Welcome to Washington Square."

Relieved, she tipped him handsomely and made for the stairs. Walter hurried to point out the elevator, but she waved this away, assuring him that climbing was good for the circulation. Mind you, by the time she reached the sixteenth floor she was kicking herself for her pride. Fifty-eight was no age to be straining one's heart like this; she must learn her limitations.

Sucking in deep breaths, she approached 15A. They key turned with a satisfying click and she stepped inside, closed the door, and let out a giddy whoop. Clapping a hand over her mouth, she looked around, but of course there was no one here to see. Not one person! Even Tommy was off with Henry for a much-deserved vacation, and for one glorious afternoon Eleanor was all alone.

She still felt guilty, mind you, being so happy when the world was in crisis. The war was going terribly and the odds for every young soldier felt far too short. Joe Lash's number had come up for the Army and last week Eleanor had thrown him a going-away dinner, trying to drown her fears for the safety of this sensitive young man in good food and wine. It had not worked. She prayed for him, alongside her sons, and every single recruit every night. But the world was at war and she wasn't sure God was listening to the fools so carelessly destroying his creation. Somehow, they had to sort it out themselves.

In North Africa, British troops were struggling against the formidable Generalfeldmarschall Rommel. The only good news had come from Russia where the Red Army had valiantly turned the Germans away from the very gates of Moscow and, aided by the ferocious Russian winter, forced them into retreat. But the Germans were regrouping and as soon as the spring thaws came they would go again.

Stalin was flinging every man he had against the invader. Millions were being crushed, but there always seemed to be millions more. Moscow was screaming for Britain and America to open up a second front in Europe to draw Nazi fire, but neither Franklin nor Winston were ready and, really, Marshal Stalin should not have allied himself to Hitler at the start of the war. Eleanor had little sympathy for him, though every sympathy for the people he was throwing to the wolves.

Meanwhile, in the Pacific, the Japanese were running rampant and had taken Guam, Wake and Hong Kong. General MacArthur had been pushed to the furthest tip of the Philippines and last week Singapore had fallen. Churchill was distraught. The resources-rich island was one of the jewels of his precious empire—or had been—and although Eleanor and Franklin had little truck with that, the loss of the huge military base was a severe blow to the Allies.

Worse, the defeats had aroused the ever-ready paranoia of the State Department, and Breckinridge Long had talked Franklin into signing an executive order to send one hundred and twenty thousand Americans of Japanese ancestry on the West Coast into "relocation centers"—a polished-up name for concentration camps if ever Eleanor had heard one. It had occasioned the worst argument of their residency in the

White House, and the second worst of their entire married life.

"It's a precaution," Franklin had told her, icily calm.

"It's an abomination, Franklin! More than half those people were born in the States. They're as American as you and I."

"They may have friends and relatives in enemy territory," he'd stated, robot-like.

"As might the hundreds of thousands of German and Italian immigrants across America but I don't see any of them in camps. This is racism, pure and simple."

"I am not a racist!"

"Doesn't look that way to me."

The argument had ground on for weeks with Franklin uncharacteristically recalcitrant, despite the obvious distress caused by the draconian policy. Eleanor's horror had been slightly appeased when the Quakers had volunteered to run the camps, ensuring they would be humane. But she was deeply ashamed of the decision and campaigning for every right she could secure for the new victims of American paranoia.

Shaking the thought away, Eleanor began determinedly investigating her new rooms. There was only so much suffering you could absorb before you went mad and she tried to focus on what was directly before her. She would have to get furniture and curtains and hang some of the many photographs she had of her family and friends. Drawing a tape measure from her handbag, she began to measure up, sketching rough diagrams on a small pad and neatly marking the dimensions, glad to assert some control, if only over her limited private life.

Last week she'd had to resign from the Office of Civilian Defense after complaints in Congress had become too loud to ignore. They'd found out that she was employing "friends" to help with the project and gone wild. It was true, to be fair, but Eleanor had a very wide circle of acquaintances, enabling her to appoint people with the best skills for the jobs. Not that that mattered. Men could appoint the members of their precious private clubs to every job in town without censure because "that was how business worked," but when women did it, it was empty-headed nepotism. Oh, it made her mad.

Everything, these days, made her mad!

She had no idea how Franklin coped with the petty government infighting and, although she'd been sad to give up the projects she'd held dear, she'd not been sorry to leave her official position. It had meant a lot to her to be actively involved in the defense of America, but it seemed to be impossible to get anything meaningful done without irritating people, especially when you were female. She had long got used to being called a "nag" or a "harridan." It did not worry her personally but it did infuriate her that being persistent in having your voice heard was seen as a sign of assertiveness and authority in a man but of petulance in a woman.

Eleanor sank gratefully into a battered armchair left by the previous tenants and looked around her tiny kingdom. This central living room had a wood-burning stove and beautiful built-in bookcases that she could not wait to fill. To one side was a fine kitchen and dining room and to the other four well-sized bedrooms. She had already selected the one looking over the park for hers and another for Tommy. A third would be a guest room and the fourth would be for Franklin, should he ever get time to visit.

The apartment was theoretically here for them to move into when his third term was up in 1944 but it was almost impossible to imagine what the world would look like then. Surely another two years would be enough to defeat the Nazis and bring the world to peace? But it was hard to imagine. Would Franklin have to stand for a fourth term? Surely not!

Eleanor and Franklin had lived in the White House for nine years, the longest they'd been consistently in any home since their marriage. It belonged to the nation and they were merely temporary tenants, but it was impossible for certain habits and attachments not to form. For all its pressure and frustration, the White House was an invigorating place to live and Eleanor could not see them sitting out old age as a private couple after so much stimulation. It had been Franklin's dream to be President. Who wanted to wake up from a dream?

She stood up, shrugging this away. A mirror hung on the opposite wall and she caught sight of herself in it—a tall woman, in a handsomely tailored suit, with hair more white than gray and lines around her eyes that told the world she was growing old. Well so what? She had no intention of giving in to age. Her mind was as agile as ever and physical infirmities could be overcome; just look at Franklin!

He was lonely, she knew. He was talking of bringing Missy back to the White House but the doctors said she would return as an invalid, not as a bright spark to pull him out of his infirmities. He missed his mother, and with the children away on war duties, he had little close companionship. His cousins Polly and Daisy were often around to offer the devotion he craved, but apart from them, his only intimate was his Scottie dog, Fala. Indeed, Fala was probably more wife to Franklin than Eleanor, happy to sit forever at his feet and love him without condition or question.

More fool Fala.

A scent of violets wafted through Eleanor's mind and she grabbed her handbag, riffling past her knitting and notebooks and drawing out three framed photographs. They weren't much but they would serve to make her new apartment homely. Carefully, she arranged them on the bookshelves. The first was of the children at Campobello, the second of the whole family on the Springwood porch the night Franklin was first elected President, the third of the two of them shortly after their engagement, when their love had still been secret. She stared at it, twisting her wedding band around and around, pushing the rotting violets away. They *had* been in love. Franklin had been ardent in his proclamations and for the first time in her life Eleanor had felt truly happy. Truly secure.

It had not lasted.

Eleanor shook herself crossly. Such introspection was good for no one. Plenty of women had gone through the same as she had without making such a fuss. Few, perhaps, with such high-profile lives, but that only mattered if you cared what others thought and Eleanor had long since learned not to waste her time doing that. She and Franklin had a partnership and if, sometimes, she felt a longing for the sort of storybook love that had made her giddily happy for a number of years, she soon shook herself out of it. Love was like a strong cocktail—potent but dangerous. And apt to make you behave like a fool.

Through the window, she could hear the faint buzz of New York, and went over to look down upon the bustling people sixteen stories below. This apartment truly was wonderful—so close to the life of the city but so blissfully detached from it too—and she was determined to enjoy it. What was the point in fighting for your way of life if you did not live it to the full when you could?

Eleanor stashed the notepad full of measurements carefully in her bag and smiled at the indulgent thought of the pieces she would order delivered to her new home. She would lay it out exactly as she wanted and it would be hers, no matter who else cared to join her. But as she took a last look around, she couldn't help noticing the step between the living room and the corridor to the bedrooms. That would be hopeless with a wheelchair.

She sighed. Franklin was blockheaded and infuriating, secretive and devious, but he was also—usually—warm and forward-thinking. The man of the New Deal was not the man locking Japanese-Americans into camps, and she had to assume that the pressures of the war were taking their toll. Her husband, deep down, was every bit as engaged with the world and its many problems as she was, and if he could step away from the presidency, she might see the real him once more.

Whipping her notebook back out, she made a note: "Carpenter for ramps." She could do nothing to bring her husband to Washington Square, but everything to make it welcoming for him if he ever did come.

SEVENTEEN
WASHINGTON, JUNE 1917

"Coffee? Would you like sugar in that? Two? Of course. You'll need your energy once you're on your way!"

Eleanor gave the soldier a bright smile, trying not to notice how young he looked, or how his hand went continually to his top pocket where, no doubt, a photograph of his sweetheart nestled. Union Station was bursting with soldiers heading for the coast and faraway Europe. Some of them were blasé, boasting of how many enemies they were going to kill, others were openly terrified. Most sat somewhere in between, bravely hiding their vulnerable humanity beneath the comforting homogeneity of uniform. Eleanor had volunteered to go with them to nurse on the battlefields but approval for her appointment had got tangled up in government red tape, so here she was, serving cups of coffee to the men heading into the fray.

"Coffee? Would you like sugar in that? No? How about a cookie then? Home-made this morning."

The soldier accepted this with alacrity, taking a large bite and praising her domestic skills. He moved away far too fast for her to explain that it had not been home-made by her—she was useless in the kitchen—and she was left feeling vaguely fraudulent. It was not an unfamiliar feeling. Most of the time as she went about family life, she felt as if she were acting out a part. She loved her children dearly but feared she wasn't naturally maternal and was looking forward to them growing into adulthood when she could engage with them as equals.

Anna and Jimmy, at eleven and nine, were becoming quite a handful, though they would be sent to school soon. Elliott, born just ten months after poor little Frankie's death, was seven, and the new Franklin Junior was three. Eleanor had wanted to preserve that name for her lost son, but Franklin had insisted and, really, with their lone daughter called Eleanor Anna after herself, she had hardly been able to object. She was used to it and young Frank, as she'd carefully taken to calling him, was a charming, easy child, who definitely took after his father, unlike Elliott who could be rather wild.

Eleanor feared Elliott's instability was her fault. Still struggling with the loss of little Frankie, she'd not been able to give in to the joy of her new baby in case he, too, was taken from her and perhaps his erratic behavior was a result of her inattentiveness. Would she never learn her lesson? Her sixth baby, John, was just one year old, and here she was applying to travel to the war zones of Europe. She wasn't a natural mother! But she did love them all and should probably not be putting herself in danger just to satisfy her itch to help the wider world.

Perhaps Franklin had buried her application. To his delight, after being elected to the state legislature in 1910, he had recently been appointed Assistant Secretary of the Navy. It was a job he loved and apparently one that made him too important to "waste as cannon fodder." Eleanor had been shocked at the stark analysis but they were four years into the war and no one, not even Americans fresh into combat, was under any illusion about the brutal nature of the fighting. So, she was not in Europe and he was not in Europe, but he, at least, was on track with his career and pursuing his goal with steady but fierce determination. The fact that it meant he only spent a few hours every week with his children apparently made him a perfectly natural father. Perhaps Eleanor should have been born a man...

"Coffee? Would you like sugar in that? Here you go!" Eleanor doled out more cups of thick black liquid, remembering to smile.

"Send Soldier off with a cheery beam," the Red Cross superintendent had urged in training. "It will be bleak out there and the memory of your pretty face will keep his morale strong."

It had been anodyne stuff. Eleanor knew her face was not pretty, and her smile showed far too much of her protruding front teeth, but the soldiers seemed to like the interaction so she did her best.

"You remind me of my sister," the next lad said gratefully.

Sister. That was not so bad, was it? A sister was a solid, comforting, dependable sort of a dame. She was someone you could play with and tease and, if the chips were down, ask for a hug.

"Like her, I'll pray for your safe return," she assured him, and slipped him an extra cookie.

A thought crept, unwelcomed, into Eleanor's head: *No one would call Lucy a "sister."*

Lucy Mercer was her secretary, or had been until recently. Employed when Eleanor had been snowed under with work supporting Franklin's campaign to the state legislature, the composed young woman had swiftly become part of the Roosevelt household. The kids had loved her. She was warm and easy, quick to laugh and rarely ruffled, and she seemed to have endless patience for doing jigsaws and playing the sort of make-believe games that Eleanor didn't have the imagination to sustain. She was also good-looking in that petite, bright-eyed way that men liked, and smelled prettily of violets.

The Red Cross would have loved to employ Lucy to send off the boys inspired to fight, like a modern-day Helen of Troy. Well, *tough, because she wasn't available—and not because Eleanor was keeping her for herself. Quite the reverse. She'd been forced to let her go as her secretary when she'd been alerted to gossip about her and Franklin becoming "close"—whispered with gleeful emphasis at a cocktail party she'd already been hating.*

The children had been furious to lose her and Lucy so tearful Eleanor had feared she'd been a fool, but the girl already had a new job. She'd joined the Navy as a yeomanette (the term every bit as prettily flirty as she), and been immediately assigned to the office of the Assistant Secretary... Now, instead of Eleanor having Lucy under her supervision, the bright, clever, attractive young woman was with Franklin day in day out in the safety of his tight ship of an office. Eleanor had absolutely no idea what to do about it. She was a worker, not a flirter; a sister, not a lover. But then, what did such petty concerns truly matter, with the world at war?

Wiping away a tear, Eleanor forced herself on with the job at hand. "Coffee? Would you like sugar in that?"

EIGHTEEN

THE PRESIDENTIAL TRAIN, SEPTEMBER 1942

Eleanor liked trains almost as much as she disliked boats, and the specially commissioned presidential train was a particularly fine one. The ten-carriage locomotive was equipped in high style with elegant bedrooms, a beautiful living area and a fine kitchen.

"Is it a bit *too* opulent?" she asked Tommy as they climbed on board and went to get themselves settled in their adjoining rooms.

"No," Tommy said crisply. "Kick aside your puritan streak for once, woman, and enjoy a bit of luxury."

Eleanor laughed. That was her told! And, besides, the schedule for the tour was a punishing one so it would be good to be able to relax in between. She was joining Franklin for a trip south to inspect a huge range of factories, army camps and naval yards busting a gut for the war effort and in need of a boost. It wasn't the sort of thing they usually did together, as they could cover more ground if they worked their own schedules, but Franklin had especially asked her to come with him.

It had taken some juggling to free up the time, but she was

glad to escape Washington. It was important to travel America, or you began to think everyone lived like they did and became terribly out of touch. She'd recently put in a proposal to visit Great Britain to learn from their clever home front organization and was praying Franklin would authorize the visit. Perhaps this trip would be a chance to discuss it.

"It'll be good for you," Tommy had said, when Eleanor had mentioned coming on the train. "You don't see enough of each other with this damned war taking up everyone's time."

"You think?" Eleanor had asked, surprised. For years, she'd spent around two hundred days away from her husband, traveling America on lecture tours and projects, as well as running these sorts of inspections and visits as they were far easier for her than for Franklin. "We're hardly a sit-down-to-dinner-every-night type of couple, Tommy."

"No. But these days you're lucky if you dine together once a month. And hardly ever alone."

That much was true. There were always important guests to entertain—generals, congressmen, ambassadors, exiled princes and princesses. Crown Princess Martha of Norway had sought refuge in America and was often in Franklin's company, offering the sort of flirty compliments he so loved. It was rather nice therefore that, given such enticements, he'd asked Eleanor to come on the train. But, then, she was the First Lady. And lots of people had sent them very kind invitations to all sorts of things once they'd heard she was going to be coming.

"Because they love you every bit as much as him," Tommy had said. "And he knows that, even if you don't."

It was nice of her to say so, but with poor Missy "honorably retired" to her sister's house she thought he might just be lonely. Even so, as the train got underway and Franklin sent to ask if she'd like to take tea with him, it really did feel as if he wanted her for herself.

"How are you?" she asked him, taking a comfy armchair at his side in the lounge-car. Franklin was poring over one of his treasured stamp albums so she gladly took up her knitting and settled in. She was becoming quite proficient these days and very much enjoyed how it was both relaxing and useful.

"Good. I'm good. Better when I look west than east."

Eleanor nodded. The first half of this year had seen considerable success in the Pacific. Her dear son, Jimmy, had been part of the brilliant reclaiming of Midway Island from the Japanese. She'd trembled to imagine the dangerous work of his "raider" corps, but the operation had been a huge success. Across America people had celebrated the avenging of Pearl Harbor and Franklin had been very proud. Now, though, all eyes were turning to the European arena.

In North Africa, ruthless Rommel had stolen the key port of Tobruk from the British, and was advancing on Alexandria, where, worryingly, Anna's husband, John, was stationed for the War Office. Earlier this year, he'd buckled under the pressure to "do your bit" and taken leave of absence from his newspaper to sign up. Anna was not happy about it and neither, from the sounds of his letters, was John now he was actually faced with a combat zone. When, Anna and Eleanor had opined together, would men stop seeing the front line as glamorous?

The answer might come horribly soon for Franklin had authorized an invasion of North Africa this November – the first mass U.S. service of the war. His approval had been at the urging of Winston Churchill and against the advice of all senior military advisers in Washington. If it went well he would be a hero; if it went badly he would go down in history as the President who sent thousands of American boys to the slaughter.

"How are things in Africa?" she asked nervously and was surprised by a glimmer of a smile.

"Improving. General Montgomery has taken command and I'm told he's licking the men into shape. It's been a long campaign out there and maybe they need a fresh commander to turn things around."

"He's good then?"

"I believe so. Classic Brit, all stiff upper lip and curt orders, but that gets the job done."

"Good. He'll pave the way for our boys to invade?"

"God, I hope so. That General De Gaulle man has been romping around Africa recruiting his colonials, but mainly in the west. In the east where, note you, there's the most immediate danger, he's failed to gain much support. It's a worry."

"I can see that," she agreed, setting down her knitting. "But Eisenhower is a fine general. He knows what he's doing."

"God I hope so," he said again.

He looked around but, bar the maid with the tea, they were alone in the carriage. Tommy was in her room sorting Eleanor's correspondence and Franklin's aides were, by the sounds of them, in the adjoining bar making the most of the presidential liquor supplies to get the long journey south going with a swing.

Franklin leaned in. "Do you think I did the right thing, Eleanor?"

She almost choked on her lemon slice. Franklin often canvassed her opinion in advance of his decisions, and she'd frequently heard things they'd discussed suddenly appearing in important speeches, but he had never before questioned a decision once made. Not to her, nor to anyone.

She reached out and took his hand. "I do, Franklin."

"Truly?"

Truly, she had no idea. She still avoided the Boys-Own map room and had little clue about military strategy, but she did know something of humankind.

"We have to get into the war in Europe. The draft was nearly a year ago and the anniversary of Pearl Harbor will soon be upon us. If we allow that to come around without any direct action against the Nazis, the public will be very disappointed."

Franklin gave her a faint smile. "It's good of you to say so but we declared war on Japan, not Germany."

"Then Germany declared war on us, so we had little choice but to fight them too. We have to find a way of attacking him. And not by launching our boys into France—not yet."

"No."

"So... Africa."

"Africa, yes." His words were positive but his tone forlorn.

"Are you feeling well, Franklin?"

It was the wrong thing to say. He pulled back, his shoulders tightening. "Quite well. This is not about me, it's about the strategy of the war."

"Of course it is," she said hastily. "I've just never seen you question a decision once you've made it before."

"Maybe I've never made one against the advice of every expert in my team."

"Churchill is, surely, in your team?"

Franklin rolled his eyes, but his shoulders loosened again. "I suppose he is, yes."

"And he understands the situation on the ground in Africa, does he not? He and his generals."

"Yes, but they've got their backs to the wall so they're going to want help however risky it might be."

Eleanor considered. "I'm not sure that's true," she said eventually. "Winston is a bullish man but a crafty one. If he thought Africa was a lost cause, he'd be pulling out and regrouping, as he did at Dunkirk."

"He had little choice at Dunkirk."

"But will have learned his lesson. That man has a brain the size of a whale."

Franklin let out a sudden bark of a laugh. "The size of whale, Eleanor? Where on earth did you conjure up that image?"

Eleanor laughed too. "It was the biggest thing that came to

mind. Sorry. I'm no expert with words, Franklin—that's your job."

He leaned forward again, retaking her hand. "Oh, I think you are very good with words, my dear. And very, very good with people. I'm glad you're coming with me on this trip."

"Me too," she said, and she meant it. Tommy was right. They'd spent far too much time apart recently and it was nice to reconnect.

The trip went very well. The army camps and naval bases were alive with activity and the men delighted to be visited by the first couple and eager to demonstrate their new-learned skills. Eleanor liked talking to them, but hated the thought of them soon being on ships to North Africa and much preferred the factory visits. Production was booming and Eleanor was particularly glad to see so many women on the shop floor, running complicated machinery with skill and bounce.

"Is that not terribly hard?" she asked one woman, operating a rivet gun as skillfully as the famous Rosie the Riveter of the posters urging women into the workforce.

"Not anywhere near as hard as trying to get a toddler to eat broccoli," the woman shot back and Eleanor laughed and asked if she could have a go. The gun was hefty if, indeed, relatively simple to use, and the clunk of the rivets was very satisfying. Plus, next time Eleanor looked up to a plane flying overhead she would be able to think that it might be held together by her own labors and that was a fine thing.

The only real complaint from the women was a lack of childcare. Grandmothers and great-aunts were weighing in where they could but it was far from perfect.

"What we need is onsite nurseries," Mrs. Williams, a hard-faced woman, said to Eleanor on the last visit of their trip.

"Tell my husband," Eleanor suggested.

"Very well, I will."

The woman marched up to him, beefy arms crossed, and told him in no uncertain terms that he couldn't have it both ways—women either stayed at home and looked after their children, or came to work and built the machines that would help the country win the war.

Franklin, to his credit, listened to her carefully. "I see the problem," he said.

"Do you though?" Mrs. Williams demanded loudly. "Imagine if you had to run all those meetings you must have in the White House, while worrying about whether your kiddies were running amok."

"That would be very difficult," he agreed again, but she wasn't to be placated.

"That's easy to say, Mr. President, but *really* imagine it. You're IT, the backstop. If you don't look after your toddler, no one will. No one. We don't all have nannies or nurserymaids."

"Of course not," he said, abashed. "I see your point, Mrs. Williams, though it may be harder to make Congress see it."

"I'll come and tell them. And I'll bring my four little horrors for them to take care of. See if that helps broaden their vision a little."

Eleanor and Tommy had to fight hard not to burst out laughing at the vision of four mini Mrs. Williamses running rings around Congress.

"I might give you a call," Franklin said and ordered an aide to take a flushed Mrs. Williams' contact details as he moved gratefully on.

"You will consider childcare, won't you, Franklin?" Eleanor urged that night.

The train was heading home to Washington and most of the party had retreated to the bar for a last hurrah. Eleanor sat on at the dinner table, curiously unwilling for this trip to come to an end. They'd met so many interesting people and seen so much activity and it had been invigorating. Plus, the train had proved the perfect place to keep up with work—at least if you did not find the bar seductive. Tommy, she was aware, had been harder pushed to resist its allure. Her secretary loved a good whiskey, as well as the nonsense chatter that the Scottish water always seemed to induce, and tonight Eleanor had been glad to dispatch her to cut loose. She was, therefore, alone with Franklin and seized the chance to press Mrs. Williams' well-made points.

"I will," he promised. "Although it won't be easy. Your average congressman believes that a child is best with its mother."

"But not its father?"

"Eleanor..." His weary tone implied she was being foolish, which was very irritating. Just because women carried babies in their bodies for nine months did not, surely, mean they had to carry them for the next eighteen years as well? She mentally counted to ten.

"The point is, Franklin, that right now mothers are not so much mothers, as workers. If we wish them to work productively we have to enable them to concentrate on their factory job without having to do a second one in the home at the same time. It's not possible."

"I suppose not," he said, but it was clear he wasn't convinced.

"Fine." She stood up, flicking the skirt of her black silk gown away from her heels, and lifted Franklin's Scottie dog from his warm bed into his master's arms. "Hold Fala. Now, we're having a meeting over here. Come and join me please. No, no—you can't put Fala down. He can't support his own head."

"Eleanor..."

"Come on, this way. Oh and you'll need to make notes. And it will be a good five hours long."

"He won't let me hold him that long." Franklin laughed.

"He'll need a pee and his food and... Oh I see. Very good. Very clever."

She sighed. "It's not a game, Franklin. It's life. Remember Anna when she was little? Or Jimmy or Elliott or any of them."

"I remember it well," he agreed, releasing a wriggling Fala.

"So imagine: You're in sole charge of them, your mother, who's meant to be having them today, has sent a message that she's sick, and in thirty minutes you should be driving rivets into an airplane in a factory twenty-minutes' bus-ride away. What do you do?"

"Call a neighbor?"

"She's already on the way to her own job."

"Sweet-talk the neighbor's mother?"

"She's got six kids already and she's eighty-four with a weak heart."

"Take them with me...?"

"Into a factory full of welders and drillers?"

"Right." He thought about it. "I guess, then, I don't go to work."

"Exactly! Then the planes don't get made and the Army don't have them to fly in cover of their infantry and the Germans defeat us and shoot half our boys dead, then come for our country."

Franklin gave her a rueful smile. "I don't know about Mrs. Williams, but perhaps I should take you into Congress with me, Babs."

Eleanor shuddered. "I've had my brush with government work and I'm not going there again. You'll find a way around them, Franklin, you always do."

He smiled again, more openly this time. "Thank you for your faith in me."

She looked at him, his face pale in the flickering lights as the train chugged them back to the White House. "I've always had faith in you, Franklin. Always."

"I know." He drew in a deep breath. "I've liked having you with me these last few weeks, Babs."

"It's been good."

"I like having you with me generally. You do know that?" His blue eyes fixed on hers, now beneath gray eyebrows but burning as brightly as she remembered back at the start of their courtship.

She shifted. "In what way?"

"In every way that counts. You're the most interesting woman I know."

"But not the best company."

"Oh Babs, yes. You *are* the best company. A little tiring, perhaps, but only because you care so much about the world. You're my conscience, my darling girl, my agitator, my good angel. I'm a better man for having you at my side, and most certainly a better president."

A lump came to Eleanor's throat and she tugged at the collar of her blouse. "I don't pander to you."

He chuckled. "No. But there are plenty to do that." He wheeled himself around to her side, reaching for her hand. "This has been fun, yes?"

"Yes," she agreed cautiously.

"So how about doing it more often?"

"How do you mean?"

"How about us being man and wife again. Properly. Oh, not in *that* way—I'm an old man, Babs, and my vigor must go into politics—but living together more... permanently."

She looked sideways at him. "You mean me giving up my projects to stay in the White House with you?"

"Not giving them up, just... cutting back. Not traveling as much."

"Not going to Great Britain?"

"Why should they get you, hey?" He shot her his finest smile. "I'd love to have you in the White House to host cocktail hour with me every night and dine with our guests and spend weekends together."

"Doing what?"

"Relaxing, Babs. Going to the theater, eating with friends, collecting stamps... knitting!"

He indicated her half-completed jumper in the corner. Eleanor tried to smile back but found herself fighting for breath. She liked all of those things, but they weren't terribly useful. Besides, what would people say if she canceled her hectic schedule of events? She'd be letting them down –and just to go to the theater!

On the other hand, this was her marriage. It had been through a lot and taken on a shape that not many would recognize, but that had worked well for them so far. Perhaps it was time for it to shift again?

"Consider it, Babs," Franklin said. "That's all I'm asking."

"The thing is, Franklin, you'd still be President, doing everything you have to do, but would I be First Lady?"

"You'd be *my* First Lady." She bit her lip and, seeing it, he surprised her by leaning forward and kissing her. "I love you, Babs. Always have and always will. I know I did a really bad thing, but that was a long, long time ago. Maybe we could forget? Move forward? Find a way back to each other?"

"You think we could?"

He smiled. "I think you and I can do anything we put our minds to. Surely the man and woman who brought America the New Deal can do a new deal for their own marriage too?"

Lord help her, he was persuasive.

"Remember what it was like when we were first married?" he urged softly.

She did. She really did. She'd been so happy, so innocently, trustingly happy. It would be wonderful to feel that way again.

But was that possible?

"Those letters, Franklin."

Her words came out on a moan and she heard him sigh.

"Can you not let go of the letters, Babs? Please? It was twenty-four years ago."

"Was it?" Eleanor looked at him, surprised. For to her, that painful discovery still felt like yesterday.

NINETEEN

NEW YORK, SEPTEMBER 1918

Spanish flu! It sounded so innocuous, like something you caught on vacation, but the reports in the papers described a killer virus sweeping through the troop ships bringing the men home from war. It was a dark irony that the lads who had survived the killing fields were being struck down by a mere bug, but perhaps it was nature having her revenge, punishing man for wreaking such destruction on the world. That, at least, was what Eleanor had thought last week, but now Spanish flu was staring at her from the pale face of the person she loved most in the world and it looked truly horrific.

Franklin had only been sent to Europe to take charge of closing up the naval bases now the war was won. He'd sailed off in high spirits, thrilled to be at sea, but sailed back into New York harbor eight weeks later as a wraith—pale and drawn but burning up as if there was hellfire in his belly.

Eleanor dipped a cloth in the bowl of cold water by the bed and mopped his brow. He jerked his head away, flinging an arm up to ward her off, but she was practiced now and, catching it, kept it pinned to his side as she labored to suck the cruel heat from him. The doctor had said that if she could keep his temperature below a dangerous level he might have a chance.

Might.

Eleanor had barely slept for fear of letting him burn up. She'd hired a nurse, who was very competent, but it wasn't the same, was it? Only Eleanor knew how much Franklin mattered —to herself, to the children, to the world. He was going to be President one day. They'd discussed it over and over, planned it with such care, and he was on his way. He couldn't die.

"Come on, darling," she crooned as she whipped off the cloth, now boiling hot, and applied a fresh one. "You can do it. You can stay with us."

He moaned and his eyes opened but did not seem to be able to fix on her. Outside, the sun was rising, but day and night had no meaning for Eleanor; her only clock was her husband. She wished there was more she could do but the doctor said there was no medicine that could help, just his own body fighting the infection with this fever that might, ironically, kill it in turn.

"Come on," she urged again.

He'd been like this for three days and nights and there was surely only so much more he could take. To make things worse, the younger children had caught it too. They seemed, thankfully, to have a mild dose that was merely making them irritable and tetchy, but Eleanor had to dart off to the nursery constantly to be sure that none of them had worsened. Memories of losing Baby Frankie still haunted her and she could not bear to have that happen again. At the moment, though, it was their father who was in the greatest danger.

The nurse arrived, saying Eleanor should get some rest, but how could she with her husband at death's door? And yet, she could feel herself swaying from tiredness and was unable to protest when the nurse tucked her up on the padded window seat and assured her that she would wake her immediately if there was any crisis. She was asleep within moments.

When she woke, the sun was high in the sky and the nurse was smiling. "I think the fever's broken!"

Eleanor leaped up and ran to Franklin. He was lying completely still and for a terrible moment she thought he was dead, but when she put a hand to his forehead, it was merely warm and not coated with a clammy sheen of sweat. He'd done it —he'd fought the Spanish flu and won. From what she'd read in the papers of the many, many cases, the worst should be over. The vicious bug had killed around fifty million people worldwide— more than the whole war—and would kill many more yet but Franklin would not be one of them.

"God be praised." She pressed a gentle hand to his heart to feel it beating beneath her fingers, then kissed him and tiptoed off to the nursery to check on the children.

They, too, were recovering and for once Eleanor was delighted to see Elliott and Frank wrestling violently. She would order beef for dinner to get everyone's strength back up. And she would send to Sara that it was safe to come through from her side of the house at last. They'd kept her away, for the flu was merciless with the older generation, and she would be so relieved to see them well. She was a controlling, interfering matriarch but she loved them dearly.

Returning to Franklin's room, Eleanor sent the nurse for a break and sat down at his side. She could see his chest rising and falling more normally, and he was no longer thrashing or moaning. Smiling, she looked around the room. Goodness, it was a mess! In the horror of nursing Franklin, they hadn't even unpacked his suitcase and it was sitting on the side spilling clothes onto the floor in a most unseemly way.

Relieved to have something constructive to do, Eleanor began pulling out items and sorting them. The naval laundry service had clearly not been functioning with so many sick men onboard and she fetched a basket to send most of it for washing. Every so often she glanced to the bed, but Franklin was still sleeping peacefully. She almost went over and crept under the covers to curl up next to him, but that would hardly aid his recovery.

Finally, the case was empty of all but the sundry items in the two capacious pockets at the back. Eleanor removed his toiletries bag and lifted out a pair of framed photos—one of herself in their early courtship looking ridiculously fresh and young, and one of the children on the beach at Campobello. She set them on his bedside table and, kissing him again, went back to the final items: a compass his father had given him, a silver hip flask and then, buried at the bottom, a package of some sort. She caught a waft of sickly sweet violets as she pulled it out and felt her gorge rise.

They were letters, carefully bound with a ribbon, addressed to Franklin in a curving, surely feminine hand, but they were not from her. Hands shaking, she fumbled with the ribbon and the letters dropped out and fanned across the inside of the empty case. Picking up one, she pulled out the contents—three sheets, words spidering passionately across the page. Eleanor's eyes blurred but phrases leaped out at her, cruel in their clarity.

Darling I miss you so much.

I cannot wait for us to be together again.

I long to press my lips to yours, to feel once more the delicious sensation of your tongue creeping lower and lower until I must beg you to...

Eleanor threw the letter down, clutching at her chest as if her heart might burst out of it. She forced herself to scrabble for the final page, though she knew already what it would say and, sure enough, written brassily bold:

Ever yours my darling Franklin, Lucy.

Now it was not just her heart that was threatening to burst out of her body, but her whole self being turned inside out. She'd known he had a soft spot for pretty Lucy, known he liked her company, liked flirting with her even, but this... This was a betrayal of their marriage, of their children, of their whole life together. Worse than that, it instantly exposed everything that was wrong with Eleanor. She could never have written to him with such wanton abandon and she could never, ever, have let his tongue run... Well, wherever it had run.

Leaping up, Eleanor ran to the bathroom and vomited, though there was so little in her stomach after three tiring days of nursing, that she could only retch emptily into the bowl. How apt, she thought miserably. How very apt. She was a dried-up husk of a wife and Franklin had traded her in for a younger, prettier, brighter model. For a moment, she almost wished he had died but then she remembered—he was going to be President. It was going to be a wonderful thing for the world. He just, it seemed, wished to do that with someone else now.

When she eventually went back to the room he was awake and sitting up.

"Eleanor!" He gave her his usual cheery—treacherous—smile. "I'm sorry. Have I been an awful nuisance?"

In reply, she lifted the letters from the case and scattered them across his bedsheets. He went whiter than he had from the flu.

Divorce. It was such an ugly word, especially once you'd heard it over and over and over until it seemed to take on a life of its own—an ugly, hairy monster threatening to eat up all your happiness, save that it was already gone and the beast was just feasting on the remains.

Eleanor offered it to Franklin quite calmly the first time, using it as a knife to cut through his apologies and promises to change. For agonizing days she'd been forced to listen to his blustering explanation that Lucy had been alternately "a madness," "a silly bit of fun" or "a terrible mistake." In the end, tortured by his blithe dismissals of the affair that had torn her life apart, she went on the offensive.

"I think we should get a divorce."

The scary bit was the silent twenty-four hours after, in which she truly thought he might take her up on her offer. She told herself she should want a divorce, that she should not allow herself to be treated this way, but all her life—until Franklin— she'd been treated poorly and underneath her determined surface bubbled the craven little girl wanting to take whatever scraps of love were left over. Her mother had left her, her father had left her; she wasn't sure if she could bear for Franklin to leave her too.

Then came the other people, flooding in with their opinions, advice and "support." Their marriage had always been lived within a wider sphere, their brief intimacies like bubbles within the sea of public life, so why should its demise be any different? Franklin's advisers were horrified at the thought of a divorce, his mother, once she'd been mortifyingly appraised of the situation, even more so.

"That cannot happen," she pronounced. She offered no moral judgment on her son, and no appeasement to her daughter-in-law, simply plowed forward with how things "had to be." "The Mercer girl is Catholic," Sara said, businesslike as she sat before the pair of them, stiff and awkward on the couch. "She will not marry a divorced man, so if you have any thought of that, Franklin, you can put it out of your head."

Eleanor wasn't so sure. She'd read enough of the letters to believe that Lucy Mercer would give up anything for Franklin, and had not even dared to look at Franklin to see if he believed the same. Was he talking to Lucy? she tortured herself wondering. Was he telephoning her? Writing to her? Meeting her? He was still weak from the flu but was taking walks around the gardens. Was she behind a tree, waiting for him? Were they plotting their future while Eleanor's turned to ashes? Her imaginings felt like poisonous insects feeding on her flesh and it was all she could do not to scratch off her skin.

The days ground painfully on and a new argument emerged.

"You will not be able to run for high office as a divorced man," Sara announced.

"You could run," his adviser corrected. "But you would not win. The people would not countenance a divorced president."

And that, it seemed, was that. Whether Lucy was behind a tree or not, Sara had set Franklin's greatest love against her—not Eleanor, nor their five children, but his political career.

"I want you, Eleanor," Franklin said when the humiliating hullabaloo died down and they were alone at last.

"Why?" she asked. By then she was not in the mood for platitudes. For thirteen happy years she had lived secure in the cocoon of her marriage, loved and wanted at last. Now, it emerged, that had been a sham and there was no more time for romance, just for cold, hard truths.

"Because you're the most interesting woman I know."

"But not the most attractive."

"Being interesting *is* attractive."

"Just not attractive enough."

"I had my head turned, Babs. I was a fool and—"

"You were," she interrupted, putting up a hand to forestall any more wasteful bickering. "But now we must decide how we go forward."

"I don't want a divorce, Babs, I—"

"Fine. If I agree to stay with you..." He gaped at her, astonished the decision was not his. "Then it is on two conditions."

"Conditions?" he asked nervously.

Eleanor drew in a deep breath. She had thought about this long and hard as the politicos had wrangled over how the breakup of their marriage might affect Franklin's career trajectory. At first she'd thought the pain of his betrayal unbearable, but every day the sun rose and the children came running and their world rolled on. No emotion, it seemed, could not be borne with a supreme effort, but she could not risk the same hurt again. She was sick of being controlled, sick of worrying about what *people thought about her. Look where that had got her! If Franklin wanted a wife solely for his career, then that's what he would have.*

"One—there will be no more intimate relations between us."

"No—?"

"No."

"So how do I...?"

"You don't. Two—you will never, ever see Lucy Mercer again."

"But she works in my office."

She stared at him.

He swallowed. "She doesn't work in my office any longer?"

"Not unless you want a divorce. I can sue for it as well, you know, Franklin."

"I thought—"

"Well don't. You've hurt me."

"I know and I'm truly sorry. I won't see Lucy, I promise. We can rebuild our marriage. I'll be good to you, really I will. I'll make you love me again."

Eleanor looked at him. She wished that were true. She really, really wished that were true, but she feared it was too hard a job even for him. Franklin had shattered their marriage into a thousand tiny pieces and it was going to take a long time to pull even a fraction of them together again, let alone to form it into a resilient whole once more. Their only hope, perhaps, was to form it in a new shape—a sturdier, less glamorous shape, but one that, pray God, might be strong enough to hold.

And there was only one way to do that—Eleanor had to step aside from pleasing Franklin and work out, at last, exactly what it was that pleased herself.

TWENTY

THE PRESIDENTIAL TRAIN, SEPTEMBER 1942

Eleanor pressed her forehead against the train window, feeling it cool against her heated skin. They were passing through a station and a muted light revealed a handful of passengers, gaping at the presidential train. A woman waved excitedly and she raised a hand in greeting.

"It's Eleanor!" she heard the woman cry, grabbing at her husband's arm and pointing. "It's actually her, Eleanor!"

Then he was waving too and the others on the platform were looking up and smiling and she felt a rush of love for them all.

"It's Eleanor."

Not "the President's wife," not "the First Lady," not even "Mrs. Roosevelt," but Eleanor. The people knew her for herself: writer, broadcaster, campaigner, friend.

Eleanor turned her wedding band, once, around on her finger and turned slowly back to her husband. "I can't give up my work, Franklin."

He closed his eyes a moment but when he opened them again he was nodding gently. "Why should you, my dear? It was foolish of me to ask it."

"Not foolish."

"Brave?"

She laughed. "Kind. And maybe, once upon a time, we could have rebuilt our marriage along traditional lines, but those weren't the cards life dealt us. I had to change, build myself a raft so I didn't drown."

"Drown?"

"In sorrow."

"I'm sorry."

"I know." She went over and sat at his side. "The thing is, Franklin, that raft didn't just save me, it propelled me into being someone I never knew I could be—a woman in my own right, with my own projects and ideas and friends."

"A man then?" Franklin suggested ruefully.

"A man, yes!"

"A husband even."

She nodded. "And I'm sorry if that means you don't get a wife, especially with Missy gone and your mother passed away."

"That's not your fault, Eleanor." He reached up to tenderly tuck back a strand of hair escaping from her evening up-do. "Your raft—if that's what we must call it—did not turn you into a new woman. You *were* that woman, that wonderful, driven, caring woman with her eyes on the worries of the whole world. That's the woman I married and I'm sorry it took stepping out of that marriage, at least in the normal sense, to let her truly come into her own. But I'm still glad she did." He shook himself. "I shouldn't have asked."

She leaned in and kissed him quietly, her lips lingering on his before she forced herself to pull away. "I'm glad you did."

"You will go to Great Britain then?"

"If you'll allow it, Mr. President."

He shook his head fondly at her. "I'd be the biggest fool not to. Lucky Brits. They'll love you."

PART TWO

TWENTY-ONE

BUCKINGHAM PALACE, OCTOBER 1942

Eleanor did not know what she'd expected from a palace but this one met every possible criteria. For a start it was vast. The White House was far from small but Buckingham Palace went on and on, with corridors and rooms in every direction, all with fancy wallpaper, fine furniture and fairytale gilding. Wandering dazedly around, she and Tommy agreed that although, logically, they'd known British history was far longer and deeper than American history, coming face to face with it was impressive.

"This chair predates the Declaration of Independence," Eleanor whispered to her secretary when they sat down to dinner.

"Not surprising," Tommy whispered back. "It was the owners of these chairs we fought for that independence!"

The whole palace sat in a vast, enclosed courtyard at the heart of London and was guarded by khaki-clad soldiers. Princess Margaret, a precocious twelve-year-old, had told Eleanor scornfully that they were "drab these days" and taken her down a maze of corridors to see a model wearing a delicious scarlet uniform and huge, furry bearskin hat that was apparently the peacetime uniform of the King's Guard.

"Much nicer, aren't they?" Margaret had said and Eleanor had had to agree that they were far more fun.

But this was London in wartime and little was fun. Or, rather, little should have been. The Londoners, however, seemed to have an extraordinary ability to get on with both work and play amidst the rubble of the Nazi bombings.

There were not, thankfully, many raids any more, but the evidence of the damage and suffering they'd inflicted was everywhere. King George and Queen Elizabeth took them out to visit some of the worst-hit areas in the East End and Eleanor was horrified to see whole streets reduced to rubble. Children were playing among the broken bricks and families living in sheds, tents and all manner of makeshift accommodation, cooking on open fires like their forefathers (or foremothers) of centuries long past. Many were wearing roughly knitted jumpers which Eleanor assumed were from the Bundles for Britain program. She hoped she didn't see any of her earlier efforts on display. Though she'd been proud of them at the time, they had been quite terrible and the poor Londoners had suffered enough.

As soon as the King and Queen were spotted, an excited cry went up and crowds gathered, pressing for a handshake and calling out blessings. The security staff fretted but their majesties waved aside their concerns and chatted to their people as if they were the greatest of friends. They then introduced Eleanor and she was gratified that many of them had heard of her.

"American soldiers are very big and strong," one little lad said to her. "And they have chocolate!"

His voice had taken on a reverential tone and the Queen explained that chocolate had been rationed in Britain for several years and the children missed it.

"Not just the children." She laughed. "I'm rather partial to a nice chocolate myself, so the sooner this war is won the better."

The crowd cheered with the sort of merry optimism that

people living in rubble should surely not find possible, and laughed over their shared depravations. Eleanor assumed the Queen was being tactful, as surely any palace could secure chocolates at will, but that evening over dinner it was clear the royals were adhering strictly to rationing. They were treated to three plain courses—fishcakes, cold chicken with salad, and a sponge pudding—with just a single bottle of wine. Eleanor heartily approved.

She was, mind you, rather less pleased when, going to take a bath the next morning, she found a dark line drawn a mere five inches up the side and was told by the maid that the water was not allowed past it.

"Water is rationed too?" she gasped.

"Yes, ma'am. We need it to put out the fires."

Eleanor did not complain further. How could she in the face of such stoic coping? And she wrote about it as vividly as she could in the column Tommy wired home every day, hoping to impress upon Americans how easy a war they were having in comparison to their British cousins.

The royal family were charming to her. Despite living in a veritable museum of a house, the King and Queen, their two princesses and their pack of short-legged corgi dogs were as straightforward as an everyday family. The King always looked smart in his wartime naval uniform, and the petite Queen elegant in a parade of floaty pastels that made Eleanor feel very conscious of her height and the conservative nature of her tailored suits and dark dresses. Queen Elizabeth floated through the crowds with a pretty tilt of her head and the smile of an angel—although she was not an actual angel; quite the reverse. In the privacy of her home, Elizabeth teased her husband, loved a flutter on her beloved horses, and had a wicked sense of humor.

She and the King clearly doted on their daughters, but had brought them up very strictly. The girls wore dresses made from cut-down curtains, tidied their bedrooms, and attended long hours of schooling every day. They were incredibly polite and had clearly imbibed their parents' sense of public duty. Princess Elizabeth especially, as heir to the throne, was a solemn young woman of sixteen, who engaged Eleanor in a wide-ranging discussion of the problems of the world.

"We must find a way to stop men going to war," she said earnestly over the deliciously stodgy sponge apparently called a spotted dick.

"My husband and Winston Churchill are working on a way of bringing all countries together in an organization called the United Nations," Eleanor told her.

"Oh I know," the Princess said immediately. "I was talking to Mr. Churchill about it last month. I think it an excellent idea and have been discussing something similar for the Commonwealth with Papa."

"You have?" Eleanor said, astonished.

"For the future, you understand, when the war is over and we can focus our minds on how to move forward. As we help countries to gain independence, it behoves us to promote the Commonwealth as a means of joining together in friendship, loyalty and shared peace."

"I see." Eleanor was genuinely astonished. Franklin had told her after one of his late-night drinking sessions with Winston that, despite granting theoretical freedoms to its dominions, Britain was welded to its empire. And yet here were the King and his heir already with forward-thinking ideas. It was most refreshing. "That sounds wonderful, ma'am."

Elizabeth flushed. "It is our duty, do you not think, as leaders, to actually lead—to show the people in our charge the way it is possible to be?"

"I do," Eleanor agreed. "I think it is excellent that you are looking at ways to... modernize your empire."

"Thank you. Perhaps America will do the same with its attitudes to segregation?"

"Elizabeth!" King George snapped, but Eleanor was not offended.

"The Princess is absolutely right. It's something I've been fighting for, for some time."

"I hear Mrs. Roosevelt once broke ranks in a segregated conference," King George said.

"Broke ranks?" the Princess asked, gazing at her.

Eleanor flushed. "I wished to sit with my good friends on the black side but the southern authorities forbade it. I could hardly fight for fear of embarrassing my husband, so I set my chair in the aisle instead."

"All alone?"

"Yes. It was a little frightening but sometimes you have to stand up and be counted, do you not?"

"You do," she agreed warmly. "And you did! Well done, you."

Eleanor found herself strangely moved by the young woman's praise, but still ashamed she had not done more to stop racial inequality. The people of Britain had been shocked at the fact that the American Army was still segregated. Some publicans were banning white GIs, in protest at their high-handed treatment of their black brothers, and those white GIs were enraged.

"Not nice being singled out merely for the color of your skin, is it?" Eleanor said mildly to one young man at a training center.

"But, but my skin's white?"

"A color developed, I believe, when the original humans moved from Africa into cooler climes."

"Original?"

"Oh yes. Did you not know? The Africans came first."

"I... I didn't know." He looked down, abashed, and Eleanor

prayed he would think about it in the privacy of his room and realize the foolishness of discrimination. It could only lead to problems—look at Hitler.

It was hard *not* to look at Hitler over here. The papers seemed to carry nothing but war news, quite understandably, as it felt so immediate. Everyone was on rationing, every city, town and village was blacked out at night, war posters were everywhere, and so were soldiers—in training camps, on leave, on their way back to war. Some were injured, many had sweethearts clinging to their arms, most had the weary but determined look of a people who had stood alone against Hitler and were desperate to see him finished off. The war at home was still theoretical; over here, it was personal.

The end of Eleanor's very enjoyable weekend in Buckingham Palace was to be marked by a cocktail party in the main hall, although it was, Queen Elizabeth told them, to be attended entirely by women working in the higher echelons of war provision.

"No men at all?" Tommy gasped, delighted.

"Only my husband," she said with her angel smile. "I tried to ban him but he outranks me, you know!"

"Mine too," Eleanor said ruefully and they both laughed.

"With yours, at least, he will one day be out of office and you can rule the roost again. Mine will never have the privilege of retiring." She looked sad.

"You did not wish to take the throne, ma'am?" Eleanor dared to ask.

Queen Elizabeth looked straight at her. "Good lord, no. Neither Bertie nor I could imagine anything worse. We were very content living a family life and attending to our duties as necessary, until bl— until Edward decided he'd rather have

Wallis than the throne." She sniffed crossly. "Neither of us wanted the spotlight of leadership."

"And yet you are both so good at it."

The Queen blinked and looked away. "Thank you," she muttered faintly, but then her shoulders straightened and she turned back. "It is an honor."

"But a chore too."

"Sometimes. You will know that yourself, Mrs. Roosevelt."

Eleanor nodded. "I confess I love the chance to help shape the country."

The Queen gave a tinkling laugh, with a brittle edge. "That is where we differ. Bertie and I cannot shape the country, merely soothe its inhabitants when that shape impacts their lives."

"It sounds frustrating."

The Queen looked her up and down and smiled. "I can see why you make such a good First Lady, Mrs. Roosevelt."

"Oh, I—"

"And I am pleased to say that Mrs. Churchill will be coming early to the palace so you can meet her before the wider jamboree."

That caught Eleanor's attention. She'd been dying to know what Winston Churchill's wife would be like. Now was her chance and she hurried off to get ready. She had an hour, so enough time to write her column and reply to a few letters before she had to dress.

"You don't want to take slightly longer over your toilette?" Tommy suggested. "There'll be a lot of important women there."

"Women," Eleanor echoed her. "So they won't judge what I look like."

"I wouldn't be so sure," Tommy said, but she sat down at her typewriter all the same.

. . .

Fifty-eight minutes later, Eleanor zippered up her gown, pushed a stray hair back into her bun and hastily applied lipstick. Her column was done and she'd whipped through replies to fifteen letters, which meant she wouldn't have to worry about them later on. She swept down the stairs to the designated reception room to find the Queen welcoming a woman she assumed was the intriguing Clementine Churchill.

She paused in the doorway, wondering if Tommy had been right about spending more time on her appearance. These days she was less worried about blending into the background and even enjoyed the couture dresses Tommy ordered to "befit her station," but she was not a patch on the Prime Minister's immaculate wife. Mrs. Churchill's gown was stunning, her accessories perfectly coordinated, and her hair beautifully styled. She stood as tall as Eleanor, which was a welcome relief, although she seemed to carry it rather more graciously. Her shoulders were back and her chin high. She had doubtless been coached in "deportment," Eleanor thought, grateful her school had been keener on debate, though she did try not to hunch over as she entered.

Mrs. Churchill turned and Eleanor saw that, to cap it all, she was a beautiful woman, aging it was true but with perfect cheekbones, a slim mouth and stunning blue eyes. She felt unaccountably shy—like a schoolgirl faced with the most popular girl in class—then told herself to stop being silly. She was a grown-up, First Lady of the United States of America, and she was here to discuss vital war work not play society games.

She strode forward. "Mrs. Churchill, wonderful to meet you at last."

"And you, Mrs. Roosevelt. My husband has been so very grateful to yours for all the support he's offered."

"It was rather late coming, I'm afraid."

"He was hampered by Congress. I know how it is. Winston

is forever raging against Parliament, although he loves it like his own child."

She laughed, a surprisingly hearty bray, and Eleanor found herself laughing too. Clementine Churchill might look immaculate but she was clearly not some simpering socialite. Thank goodness! This, it seemed, was a woman she could do business with.

"It's very refreshing to be invited to an all-female party," she said, bowing her head to the Queen, who smiled.

"Women, do you not find, are often the ones who get things done. We are merely recognizing that fact," said Her Majesty.

"Everyone you will meet today," Mrs. Churchill added, "is running an organization, doing key work with a charity, or broadcasting vital news."

Eleanor seized on this. "I've been working for years on promoting the work of female journalists."

"So I've heard," Mrs. Churchill said. "And I believe Mrs. Jenny Miller will be here tonight, in both her roles, as broadcaster and running the Bundles for Britain charity."

"That's excellent," Eleanor said. She was glad at least one American woman was standing up to be counted and looked forward eagerly to seeing the way the British were utilizing women's skills, and how they could replicate that back home. This was going to be a most inspiring trip.

The party was fun, filled with so many fascinating women that Eleanor had to work hard to talk to them all. It was good to see Jenny Miller again, although the poor girl was fretting about some sort of problem with the hem of her dress. How curious. What did a hem matter when there were so many people to meet? Still, she was doing an excellent job with Bundles and looked sweetly delighted when Clementine offered to introduce her to the Queen.

"Thank heavens," Queen Elizabeth said gaily to Jenny,

"someone my own height. I swear, you have to be Amazonian to support the rulers of the known earth these days."

Eleanor exchanged looks with Clementine and felt a rush of kinship for this other woman also cursed—or perhaps blessed—to stand above everyone else in the room.

"Merely Amazonian of the heart, your royal highness," Jenny said.

The Queen clapped her hands delightedly. "Amazonian of the heart! I like that. And you are?"

"Mrs. Jenny Miller, ma'am. I run Bundles for Britain here in London."

"Wonderful. I'm quite jealous of some of those fabulous jumpers I've seen on our sailors. The palace can become so drafty, you know! Not that I'd dream of depriving the boys serving bravely in those horrible northern seas."

"It must be very cold up there."

"It is. The King was posted to Scapa Flow in the Great War and said it took months to thaw out."

"The King was in the Navy?"

"He wasn't King then—nor ever meant to be."

The Queen's brow darkened and Clementine stepped smoothly in.

"But thank the Lord God that he is, for your husband is the best possible monarch we could ever hope for."

"And yours the best Prime Minister."

Clementine smiled gratefully, then turned to Eleanor to add, "And yours, of course, the best President."

Eleanor was lost for a reply to this rare outpouring of British sentiment and glanced to Jenny for help.

"What a dazzling set of men you have," Jenny trilled.

Dazzling, Eleanor thought. She supposed they were, in their own way, but what use was dazzling?

"And what a responsibility," Clementine commented, which was far more to the point.

Silence fell. The palace party buzzed around them but here, at its center, all was still.

The Queen recovered first. "What a good job, then," she said stoutly, "that we have Amazonian hearts."

Clementine laughed first, the explosive bray Eleanor had heard before and that, again, set her off too. Queen Elizabeth joined in and suddenly Eleanor did not feel like the awkward kid at the back of the class, but like someone at the heart of the main gang. It was exceptionally pleasant and she sent up a prayer of thanks to God for bringing her to meet these warm, strong, powerful women.

A week later and life no longer felt like a cocktail party. She had toured London and the south of England, visiting barracks and hostels, hospitals and orphanages, factories and Red Cross units. She'd then been to the cities of Bristol, Birmingham and Liverpool and flown out to the naval base at Londonderry in Northern Ireland from where she'd made a radio broadcast emphasizing the importance of working for a lasting peace. Her picture had been in all the papers the next day, with the journalists estimating that over half of the British adult public had listened to her. It was most kind of them, especially considering she'd had a horrible cold and they'd probably not been able to understand a word she'd said.

Someone had found her some lemon and honey, and the tour had moved inexorably on. She'd seen women running wards, manning guns and flying planes. She'd attended a Red Cross Club dance and been followed around by a drunken soldier desperate to waltz with her. The major had chucked him out, horrified he'd offended her, but she'd assured him she'd been most flattered. The lad had been young enough to be her grandson!

She'd been to factories with nurseries on the premises and

watched mothers gratefully depositing their children into the hands of smiling caregivers before turning to their work, secure in the knowledge that their little ones were not just safe but happy. It was similar on military bases where women in smart uniforms carried little girls in pretty dresses and bobby socks into work and saw them run to play with friends before heading to the drill-yard. It looked peculiar at first, but once you got used to it, it was a sight to truly warm the heart. Everyone was content; everyone was productive.

Today, Eleanor's last day in London before she headed to Scotland, she was visiting a WRVS clothing store, set up to provide for those who'd lost their wardrobes to bombs, or with children growing faster than rationing allowed. It was a clever, well-run enterprise and Eleanor was delighted to inspect it, though Clementine looked weary and did not even come up the stairs to the main store, staying behind to talk to a small girl instead. Still, Eleanor supposed it wasn't as novel for her British counterpart, and she had to admit, those stairs had been quite steep! Visit over, she sunk into the soft leather of the waiting car with a grunt of relief then looked, embarrassed, to Clementine, sitting elegantly on the other side.

"The old bones aren't what they used to be," Eleanor apologized.

"It's good to see you're human," Clementine replied.

Eleanor blushed. She'd been dashing around a lot, she knew, but only because there was so much to get through.

"Do I come across as a machine?" she asked nervously.

"No! Heavens, no. I simply mean that you have unending stamina."

Eleanor laughed. "I expect it comes from being plain."

"You're not—"

"I am, my dear. Always have been." It was nice of her glamorous new friend to protest, but she did not need to fret on Eleanor's behalf. "I learned early on not to worry too much about what other people think of me and that is most liberating. Other people's opinions can be very draining."

"That's certainly true, but, really, you're a very striking woman, Mrs.... Eleanor."

She was still trying to make her feel better! The English and their overly polite social conventions made her smile. Clementine even struggled with calling her by her first name, which seemed rather silly after they'd spent so much time together.

"You're too kind, Clementine," she told her, "though worrying about how you convey your opinions of others can be very draining too. You needn't worry with me. I'm not easily offended."

"Well, I honestly think you're amazing to get so much done."

Eleanor sighed. "The problem is that there's so much *to* do, is there not? It nags away at me day and night, and I simply cannot escape feeling responsible for it." She surprised herself with the confession but it was so warm and comfortable in the car and Clementine felt like the one person who might truly understand.

Sure enough, she was nodding. "I invited that young girl, Daisy, and her mother for tea," she said, "and they positively glowed. They've had a frightful time with the bombing and something as ridiculously easy as having a cup of tea with me can make them happy. If that's true, I should be having tea with people every single day, yet I would still leave far more out than I saw!"

"The power to effect change is a privilege," Eleanor agreed. "But it's a weight as well, and it's so hard to do at a micro level. We have to change the inherent way we run the world. We need a united nations group to create international cooperation and settle disputes in a civilized way long before they have to come to war. Maybe that's a woman's way of looking at it, but if so, I'd say it's time women ran things."

"Time you did, certainly," Clementine told her.

But at that Eleanor shook her head. "I'd be useless. I've been butting my head against injustices in my country for decades. Franklin says I take it too much to heart. He's a consummate politician. He can balance what he wants to get done against what is practical for the time and situation. I cannot. If I were president, I'd go charging in trying to sort everything immediately and so many people would object that I'd be out on my ear before I could manage even one solid reform. That's what frustrates me."

Clementine fiddled with her earring then turned and faced her, full on. "It seems to me, Eleanor, that you are a better politician than you think."

Eleanor was stunned, and not a little touched. This woman was at the heart of the British establishment and, more importantly, she was intelligent, warm and insightful. Eleanor realized Clementine's good opinion meant a lot and tried to find a way to say thank you, but she was still talking.

"For myself, I'd like to step away from public service and live my life with Winston and the children, as a family."

"Ah," Eleanor said, her heart falling. "Well, that's where you're lucky."

She thought of Franklin asking her to "be his full wife" again, in whatever way he had meant it. She suspected that, despite all he said about how "interesting" she was and how much he admired her, behind the request had been his usual, driving need to have someone hanging on his every word. She was not that woman and even when she'd tried to be, she had not measured up to Lucy damned Mercer.

Eleanor turned to the window, horrified at her violent thoughts. She reminded herself that she had an "Amazonian heart" but right now it felt more pygmy. She wanted to scream and shout and run amok around the stoic Londoners, and clenched her hands tightly to hold herself together. She looked for words to explain to her new friend how lucky she was to have a love-match with Winston, but none would come. Perhaps she was more English than she realized?

To her surprise, Clementine reached out and quietly placed a warm hand over hers. Eleanor felt her composure returning. Love had many forms and, after that second dreadful illness, she and Franklin had found their own version. It was formed more of respect and shared drive, perhaps, than any sort of romance, but in the end that was a more solid foundation for a life lived together.

Wasn't it?

TWENTY-TWO
CAMPOBELLO, AUGUST 7, 1921

The kids were wild with delight. Finally Pa had made it to Campobello and the summer could truly begin. They'd come out together a month ago, determined to have some family time, but within days Franklin had been called back to government business. Eleanor had been entertaining them since then and, although they'd had a lovely time, she did not have Franklin's endless enthusiasm for fishing, hiking and swimming and had been painfully aware of her inadequacies in her children's eyes. But now he was here and all would be well again.

Eleanor waved them off in Franklin's fishing boat with an extravagant picnic and a mound of warm clothing. It was a glorious day but the Canadian waters never got much above icy and Franklin was apt to forget how small the younger ones still were. Frank was seven and John only five, and they did not warm up as fast as their big, fit father so she'd urged fifteen-year-old Anna to make them put on jumpers when they came out of the water—then felt guilty for putting the responsibility on her only daughter. Why should she care for her brothers? It wasn't as if they'd be grateful. Eleanor should be going with them, but she had so much work to catch up on and that, if she was honest, was far more enticing than a fishing trip.

Earlier in the year, Mrs. Vanderbilt had invited her to join the New York League of Women Voters and the meetings had been a revelation. She'd met so many interesting people and learned so much about politics. She'd always read the news and formed opinions but had only ever voiced them with Franklin before. Nowadays, she was being encouraged to share them with the world, and the world—at least the league's corner of it—was listening.

It was liberating and, even better, it was slowly restoring the confidence that Lucy Mercer's letters had slashed out of her three years ago. Franklin had, true to his word, dismissed Lucy from his office and they'd got word that she'd found employment as a governess to the six children of wealthy widower Winthrop Rutherfurd. Last year news had reached them that he had married her. Eleanor had been unsurprised and indulged herself in a few catty remarks to her new friends, then put the woman out of her mind. Franklin had been reassuringly surprised and, if he'd been hurt, he'd not shown it.

He'd stuck to the other part of their bargain as well, leaving her in luxurious peace in her bedroom. The rift between them still hurt like a raw wound in her flesh, but they'd found a way back to companionship through shared debate, and that was some balm. More forceful yet was their shared passion for getting Franklin to the White House.

The Women's League of Voters, although mainly Eleanor's project, would also feed into Franklin's fortunes and, as one of the women had pointed out the other day, it wouldn't only be Franklin in the White House. If they could get "one of their own" there, the world would be a better place. Eleanor had been so excited at being considered part of their stimulating gang that she had not analyzed the words too closely. Besides, she and

Franklin might have a foot on the path to the presidency, but there was a long way to go yet.

Keen for closer involvement, Eleanor had been to the league's convention in April and found their leader, Mrs. Catt, utterly inspiring. In her final address, she had said that women must, "consecrate themselves to put war out of the world." "Men were born by instinct to slay," she'd told the huge group, "and it seems to me that God is giving the call to women to come forward, to stay the hand of men, to say: 'No longer shall you kill your fellows.'" The convention had erupted in cheers, Eleanor the first among them, and she'd eagerly volunteered to help.

"I just want to be useful," she'd told Mrs. Catt.

"An honorable aim," Mrs. Catt had said. "And much underrated."

It had been quite thrilling. Eleanor had been tasked with going through various reports and studies to help inform women voters in the next election, and a whole day to dedicate to them felt like a great luxury. Waving as her family hoisted the sails to catch the brisk breeze blowing across the waters, she turned eagerly back inside to coffee, peace, and the joy of useful employment.

She was so busy that she barely looked up until the housekeeper came to ask her if she wanted dinner delaying seeing as the master wasn't back yet. Glancing at the clock, she saw it was almost six and hastened worriedly down to the waterside. Sara, who'd been off lunching with a friend, joined her, scanning the horizon. Eleanor shivered in her simple cotton frock, her mind racing as fast as the rising breeze. Had they capsized? Should she send someone after them? But who? There was only one motor boat on the island, run by old Mr. Calder, and he would be busy ferrying people from the mainland.

Sara fretted at her skirts, unusually discomposed. "What if they've—"

"Don't!"

Sara jumped, but closed her mouth. Since divorce had been sidestepped, Eleanor had learned to stand up to her mother-in-law and Sara, perhaps out of sympathy, perhaps simply to make it easier for her precious son, had not objected. She did not like Eleanor's new friends, and had exclaimed in horror when Eleanor had, at their recommendation, bought herself a pair of pantaloons, but there was little she could do. Eleanor had suffered a terrible hurt but, on the upside, nothing could hurt her in the same way again. It was a form of power and she was learning to use it.

"Franklin is a very experienced sailor," Eleanor said, "as are Anna and Jimmy. Even Elliott is competent, so between them they will get themselves home safely."

"I hope you're right," Sara snapped.

So did Eleanor and, despite her enforced calm, she'd never been more relieved than when she heard a cry of "hullooo!" and saw her family coming, intact if rather ragged, around the bay. She ran to meet them and the children tumbled out of the boat. Their hair was wild, their faces pink and their clothing ominously sooty.

"What on earth happened to you?" she demanded.

The whole story came out as she hastened them up the path, calling for the maids to draw baths. They'd been happily fishing when they'd spotted a wildfire on an island and rushed to beat back the flames. They'd secured the victory, they assured her, but only after hours of battle and then, black from the smoke, had sailed to their favorite lagoon for a cleansing dip.

"The lagoon?" she asked Franklin, as the maids gathered up the children. "Why not a bath?"

"Oh," he said blithely. "A bath is far less fun."

"Maybe, but I suggest you take one anyway. You look exhausted."

He did. His skin was gray beneath the patchy soot clinging to it, and he was shivering. He'd come to Campobello via a scout *jamboree, trekking up Bear Mountain for games, campfires and a night under canvas, and although he'd loved it, it must have been tiring. Today, on top of that, would wear out most people.* She put a hand on his arm to guide him after the children but he shook her off.

"I'm fine, Eleanor." She jumped back, stung, and he bit his lip. "That is, thank you for your concern but I'm fine, really. I have a few papers I need to look over so I'll do that while the children are getting sorted and then we can have dinner together, yes?"

Eleanor looked to Sara and was, for once, grateful when she waded in.

"At least change your clothes, Franklin. What sort of an example are you setting?"

"Fine, fine. Send my valet to my study with something fresh."

It had been all they were going to get but while the children came to the dinner table fresh and full of renewed energy, Franklin looked worn out and retired to his bed unusually early, still shivering. Eleanor lay awake worrying and eventually, at dawn, crept in to check on him.

"Morning," he said with encouraging cheer, though when she looked at him trying to rise she saw it was forced. He struggled to push himself up from the mattress and then, two steps across the room, his left leg buckled and he fell to the ground.

Eleanor ran to help him up and found him hot with fever. "Bed!" she instructed fiercely.

It was testament to his weakened state that he did not raise even a murmur of protest.

Instantly, Eleanor was transported back three years to the Spanish flu and how it had raged through him. But he had beaten that, she reminded herself, and he could beat whatever chill he'd caught here too. She just had to get him warm and he would soon be his usual perky self. She summoned maids and sent for blankets, hot water bottles and cocoa. The children came in when *they woke, intrigued to see Pa laid up, but soon lost patience and ran out to play. The sun shone and the day wound on to the sound of their happy shouts through the window, but Franklin did not improve. If anything, he got worse.*

Eleanor sent a boy to Mr. Calder, begging him to fetch a doctor, but when he took his boat to the mainland, it emerged that Dr Bennet was on holiday. They were on their own. The only telephone on the island was in the general store at Welshpool, a mile away, and with no bridge and no means of air transport, they were trapped.

Franklin complained he could not feel his left leg, and then his right one. Within two days he had lost all sensation below the waist and Eleanor, guided by a doddery retired nurse, had to learn to insert a catheter. The children stopped playing and sat around listlessly on the lawn. Eleanor set up a bed in Franklin's room and mopped his brow, just as she had before. The fever dropped but the paralysis remained. It was terrifying. At least with the flu they'd known what it was; with this, they had no idea.

Finally Mr. Calder found Dr Keen, a Philadelphian physician on holiday in Maine, and persuaded him to visit. He diagnosed a clot on the spine and recommended Eleanor massage Franklin's legs to restore sensation. The first time she pressed her fingers gently into his thighs, he cried out in agony but when she pulled back, he grabbed at her and insisted she try again. And again. And again. Their perfect family summer slowly unraveled in a misery of Franklin's suffering that radiated through them all.

"What's wrong with him?" Sara wailed every single day.

"I don't know," Eleanor shot back through gritted teeth. "I'm doing my best to find out."

She sent word to her Uncle Fred in New York, begging him to find a specialist, but with everyone on vacation it took three horrific weeks before he delivered a Dr Lovett to the island. The man was calm and confident. He took Eleanor's hand and *assured her that he would find out what was wrong with her husband, then he shut himself in the bedroom to examine Franklin. It seemed to take forever but eventually the door opened and he invited her inside.*

"*Do you know what it is?*" *Eleanor asked.*

He nodded. "*I'm afraid I do.*"

"*Afraid?*"

"*There is not a shadow of doubt in my mind that Mr. Roosevelt has contracted polio—infantile paralysis.*"

"*Infantile...? But he's not a child.*"

"*No. It's unusual, but not impossible.*"

"*Is it curable?*" *She had no idea why she was asking. They'd all seen the polio children lined up in wheelchairs on newsreels, reporters solemnly saying they were doomed to never walk again. But surely a grown man could throw it off?*

"*I'm afraid not. Your husband will be in a wheelchair for the rest of his life.*"

Eleanor ran to the bed. Franklin was white and as his eyes found hers, she knew they were both thinking the same thing: America might not approve of a divorced president, but they sure as hell would never countenance a crippled one.

Franklin's dream, it seemed, was over.

TWENTY-THREE
THE ENGLISH COUNTRYSIDE, NOVEMBER 1942

"It must be around here somewhere, Mrs. Roosevelt ma'am," the driver said, anxiety clear in his Texan drawl, curiously out of place in the wilds of Suffolk.

He'd been assigned to take her to the base where Elliott was part of a team of reconnaissance pilots preparing to support the upcoming invasion of North Africa, but the base was proving elusive. Security was important, Eleanor knew, but a unit that could not even be found by its own military seemed useless.

"Someone must know where it is," she said crossly. If they didn't get there soon, she'd be late for her overnight train to Glasgow. It wouldn't leave without her, but she couldn't bear to keep people waiting. It was so inconsiderate. Plus, Elliott would be past his curfew and she'd lose her chance to see him before he headed into a war zone. Her heart contracted.

The situation in North Africa was much improved since Franklin had made the tough decision to invade. General Montgomery had rallied his troops and secured a victory at somewhere called El-Alamein. It had turned the tide against the German advance and forced them to pour more troops east, so the American boys, landing in westerly Algeria, would face weaker defenses. It was comforting, although not as comforting as no defenses. She had to see Elliott.

"Get on the radio again and ask for top command this time."

"Yes, ma'am." The driver picked up his radio. "Rover has lost his pup. Repeat, Rover has lost his pup."

Eleanor rolled her eyes. Whoever came up with the codes had a facile sense of humor. "Rover is going to lose her cool soon," she said crisply. "Give it to me."

Some wrangling ensued—coded of course—but eventually new coordinates were secured and Eleanor turned a torch onto the map in the glove compartment and attempted to guide them in. It wasn't easy. All road signs had been taken down in 1940 to confuse Nazis in the event of an invasion, and the only way to establish their current location was for Eleanor to march into a public house—the driver scurrying anxiously in her wake—to ask the name of the village.

"Have I had too much to drink, or are you Eleanor Roosevelt?" the elderly man at the bar said, gaping.

"Oh, I'd say you must have had too much to drink, wouldn't you?" she retorted with a wink, and went on her way.

This time they found Elliott, and Eleanor was able to have a precious hour with him. He pored over the pictures she'd brought of his second baby son. "He'll be walking by the time I get home, Ma!"

"Just make sure you do," Eleanor said.

He looked at her, surprised. "Not like you to be negative."

She was mortified. "Sorry. I'm so sorry. It's being over here. The war feels so much more threatening."

"Because it *is*, Ma," he said gently. "And it'll be even more so in North Africa."

"Do you have to go, Elliott?"

"I do, you know that, same as any other airman."

She did know that, but it didn't make it any easier. She'd been brought up to do her duty, but when that duty was putting your life on the line—or even worse, your child's life—it felt so very hard.

Elliott pulled her in for a hug. "Don't you worry. I'm a damned good pilot and I'm flying reconnaissance, not open battle. I'll be dandy."

Eleanor left the base feeling rather wobbly. She wished she could talk to Franklin about their son's imminent departure for Algeria, but it would be the middle of the night in America. Besides, she had a train to catch to Scotland, so she told herself not to be so silly.

It was a relief to reach Glasgow and hit a packed schedule of duties. The Scots were raucously welcoming and she thoroughly enjoyed her tour of the bustling docklands. Everywhere, boiler-suited men and women came to cheer, praising America and offering the V-sign that Churchill had made so popular. V for victory. She prayed it would come true. Any day now the Americans would be entering active combat in the European field and the stakes for every family back home would rise. She couldn't help but remember Franklin sitting in the presidential train, staring at her with fear in his eyes. "Did I do the right thing, Eleanor?" Well, God help them, they would find out soon.

She was inspecting a marvelous nursery school set up in the bowels of an old merchant ship on November 8, when a boy came running in waving a news-sheet.

"Invasion!" he shouted.

Everyone jumped, bar the toddlers, who carried on bumping scooters around the lower deck.

"Invasion of North Africa. The Americans have landed!"

There was a throaty roar of a whoop, then everyone looked guiltily to Eleanor. She waved them on and went up to the boy, scanning the news-sheet for details. They were thin on the ground but the gist was that thousands of troops had been safely landed on the beaches and were establishing secure bases.

Reconnaissance, it said, had enabled secure landing sites to be pinpointed, which made Eleanor think with pride of Elliott. Then, instantly, of Franklin.

"Would it be possible," she asked the commodore, "for me to get through to the President?"

All heads turned and he saluted smartly. "I'll see what I can do, ma'am."

It took time, but eventually Eleanor found herself in the signals room of a large destroyer, waiting patiently while the radio operator connected to America. It would be early morning and she imagined Franklin sitting up in bed, scanning his official briefings for news of the men.

Then suddenly his voice came through, loud and clear, making her jump. "Eleanor? Eleanor, is that you?"

"It's me," she confirmed as the sailors shuffled out to give her privacy. She felt guilty for making such a fuss but, really, Franklin had borne the whole weight of the decision to send the men into North Africa so he deserved her support. "I've heard the news. It sounds as if it's gone well."

"Thank God," he said.

"When did you hear?"

"Last night. I was so relieved. Polly put on some outrageous Egyptian costume she'd found in the loft and insisted on having people for cocktails, but I couldn't focus at all."

"Couldn't focus on cocktails? Goodness, Franklin, it must have been bad!"

He laughed softly down the crackly line. "I was a mess, Eleanor."

"I'm sorry I wasn't with you."

"Not at all. You're doing important work over there. Is it going well?"

"Very well. Everyone seems delighted about the landings. There's a lot of love for our GIs on this side of the water, my dear."

"Glad to hear it. Very glad. I'm going to address the nation tonight and I'll mention that."

"Good idea." Suddenly Eleanor wished she was there, with her own people. It had been astounding seeing the war close up, and amazing to visit so many valuable projects, but she felt adrift on this side of the Atlantic. "I'll be back soon," she said. The radio operator was fidgeting and she knew she was clogging up wavelengths better employed in war communications, but it was hard to let him go.

"I'll look forward to it," he said. "Take care, Babs."

"You too."

Then he was gone and the commodore was fussing because she had to get to Edinburgh for dinner with something called a Lord Provost and it all felt rather confusing. Still, a few more days and she'd be back across the Atlantic.

Or maybe not.

When she reached London, there seemed to be furious debate raging about how best to transport her home. With the Americans hitting Rommel's rearguard in North Africa, an enraged Hitler had upped the U-boats in the Atlantic and everyone was worried about how to get her safely across. Her return was delayed and, despite the kind hospitality of the Churchills, she felt adrift and gratefully accepted an invitation to a Sunday scrambled-egg supper from Jenny Miller.

"A slice of the USA right here in London," the young broadcaster promised her.

What she found, however, was something of a party, most of them far more glamorously dressed than her beige, three-quarter-length frock.

"I'm so sorry," Jenny whispered, guiding her into the kitchen. "Ned seems to have got excited and invited every American he knows to meet you."

"How sweet," Eleanor said, though it didn't feel sweet, just irritating. She'd been looking forward to a quiet night after three weeks on the go, but there was nothing quiet about Ned's broadcasting friends who, armed with a number of martini bottles, were drinking themselves into a frenzy.

"I'm working on the RAF to let me fly in one of their bombers," Ned boomed, while Jenny battled to eke out two dozen eggs for the masses squeezed into their tiny apartment. "Imagine that—broadcasting live as the hatches open to drop bombs on Berlin!"

There were noises of male appreciation that made Eleanor instantly mad.

"Will you broadcast them falling on innocent civilians, Mr. Miller?" she asked.

"*German* civilians," he retorted, waving his martini glass to cheers from his colleagues.

Eleanor stood up. "You think all Germans are Nazis, do you?"

Ned froze.

"They voted Hitler in," he said.

Eleanor nodded. "That's true. Mainly on his promise of greater economic stability, rather than his remarkably understated policies on exterminating Jews or taking over the whole of Europe."

"Well, yes, but that's clear now and he's still in power."

Eleanor sighed. Were even their top broadcasters so poorly informed?

"Because," she told him, "the elections of both 1936 and 1938 offered the electorate merely the chance to confirm the Nazi leadership, with no alternative option."

Ned swallowed. "Is that right?"

"And even if not, German democracy, at least nominally, is the same as ours—victory by majority. How many people in America do you think voted for my husband two years ago, Mr. Miller?"

Ned looked desperately around for help but his colleagues

had melted to the edges of the apartment. Cowards, the lot of them.

"Around twenty-seven million," she supplied, remembering the tense evening waiting for the counts to come in. "That's not quite 55 percent, and it was considered a good victory—55 percent. That means that 45 percent of Americans did *not* vote for the current President. Is it not safe, then, to assume that a similar number of people did not vote for Adolf Hitler in Germany?"

"I'd have to look at the numbers," Ned stuttered.

"You won't find them. Goebbels is in charge of Nazi numbers so they will state that the Führer carried 99 percent of the vote—that he is, against all possible logic, the most wanted leader in any country in all of history."

"I see your point, ma'am."

Ned was looking cowed, clearly regretting inviting his buddies over to impress them with his presidential friend, but so he should. She would never glorify war.

"I'm told by the German resistance, for example—" she went on.

"German resistance?"

"Oh yes. There are brave youngsters out there trying to combat the worst of Hitler's many excesses in the back streets of their country. They send us reports when they can, and they estimate there may be some twenty thousand Jews hiding in private homes in Berlin. That's thousands of Germans prepared not only to dislike Hitler but to actively work against him, at huge danger to themselves. Some of your bombs may fall on them, Mr. Miller."

"I…" Ned floundered and fell back on an old stand-by. "I'm merely there to record what's going on."

Eleanor let it go. This was a party, not a convention, and she was being very rude to her hostess in hectoring her husband.

"And I'm sure it will make excellent radio," she said, with

her sweetest smile, then turned to Jenny. "Those eggs look wonderful, my dear. Shall we eat before they spoil?"

The evening recovered as the food was served. Eleanor asked the CBS staff about the difficulties of broadcasting from war zones and let them retreat into talk of signals and amplification, studiously steering around who, or what might be amplified. The eggs went down well, the martinis were finished, and someone produced a packet of excellent coffee—the best Eleanor had tasted since landing on British shores. Even so, she was glad to take her leave of the gung-ho group and head to her appointment with a group of fire-watchers on the roofs of Whitehall.

When she got to Downing Street, however, she found aides dashing around and Winston on the telephone to Franklin. Her husband's voice came down the line, achingly familiar, although unusually angry. "I don't care how you send her home," he bellowed to Winston. "Just send her."

"I'll see what I can do, old chap," Winston said and looked over at Eleanor. "Best forget the fire-watching, I'm afraid. Time to go and pack your bags."

Eleanor didn't need asking twice.

In the end she flew home jostled into the hold of a bomber, with several ferry pilots. The men produced flasks of bourbon and supplies of biscuits and chocolate to share and Eleanor was reminded of the little lad in London's bombed-out East End who'd reverently told her that Americans came with chocolate. She prayed their combined forces would be able to release him and his friends from such a restricted, fear-filled childhood.

As they came in to land, she peered out the window to see the sun coming up over the USA, lighting up houses and roads and people going about their daily business. Home! She pressed her face to the glass, straining to see the airbase, and then suddenly there was the runway and at the end of it, stark against the utilitarian hanger, a group of long, black limousines. That could only mean one thing.

"Franklin," she breathed.

He'd come to meet her! She felt an urge to powder her nose, as immaculate Clementine Churchill might do, but she could hardly pull out a pocket mirror in front of the airmen and, besides, the pilot was calling to brace for landing and she had to clutch at the webbing on the side of the plane to keep herself from tumbling gracelessly into their laps. Before she could catch her breath, the doors were opening and the lads were jumping out and turning to help her after them.

She was delivered to the tarmac like a dancer in a show and, embarrassed, only managed to murmur her thanks before they melted away. Then there he was: Franklin, President of the United States and her husband. Not, perhaps, a devoted husband in the way Winston was to Clementine, but a far less controlling one. She'd asked him for her freedom in 1918, and again last month, and he had offered it openly and without rancor. So if, sometimes, her foolish heart hankered to see him look at her as Winston looked at his wife, freedom was worth a very great deal. Even so, she couldn't stop herself giving a rather girlish skip as she rushed forward to bend and kiss him.

His arms went around her and held her tight. "Welcome back, Babs. I missed you. I don't mind you going off saving the world—"

"Don't joke, Franklin."

"I'm not joking. I'm deadly serious and I don't mind it, as long as you always come back to me. Promise?"

"I promise."

Funny, how you could leave someone and yet still be as happily tied to them as ever. Eleanor's head was spinning, and she was delighted when Franklin said he'd arranged for them to have dinner alone, for there was no one on this earth she would rather explain her trip to. Perhaps the long and tangled path of their marriage was leading them slowly, inexorably back around to each other? She had to admit, the thought sent a tingle through her body and she settled into the car at his side feeling happy indeed to be home.

TWENTY-FOUR
SPRINGWOOD, AUTUMN 1921

Withered.

Withered, withers, withering. They were words Eleanor had heard enough of to last a lifetime, but every doctor that came to see Franklin insisted on using them again. "I'm afraid the muscles have withered," as if they were a bunch of flowers no longer in full bloom.

It was true of course. Within only a few weeks, Franklin's strong, athletic legs had withered (there was no other word) to scrawny stumps and he could not, with even the greatest of effort, move so much as a toe on the end of them. For a terrible time it had looked as if the paralysis might go higher, into his upper body, but thankfully that had not happened. Sensation had also returned to his genitals making, as the doctor had excruciatingly told her, all urinary, bowel and sexual functions possible.

"You'll be able to live a normal marital life once he's stronger," he'd assured her.

Eleanor had wanted to say that there was nothing normal about their marital life, but had curbed her tongue. It was not about her at the moment. And, besides, in the long hours sitting by his bedside, they had talked almost as much as when they'd first been courting. Franklin, it had emerged, had not given up on his dreams of a life in politics. The problem, as they both knew, was that most of America looked upon physical disabilities as indicating mental ones. Franklin's brain had most certainly not withered with his legs, neither had his passion for making the world a better place, but neither of them had any idea how on earth they would convince anyone else of that.

"I have to walk again," Franklin would say, over and over.

"Or at least look as if you can walk again," Eleanor suggested.

She'd been talking to the doctors. There were leg braces that could support him with the additional aid of crutches, or a strong arm from a friend. They were cruel-looking iron things, but available to those with money and determination, and Franklin had plenty of both. That's to say, he had plenty of determination and his mother had plenty of money. The question was whether she would part with it to put her precious son in irons.

Sara was finding Franklin's paralysis harder than anyone, and was forever pacing up and down, wringing her hands and saying how glad she was his father was not alive to see this. She was always asking the doctors what adaptations could be made to Springwood, and neither Franklin nor Eleanor had yet found a way to tell her that he had no intention of retiring to the country. He was only thirty-nine, with a young family and big ambitions; he was not ready to be a country squire.

The other thing Sara did was pray, leading the family in an ostentatious nighttime ritual that they all hated.

"I think God may have already spoken, Babs," Franklin said to her one night after a particularly dramatic set of prayers.

"How do you mean?"

"I think this might be retribution. For, you know..."

She rolled her eyes. "I know, Franklin, and although I've wanted to punish you for it ever since, I don't think the Almighty is that intricately involved in individual lives. He's benevolent. He wants the world to be as good as it can be. It's only when man makes mistakes, or follows the evil side of his nature, that bad things happen."

"But I did follow the evil side of my nature."

She hated the conversation, but it felt important and she forced herself not to shy away from the memory of those terrible letters. "And you lost me."

"Yes." He lapsed into thoughtful silence, then said quietly, "That was a greater punishment than this."

Eleanor cried then, for the first time since the morning he'd collapsed. He reached for her hand and they sat there, curiously together in their sorrow over them being torn apart.

Eventually Eleanor composed herself. "And yet, Franklin, here I still am."

"Here you still are."

"And I'm not going anywhere."

"Thank you, Babs," he said quietly, then added, "I'm afraid."

Eleanor's heart squeezed. She still loved him, however foolish that might be, and this admission hurt. Then she remembered something. "I've been reading Thoreau recently."

"Thoreau? How intellectual."

"Hardly. There's been a lot of time, you know, waiting, and a friend sent it to me."

"And does Thoreau have anything to say on paralysis?"

She shook her head. "Of course not. But he does have something to say on fear." She screwed up her forehead, trying to remember. "It's something like: 'Nothing is so much to be feared as fear.'"

"Nothing is so much to be feared as fear," he repeated. "I like that. It makes sense. This is rock-bottom, right? So the only thing stopping me pushing upwards is fear I won't be able to do it."

"Exactly. And you will be able to."

"Thank you, Babs," he said again, looking so pathetically grateful she felt most uncomfortable.

"Don't thank me," she said, patting his hand. "Just get on with it!"

And he was doing so. This morning, Eleanor could hear him grunting and panting, and knew he must be doing his exercises. With the tantalizing prospect of the braces, he was determined his arms would be strong and had had a system of leather straps and loops fitted above his bed so he could work on them. As his legs withered, his arms and shoulders were becoming as muscular as an ox—only serving to exaggerate the contrast. If you stopped to think about it, it was a tragedy that could hardly be borne. But they were learning not to do so, and Eleanor went to find their youngest two to see if they fancied another chapter of Treasure Island.

The children, after their initial trauma over their father's illness, were adapting. Frank and John had been delighted to find that, if they jumped onto his bed, Pa could still wrestle them and had been easily soothed by his relentless positivity. Elliott was withdrawn, but sometimes Eleanor would go in to check on Franklin and find her middle son sitting by his bed talking solemnly with him and hoped he was finding a way to cope with this very changed father. Jimmy, at fourteen, was stoic, determined to be the man of the family, "until you're up and about again, Pa." He was often in the bedroom helping Franklin with his exercises and had already volunteered to be his "strong arm" when he wanted to try walking again.

Anna was the problem. Already a moody fifteen before Franklin's paralysis, she'd withdrawn into sullen silence, broken only by sudden flares of temper and tears. Eleanor understood, but there was only so much she could handle and she flinched now as Anna came bursting into her room before she could so much as lift Treasure Island off the shelves.

"Pa's calling for you, in case you hadn't heard."

"I hadn't," Eleanor said mildly. Her daughter had the wild-

eyed look of someone spoiling for a fight. "Is the nurse not with him?"

"Yes! But she's not his wife, is she?"

"No," Eleanor agreed. "She's a professional, hired to use her particular skills to care for him."

"Well he wants you, and you're neglecting him."

That stung. Eleanor stood up. "I am not neglecting him, Anna. I am with him for most of every day but he is not the only one in this family and I'm about to read to the boys."

"Oh, how sweet. How very lovely. You carry on and enjoy yourselves, and never mind that poor Pa is in agonies in there!" With that she burst into tears and ran from the room.

"You best go after her, Ma," Frank said. "Don't worry about us. We can read *Treasure Island* another time. Come on, John, let's go and hunt for rabbits." He took his brother's hand and they ran outside together, leaving Eleanor with a stroppy teenager to face.

She found Anna in her room, thrown dramatically across the bed, and edged inside.

"I'm sorry you're upset, Anna."

"No, you're not."

"I most certainly am. I love you."

The girl sat up and fixed her with a red-eyed stare. "Do you?"

"Of course. You're my daughter. My only daughter. And my firstborn too. You're special."

There was a flicker of emotion across Anna's pretty young face, but then she shut it down again. "Is Pa special?"

"I'm sorry?"

"Pa? Is he special? To you, I mean. Do you love him, Mother?"

Eleanor felt as if her daughter had punched her in the stomach. She sank onto the end of the bed and flinched as Anna pulled her legs pointedly away. "I do love him, yes."

"Doesn't look like it sometimes. You're always off without him."

"As is he without me, Anna."

"He has to work."

Eleanor ground her teeth. "And I have to look after all of you."

"'Spose. But you don't, you know, cuddle him any more."

"Does he cuddle me?"

"No. But he often looks like he'd like to."

Another punch. Eleanor gripped the bedstead to keep herself steady. "Yes, well, there are reasons for that."

"Like that you're a cold-hearted bitch?"

Eleanor gasped and even Anna clapped a hand to her mouth. Eleanor stared at her. She could take the moodiness and the upset, but there was no call for rudeness. If Anna wanted a hard-hitting conversation, she could have one.

"Like that he had an affair and we are... working things out."

Anna gaped. "Pa? Had an affair? Who with?" She put a hand up. "Wait. I know. It was Lucy, wasn't it?"

That punch was almost a knockout.

"You knew?" Eleanor whispered.

"No! Oh, Ma, no." Anna came closer. "Just looking back, you know, now that I'm older and understand this stuff, I can see that she disappeared and that, well, things were a bit tense."

"A bit tense?" Eleanor echoed weakly. That was a masterful understatement. She was already feeling guilty for telling Anna. The girl should not have to know that about her father but, on the other hand, why should Eleanor take the blame for something that was not her fault and that had hurt her so much it had nigh-on paralyzed her heart? Withered it, she thought, then scolded herself for being so melodramatic. "I'm sorry," she said. "I shouldn't have added to your upset."

"You haven't." Anna put her hands on Eleanor's shoulders.

"I understand now, Ma. And I'm glad you..." She swallowed. "Glad you didn't leave."

Eleanor felt tears flow and grabbed her daughter in a tight hug. "I would never leave you, sweetie."

"Or Pa?"

"We're working it out," she said again and they were, they really were. But, oh, it would be lovely to have an ally in her daughter.

"Shall we make lemonade, Ma?" Anna suggested. "Like we used to."

Eleanor smiled. "I'd love that. Oh, but I should probably check on Pa."

"Nah," Anna said, leaping up and tugging her to the stairs. "Let him wait!"

They took lemonade up to Franklin later, calling everyone in. Whatever Franklin had been shouting for earlier had clearly been resolved and he looked bathed and bright after his exercises.

"Not quite the summer we were hoping for," he said ruefully as they gathered around.

Eleanor noticed guiltily that Anna hung back, but she loved her father and would soon come around to him. She felt bad that her little girl was having to learn the harsher ways of the world but there wasn't much she could do, bar try to guide her through it.

"At least we're together," Eleanor said. "And the sun is shining."

"But not like it did," Elliott said miserably. "I have to go back to school in three weeks."

Eleanor looked at him, startled. He was right. She'd been so caught up in Franklin's illness she hadn't noticed the passing of time. Now, she noticed, some of the leaves on the trees were turning red.

"There's much to look forward to," Sara said.

Eleanor looked at her mother-in-law in surprise, grateful for this sudden positivity.

But then Sara added, "Hyde Park is lovely at this time of year."

"Mama—" Franklin said.

But Sara was not listening. "I was thinking you could have the front drawing room made into a ground-floor bedroom and—"

"Mama!"

Sara jumped.

"I am not going to live in Springwood."

"But... but you have to, Franklin. Everyone loves you there. They'll understand your, your..."

"Disability," he filled in, his voice hard. "How considerate of them."

Sara wrung her hands. "I mean simply that they will know it doesn't change you. You will still be able to run the estate as your father did and—"

"No." Franklin's voice was low but sure. "I am not going to become a gentleman farmer. It would bore me to tears."

Sara patted his hand. "I'm sorry about that, son, but what else can you do now that you're...?" She gestured to his withered limbs.

"Politics is about the mind, Mother, not the legs."

"Politics is about public perception," she shot back, then swung around to Eleanor. "Tell him, Eleanor. Tell him he must give up these foolish ideas of running for office and live a quiet life."

Eleanor looked down at Franklin. The whole room seemed to hold its breath. No one ever stood up to Sara Roosevelt, but this was important. This was their future.

"No," she said. "No, Mama, I'm afraid I will not tell him that. Franklin is made for the political life and would be wasted *in the country. He will not be living with you in Hyde Park, but with me in Washington DC."*

Sara threw up her hands in horror, the children gaped. Eleanor stood up to her full six foot and Franklin held so tightly onto her hand she thought they might never be able to get their fingers unlaced. Lucy's letters had almost torn their marriage apart but, one way or another, they were binding it together again. She would stand by him, as she had stood by him on their wedding day, and see him back on the path to his dream.

TWENTY-FIVE

THE WHITE HOUSE, DECEMBER 31, 1942

The mood was high as Eleanor and Franklin's guests came out of the cinema room. They had thoroughly enjoyed the private showing of *Casablanca*, a new romance thriller starring Humphrey Bogart and Ingrid Bergman. It had been rushed to release in New York City to mark the success of the Allied invasion of North Africa, and was exceeding all expectations at the box office. Franklin had secured a copy for the White House New Year party and it had gone down a storm.

"So romantic," Tommy said, unusually bright-eyed.

"And so stylish," Henry added, sweeping her into an impromptu waltz along the corridor to the Red Room where champagne was waiting to toast the arrival of 1943.

Eleanor glanced at Franklin, who threw her a wink for, unknown to the rest of the party, he was to fly to the city of Casablanca in ten days' time to meet with Churchill. Progress in North Africa had stalled in Tunis, but Algeria was secure and Churchill was eager to meet there to mark the victory and plan the next stage. Stalin was meant to attend too, but had recently sent a message that, with his troops so heavily engaged against the enemy, he could not possibly desert his country.

If it was an attempt to guilt the Western leaders into opening up a second front, it would not work. Stalin was sending increasingly irate telegrams demanding the invasion of northern France but Churchill was adamant they were not ready and everything Eleanor had seen in Britain backed that up. Hitler's "Atlantic Wall," along the coast from Belgium to Spain, was formidable and they would need far longer to amass the equipment and personnel to penetrate it. Churchill was still certain that invading Italy was the way to "soften the Nazis up" but Franklin was yet to be convinced. Hence the conference.

Franklin also felt it would do Americans good to see the President flying into the area their sons were holding, showing commitment to the cause for which they were risking their young lives. The fact that he would have to make the trip in a wheelchair was an added complication, but not one he'd ever let get in his way before.

"I have to be there in person," he'd said to Eleanor. "I have to see the troops and meet the generals. I have to look them in the eye and be sure that the advice they're giving me is sincere."

"Like when they advised you not to invade North Africa?" Eleanor had said.

He'd laughed ruefully. "That worked out, thank the Lord. But we're engaged now and I have to bow to the judgment of the commanders in the field."

"How refreshing."

"Yes, well, it will help if their judgment coincides with mine!"

It was her turn to laugh. "And if Churchill's does."

"That might be trickier. I've never met a man surer of his own opinions. But he's keen to push on and end the war and I cannot blame him for that. What I can do, is insist on unconditional surrender."

"That sounds... uncompromising."

"It is." He'd leaned in confidentially. "I borrowed it from

General Grant, leader of the confederate side in the Civil War. Read about it when I got his stamp for my collection and it seems apt here. We cannot have pockets of surrender and we most certainly cannot have wily old Stalin arranging a separate peace with Hitler."

"He won't like that."

"Then we'll remind him that he's got history in that department. If he wants Allied support, he has to stay part of the Allied team. And he has to keep on fighting until we are ready to join him."

Stalin might be wily, but he'd met his match in Franklin. The American President, with his boyish good looks, charming smile and wheelchair, might look a soft touch but this was the man who'd driven American business, kicking and screaming, into the New Deal. This was the man who'd forced Lend-Lease on Congress and dared to sign off a draft of their young men a week before his election to an unprecedented third term as president. This was the man who'd risen out of his sickbed, walked on withered legs, and fought his way into the highest possible seat of power. He was hard as nails.

Right now, mind you, he was at his most charming and looked very handsome in a white tux. Eleanor had treated herself to a new dress, daringly zigzag striped in white and silver, and felt pleasingly elegant. It was five minutes to midnight and their guests were gathering around Franklin's throne-like leather armchair. The staff were handing around champagne and Eleanor stepped forward to take her glass. Although she wasn't a big drinker, she did like champagne, mainly the way the bubbles tickled your nose, and the fact that it was only drunk (unless you were Winston Churchill) at times of joy.

Could you call a wartime new year one of joy? she wondered briefly, but then scolded herself. Much had happened in the last year and there was much to happen ahead, but they were safe in their home—America's home—with friends and music and the clock ticking to midnight, and that was joy enough.

"Ten..." Franklin called, "nine..."

Then they were all counting down and crying "Happy New Year" and hugging one another.

"A toast," Franklin proclaimed, as he always did. Everyone raised their glasses. "To the United States of America."

"The United States of America!"

They drank and Eleanor proposed her own, "To those family and friends who are in other parts of the world and unable to be with us tonight."

Everyone let out a cheer and drank deep. They might be in the White House, but they all had sons and daughters, friends and relatives off somewhere working to aid the war effort. Pray to God they could have them home safely to see in 1944.

Eleanor set down her glass on the side and went to check on supper, set out on the sideboard, but Franklin cleared his throat and she stopped and looked curiously back to him.

"I would like to propose a final toast," he said, beckoning her to his side. "A long, long time ago, when polio stole my legs from me, it looked as if my dream of being President was over. It was not." Their guests gave a small cheer and he smiled, but put up a hand to stop them. "It was not, thanks largely to the tireless work of one person—one person who never asks for acknowledgment, but just gets on with the job. Any job. *Every* job!" A ripple of laughter, but again Franklin put up his hand. "And so tonight, as we step together into 1943, I ask you to raise your glasses to Eleanor—the person who makes it possible for the President to carry on."

Glasses were duly raised, approval loudly given, and champagne drunk. Eleanor sank onto the arm of Franklin's chair and looked down at him, tears in her eyes that she did not, for once, bother to try to hide.

"You must be getting soft in your old age," she said, nudging him.

"I must," he agreed. "Make the most of it, Babs. It won't last!"

"Nothing does," she said lightly. "Not even our time here."

"Thank God," he chuckled, but then looked around him, misty-eyed.

Eleanor followed his gaze, trying to remember the exhausting chaos of the last year in the White House, but all she could see was the pretty Christmas tree, the smiling staff, and her dear friends. On nights like this, she had to admit that living out Franklin's dream wasn't bad at all.

TWENTY-SIX

PORTLAND, SUMMER 1943

Eleanor leaned forward in the car, looking eagerly up the road to the Swan Island Center. This would be America's first purpose-built workplace nursery and she couldn't wait to get there. She wondered if she could demand that Brandon, her plodding driver, went faster but feared that might be deemed reckless. How she wished she could be driving her own delicious Buick roadster, but with a war on it had been deemed too risky. Eleanor wasn't sure what they thought was going to happen to her.

Perhaps, in truth, it was more what they thought she might make happen. Breckinridge Long and his reactionary cronies were highly suspicious of her, mainly for the "crime" of seeing good in people until proven otherwise; the very reverse of their mean policies. Recently she'd paid a visit to Joe Lash, on leave from his training as a military weather forecaster, and he'd discovered her hotel room was bugged. She'd long known that the FBI kept a chunky file on her, based largely on her "treacherous" embracing of the causes of the African-Americans and the poor. Usually she and Franklin found it funny, but it had not been funny this time. Her privacy had been invaded and, furious, Franklin had ordered an immediate shake-up of the security services. That had been good news for her, but less so for Joe who, also under suspicion as a "red," had been posted to the Pacific barely a week later. He was stationed on the Solomon Islands, recently retaken by the Allies but under continued attack from the enraged Japanese, and she worried about him constantly.

It drove her mad that the authorities were so suspicious. Earlier this year, Ned Miller had broadcast a horrific program declaring, with convincing proof, that the "labor camps" the Nazis were shipping millions of Jews to every day were in fact "extermination camps," complete with gas chambers to poison them like vermin. It had seemed to Eleanor a fact that should have the entire world screaming in fury, but it had made barely a ripple.

"It can't be true," everyone she tried to talk to about it said.

"Why can't it?" she'd challenge. "Because it's too uncomfortable for you?"

"Of course not. But not even Hitler could be that monstrous."

They wouldn't see and they wouldn't do anything about it.

"We just need to defeat the bastard, Babs," Franklin had consoled her and he was right, of course, but... gas chambers? She didn't want to believe it was true either. But that didn't mean it wasn't.

Still, today she must focus on the job in hand and, for once, it was a joyous one. Ever since her return from England, Eleanor had been nagging for childcare facilities. Franklin had taken the issue to Congress several times, but they'd been predictably negative. Eleanor had sat in the gallery and listened as fat bellied, red-faced men had blustered about the "erosion of Western society" and the "betrayal of America's children," as if putting them into play centers under the supervision of trained staff was like tossing them into Hades.

It was as pathetic as their paranoia about immigrants. Eleanor had visited one of the Japanese internment camps and found a wonderfully ordered, peaceful community, doing their best to grow healthy food, educate their children and keep their minds and bodies active. Franklin, finally shamefaced about his foolish decision to lock them up, had quietly authorized her visit and was doing his best to facilitate the release of those proving their loyalty, some twenty thousand of whom, with no apparent sign of rancor, were now fighting in the U.S. Army. But still, Congress, in its marble palace on Capitol Hill, refused to believe that anyone not exactly like themselves could possibly be decent. It made her blood boil.

"Perhaps we should call up Mrs. Williams and her brood for all those complacent males to deal with for a day," she'd said to Franklin. "Then see if they change their tune."

"There might be more diplomatic ways forward, Babs," he'd laughed.

"That, Franklin, is why you are the President and I merely your agitator."

"A shame. Your methods would be far more entertaining."

"And would get us kicked out of the White House in months."

That was the issue. Democracy meant all measures had to be voted on by the country's chosen representatives and she had to respect that, much as it infuriated her. But, on a sleepy day in January, Franklin had finally managed to get the Community Facilities Act passed, allowing government-funded ancillary services for war plants, of which childcare could quietly be deemed one. Even so, there had still been little positive movement—until she'd met the Kaisers.

Henry Kaiser and his son Edgar ran Oregon Shipyard Corporation on Swan Island in the Willamette River. It was reliant on female workers to provide the destroyers and aircraft carriers needed by the Navy and, unlike many, the Kaisers did not think women should be asked to juggle childcare and welding. Edgar in particular, aged thirty-four and father to six, had proclaimed himself eager to build "the best childcare center in the world," and today Eleanor would get to find out if he'd succeeded.

"Here we go, ma'am."

At last Brandon was pulling through big gates and there, on what had previously been wasteland, stood a stunning building.

"Oh!" Eleanor said out loud. "Oh, yes!" Brandon looked at her strangely but she wasn't going to let him spoil her joy. "Is it not marvelous—a place where children can play while their mothers work?"

"Mothers should be playing with them if you ask me," he muttered.

"Is that right?" Eleanor swung around in her seat and eyeballed him. "And how, then, do you think we'd get the ships to defeat the Nazis?"

"There's plenty of men not gone to war."

"True. The old and the infirm. I'm sure they'll be marvelous with heavy machinery."

He shifted. "It's still not right."

Eleanor let out a cry of frustration. "Of course it's not right, Brandon. This is war. War is, by definition, not right. Do you think it's right for eighteen-year-old boys to be facing tanks and guns?"

"Well no, but it's..."

"Yes?"

He leaned back, trying to get as far away from her as possible. "It's natural."

"Men shooting each other is natural?"

"If they have to, yes."

"But women putting together a ship is not?"

"No. Definitely not. Women are soft and caring and sweet."

Eleanor had to resist an urge to laugh. "Are you married, Brandon?"

He shifted nervously, making the leather squeak. "I am, yes."

"I see. Do you have children?"

"Three, ma'am. Lovely lads."

"Excellent. And your wife is at home looking after them?"

His eyes narrowed. "No," he burst out. "She is not. She's got a job nursing and she's out all hours of the day and night running around after injured soldiers while I have to have the mother-in-law watching the kiddies. She's a tyrant too. Won't let me put my feet on my own coffee table and heads for home the minute I'm in the door, leaving me to put the three of them to bed by myself."

Eleanor really was going to laugh. It seemed that Brandon's objections to women working were far less about the comfort of his children and far more about his own.

"How lovely that, as their father, you're getting to spend time with them," she said crisply. "I hope you have dinner ready for your wife when she comes in from her shift. Nursing is exhausting work, not like sitting in a nice cushy car all day, hey?" She opened her door and climbed out, leaving Brandon gasping at what he doubtless saw as her uncaring insolence. Well, as far as she was concerned, it was time men woke up and valued their women as people, not simply caregivers. If the President of the United States could manage it, so could they.

"Mrs. Roosevelt! Welcome."

Edgar Kaiser was coming toward her, arms outstretched, and this was not a time to be dwelling on America's retrograde males but to be embracing the progressive ones.

"Edgar! This looks marvelous."

The brand-new building was built like a wheel, a play garden as the hub, surrounded by the spokes of fifteen great big playrooms. They had huge windows to let in daylight, the walls were covered with bright pictures, and the rooms were equipped with all manner of books and toys. There were desks and sandpits and squishy cushions. In the garden there was a climbing frame and swings, plus skipping ropes, hoops and balls. It was a child's paradise.

"This is amazing," Eleanor couldn't stop herself saying over and over as Edgar showed her around. "How did you think of everything?"

"Simple." He laughed. "I asked my children what they'd want."

Eleanor could have kissed him. It *was* simple. Why ask adults what to put in a children's facility when you could go straight to the kids?

"It's amazing," she said again.

She wasn't the only one impressed. The lucky children who were to be the first attendees were rushing around excitedly, testing out everything, while their mothers looked on, agape. Even better, the center was to be fully integrated and white children were playing alongside black ones, without blinking an eye. Perhaps they should ask children what to put into the adult world as well, Eleanor reflected ruefully.

There were many journalists, scribbling frantically in their notebooks and taking photographs. The Swan Center would be all over the papers tomorrow and Eleanor vowed to do her bit by giving it a glowing review in "My Day."

"I've been contacted already by other businesses looking to do something similar," Edgar told Eleanor. "I tell them all that this center can give children a wonderful education, while also enabling their parents to work for the country. It's a win-win."

"It is!" Eleanor agreed. "Thank you so much, Edgar."

He blushed. "For what?"

"For taking a chance, for being bold and forward-thinking, for showing the world what's possible."

"Yes, well, for all its evils, sometimes war can liberate us."

Eleanor looked around, fascinated. Maybe he was right. After all, without war there would be no women building ships, or driving trams, or nursing around the world. Apparently, some small teams of Wrens in Liverpool had proved so effective at tracking U-boats in the Atlantic that they were retreating into German waters. And the other day Eleanor had entertained Jacqueline Cochran who, along with a determined group of women, were proving they could fly every bit as well as men. Childcare released women's skills to the world and, with centers like this, children would benefit too.

Edgar was calling everyone to the entrance for Eleanor to officially declare the center open, and she stepped up to the microphone with a huge smile.

"We stand here today," she told the huge crowd, "not just on the doorstep of the best nursery I have ever seen, but on the doorstep of our future."

She got back to the White House in the early evening, still buzzing. After all the troubles, frustrations and sufferings of the war, she'd finally found something good and she was dying to share it with Franklin. Happy chatter was ringing down from the presidential study, and a glance at her watch told her it was cocktail hour. Damn—that meant "no business talk." Franklin was brilliant at putting aside his job to talk hooey over martinis and manhattans. Eleanor had no idea how he did it. Gossip and trivia just felt irritating to her, but it helped him cope with the strain of being President so she tried her best to obey the rule—usually by not coming down until ten minutes before dinner. Tonight, though, she had to share.

She made for the study but paused in the doorway at the sight of Franklin laughing uproariously with Polly while Daisy tried to make Fala walk on his hind legs. The poor dog looked upsettingly confused but Franklin, his cousins, and the usual cluster of secretaries and aides seemed to think it hilarious.

"Try again, Daisy," Franklin urged, though his poor Scottie was looking at him in a desperate appeal.

Eleanor strode inside. "Good evening."

All heads turned her way. For a moment she felt self-conscious in her cotton day-dress, with everyone else in evening wear, but that was just clothing and she brushed her silliness aside.

"Eleanor." Franklin sounded surprised, and not happily so, but his manners were well drilled. "Would you like a drink?"

"I'd love one," she said. "Do we have any champagne?"

Everyone gaped as if she'd asked for the juice of a bongo-bongo tree. It was rather unpleasant but at least it gave Fala a chance to wriggle free of his tormentors and escape the room.

"We can find champagne," Franklin said, recovering first. "Are we celebrating?"

"We are! The opening of the Swan Center at the Kaiser shipyard in Portland. You should see it, it's—"

"No business talk!" Polly said imperiously, tossing back her trademark hair, today dyed a deep blue.

"I know," Eleanor agreed, "but surely children aren't business?"

"Children?"

"It's a children's center and it's marvelous. There's a central garden and—"

"Children are even more boring than business, Eleanor darling!"

"They are not," Eleanor protested, but her words were lost in a gale of laughter.

She looked to Franklin but he was laughing with the rest. His color was up and his eyes unnaturally bright. He had been ill recently and was clearly on the verge of it again. She should not bother him, but how could something like this possibly be a bother?

"Franklin," she said, striding over to him, "it truly is marvelous. Better, even, than anything I saw in England. Our children would have loved it."

"How nice," he said absently, then, with clear effort, "Well done the Kaisers. Ah look, here's your champagne!"

"Marvelous," Polly said, seizing the bottle from the server. "Let's make champagne cocktails."

"Marvelous!" Franklin agreed.

Eleanor turned away. Her husband was in a flirty mood and she could do nothing with him when he was like this. She no longer wanted champagne and she most certainly did not want a champagne cocktail.

"I'd better go and change for dinner," she muttered and fled, feeling a curious kinship with Fala.

She could not complain, she supposed. Franklin had asked her to stay at home, to host his cocktail hours and "relax" with him at weekends, but she had turned him down. She could hardly blame him for finding other women to do the job. She'd put two conditions on their continued marriage—that they no longer had to be intimate, and that he never again saw Lucy Mercer. She should perhaps have specified more, but that was all that had truly mattered to her and she must stick by it. Even so, she'd thought they'd grown close recently and it was disappointing to be so ignored.

"Eleanor." She was at the door but turned back at his voice. "I'm glad you had a good day. The Swan Center will be a huge boost to production in the shipyards. It's marvelous that you're helping Americans apply what you learned abroad."

"You should travel more." Polly laughed.

"I should?"

Shallow Polly had already turned back to wasting the lovely

champagne by adding garish ingredients, but Franklin looked thoughtful.

"You should, actually. Have you thought about the Pacific?"

"The Pacific?!"

"There are many boys stationed out there and Jimmy says they're going mad with inactivity now the Japanese have backed off. Sending you out might be the perfect way to appease them."

"Appease?"

"Entertain then."

That was even worse!

"If they need entertaining, send a pretty singer," she suggested.

The room seemed to wait for his response. "Pretty singers lack your solidity, Eleanor."

"Solidity?!" Eleanor heard Polly snickering but refused to rise. Solidity wasn't a bad thing. You couldn't build a new world without solidity. But the Pacific islands? They were so far away. Although... "Maybe I could visit Jimmy?" she said eagerly.

"Maybe," Franklin agreed, "though the Marine raiders are famously hard to pin down."

Her heart sank, but then she remembered something else. "Joe Lash is out there!"

"The Youth Congress lad?" Franklin wrinkled his nose. "Isn't he forecasting weather or something?"

"A vital job if you're launching planes against tricky targets," Eleanor retorted furiously.

"Of course, of course. I'm sure he'd love to see you."

He would and it would be wonderful to see him too, but she still felt as if she was being maneuvered.

"The Pacific?" she repeated again.

"Absolutely." Franklin was nodding keenly, as if this trip had been his plan all along—which maybe it had. "You're a wonderful ambassador for our country, Babs—for *me*. You always have been." He gave her a beaming smile. "Think about it."

She nodded assent, because what else could she do? He was right, she'd stood up for him when he'd been unable to stand up for himself and she would happily do so again. But as Franklin turned to accept a cocktail made with her champagne, and everyone giggled around him, she couldn't help feeling there was something else going on here, and for once the White House, vast and imposing as it was, felt sickeningly claustrophobic.

TWENTY-SEVEN
NEW YORK, SUMMER 1924

"*Go slower, Eleanor, or the teapot will fall off!*"

Eleanor laughed as Marion Dickerman hung out the window of the old Ford to clutch onto the giant papier mâché teapot strapped to the roof. She couldn't afford to slow down too much; they had to get to Union Square before Teddy Roosevelt junior began his speech or the teapot would be wasted.

It had been Nancy Cook's idea. Nancy and Marion were friends Eleanor had met through the State Democratic Party Women's Division and had taken Eleanor under their wing, helping to forward her "political education." Eleanor was attending rallies and conventions, and even occasionally daring to speak at them herself. With Franklin fighting to walk again, Eleanor's involvement was keeping the Roosevelt name in the public eye and he was encouraging her in everything. Even the teapot.

"We need to show how corrupt the current administration is," Nancy had said. "We need to remind people again and again, in the most dramatic way possible, that the opposition are cheating, self-serving bas—"

"Thank you, Nancy," Marion had interrupted hastily.

"I'm right though, aren't I?"

"Of course you're right. They're only in government for their own gain and at last the inquiry is proving it."

She was referring to what had become known as the Teapot Dome Scandal, after the name of Navy oilfields in Wyoming that the Secretary of the Interior had merrily leased to private companies at a low rent and with no open bidding. He had, "coincidentally," much improved his own private worth around the same time and two years of inquiry had finally proved that he'd taken huge bribes for the deal. The papers had been full of the Teapot Dome Scandal and the Democrats had to make the most of it as the public went to the polls.

"Let's make a giant teapot!" Nancy had suggested. "We'll stick it to the roof of a car and follow their candidate around to every speech and rally so whatever lies he spouts, our teapot will be there to remind everyone not to trust them."

So here they were, driving around New York with a giant teapot, attracting endless attention—as was intended. Eleanor turned the Ford into the large square where the Republican candidate for New York Governor, Teddy Roosevelt, eldest son of the onetime President, would be speaking—or trying to. Uncle Ted had died five years ago, barely into his sixties. Eleanor had been so sad about that at the time but was now guiltily relieved he couldn't see her harassing his son as the opposition candidate. Still, all was fair in love and politics.

Well, in politics.

Nothing, as far as Eleanor could see, was fair in love.

"There he is!"

Her musings were thankfully cut away by Marion pointing to a young man on a podium. Eleanor carefully maneuvered the car as close as she could get it, smiling as people turned to point, distracted from the young candidate's speech.

Nancy leaned out of the window, megaphone in hand. "Don't believe a word he says!" she boomed. "The Republicans *are lying swindlers, who only want to be in government to collect bribes and backhanders to fill their own purses!"*

More of the crowd looked over and Eleanor saw her cousin groan and wave for the police. Well, let him! There was nothing illegal about driving around with a giant teapot and she was going to keep on doing it until people realized the Democrats were the only ones who could be trusted to govern for the people, rather than for themselves. She couldn't wait to telephone Franklin and tell him what a success their crazy idea was proving.

Franklin's torture-chamber iron braces had been made and every day he forced himself to take a few steps in them. It wasn't really walking. His legs quite simply did not work, but his hips were strong and, with huge effort, he could force the useless limbs to move forward using the muscles at the top. It was a stilted, swinging gait but, with the right "window-dressing" it looked a bit like walking. The idea that the state of Franklin's legs supposedly conveyed his ability to lead was a deep irony to Eleanor. He could walk in braces, he could drive a specially adapted Ford, and he could arrange himself so that no one really had to think about his disability, but the truth was that his strength in overcoming it proved far more than any natural gifts that he was special.

Appearances were everything, however, and two weeks ago he'd been determined to take enough steps across the stage at the Democratic Convention to convince the party he was returning to full mobility.

"Nothing is so much to be feared as fear itself, right, Babs?" he'd said to Eleanor as she'd fussed around him in the wings.

"Right," she'd agreed. Then she'd stood there, heart in mouth, and watched him, leaning heavily on Jimmy's strong young arm, trace the agonizing path across the stage to make a bold speech in support of Al Smith as their candidate for President. Clutching the podium like a life-raft, Franklin had lifted his head high and *pronounced Smith to be the "Happy warrior" that America needed to move forward. The Democrats had gone wild and the next day the "Happy Warrior" had been all over the papers—attributed not to Smith but to Franklin himself. He had a long way to go yet but he was "walking" and he was making headlines and that was certainly a step back onto the path his mother had wanted him to abandon.*

It had been a triumph, but the effort had taken a lot out of him and he was in Georgia, visiting a thermal spa known as Warm Springs in the hope of relief for his ever-aching legs. His secretary, Missy, was in close attendance and Eleanor wasn't sure she liked that much. Sometimes she thought of the doctor telling her, right at the start of the polio nightmare in Campobello, that he would be able to have a "normal marriage" and wondered what he got up to with his attractive secretary, but most of the time she put it out of her mind. She was far too busy making new friends, furthering her political education, and keeping the Roosevelt name alive to spend indolent weeks in Florida or Georgia. If that meant Missy and Franklin were up to an activity she'd never much enjoyed anyway, it was a small price to pay.

Her heart squeezed but she ignored it. It would be nice to be one of those sensual women like Missy or Polly, or even damned Lucy, who seemed to enjoy the business of the bedroom as much as men, but she just wasn't. The words of that letter haunted her more than she would care to admit. "I long to press my lips to yours, to feel once more the delicious sensation of your tongue creeping lower and lower until I must beg you to..." Eleanor didn't see what was so good about begging for anything, but the pain of even half-imagining what they'd done together had been too great to stand and she was numb to it now. It was the only way.

"Press the button, Eleanor!" Marion urged.

Eleanor leaned forward and pressed the button that sent

steam out of the teapot spout with a loud toot. The crowd gasped and pointed. Almost no one was looking at Teddy Roosevelt. Excellent! Eleanor laughed out loud. If her pre-Lucy self was in that crowd, watching her spouting steam from a giant teapot with a group of wild-spirited friends, she wasn't sure she'd recognize her. Then again, perhaps it wasn't the Lucy incident that had liberated her, so much as Franklin's polio and the way it had forced him to rely on her, not as his wife, but in the far more valuable role as the keeper of his political hopes and dreams. Dreams that might be back in play, thanks in no small part to her.

Maybe they were both learning to walk anew.

TWENTY-EIGHT

THE PACIFIC, AUGUST 1943

Eleanor clutched at the strap that was her only means of steadying herself in the shaking military plane, and prayed for safe deliverance to her next destination. Below her, the Pacific stretched out, gloriously turquoise but scarily featureless, the Cook Islands already mere dots of sand and vegetation. Beautiful as they were, she was glad to leave. The colonel appointed to show her around had crisply said that he didn't see the point in "do-gooders interrupting the men's days" and driven her at top speed around hair-raising mountain roads, clearly determined to scare her charitable tendencies out of her. It hadn't worked. Eleanor had gritted her teeth, held onto her hat, and told him at the end that it had been "most exhilarating." He'd looked amusingly put out.

Even so, his low opinion of her had stung and he hadn't been the only one. Right from the first flight it had been a battle. She loved planes and all they represented in terms of progress and efficiency, but her two-thousand-mile trip to Honolulu in a shuddering army Liberator had been terrifying. She could swear the men traveling with her (all decorated for bravery but not one with an ounce of manners) had taken great delight in seeing her perched on a mail bag in her Red Cross uniform, and had cursed that the gray suit came with a restrictive skirt and not the trousers that enabled the rest of them to be warm and comfortable. Mind you, the thick overcoat, lined with red flannel that Anna had laughed at when she'd seen her off in San Francisco, had been perfect to wrap around herself at altitude so she'd survived the journey fine.

The uniform was, in fact, a blessing. It made her feel less like a sore thumb in military installations and saved her having to worry about what to wear every morning. Plus, it had reduced her luggage so much that she'd had room within the allowance to bring her typewriter—vital if she was to complete her column every day. She was useless on it compared to Tommy but she'd had to leave her dear secretary behind because Congress had been grouching about the cost of her "jaunt," as if she was flying off to the war zone of the Pacific to lie on recliners sipping cocktails.

Every general and admiral, and plenty of ranks beneath them, traveled with an entourage of valets and secretaries but she, the First Lady of America, was expected to do everything for herself. She didn't mind—she'd been doing everything for herself for years—but the hypocrisy of it was despicable. Plus, she was lonely. Being the only woman in a mass of military men wasn't easy, especially when most of them wanted you to fail, and on her first night on Christmas Island when she'd found her room crawling with bugs, she'd had to summon up all her courage not to scream and confirm their suspicions about females at the front.

Now she was on her way to Pacific HQ on New Caledonia to meet the Commander-in-Chief, General "Bull" Halsey, and couldn't say she was looking forward to it. Franklin had been so certain that she would be "a huge help" to the men, but it was clear the top brass felt that ferrying her around was an imposition on their valuable time (though as far as she could see, there were plenty of *them* on recliners with cocktails!) and she was beginning to wish she'd never come.

"Five minutes to landing, ma'am."

The plane dipped down and wobbled alarmingly. Eleanor clutched at her strap—as if that would help her if they plummeted to the ground—and held her breath.

"Just a thermal," the pilot called cheerily.

But Eleanor could feel her heart pounding wildly as the runway loomed. She didn't want to die and she especially didn't want to die thousands of miles from those she loved. Before she'd departed, she'd written a list of who she'd like her jewelry and precious possessions to go to if she didn't make it back. She'd asked Tommy to take care of it, and Tommy had come over all funny and had to lean on Henry. It had been rather touching.

"Make sure you do come back," she'd told her fiercely and of course Eleanor had promised she would, but it was hardly in her hands. If her pilot messed up, or the plane failed, or they were attacked by Japanese fighters, there would be little she could do to save herself. It was a stomach-churningly vulnerable feeling.

To her huge relief, the wheels connected with the runway and the plane ground to an only mildly bumpy halt.

"Here we are, ma'am." The pilot looked back and gave her a shy smile. "General Halsey can be a little... brusque," he warned. "Not a man for social niceties, if you know what I mean. Don't... don't let him intimidate you."

Eleanor smiled, grateful for this small show of solidarity.

"We're glad to have you here, whatever the Bull says."

"Thank you," she said nervously. Clearly the general had been briefing his troops about her visit with some scorn. She busied herself fetching bags to hide her tears. Outside the little plane, the sun was shining from a beautifully blue sky but Eleanor longed to turn around and go home. She had five more weeks of dragging recalcitrant generals out of their comfy bases ahead of her and it felt like forever. Why on earth had she agreed to this?

Franklin hadn't even been there to wave her off as he'd been dragged into a "vital" meeting on Italian strategy. Eleanor understood that. Finally, Churchill was getting to stick his sword into the soft underbelly of Europe and it was all go. With Hitler's decimated troops forced to surrender in North Africa—the first Nazi surrender of the war—the Allies had launched an attack on Sicily at the start of July. It was vital Franklin was involved, Eleanor understood that, but surely he could have spared half an hour to say goodbye?

She was heartily glad she had not agreed to be his "proper" domestic wife, for she'd have been stuck pouring tea and ordering dinners to make the "important" men's lives easier for them. She couldn't imagine anything worse. Although, looking at General Halsey's drawn brow as the plane door opened, maybe she could...

"General!" She covered her nerves with fierce bonhomie. "Wonderful to meet you."

"And you, ma'am," he said stiffly, "though you find us at a very busy time."

"There's been an attack?" she asked, knowing full well there had not. She might dislike Franklin's map room but she kept abreast of the information it provided.

Halsey bristled. "Not yet, but we are on the offensive in Guadalcanal. It's a critical time."

"So I gather from my husband," she said, reminding him on whose authority—indeed whose instruction—she was here. "He was keen for me to visit the men there and offer his personal encouragement to them."

That wasn't quite true. Franklin's instructions had been characteristically vague, but Joe Lash was stationed on Guadalcanal and she'd love to see him.

"That won't be possible," Halsey said sharply. "I couldn't possibly send a woman into danger, especially not the President's wife."

"But—"

"Come on, let's get this visit over with as fast as possible, shall we?"

He tried to turn away but Eleanor stood her ground. As far as she could see, this man's nickname should be "bully" not "bull" and she wasn't going to stand for it.

"I suggest, General," she said sharply, "that we get this visit going in the most positive possible way. I am here as a representative of the President of the United States of America, and, more importantly, as a representative of every one of her mothers, keen to offer boys miles from home comfort and encouragement."

General Halsey swallowed. "Of course, ma'am. They can't wait to see you. Not that we've told them who's coming, of course—security, you know—just that it will be a lovely female treat for them." He smiled patronizingly.

Now it was Eleanor's turn to swallow. Great. Just great! These poor lads would be expecting some gorgeous blonde starlet with pretty red lips—someone like Lucy Mercer Rutherfurd—who would flirt with them and sing for them. Instead, they'd get dumpy old Eleanor Roosevelt. With renewed misgivings, she followed the general to a swanky car to start her tour of the base, wishing with all her heart that she was back home in the White House.

The boys, it turned out, did not want a starlet and came rushing to meet her, eager to shake her hand and touchingly bashful when she told them, again and again, how proud she and the President were of their hard work out here.

"Thank you, ma'am," she heard endlessly. And, "It sure is good to see you, ma'am."

Some of the bolder ones offered more. "It's swell to see a woman among all these hairy men," one cheeky lad said to her.

"I'm afraid I'm more a mother than a sweetheart," Eleanor said.

"Gee, ma'am, a mother is what a fella needs when he's sweating his... er, his head off waiting for the enemy." He gave her a shy grin, then suddenly asked if he could have a hug.

He couldn't have even been twenty, Eleanor realized, and she was happy to oblige. For all his apparent confidence, he held on to her so tight she thought he might squeeze the breath out of her.

"Enough, soldier," his sergeant snapped, but Eleanor hugged him a little longer.

"Can there ever be enough home comfort, sir?" she asked mildly and, to her huge surprise, all the boys cheered.

For the first time, Eleanor actually felt glad she'd come and she went around the base chatting to as many of the lads as she could. Dinner that night was a stuffy, formal affair and she excused herself as early as possible, claiming travel weariness. The men were quite content over their brandy and cigars and it enabled her to get enough sleep to be up at 5 a.m. for breakfast in the canteen.

It was Elliott who'd suggested that to her.

"Queue in the mess, Ma," he'd urged. "That's how you'll meet the ordinary lads. They'll talk to you properly when they're not on parade."

She'd seen the sense in that, so here she was, but as she took her place in the queue, she felt ridiculously exposed. Everyone turned to stare, but she met their eyes and smiled and the lad one ahead of her turned and said, "Good morning, ma'am. Did you sleep well?"

She thought about it. "Not very. It's so hot out here, isn't it? So airless. I've no idea how you fight in this."

"It's not easy, ma'am. It's not like home."

"Not like home at all," the lad behind agreed and within moments everyone around her was chatting away about the discomforts of drilling in the boiling sun, mosquito bites, and even their stomachs' poor reaction to local food. Eleanor relaxed and listened to all they had to say. She was served her breakfast by a beaming private and found boys clamoring to carry her tray to a table.

The food was good, which was to say it was hot and filling. Eleanor noticed little else as she listened to the boys' chatter and only looked up at a sharp "What the hell is this noise?" from the door. She turned to see General Halsey standing, stick under his arm, looking furiously around the buzzing hall.

She rose. "Blame me, General. I'm the one creating the fuss."

Halsey huffed dramatically but looked at her packed table with interest. "You're up early, Mrs. Roosevelt."

"Keen to eat with the men, General. Breakfast is such a convivial meal, is it not?"

His eyes widened but he didn't comment further. Eleanor suspected it was a long time since he'd known what convivial meant.

"Your car will be ready at 7 a.m. for our trip to the hospital," he said crisply. Then added a surprising "bon appetit" before doing a smart about-turn and marching out.

The hall released a collectively drawn breath and everyone began clamoring to talk to Eleanor again. It was all she could do to get herself away on time and, once again, she missed Tommy who always kept an eye on the clock when Eleanor was distracted by fascinating conversations. Luckily, the first lad from the queue took a proprietorial care of her and shepherded her out of the canteen at precisely 6.55 a.m., delivering her to the car with a smart salute and a "God bless you for coming all this way for us, ma'am."

General Halsey, sitting upright in the car, raised an eyebrow but said nothing more than, "I hope your stomach is strong, Mrs. Roosevelt. I'm afraid you'll see some horrific injuries."

"I'm afraid of that too, General," she said, "but what can we do? There's a war on and if the men are brave enough to put themselves in the line of fire, surely I can manage to console them for the results of that bravery?"

The general gave her a small smile. "Do you know what, ma'am, I'm sure you can."

His confidence bolstered her but, even so, when she was shown into the first ward, it was a struggle to hide her shock. The men in the beds were maimed and burned in ways that might make them unrecognizable to their own mothers.

"But they would still love them and care for them," Eleanor reminded herself. Those mothers could not be here to offer their boys the comfort they so badly needed, so it was up to her to do it.

"Chuck Zimmerman," the matron introduced the first lad. "Brought down in a burning plane, God bless him."

Chuck's entire left side was encased in bandages and his right eye peered out of a shriveled socket. Eleanor moved to his bed, imagining that he was Elliott or Jimmy, Franklin or John.

"You're so brave, Chuck," she said, gently taking his undamaged right hand.

A tear leaked out of his eye. "I'm not brave, Mrs. Roosevelt ma'am. I cry myself to sleep every night."

"As would I," she said. "But you sustained these terrible injuries fighting in defense of your country and that country is hugely grateful and will take good care of you. We have the best doctors in the world and will spare no expense to mend you."

He gave her a weak smile. "I think I'm past mending, ma'am."

Eleanor shook her head firmly. "Not true. We're not going to give up on you, Chuck, so you must not give up on yourself." She bent down to drop a careful kiss on his forehead. "Your mother wouldn't want that, would she?"

He shook his head. "No ma'am. She's always writing about how much she wants me to come home so she can care for me."

"We will make that happen. I will tell her so myself."

His one eye widened. "You will?"

"Of course. What's her name and address?"

Eleanor looked around for Tommy but of course her redoubtable secretary was not here. A young nurse, however, scurried up and offered to take notes.

"Thank you," Eleanor said gratefully. "Now, Chuck, your mother's name please."

He gave it with tearful gratitude and Eleanor promised to write to her the moment she got home. The boys in the next beds were sitting up to see what was going on and she suspected the nurse's notepad would be full of addresses by the time she was done, but so what? A letter or two would cost her little and would mean so much.

For the first time, Eleanor could see the true impact of war. She had, to her shame, enjoyed her civilian defense project, loved seeing women working in factories, and raved about nurseries like the Swan Center. All of those were an indirect result of war, but these young men, broken and burned in the most hideous of ways, were the true result. And the true reason why this must never be allowed to happen again.

TWENTY-NINE

NEW CALEDONIA, SEPTEMBER 1943

"Welcome back, Mrs. Roosevelt. Lovely to see you."

Eleanor fought to hide her surprise as General Halsey came forward, hands outstretched in what looked like genuine pleasure. Conviviality even. She smiled and shook his hand.

"And you, General."

"How was your trip?"

Eleanor had no idea how to answer. Her trip had been many things—long, exhausting, thought-provoking, exhilarating, endlessly heartbreaking. For the last four weeks she had traveled around Australia, New Zealand and more of the small islands that made up this beautiful but desperately isolated sector of a world at war. She'd been up every morning with the dawn, meeting men and women working in very difficult conditions, far from all they knew and loved.

Franklin had sent her regular telegrams saying how well her visit was being reported back in the States, and she'd been glad of his encouragement, but the opinions of midwestern housewives had felt far less important than the suffering of the people laboring on these far-off islands. She'd told them how scared she'd been coming out here for a visit, let alone for a permanent station, and they'd cried and blessed her for doing so.

It had been lovely of them but she'd not felt so much blessed as helpless. For every ounce of comfort she could offer, there were a million more needed, and she'd replied to Franklin about the importance of impressing upon the men—and, if they were lucky, women—who would eventually carve out the peace how much war cost. Surely anyone looking into the burned face of a man brought down in a plane, or the exhausted eyes of the women trying to ease his suffering, would yearn for peace? Surely anyone sitting listening to the wails and cries of the wounded in the night would fight to be sure this never happened again? Surely nothing would unite nations more than the mutual suffering of their sons and daughters?

The general looked at her expectantly.

"Sobering," she said.

He nodded. "War looks very fine on maps and planes; not so fine in the fields on which it is actually fought."

"You must be very proud of your men."

He blinked. "I am. Thank you. And I'm proud of you, Mrs. Roosevelt." He flushed. "That's to say, I'm delighted with what you've achieved. I've had glowing reports from every base and hospital you've visited. I'm told that the Māori christened you "kōtuku rerenga tahi."

"What does that mean?"

"The white heron of the one flight—someone only seen once in a lifetime, if one is very lucky."

Eleanor smiled. "They are too kind."

She'd loved the Māori people of New Zealand, who'd been so welcoming, keen to show her their homes and feed her their food. Their traditional greeting was to touch foreheads and she had gladly done so with their leader. It was an excellent tradition, respectful but curiously intimate, but of course the press had seen it differently. The flashbulbs had popped and a week later someone had shown her a Texan paper deriding her contact with people of color in the most unpleasant of ways. In the privacy of her bedroom, she'd made a rude gesture to the idiot journalist who'd put such an ugly skew on a happy moment, then gone back out and talked to the lovely Māori again.

"You've made the troops very happy," Halsey went on. "You've brought a little of America to the Pacific—the America of front porches and little league games, of bake sales and Saturday-night dances and those small things that make life the rich thing it should be." He blinked, perhaps surprised by his own eloquence.

Eleanor patted his arm. "Thank you, General. It's very kind of you to say so."

"Words are easy. Actions are better. And so, I have arranged for you to visit Guadalcanal."

Eleanor gasped. "You have? I thought you said it was too dangerous for a woman."

General "Bull" gave a soft laugh. "I did, but it seems that you, Mrs. Roosevelt, are not an average woman. You will fly at first light."

"Tomorrow?"

"Yes. We do not want the Japanese getting wind of the location of the most important woman in the known world."

Eleanor shook her head. "Now you're overdoing it, General."

He laughed again, but as she was escorted to the car, she heard him say, "I'm not sure I am." She had no idea what she'd done to impress him, but she was certainly grateful for it. Tomorrow she would be in Guadalcanal. Tomorrow she would see Joe.

In fact, the trip was convoluted. She was flown first to the Vanuatu Islands to visit the hospitals on Efate and then the headquarters of the Navy air force on Espiritu Santo, whence she would fly on to the Solomon Islands. Eleanor, used to the grand land mass of America, was starting to find the endless ocean disorientating. Guadalcanal would be her seventeenth Pacific Island—though the first one engaged in live combat.

U.S. troops had taken back the southern islands of Tulagi, Florida and Guadalcanal earlier this year and seized control of a big airfield, from which they planned to neutralize the major Japanese station on New Britain, but the Japanese were not surrendering lightly. Although they had vacated the islands, they made regular retaliation attacks. Eleanor had to get up at 1 a.m. to fly in under cover of darkness, landing on a runway lit at the last minute by low torches from whence, still saying prayers of thanks, she was delivered to breakfast with General Nathan Twining.

The general personally took her on a tour of the island and gave her lunch with the senior officers before she was released to visit the weather station to see where Joe and his fellows worked. She had an enjoyable afternoon with the enthusiastic group but little chance to talk properly to Joe before she was rushed off again to meet General Halsey, who seemed to have followed her to Guadalcanal, with several sweating senators in tow. Eleanor bet they had secretaries with them but managed to stop herself from asking.

A visit to the hospital was on the itinerary. One of the senators asked to visit the weapons room instead, but Eleanor wasn't having that.

"Better, don't you think, to see the impact of the weapons rather than the weapons themselves?"

It was clear he did not, but he could hardly say so and trailed behind as they went around some of the worst injuries Eleanor had seen yet. The senators hovered at the end of beds, but there was no way she was making the patients feel less human than they already did by shying away from their suffering. She focused on their eyes, avoiding the gaping wounds, the raw scars and the amputated limbs, looking instead into the souls of the men behind them.

"I'm OK," they all said, using the strange new expression that was meant to mean fine, but clearly did not.

"We'll get you home," she responded every time, though God only knew how, and she took more addresses of more grieving mothers and promised to write. It would take forever but it was the least she could do.

She was exhausted by the end and horrified to discover that another fancy meal was planned for the evening.

"I'll find you later," Joe promised and, sure enough, when she gratefully made for her little hut after dinner, there he was, waiting on her porch.

She sank into a chair at his side, scanning his face in the low lamplight. "You look tired, Joe."

"Not half as tired as you, Eleanor."

"I'm a little worn out," she admitted. "I'm not as young as I used to be."

"You could be as young as me and still be utterly floored by the schedule you've followed. The papers are saying you've seen over four hundred thousand men. And spoken to every single one of them."

Eleanor smiled faintly. "Is that so? Aren't I lucky?"

"Aren't *they*?"

Eleanor could feel her eyes closing and stood up to keep awake. "How are you really?" she asked Joe, giving him a hug.

"I've been better," he admitted. "It's a weird life on a military base, almost all men and with little conversation except who's best on the darts board, or who can run faster, or who's shot the most planes down. I'm not the competitive type, Eleanor, as you know, so I'm not exactly in my element. Hardly anyone reads and they'd rather talk about sex than politics. Not that I'm in any way averse to sex, you understand but..." He trailed off and cleared his throat awkwardly.

"They're not your sort of people," Eleanor filled in.

Joe was a sensitive soul, at home with poetry and politics, and she could see how military life would suit him poorly. As it must do many young men. Her sons were robust, athletic lads who seemed, from their letters, to thrive on the adventure of their various roles. That worried her too as there was little better way to put yourself into death's path than by trying to be a hero, but at least they were secure in their day-to-day life. Joe looked tortured.

"Then there's the bombings," he went on. "The Japanese planes come out of nowhere, Eleanor, screaming in on you, flinging bombs and firing everywhere. It's not so much a war as a lottery."

"We can only pray it will be over soon," Eleanor said.

"Not with the Japanese," Joe said darkly. "They demand not just loyalty but madness. I've seen pilots willingly fly suicide missions into key targets. They see the good of the country—as they've been told it—far above their individual merit, so God only knows what it will take to make them surrender."

Eleanor had an idea, but not one she wanted to think about. Back in July, an earnest young physicist by the name of Irving Lowen had turned up in the lobby of her Washington Square apartment, asking to speak to her. He was part of some top-secret project, working in the desert to produce something he called an atomic weapon—a "superbomb" capable of wreaking huge damage on the enemy—and was desperately worried that German scientists were pulling ahead of the U.S. He'd begged Eleanor to impress upon her husband the need to proceed with greater speed and Eleanor had duly spoken to Franklin who'd invited the young man to his office.

Two weeks later, Lowen had turned up at her apartment again and the security team had panicked. The last she'd heard, the poor man had been transferred off the project and sent away. What was happening to the "superbomb," however, she did not know. It felt as if they were depressingly trapped in a cycle of violence.

But tonight she tried to put it aside and talk to Joe about a united nations and how a peaceful world would look were they lucky enough to have some part in shaping it. Soon her eyes were closing again and at 11.30 p.m. she had to give up and go to bed, her precious time with her friend all too brief as the world called for her once more.

The trip back to San Francisco was long and bumpy, filled with too much fear and too little sleep and Eleanor finally landed, exhausted and longing for her own bed. General Halsey had sent her with a letter for Franklin that very kindly stated she had "accomplished more good than any other person or group of civilians who have passed through my area" and she found herself keen to show it to him. With a two-hour wait before her plane to Washington, she requested a phone line to the White House and finally got through.

"Glad you're back safe," Franklin said, as if she'd been on a hop to Chicago.

"It's been rather exhausting."

"But fun, I hope, Babs?"

"Fun?"

He sounded distracted. "Pretty, you know, all those tropical islands."

She ground her teeth. "Oh yes, it's very pretty in makeshift hospitals full of bleeding men."

"Right, yes. Poor things." He coughed. "I hear Halsey let you go to Guadalcanal to see your pal, Joe."

"My 'pal,' Franklin?"

"Your special friend." His voice had an unusually nasty edge to it, something almost like jealousy.

Good God, she had no time for this. She twisted at her wedding band, but it was stuck to her finger; flying must have swollen her joints. "Joe is special," she agreed. "And do you know why?"

"Because he's handsome and earnest and—"

"No!" she shouted him into silence and drew in a deep breath. "Because he was born in the fall of 1909."

She could almost hear Franklin swallow. "He was?"

"Yes. And what else happened in the fall of 1909?"

"We lost Frankie."

"We lost Frankie, yes." Tears welled in her eyes but she fought them back. She was crying far too much these days. "So forgive me," she said icily, "if in Joe Lash I cannot help but see the son that was taken from me."

"I'm sorry. I never thought—"

"Well perhaps sometimes you should."

"I'm sorry," he said again. "It's been very busy here. We've invaded Italy."

"I'm aware of that."

"And it's been non-stop."

"Probably more so for the lads facing the guns."

"Yes."

She could hear his discomfort. Well good!

"You should see some of the injuries, Franklin," she said, distress making her voice squeak. "There are boys with missing limbs, boys with half their stomach torn out, boys with their skin burned right off their faces. It's hideous."

"Of course. Eleanor, I'm sorry, I'm not getting this right. I—"

"We waltz around ordering the production of planes and guns and bombs, praising the figures we hit and gleefully noting that we're at near full employment, and we never for once think about what happens at the other end, when we explode those bombs into people's lives."

"Into the enemy's lives."

"They're still *lives*, Franklin. Or they were. Plus, for every one we drop, they drop another. And half of them fall on civilians—women and children who think war is a futile macho pursuit that can bring only harm. And who are damn well right!" Her voice had risen and the few people in earshot looked around as if she were crazy but she wasn't the crazy one here, it was everyone else who thought war was noble, or heroic or, worst of all, normal.

"I'm sorry, Eleanor." Franklin was conciliatory now. "It must have been horrible. Come home. Rest."

She drew in a deep breath. Rest! That sounded wonderful. But she couldn't help a nagging feeling that the men out on the front lines, not to mention the resistance fighters in the occupied territories, could not rest. And if they could not, why should she?

"Will you be there for dinner?" she asked Franklin.

Face to face she'd be able to discuss what she'd seen more clearly, explain what the war looked like for Americans thousands of miles from the security of the White House.

"I'll... try."

"You'll try?!"

"There're a lot of meetings tonight and—"

Anger flared, red-hot, inside her. "And I've been twenty-five thousand miles around the world at your request. I'll see you at dinner."

"Right. Yes. See you at dinner, Babs. Safe trip."

Eleanor hung up and folded her hands into her lap, looking for fortitude. Her whole body ached with tiredness and her brain felt heavy with the sorrow of too many young people lost and damaged.

"Your plane home is ready for you, Mrs. Roosevelt ma'am," a young soldier came to say.

"Home?" she asked, looking up at him, confused.

"Home, ma'am, yes. The White House."

"Ah. That home."

She got up obediently, because who was she to make everyone else's life awkward, but it was an effort to walk out to yet another plane to fly to what was, let's face it, yet another government installation. She'd lived in the White House for ten years but it wasn't her home, just the place from which she failed to improve the world, and she strapped herself in to return to it feeling wearier than ever in her life before.

THIRTY

WASHINGTON, NOVEMBER 1928

Eleanor paced the Democratic Party HQ and then, seeing Franklin enviously watching her from a chair at its center, forced herself to stop. He could only pace inside his head, poor man, and she went over to sit with him, although her feet itched to be on the move again. This was unbearable.

The country had gone to the polls today and the count was underway. The first results should come in soon but it would be hours before there were enough to give a real indication of which way they would fall. The Democratic candidate was Al Smith, the "happy warrior" of 1924. He had not been elected then and, if the party was honest with itself, had little chance now either.

America was in boom. Share prices were rising and the Republicans were getting the credit. There were more cars, bigger houses, fancier dresses and party after party. In theory the country was in prohibition but there were speakeasys aplenty keen to take the money of the ridiculously rich. Al Smith had told America it couldn't last, but that was not what America wanted to hear. Neither did they want to hear about how the poor were suffering—it spoiled the party mood. The poor had a vote too, of course, but the Republicans were promising riches for everyone and that was hard to beat. To make things even harder, Al was a Catholic and America was staunchly Protestant. At a big Washington rally, thousands of hooded Ku Klux Klan members had turned out in ominous protest at his candidacy. It would be an uphill climb.

Nonetheless, Franklin and Eleanor had thrown themselves into Al's campaign. Eleanor and her friends had led a drive to get women out to vote, as far more of them were natural Democrats. And Franklin—Franklin was standing as Governor of New York State. Al Smith currently held that office, helped by Franklin's support and Eleanor's teapot antics four years ago, and had invited Franklin to stand in his place now he was going for the big job. Franklin had agonized for weeks over whether to accept. His advisers thought it too early in his rehabilitation, especially with the Republicans riding so high, but Franklin had been champing at the bit.

"It's been eight years, Babs," he'd said to her. "Eight whole years of doing nothing but trying to get two steps further down the drive. I want to get out there again. I want to be in public service. I want to get back on the path."

"The path to the White House?" she'd asked, trying not to sound surprised.

Franklin had sighed. "Just to office of some sort. I doubt America is ready to vote a cripple into the White House."

"Don't call yourself that, Franklin."

"Why not? I am."

"Maybe, but it makes it sound as if your brain is crippled too and it most certainly is not."

"Which is why I think I have to run. There's nothing to fear but fear itself, right?"

He'd updated her Thoreau quote, she'd noticed but, then, it was fast becoming his mantra so why not rephrase slightly?

"Your mother will have a fit."

He'd winked. "All the more reason to do it!"

She'd laughed and gone with him to sign up as the Democratic candidate. It had felt exciting then, thrilling even. They'd talked about how life might be in the Executive Mansion in Albany, the capital of New York state, and Eleanor had realized, with a shudder of delight, that she would be free of Sara if they moved there. She'd taken several secret trips to stand and stare at the magnificent house that might represent a whole new future for them.

Now, she wondered what on earth they'd been thinking.

Franklin's chances were not much better than Al's in the current climate but he'd campaigned tirelessly, visiting every town in the state, talking to rich and poor alike, and he'd received a good reception. They'd dared to hope, but the early counts were going to the Republicans. Eleanor glanced to Sara, sitting staunchly in a large armchair. She had not been happy Franklin was running but, to give her her due, had stood by him and was still doing so.

"I suppose it's all experience," Eleanor said to Franklin as the packed HQ echoed with moans.

"Not a very good experience," he replied.

"No."

To her surprise, his hand crept into hers and they sat there together as more and more losses came in. The speech writers huddled in the corner, miserably working on a gracious concession.

"We didn't want to live in Albany anyway, did we?" he said to her later as it began to look as if the Democrats were facing a landslide defeat.

"Hated the thought of it," Eleanor said through desperately gritted teeth.

She loved New York City, she reminded herself, and she was very lucky to have a gorgeous house in the heart of it, even if it was one that her mother-in-law could step into at any moment of the day, or night.

Midnight chimed and with it the count from the last of the big electoral colleges—Republican.

Al Smith got wearily to his feet. "At least we tried," he said to Joseph Taylor Robinson, his running mate. He shook his hand and came over to Franklin to do the same.

"My count isn't in yet," Franklin pointed out.

The gubernatorial elections ran alongside the presidential one, so theoretically it was possible for Franklin to take office even if Al did not. But across the country governorships were falling to the Republicans and it seemed the writing was on the wall.

"Shall we go?" he asked Eleanor.

She nodded and looked over to Sara. "Are you coming home, Mama?"

Sara glared at her. "Home? It's not over yet."

"It might as well be."

Sara tossed her head. "You youngsters give up far too easily."

"You old folk," Franklin teased back, "are far too stubborn to ever give up."

Sara folded her arms and set herself further back into her armchair. Franklin looked uncertainly to Eleanor, but he was pale and telltale drops of sweat were starting to appear on his temples. It had been an exhausting campaign for a man who'd forced himself to stand on soap boxes across the state and it was time to rest.

"Home," she said firmly.

They were fast asleep when the phone rang. Eleanor leaped up to take it from the bleary-eyed maid.

"Mama?" Thin threads of dawn were coming through the heavy curtains. "Are you still at HQ?"

"Damn sure I am. Give me Franklin."

"He's asleep."

"Well, he shouldn't be. He's got a lot to do."

"But—"

"Give me Franklin."

Heart thudding, Eleanor dragged the telephone into Franklin's bedroom, the cord tangling in every bit of furniture. Franklin blinked awake and stared at Eleanor wide-eyed.

"It's Mama," she said and was surprised to hear her voice come out calm—every part of her was pulsing with what this might mean. Surely Sara would not call with a defeat? Then again, who knew what Sara might do.

"Mama?" Franklin said into the receiver.

"The old were right to stay," she told him crisply. "And you need to come back." Sara's voice cracked and Eleanor thought she caught a small sob, though perhaps it was a fault on the line. "You did it, Franklin. Only by the slimmest of margins but you did it. You're the Governor of New York State."

Eleanor half-heard Franklin stuttering an astonished reply to his mother. Her head was spinning and she ran to the window and threw open the curtains. It was a gray day in New York, but over the rooftops the clouds were scattering and, as Eleanor watched, a ray of pure gold broke through, as if God himself was reaching out to them.

Eleanor lifted a hand to the light. Finally!

Ten years ago, she had opened Franklin's case and her world had fallen apart. Three years later polio had taken what had been left of their plans for the future, but they were back on track. And as very different people. Franklin knew more about suffering and endurance, and his inherent democratic principles had found stronger form as a result. As for Eleanor... she felt like a totally new woman. She had friends and activities of her own. She had an identity as more than a wife and mother. She had a purpose. Her dreams were no longer entirely his dreams, though it seemed she might get sucked into his all the same.

She spun back to Franklin as he hung up. "We'll have to move to Albany."

"What a shame..." He held out his hands and she went back to him. "Governor and First Lady of New York State, hey?"

"First Lady?"

"Of the state, yes. You'll need new frocks, Eleanor."

He was teasing she knew but she felt her heart shrivel slightly. "Will I have to be the little wife now?" she asked.

Franklin burst out laughing, the sound rich in the increasingly golden dawn. "You will never be a 'little wife,' Eleanor, and neither would I want you to. You will be a great big wife and I will treasure you for it."

"You will?"

"Always."

THIRTY-ONE

SPRINGWOOD, SEPTEMBER 1943

"Winston! Clementine! Come in, come in," Franklin boomed. "We're so happy to have you with us in our country home."

Eleanor smiled along with her husband and wished she could mean his words as sincerely as he seemed to. She was struggling to get over the dark lethargy that had wrapped its tentacles around her in the hospitals of the Pacific and still wasn't sure Franklin understood how much the visit had cost her. He'd dutifully joined her for dinner on her return and asked her a thousand questions but it had felt like an act—the smooth president putting her at ease, not her Franklin, truly engaged with what she'd seen and experienced.

To be fair to him, he hadn't been well. His sinuses, ruptured by polio, had been playing up, making it hard for him to sleep, and his skin looked worryingly gray. He missed Missy and, although quiet Daisy was often there to fuss around him and vibrant Polly to jolly him along, neither of them could manage his life in the easy way Missy had done. He'd started being secretive about his movements, and Eleanor felt more detached from him than she had since the first bitter days after their nearly divorce.

He was very busy, of course, as president of the most powerful of the Allied countries at a critical point in the war. The invasion of Italy was underway and going well. The Germans had retreated to the north and pulled troops from Russia to shore up their defense, so even Stalin was pleased. It was hoped the Allies might liberate Rome before Christmas and top minds were turning to the "big" invasion into northern France. Conferences were being planned and the world was waiting on Franklin's decisions. Why, in the face of such pressure, should she expect him to pay attention to a woman who had refused to be his "full wife"? Yet, hadn't he always said she would be more than that? So why, at this critical moment, had he pulled away? It didn't feel like spite so much as simple disinterest. She wasn't sure which was more hurtful.

In the meantime, she was expected to play the wife role when it suited him, like today as they entertained the Churchills on what was apparently their thirty-fifth wedding anniversary. Franklin had a small party planned in their honor, but for now he was proudly showing them around their home. Well, Sara's home. Springwood still didn't feel like Eleanor's, even with her mother-in-law gone for a year, and she found herself looking longingly out the window toward Val Kill on the far side of the estate. How she'd love time there alone.

She was delighted to see Clementine, but Winston was as bullish as ever, overexcited about victories in Italy—as he should be, she supposed—and determined to dominate any conversation. She should sit back and let him ramble on while she conserved her strength, but when he went into one of his wilder rants, she could never resist taking him on. She'd been quietly gleeful when he and Franklin had got into an argument over De Gaulle. Churchill was a supporter of the man but Franklin, who'd met him at Casablanca, thought him arrogant and self-seeking.

"Stalin is arrogant and self-seeking," Winston had snapped. "But you like to cozy up to him."

Tensions, it seemed, were rising at even the highest level.

Clementine, at least, was lovely and Eleanor had drawn strength from her quiet grace. In Washington, she'd suggested she join her all-female press conference and, although Clementine had looked almost amusingly terrified at the prospect, she'd been marvelous.

"You're a natural," Eleanor had told her, taking her arm afterwards.

She'd felt Clementine stiffen—really the woman was so old-fashioned about intimacy—but she'd smiled.

"They weren't as... intimidating as I thought they would be. Did I say the right things?"

"You said the true things," Eleanor had assured her, "which is what counts. I find that if you share what you can, the press respect you. It's when you're too aloof that there's trouble."

Clementine had laughed. "Perhaps that's my problem. I was brought up with aloofness being the gold standard of behavior."

That had made Eleanor laugh too. Clementine reminded her so much of some of the girls she'd met during her time at school in England. They'd been shy of saying anything for fear of sounding "improper" and shy of doing anything in case it was "unladylike." Eleanor had found it most confusing and, luckily, so had the headmistress.

"The world is yours to take by the shoulders and shake into shape," she'd tell them over dinner. "Being ladylike is all very well, but don't let it get in the way of being an actual person."

They were words that had served Eleanor well and more and more these days she was reminding herself of them. General Halsey had not wanted her in the Pacific for fear she would be too fragile to cope and she had showed him what she was made of, hadn't she?

The problem was, that out there on the Pacific front line,

she'd just had to get on and do it—see the men, talk to them, tell them their injuries didn't make them any lesser. She'd been on the go, and she was always better that way. Now, stuck in domestic duties, there was too much time to think. She'd written hundreds of letters to the mothers of the boys she'd met on the islands and with every one she'd felt again the sadness of their wounding in the name of a few megalomaniac leaders' petty desires.

As she watched Clementine Churchill being shown around Springwood by a beaming Franklin, it felt such a stark contrast to the front lines. The British woman's designer dress and matching jacket were beautiful but felt jarringly elegant after six weeks among uniforms. Eleanor missed her Red Cross suit and felt frivolous in the floral frock she'd chosen to try to cheer herself up this morning. Life in Hyde Park was all so very sweet. But of course, she told herself sternly, that was exactly as should be. There was no point fighting for homes you did not care about.

Looking around, she wondered what the cultured Englishwoman made of Sara's house, with its dark wood paneling and fussy ornamentation. She'd seen Clementine's taste when she'd visited last year and knew it ran to light, open rooms in pretty pastels, so Springwood must look horribly gloomy to her.

"Ghastly, isn't it?" she whispered when Franklin led them to a display of his favorite stamps. "Why don't you come and see my place?"

"Your place?"

Clementine looked surprised, but already the thought of taking her to Val Kill was cheering up Eleanor and she linked an arm through hers.

"*My* place," she affirmed happily. "I think you'll like it."

The men were happy to settle in on the back porch to talk war and Eleanor showed Clementine to her sporty little Buick and drove her the two miles across the estate to her cottage.

"How charming!" Clementine said. "And this is all your own?"

"All mine," Eleanor confirmed.

"Lucky you. We have Chartwell, but Winston chose it. It's cost us a fortune and I find myself resenting it for that. Resentment rather ruins one's joy in a place."

That, Eleanor could understand.

"Val Kill brings me much joy," she said. "Shall we have tea?"

"Lovely."

They took the tray out onto the lawn.

"This is heaven!" Clementine said, kicking off her shoes and wriggling her toes free in the September sunshine.

Eleanor was delighted to see Val Kill working its magic on her uptight English friend. "That's the idea," she agreed. "I built it back in the early twenties when things with Franklin were, well, not the best. He was..." She cut herself off, feeling disloyal.

"Demanding and awkward?" Clementine suggested.

"More like inattentive and unfaithful," Eleanor burst out, surprising herself. She'd nearly spoken to Clementine about it in London last year but had not been able to find the words. Here, in Val Kill, they seemed to tumble from her.

"I'm so sorry," Clementine said.

Eleanor shrugged and looked around. The leaves were turning red and orange, beautiful in their decline. Maybe people were the same. Middle age might make you less fresh and vibrant, but it had its own russet charms, one of which was undoubtedly the freedom to be honest.

"I was devastated at the time," she admitted. "But it's worked out for the best. Or, at least, it's worked out. I never would have been able to do half my projects if I'd been more intimately entwined with Franklin. We women tend to put others first, don't we? It's very kind of us but makes it almost impossible to get our own things done."

"How do men manage it then?" Clementine asked. "I believe most men care for their wives."

"Of course. I'm not denying it. But they still put themselves first." She thought about Franklin. He had told her on their wedding day that he wanted to be President, and their lives, even at their rockiest moments, had been carved out by that wish ever since.

You will not be able to run for high office as a divorced man, Sara's voice said in her head, an unwelcome echo from the most painful year of her life. Franklin's ambitions had shaped almost everything she'd done since. Yet, they had also freed her to become something she would never have been without them. His ambitions had, in a way, enabled hers and, to his credit, he had fought to allow her to follow them.

"Really," she said to Clementine, thinking it through, "it's much the most sensible way. If we all put ourselves first and those we loved a close second, I suspect it would work out fine. That's what Franklin and I have found, anyway. We have our own friends, our own... intimates, but we're still very much a team."

Was that true? Was she playing the smooth First Lady, offering up a picture that sounded neater than it truly was? And if so, did it matter? It kept her going, kept her fighting, and that was what counted. There were far too many people in the world needing just a tiny bit of love, to go around selfishly wanting it all for yourself. But she could see Clementine regarding her curiously, safe from within the cradle of Winston's utter devotion, and it made her feel far less sure of her position.

"Any which way," she said, standing before they could twist themselves up in emotional twaddle, "I find that one of the keys to my sanity and my energy is having time to myself."

"That I could not agree with more." Clementine gestured to the pool. "Can we swim?"

"We surely can."

They returned to the Big House two hours later, refreshed and invigorated, to dress for dinner. Clementine emerged looking beautiful in a blue evening gown that matched an exquisite sapphire pendant and earrings Winston had gifted her for their anniversary. Her eyes were sparkling as much as the jewels and, despite usually drinking as little as Eleanor, she accepted one of Franklin's manhattans and pronounced it delicious.

"A toast!" Winston proposed, putting his arm around his wife's waist and raising his glass to hers. With Clementine in pretty heels, he was at least a foot shorter than her and it ought to look ridiculous, save for how very well they seemed to fit against each other. Winston had, in honor of the occasion, eschewed his peculiar "rompers" for finest evening wear and they looked almost regal standing there together. Eleanor looked over to Franklin, but he was too busy watching Winston to catch her eye. She felt something unpleasantly like jealousy well up inside her and gave a tiny stamp of her foot to chase it away.

"Everything OK, Eleanor?" Franklin asked, using the peculiar new expression fashionable among the soldiers.

It reminded her of the boys lying in hospital beds on Guadalcanal, fighting to stay alive within their maimed young bodies. "I'm OK, ma'am," they'd say to her, so very bravely.

"I'm fine," she said tightly. Franklin had sent her on that trip but had paid precious little attention to her reports when she got back. On the other hand, he had trusted her to be his representative, to travel America and her outposts on his behalf, and her life was so much richer as a result. Oh, it was all so very confusing!

"A toast!" Winston cried again, pulling her back into the room where she should be.

She hastily grabbed a glass from the side and stood to obedient social attention. She was a terrible hostess.

"To the most wonderful woman in the world!" their guest proposed extravagantly. "I knew from the moment I first saw the beautiful Clementine Hozier that she was the one for me, and I was bloody well right. I couldn't have done half what I have without her."

"Bravo!" Franklin cried, and the select crowd in the room clapped and sighed happily.

Clementine's eyes sparkled even more prettily and she reached down to kiss her husband.

Eleanor shook her head. "The question is, Winston," she said darkly, "how much might Clementine have done without you?"

Clementine might have heard her, Winston certainly did not. He rarely heard much over his own voice, but tonight that was just as well. They were bitter words, unworthy of her as a friend and hostess, and unfit for attention on this happy night.

Though still, of course, true.

THIRTY-TWO

WASHINGTON, DECEMBER 1943

Eleanor took the newspaper eagerly from Moses hoping it would hold the first pictures of the conference. She was dying to see what the mysterious city of Tehran looked like, though all the press would offer, of course, would be pictures of important men posing.

The capital of Iran was the unlikely location for the first ever meeting of the "Big Three"—Franklin, Winston and Josef Stalin. It had been chosen by Stalin who had refused to travel anywhere further west, leaving Franklin, in his wheelchair, to cross the Atlantic by ship, fly from Oran to Tunis, then on to Cairo to meet Winston for the final leg.

Franklin hated planes. Without legs he could only brace himself against their bumps and twists with his arms, and if anything ever happened he would be helpless to escape unaided. The final leg of his journey had been an exhausting 1300-mile flight to Tehran, in which the pilot had had to trace a hair-raising path between the mountains to avoid going over 9000 feet—the height at which they'd feared Franklin's lungs would give up on him. But he was prepared to bear all that for the future of peace. The fact that Stalin wasn't did not, to Eleanor's mind, bode well.

She'd been keen to go along, ostensibly to keep an eye on Franklin's wavering health but also, if she was honest with herself, to be at the heart of the decision-making. With the Russians throwing the Nazis out of Russia, the stage had finally been set to plan the invasion of northern France and, even more critically to Eleanor's thinking, the first stages of the peace. The chance to be involved in that had excited her but when she'd asked Franklin, the answer had been an implacable no.

"There'll be no women there, Babs. Sorry."

Anna, keen to see her husband, who was stationed in Cairo and still not enjoying war work, had also asked to go and received the same answer. Meanwhile, with Jimmy busy winning medals in the taking of Makin Island, Elliott had been called back from duty to attend his father. Franklin had wanted Frank too, but his earnest third son had been bringing his destroyer back to America for a refit and had said he could not abandon his men to stand around serving drinks to generals. Eleanor had been proud of him, but it had done little to soothe her infuriation. When would these men understand that they were arranging events for the entire population of the world, not just their half of it?

Eleanor made it to her office and, sitting down with a nod to Tommy, already hard at work, she unfolded the paper and laid it out before her. Sure enough, a picture filled the front page, showing Franklin dead center in a pin-striped suit, Churchill and Stalin either side of him in full uniform. The three leaders were seated between the imposing pillars of some grand building that could, frankly, have been anywhere, but they were sitting there together.

"They're smiling at least," she said to Tommy.

"Foxes smile," Tommy said caustically. "Is Elliott in it?"

Eleanor looked eagerly back to the picture, scanning the

ranks of men ranged behind the "Big Three," then gasped. She couldn't see Elliott's clipped curls, but right there, behind Franklin, was a woman—a rather striking young woman in a smart WAAF uniform.

"Who's that?" The girl looked vaguely familiar but when Eleanor scanned the list of names helpfully printed below, she saw that she was simply "Sarah Oliver." A secretary perhaps, though she looked very at ease among the great and good.

Tommy looked over her shoulder. "Sarah Oliver? That's Winston's daughter, isn't it?"

Of course! Eleanor peered at Sarah, rage bubbling dangerously in her stomach. Winston Churchill had taken his daughter on the men-only trip. Bluff, arrogant, backward Winston was prepared to break the mold to champion his girl, and Franklin, for all his supposedly modern ways, was not.

"Telegram," she snapped to Tommy, who grabbed her pad. "Congrats on grand photo. Stop. Amused to see Sarah Churchill in attendance. Stop."

"Amused?" Tommy questioned, eyebrow raised.

"He'll know what I mean," she said darkly.

He knew exactly and did not take it well.

"It was not conference rules, Eleanor dear," he said loftily on his return, "but U.S. Navy rules—no women on ship."

"In which case, Franklin *dear*, U.S. Navy rules are outdated and, frankly, insulting to all those women doing amazing war work around the globe."

"Imagine the chaos if women were canned up on board with men!" he snorted.

"Yes, imagine! People chatting, laughing and dancing, instead of drinking, gambling and fighting."

"I've no time for this," Franklin said furiously. "I've got a country to run."

"Then let's hope you run it better than you'd run the Navy."

The argument rumbled on as the children arrived for Christmas. Anna was first and equally cross with Franklin, which was good, save that Anna's ability to forgive her father far outweighed Eleanor's. Barely two days after she'd joined the debate—if it could be called anything as wholesome as a debate—Eleanor found the pair of them laughing over breakfast.

"You two sound happy," she said, unable to keep the disapproval out of her voice.

Franklin did not react.

Anna looked shamefaced. "Pa says he's going to look into reviewing navy protocols, Ma. That's good, isn't it?"

"Look into" sounded, to Eleanor, remarkably like a brush-off, but Anna was so eager to believe him that it felt mean to say so. And, besides, they were at war. Young soldiers were being shot on the frontline every day. Jews were being herded into camps and murdered. Her own petty pride counted for little against all that. Plus, it was Christmas—time for love and forgiveness.

"That's very good," she agreed through gritted teeth.

Franklin looked at her. "Maybe you can come next time?"

"Maybe."

It was enough for Anna, who was bouncing around like a puppy, delighted at the détente. "And guess what, Ma, Pa's suggested I move into the White House to look after him now that Missy can't."

Franklin was holding her eye. *And you won't*, was the unspoken text but that was fine by her. He'd drawn up the lines a long time ago and if, as she'd battled to accustom herself to them, they'd become as rigid as the naval ones, whose fault was that?

"Wonderful idea," she said, breaking eye contact with her

husband and hugging her daughter. "It will be lovely to have you here with me all the time."

"Here with *us*," Franklin said, but she was hugging Anna too tight to listen.

In time, the frost thawed, as frost always did. The younger boys made it back for Christmas with their wives and children and they celebrated in Hyde Park for the first time since 1932. The warmth of her family's love reminded Eleanor of everything good about what she and Franklin had created together, and she sat proudly at the end of the Christmas table opposite him. (The second chair was finally hers, though she was sure she could feel Sara's indignant ghost prodding her.) Franklin was not perfect, but which of us were, and at least he was here.

Shock news had come in that Winston was seriously ill. The poor man had caught a chill on the plane home from Iran and collapsed at his stopover in North Africa. Franklin had offered Eisenhower's villa in Tunis and doctors had been rushed to the Prime Minister from the major British camp in Egypt. They'd diagnosed pneumonia, and he'd been so close to death that Clementine had been flown out in what must have been a terrifying rush. For days, the whole of Allied command had held its breath but Winston had, thankfully, pulled through. The next pictures had been of him grandly celebrating Christmas in his dressing gown in the African sun, but it had shaken Franklin.

"That could have been me, Babs," he said as they prepared to take the train back to Washington for the new year.

"It could. But it wasn't. And it won't be."

"You're right," he agreed, nodding firmly and setting his sights back on the White House.

Anna, traveling with them, didn't look so sure, and certainly Franklin was far from the peak of health. His hands shook regularly these days, he coughed a great deal, and he was often out of breath. More worryingly, he would sometimes seem to blank out, though only ever for a second or two. Eleanor had assumed he was studiously ignoring her until Anna pointed out he did it with everyone, even Fala.

"He's not good in the cold," Eleanor said.

Anna just tutted.

January brought a brief distraction when Franklin quietly secured Anna's husband an honorable release from the Army to return to Washington and work in the War Department. Anna was hugely grateful to have John back and, seeing it, Eleanor quashed her qualms about using their position to gain privileges; fighting Hitler was draining Franklin and having family around was a necessary help these days.

"The sooner we end this damned war the better," he'd gripe to her.

"You're preaching to the converted, dear," she'd tell him. "Your job is to make everyone else understand that."

He was certainly doing his best, and Anna, bolstered by John's return, increased her vigilance over Franklin's health.

"I think we should call in the doctors," she said, when spring failed to bring any improvement.

Eleanor was on her way to a meeting of the new United Nations Relief and Rehabilitation Administration, set up to start trying to deal with the many refugees all over Europe.

"Whatever you think," she agreed, pulling on her hat. "You're in charge."

Anna took her at her word and when Eleanor returned, several doctors were in attendance.

"Your heart is weak, sir," she heard one of them tell Franklin. "You need to avoid putting it under too much stress."

"I'm President of the United States," Franklin laughed. "Stress is very much part of the job."

"Then perhaps, sir, you should think of getting out? It's election year, after all."

Franklin was furious. "No more doctors!" he railed, throwing them out.

"No more doctors *here*," Anna agreed carefully. "We'll go to the experts."

Eleanor was not convinced it was necessary. Franklin had fought his way back from far worse than a few coughs and wheezes, but Anna was a terrier when she got her teeth into something, and insisted on full tests. Eleanor expected Franklin to refuse but, to her great surprise, he acquiesced. Perhaps the shadow of Winston's near-brush with death was longer than she'd suspected.

Anna drove her father up to Bethesda Naval Hospital and an inspiring young doctor called Howard Bruenn took up his case. Not yet forty, he was already an expert cardiologist and expressed himself very concerned about the President. More doctors were called and more tests ordered. There was much whispered arguing between Franklin's usual physician, Dr McIntire, and Dr Bruenn, but in the end the second and third opinions backed Bruenn and medicine was prescribed.

"What the hell are they giving you?" Eleanor asked when she saw Franklin taking a violent-green pill with his morning coffee.

"No idea," he said, swallowing.

"You didn't ask?"

"Why bother? We called in an expert, so let him do his job." He glared at her. "And let me get on with mine!"

She tried not to snap. He was very stressed, after all. The Allied command had finally agreed to invade northern France at some secret point this year and the intensity of the battle discussions had upped considerably. Every day more young men were being shipped over to Great Britain to prepare and it was no time to distress the President. No time, either, for him to be unwell.

"What the hell are they giving him?" she asked Anna.

Her daughter grimaced. "Digitalis. His heart is enlarged and Dr Bruenn says the digitalis should reduce the swelling and allow the blood to pump more easily."

"Digitalis?" Eleanor stared at Anna, confused. "Foxgloves? Isn't that poison?"

"In the wrong doses, yes."

"But they're sure they've got the right dose?"

"As sure as they can be."

It seemed to Eleanor a hell of a gamble. The fate of the world was in American hands, America was in the hands of the President, and the President was in the hands of foxgloves.

God help them all...

THIRTY-THREE

THE WHITE HOUSE, JUNE 5, 1944

The Oval Office was alive with people and had been for what felt like weeks. D-Day for the invasion of Normandy was due at any time, and the whole of America was on tenterhooks for its announcement. To make matters worse, summer had arrived on a rolling boil, and Washington was like a cauldron. It was eight o'clock and night was falling but the heat was clinging on, pulling everyone in the White House into a frenzy. Franklin had specified no evening dress for dinner, to allow the men to stay in their light slacks and the women in cotton dresses, and everyone was thankful for it. But still very hot! Eleanor, arriving to try and speak to Franklin about his GI education program, could barely even see him for the mass of people mopping their brows around his desk.

She cleared her throat and the men—they were all men—looked around and resentfully shuffled aside. Franklin was serene amidst the chaos, but Eleanor noted how fast his hand stroked Fala, seated on his knee, and knew he was feeling the tension too. The digitalis seemed, thankfully, to have worked well and his breathing was easier these days, but it wasn't a miracle cure and he still had to be careful to get as much rest as he could. Not easy with the Allies poised to invade.

"You're busy," she said. An understatement.

"A little," he agreed with a small smile. "But I always have time for you."

That wasn't true but it was an important fiction and she played along.

"I saw that the GI bill is coming up before Congress in a couple of weeks and came to... well, to congratulate you."

"You did?" He was surprised and she felt bad about that.

"It's a masterpiece, Franklin. Like the New Deal all over again."

His smile was real now and for a moment the chaos around them faded and they were back in his first presidency, when the revolutionary "New Deal" had offered the average man help to find work. This GI Bill of Rights harkened back to that original spirit, providing a massive program of education and training for returning GIs who, by fighting for their country, had lost out on their education. It would offer them mustering-out pay until they could get a job, and social security credits for time they'd spent in the forces. It would also fund them, if they wished, to get a college education. It was a New Deal dream and, even better, it was almost impossible to deny to the heroes fighting the war for everyone—the heroes who would, any day now, be plunging onto the beaches of Normandy and into the paths of German guns.

"We can only pray enough of them will survive to take advantage of it," Franklin said somberly.

Eleanor frowned. The only other time she'd seen him this morose had been before the invasion of North Africa. Then again, it was little surprise. This decision had been made by everyone, not just Franklin, but it was still his name on the documents that might send the nation's sons to their doom.

"Everything possible is being done to be sure of that," she said gently.

"But will everything possible be enough?"

"Only time will tell."

He nodded and looked around the office, then beckoned her closer. "It's tonight, Eleanor."

Instantly the heat of Washington felt hotter, the anxiety of the men around her more palpable, the weight of power heavier.

"D-Day?" she breathed. "Tonight?" She looked around guiltily. She might live in the White House and hold the title First Lady, but she had no official status and no right to this information. Many times Franklin had kept her in the dark, so it was a mark of his concern that he was telling her this.

"How are you?" she asked.

"That doesn't matter. What matters is how *they* are."

"And how are they?"

"No idea. France feels an awfully long way away. Bloody terrified, I'd *imagine*."

Eleanor imagined he was right and now she was terrified too. If this went well, the Allies could be on their way to winning the war and finally bringing peace to the world. If it went badly, Hitler could turn the tide on them and there might never be peace again.

That night, Eleanor tried to sleep but sleep stood no chance against the army running rampant through her mind. Every time she closed her eyes, she saw the faces of all the soldiers she'd met over the last four years. How many of them were in mustering pens on the south coast of England? Or already in landing craft setting forth across a stormy Channel to face the German guns?

There had been a large-scale training exercise back in April to test the readiness of the men for beach landings. It had been an all-American initiative, set up somewhere called Lyme Bay, and it had been an unholy disaster. Somehow two German U-boats had snuck under the inadequate defenses and shot at every U.S. ship involved. Over seven hundred young men had died, many drowning from the weight of their overladen packs, and although valuable lessons had been learned, it had been at an awful cost. This time it was the real thing. Thousands of men would have to jump into the shallow waves and run up open beaches toward Nazi guns, fired from protected pillboxes at the top.

It was surely suicide.

With sleep impossible, Eleanor got up again and traced her way around the White House, feeling some strange need to check its solidity. It was eerily quiet. A few guards stood to silent attention as she passed but, in stark contrast to the last few weeks, the corridors and offices were empty.

They were six hours behind Britain so it was already 6 a.m. over the English Channel. The attack was due to be launched at dawn and the sun would surely be creeping over the curve of the earth in Normandy. She wandered into the vast East Room, imagining the elaborately decorated walls as a moonlit beachscape, and the patterned carpet spume she must jump into.

"Everything all right there, Mrs. Roosevelt ma'am?"

She jumped and looked over to see Moses sitting alone, a bank of telephones on the table next to him. She stared at them.

"I have no idea," she said eventually. "How about you, Moses?"

"No idea either, ma'am. We just have to wait."

"Wait. Yes. Agony, isn't it?"

"Yes, ma'am."

Eleanor stared at the telephones again but they were resolutely silent so she turned and went back to her room. She could, at least, catch up on her correspondence. It seemed a paltry activity but there might be many letters of condolence to write in the next few days and she should start with a clear desk.

As soon as she sat down, however, her eyes were drawn to the framed photos before her. The closest one was of her four sons standing proudly in their uniforms at the start of the war. None of them would be involved in D-Day. Elliott, who'd been in England until recently, was flying sorties over Rome, finally poised on the brink of liberation. Jimmy was in the Pacific with his Marines, and Frank and John were on ships out there. For once, they were not at the heart of the action, but the implications of the invasion would affect them all.

The idea was not conducive to concentration and, restless, Eleanor went to the window. There was the little red light twinkling away on the top of the Washington Monument. Would Hitler keep the great obelisk? she wondered idly. Would he hang swastikas down every side to broadcast his triumph to the world? Would he—?

"Stop it!" she scolded herself out loud.

Many brilliant minds had been behind the planning of this invasion. It wasn't just the military logistics, which were mind-bending, but a whole scheme of deceptions to try to convince the Nazis the Allies would attack in the Pas de Calais—the shortest point between Britain and France—rather than across the ambitious stretch to Normandy. Franklin received many reports from the Americans working at the brilliant Bletchley Park intelligence center in England suggesting that Hitler had bought the deceptions and that there were relatively few units in Normandy, but maybe Hitler was preparing deceptions of his own. There was no way of knowing.

Well, no way bar launching a hundred and fifty thousand young men into their path.

Eleanor thought she might go mad and even found herself eyeing up the brandy decanter in Franklin's dressing room, between their two bedrooms. Was this why people drank—to take the clarity out of the world when it became too much to bear? She pulled her hand away. She was perfectly safe in the opulence of America's primary residence. What right did she have to seek relief? It was carpet beneath her feet, not spume, fancy paintings on her walls, not—

A telephone rang out. And then, before she could react, another—in her room. She ran back to pick it up.

"Hello?"

"Mrs. Roosevelt? It's Moses, ma'am. I thought I'd try you, seeing as I knew you were awake."

"Yes, yes. Do you have news?"

"I have General Marshall on the line."

General George Marshall was an Army chief-of-staff and instrumental in the planning of D-Day.

"Put him through," Eleanor managed, though her hand was shaking as she clutched the receiver.

"Mr. President?"

"His wife," Eleanor said crisply. "But I will wake him immediately."

"Do so. He'll want to know this."

"He will? Is it... is it good news?"

"As good as it can be. The men have made a successful landing on the target beaches in Normandy and secured beachheads on all four."

"They have?" Eleanor felt faint and, halfway to Franklin's room, had to lean against the wall to stay upright. "And losses?" she stuttered down the line.

"Some. More than we'd like—which is none, obviously—but it could be worse." His voice cracked. "Oh Mrs. Roosevelt, it could be so, so much worse. We're on our way, ma'am, on our way to Berlin!"

. . .

Franklin woke the moment she opened his door and yanked himself up into a sitting position, his eyes wide with questions.

"It's good news," she assured him. "The beaches are secured. The men are—mainly—safe."

"Oh, thank God." He took the receiver from her, then threw his other arm around her waist and pressed his head tight against her stomach as he spoke to Marshall. He was careful to ask for facts and figures, but repeated again and again, "But the beaches are secured? The men are safe?"

"The men are sheltered," Marshall corrected carefully every time. "We hold solid positions from which to push on."

"Push on, yes. Thank you, General. And good luck." Once he'd returned the receiver to its cradle with an incongruous tinkle, he whispered again, "Push on. This isn't the end, is it, Babs?"

She shook her head. God help them, this was only the beginning. It was at least seven hundred miles to Berlin and the Nazis would not give up easily.

"Remember Hitler's speech when he invaded Poland in 1939?" she asked him, picturing herself sitting with Tommy in Val Kill, Franklin on the other end of the phone in Washington, listening to the self-professed Führer spitting bile and determination. "'One word I have never known: capitulation.'"

"I remember," Franklin said. "He's going to take some beating, isn't he, Babs?"

"He is," she agreed. "But we *are* going to beat him. It starts now."

"It starts now." He hugged her again, his strong arms crushing her against him, and then he was pulling on his sweater and picking up the phone, and doors began to bang downstairs as the American government leaped into action and the White House filled once more.

Eleanor returned to her room and kept watch over the Washington Monument as, slowly, the summer dawn rose around the great column and the news began to filter out to the wider world. The city sprang into joyous life. At first it was voices, calling to one another, then cars honking, factory whistles tooting, even fog horns blasting triumphantly across the Potomac. People streamed into the streets, waking one another with cries of victory, and a vast crowd gathered around the monument and all the way up to the White House, calling, and waving flags, and singing. Bells joined the cacophony and thousands flocked to churches, chapels and synagogues to give thanks for the landings and pray for the ongoing safety of their boys. The casualty figures were coming in and, although it wasn't the thousands they'd feared, it was hundreds and that would be too many weeping families amidst the general joy. Eleanor went to several services and bowed her head in prayer for her sons. None of them were in Normandy, but it made little difference, for this was a world war and anyone could be hurt anywhere.

That evening Franklin went on air, not to offer news or promises or false hope but simply to lead the nation in a somber prayer for "our sons, pride of our nation" and for the people to have strong hearts to "wait out the travail and bear the sorrow." Eleanor sat at his side and, later, as the mass of aides, journalists and military leaders leached out of the great building they somehow still called home, they sat quietly together, absorbing the immense impact of the day.

"Moses called you first," Franklin said into the silence.

"Only because he knew I was awake. Does it bother you?"

He thought about it. "No. You were the one keeping watch, so you deserved to be first to know."

"I don't think it was like that."

He put up a hand. "Any other wife would have been getting her beauty sleep."

"I doubt it, Franklin."

"But not you." He looked over to her. His eyes were

drooping and there was a worrying tremor in his hands. She rose to help him to bed, but he was staring at her intently and asked, "Do you like it here?"

Eleanor sat slowly back down. "In the White House?"

He nodded. "It's not a conventional home."

Eleanor laughed. "We don't live a conventional life."

"No. Do you like that?"

He was looking at her so seriously that she didn't laugh it off but gazed around, considering. She had a strange flashback to her weekend in Buckingham Palace. It had been five times the size and grandeur of the White House, but the King had been born into it as a true home, not elected into it for a brief—or not so brief—time. Living here made your life feel borrowed but also overwhelmingly privileged.

"I do," she admitted.

"You haven't suffered for my dream, then?" His hands were gripping the sides of his chair, as they had done in the early days of him trying to learn to walk again.

"Franklin, you should go to bed."

"You haven't suffered?" he pressed urgently.

She sucked in a deep breath. "I wouldn't go that far. But it's been worth it."

"Babs—"

She stood up. "I don't think this is the time for gazing into the navel of our past, Franklin. You're tired."

"No, I—"

"I'm tired too. We must rest. There are boys on the beaches of Normandy with a long fight ahead of them and it's your job to stay fit enough to lead and inspire them."

He smiled. "*Our* job."

"Oh, I don't inspire anyone. But I'm here to support you. Always. And right now, that means bedtime!"

Franklin sighed but nodded. She dropped a kiss on his clammy forehead and turned his chair to push him to the door of his room, deep in the heart of the house they had both fought so hard to inhabit. The White House had been Franklin's dream but sometimes, lately, it had felt more like a nightmare and Eleanor couldn't help feeling that this year, it might be time to finally move on.

THIRTY-FOUR
QUEBEC, AUGUST 1944

"Would you come to the Quebec conference with me?" Franklin had asked. "I'd like you there," he'd insisted. "You'll make a real difference."

She'd been delighted at the invitation, keen to be involved in the big decisions, but now she was in Quebec, Franklin was so busy he had little time to even notice she was with him. And she certainly wasn't making a difference. Not unless you counted to the shopkeepers of the city, seeing as buying scarves and trinkets was the only thing the "wives" were expected to do around here. She'd got wool for her knitting, and a few trinkets for her Christmas cupboard, but that was hardly of international significance.

"What's the point of having us here if we cannot be involved?" she asked Clementine Churchill one afternoon. Franklin had suggested Winston brought his wife along too, so they were both stuck walking the edges of the stunning hexagonal citadel in which the men were busily hammering out their ideas for a post-war world.

"So we can support our husbands?" Clementine suggested.

"Pah!" Eleanor scoffed. "I could support Franklin far better if I was in the room with him."

"A fair point," Clementine conceded, squeezing her arm. "The issue, I suppose, is that we are not elected by the people so cannot speak on their behalf."

Eleanor nodded reluctantly. Had she not always said that she'd make a terrible politician? It was just hard to be at the door of the decision-making but not allowed through.

"Your daughter is in there," she pointed out. "As is my son."

"As officially appointed aides."

"So officially appoint me!" Eleanor burst out, infuriated.

Clementine laughed. "I really hope the American people have the wisdom to do that. You'd be an excellent leader."

Eleanor cowered back, protesting. That was her bluff called!

"And in the meantime," Clementine went on serenely, "you will have to content yourself with talking to Franklin about it afterwards."

Eleanor ground her teeth. "But that's the problem, Clemmie. He doesn't talk to me about it. Not in detail."

"Ah." Clementine gave her an awkward smile of sympathy.

Eleanor felt embarrassed. Winston apparently told his wife every detail of his war plans and strategies, though, on the flip side, it must mean an awful lot of sitting around listening to him drone on and on. Missy had always done that for Franklin, but Missy had tragically died last month. Her sister had reported that she'd left the world leafing frantically through photos of Franklin, and she would never now be returning to sit lovingly at his feet. Eleanor, however, did not have the time for such devotion. Or the patience. She was champing at the bit to get back to her own work and was sure Clementine must be too.

"I'm sorry if you had to come all the way out here because Franklin invited me along," she said.

Clementine looked at her strangely. "Winston told me

Franklin had invited you because *I* was coming along. I wasn't especially keen, I admit, but I didn't want to let Winston out of my sight after him getting so ill at Tehran. So, you see, it should be me that's sorry if I took you away from your affairs."

"Not at all," Eleanor said hastily. "It's lovely to be here with you."

Which was true, but a rather different spin on her husband's invitation.

Despite her discomfort, Eleanor was grateful to Clementine when, over an unusually intimate dinner—the four of them plus Elliott and Mary, the Churchill's lively youngest daughter—the Prime Minister's wife asked, "How was business today?"

"Endless," Franklin said with a dismissive laugh.

"In what way?" Clementine asked.

He looked surprised, but Winston stepped readily in. "We're trying to decide on the extent and division of occupation zones in defeated Germany."

"Occupation zones?" Eleanor asked. That didn't sound good. Surely the Allies were trying to stop the occupation of Europe?

"Germany will have to be ruled by us until such time as we believe she can be trusted again," Winston said.

Eleanor bristled. "There must be some good Germans around. We have a number in exile in the States. You must be the same?"

"Yes, but we can't catapult them back into leading a country riddled with Nazism, can we?"

"Why not?" Eleanor demanded, indignant on their behalf. "Is France not ruling itself, despite many of their leaders collaborating with the Nazi regime?"

"Well, yes, but De Gaulle is in charge."

"And is a jumped-up, pompous ass," Franklin fumed. "Do you know—?"

But Eleanor was not to be deflected by her husband's dislike of the French commander. This was important. "Will the Norwegian government not simply return and take up the reins again in their country, despite it collaborating?"

"The exiled government has not been collaborating," Winston said. "Quite clearly."

"But some in the country have. Can we trust *them*?"

"We cannot occupy the whole of Europe, dear lady. That would make us as bad as Hitler."

"Quite!" Eleanor folded her arms triumphantly. Clementine was fidgeting at her side but the peace of the world was at stake, so a little dinner-time debate was a small price to pay.

Winston glared at Eleanor. "You would have us leave Germany to govern herself? Put in a few academics and artists we've been harboring overseas and hope they're strong enough to do the job?"

"We could support them from the edges," she suggested.

Clementine cleared her throat. "Is it possible," she asked in her quietly cultured voice, "to support from the edges? It's so much easier if one is actually in the room."

Eleanor looked at her. The damn woman was quoting her back at herself. For a moment she felt furious but it was so clever she had to laugh. "Touché, Clemmie! I asked for that."

Clementine looked very relieved, and so did Franklin.

"What are you ladies up to tomorrow?" he asked, swiftly moving the conversation into safer waters.

Eleanor groaned. "Lady Fiset is hosting a luncheon."

Lady Fiset had come eagerly to Eleanor suggesting she invited "all the wonderful women involved in the war effort" and Eleanor had known it would be churlish to say no. But the snobby aristocrat had very old-fashioned ideas of hospitality and the event was bound to be overblown and boring.

"That sounds excellent," Winston said, rubbing his considerable stomach. "I love a good luncheon."

Eleanor bet he did! But his luncheons were a break from topline business, not the entire point of his day.

"It will be rather formal," she said to Clementine. "Lady Fiset is very... colonial."

"Even better," Winston answered for her. "Gin and tonics and kedgeree. I miss those days."

Eleanor looked at him sideways, unable to resist this easy taunt. "When you British were occupying half the known world? Oh, but you still are, aren't you?"

Winston squared his shoulders and Clementine started fidgeting again, but the gentility of the evening was saved by the Churchills' lively daughter, Mary.

"Do you know," she piped up merrily, "they put taps in trees here in Canada to get the maple syrup out?"

Winston's head turned to her. "Actual taps?"

"Yep," Mary agreed. "I was talking to a darling colonel who's a maple syrup farmer when there isn't a war on and he told me all about it. Isn't that the best?"

The conversation swung to farming and, noting that Franklin looked rather gray, Eleanor forced herself to be polite. She snuck a peek at her watch. She had a lot of correspondence to get through and when the clock struck eleven, she stood up firmly.

"We should retire," she said, trying to sound reluctant. "You must have a big day tomorrow, gentlemen."

The British Prime Minister shifted in his armchair. He'd been cozily tucked up in bed this afternoon while Franklin had been in conflab with his aides, and was clearly getting into his stride. "Maybe a final nightcap...?" he suggested.

"Just one," Franklin agreed instantly. "To see us to sleep. You ladies go up."

He looked pathetically eager, like a schoolkid longing to

hang out with the big boys. It made Eleanor mad. Couldn't he see that he *was* the big boy? And that big boys took their responsibilities seriously?

"I think you said, dear, that you wanted an early night?"

"It's not late," Franklin retorted.

"It is for you." She knew it was a mistake the moment she said it.

Franklin visibly bristled. "I am President of the United States, *dear*, I think I can decide my own bedtime."

Eleanor sucked in her breath, but stood her ground. "As the wife of the President of the United States, I am simply reminding him what he said to me earlier."

"And I am simply telling you that he has changed his mind."

"I see."

Telltale beads of sweat had appeared at Franklin's temple and Eleanor knew, beyond a shadow of a doubt, that he needed his bed, but also that his pride would never let him back down. She turned helplessly away but then Clementine stood at her side.

"Winston is under strict doctor's orders not to stay up, aren't you, my dear?" she said, quietly but firmly.

"I am," he agreed reluctantly. "But—"

"And I am here to support him and ensure he stays in the very best of health. So come along, let's retire."

"Just one more...?"

"I'm afraid not," Clementine said.

She was magnificent. Eleanor saw Winston look up at her, and Clementine give him a tiny nod in Franklin's direction. He huffed but pushed himself to his feet, obedient to her wishes.

"Best do as the ladies say, hey, Franklin? They've only got our best interests at heart."

Franklin didn't look convinced but had little choice. He wheeled himself to the bedrooms alongside Eleanor but brushed her off in favor of his valet when they reached his door.

Eleanor said a stiff goodnight and stood watching as, further down the corridor, Winston and Clementine paused outside Winston's room, chattering away. Laughter floated down the corridor and then, with a flourish of a bow, Winston showed Clementine inside.

Now that, Eleanor thought sadly, was a true marriage. She twisted her wedding band, tugging it up her finger, but it stuck at the knuckle and she pushed it crossly back down. She felt an urge to throw herself on the carpet and cry and cry, but then reminded herself of the many letters waiting for her attention and, shaking off her ridiculous self-pity, turned into her room.

The men might be making the big decisions about the course of the war, but she was writing to the soldiers and their families and that, at the end of the day, counted for a great deal. Maybe the most vital work was not, in fact, the "big" stuff, but the everyday, small kindnesses. With a nod, Eleanor picked up her pen, selected a sheet of notepaper, and began writing.

THIRTY-FIVE

WASHINGTON, MARCH 1933

Eleanor looked at the car in horror. It was a fancy limousine, long and shiny and complete with a highly polished chauffeur who was bowing before her. Honestly!

"Please, there's no need to bow," she said, hastening forward to offer her hand to shake instead.

The chauffeur looked bemused but shook her hand as swiftly as he could before turning to open the back door, gesturing grandly to a cream leather interior, complete with a set of crystal glasses and two brimful decanters. What hooey!

"It's very kind of you," Eleanor said to him. "And I know you're only doing your job, so I don't blame you, but I specifically said when I arrived in Washington yesterday that I didn't need a car."

"But Mrs. Roosevelt, ma'am," the chauffeur stuttered miserably. "You're the First Lady."

Eleanor shook her head. "One: I am not yet the First Lady. The inauguration is not until March. Two: even if I were, I would not need a car to cover half a mile to the White House. It will take me barely ten minutes to walk."

"Walk?!" The chauffeur recoiled in horror and looked desperately around for help.

Eleanor sighed. She'd been enduring this sort of madness ever since Franklin had been elected to the presidency in November. With America in deep depression, Franklin had campaigned on a promise of a "New Deal" for the American people. Vitally, it was a promise he could back up with reference to the reforms and programs he'd brought into New York state over the last four years, enabling his citizens to cope with the terrible hardships better than most of America. The people approved and had voted accordingly.

Franklin had taken forty-two of the forty-eight states and had a healthy majority in both houses. Election night had been heady, but what had followed had been nonsense. Suddenly the whole world wanted to look in on Eleanor's business, and not the important parts either. She was permanently followed by journalists asking inane things like what she liked for breakfast, who was her favorite dress designer, and what color curtains she'd order for the White House.

What on earth did the color of the curtains matter?

Even today, when she was due to visit Mrs. Hoover, the actual First Lady, to look over the White House for the alterations she would require to accommodate her family, she had no intention of changing any curtains. She simply wanted to check who might have which bedroom and be sure they were equipped with the furniture her family and key staff needed to conduct their lives. And she wanted to check it as quickly as possible. She had a lecture to give later, so couldn't afford to be hanging around on fripperies.

Only one journalist had asked her for her actual opinion on anything—Lorena Hickok, a hard-hitter who'd since become Eleanor's very great friend. She was here, waiting to walk with her, and Eleanor was amused to see her peering into the car as if it were a jail-wagon. Hick understood Eleanor, and Hick was the first person she'd met who seemed to want to be with her solely for herself, not for what she could do for her. Right now, that made her an oasis in a chaotic sandstorm of public attention and Eleanor loved her for it. Also, Hick never asked her about curtain colors.

The crazy thing was that Eleanor had been expressing her opinions through her articles, her various committees and her delegations for years. Nothing she did or thought was any different since the election, but the way people chose to interpret it—and, indeed, felt they had a right to do so—was utterly changed. There had been more speculation since Franklin's landslide victory about what she, Eleanor, would do once she was installed in the White House than there had been about what he would do. And given he would be President, and taking over during the worst economic crisis ever facing America, that seemed ludicrous.

Now she wasn't even allowed to walk down the street.

"Eleanor!" a loud voice boomed and Robert, one of many Roosevelt cousins suddenly keen to talk to her, emerged from the Mayflower Hotel, arms outstretched. "Wonderful to see you, darling. Glad the car made it."

"The car made it," Eleanor agreed. "I hope you enjoy it, Robert, but I, for one, intend to walk."

"Walk?! But Eleanor darling, you can't do that. You'll be mobbed."

"I'm already mobbed," she said pointedly as two other cousins emerged from the hotel. "So I'll take my chances, thank you very much." Tightening her coat against the cold, she took Hick's arm and turned onto Connecticut Avenue, heading south.

She was not mobbed. Funnily enough, two middle-aged women in sensible coats attracted barely a second glance and she made it to the White House gates unhampered by anything more than a smart older gentleman raising his hat. And then, suddenly, there she was, confirming her identity to the surprised *guards awaiting a damned car, and walking up to the doorway of America's iconic premier residence.*

She paused, staring up at it. In the madness of the election and the hysteria that had followed, she'd had little time to absorb that this was really happening—the path she and Franklin had set out on so long ago had wound its way, torturously at times but ever-unrolling, to the steps of the White House. Hick tactfully stepped back and Eleanor went forward alone. Unbidden, a memory of her wedding came to her.

"Would you think it very arrogant of me, Eleanor, if I said that I'd like to be president one day?"

"Would that make me the president's wife?"

"It would."

"Then I think that would be fine and dandy."

Briefly, she wished Franklin were at her side, but he would be here soon enough and for now there were curtains to consider. She laughed to herself. They were facing a run on the banks, mass poverty and shocking deprivations; the curtains could stay exactly as they were.

The door opened and a uniformed usher bowed low. "Welcome to the White House, Mrs. Roosevelt."

Eleanor smiled at him and took the steps at a crisp pace. "Please," *she said, holding out her hand to the keeper of her future home,* "there's really no need to bow."

THIRTY-SIX
NEW YORK, OCTOBER 1944

The streets of New York were crammed with people eager to see the President. And running with rain. Eleanor peered out at the water throwing itself onto the city as if practicing for the apocalypse and groaned.

"You'll have to have the roof up, sir," Franklin's head guard said, gesturing to the cavalcade awaiting them in a private road at the back of Grand Central Station.

"No!" Franklin was in his wheelchair, but looked six feet tall as he squared up to his staff. "No roof."

"But, sir, you'll be soaked and your health—"

"My health is not the issue here. The people have been waiting hours to see me, so they must see me. They cannot do that if I'm huddled beneath a damned roof."

He was every inch the President and, if this went well, would continue to be so for four more years. Despite Eleanor and Anna's concerned protests, he had barely hesitated when asked if he would stand for a fourth term. It felt ridiculous to be embroiling the country in the fandango of an election as their troops were pushing the Nazis back over the German border, but that was the constitution and the constitution was sacred. Over in England, Winston was presiding over a "war coalition," a multi-party group designed to lead until the enemy was defeated. No one expected him to leave his map room to persuade the people to let him carry on; he was there until the job was done. Not so for Franklin.

"But the rain, sir—" his chief guard tried again.

"If they can take the rain, so can I."

"But you're..." The guard trailed off, unwilling to put into words what they all knew to be true—that Franklin's chest was weak, his lungs clogged and his heart struggling to beat its way to the end of a normal day, let alone a rainy October one. "They'll vote for you anyway, sir," he tried. "Nobody wants anyone else."

"Not true," Franklin snapped. "And not the point anyway. We've promised an open-top tour and that's what we'll deliver. I have my navy cape and a decent hat. It will be fine."

Eleanor wasn't so sure, but she knew Franklin. When his mind was made up there was no changing it and they were wasting time arguing.

"Let's get a move on, shall we?" she said. "Perhaps, if someone can fetch the President a change of clothes, we can find somewhere to get dry halfway through the morning."

"Exactly!" Franklin turned gratefully to her. "Praise God someone around here is thinking practically. Thank you, Eleanor." She smiled, then he added, "And I can change again when we get to Washington Square."

"Of course," she agreed, swallowing nervously.

Despite them having leased it two years ago, this would be the first time Franklin had made it to their apartment and she felt curiously anxious about showing it to him. She focused on helping him settle into the car and climbed in at his side. She, of course, had no navy cloak and she'd foolishly chosen a hat with no brim, but a little water had never hurt anyone—well, anyone in full health—and perhaps the weather would cheer up once they were on the road.

It did not.

"You're getting awful wet, sir," someone called as they drove down 42nd Street in driving rain.

"Not as wet as our lads on the front," Franklin called back and the crowd cheered. "If they can do their duty by our country, then so can I."

It wasn't the first time Eleanor had heard him say that. Indeed, it was the underpinning reason for running for this astonishing fourth term. That said, the election was far from a foregone conclusion. He was standing against Wendell Willkie, a Republican but a supporter of both the New Deal and intervening in the war. Franklin liked him and there had even been brief talk of them forming a new party together, but the concluding (pray to God) phase of a worldwide war was hardly the time to go radical.

Besides, Franklin didn't have the energy to start something new. He'd even permitted the convention to choose his running mate—a decent man called Harry Truman—and Eleanor suspected he wouldn't be too worried if he lost. He'd retire to Top Cottage, on the hill above her Val Kill, spend months in Warm Springs and maybe, sometimes, stay with her in Washington Square. They could do as he'd suggested back in 1942: Go to the theater, eat with friends, collect stamps, knit. Eleanor laughed at the cozy picture. It was hard to imagine. Though not as hard as it had once been. Perhaps she was getting tired too.

They turned up Fifth Avenue and the roar of the crowd was deafening. Who could ever tire of that?! Eleanor looked to Franklin, beaming and waving, the rain running, unnoticed, down his face. People were reaching out their hands to him as if he were a savior which, in some ways, he had been. Franklin had delivered America from the Depression back in the thirties and now he was close to delivering them from fascism. It was crazy when you stopped to think about it. No wonder they didn't have a "normal" marriage.

They paused mid-morning in the Coast Guard's Car Pool on the banks of the Hudson and Franklin was hustled into a specially warmed backroom to change his suit and drink coffee liberally laced with rum. Tommy came racing in with a fresh outfit for Eleanor, who snatched thankfully at it. Her dear friend had brought a warm woolen dress and fur-lined mackintosh and had even thought of a wider-brimmed hat so that on the second leg of their tour she could see into the crowd without rain blurring every face. A lot of people called her name as well as Franklin's. Children held out flowers and cards for her and two young men on either side were kept very busy collecting the gifts and storing them in the car behind.

"Carefully," Eleanor instructed. "I want to look over them later."

"There are an awful lot, ma'am."

"And all prepared with care. Keep them safe."

"Yes, ma'am."

It was a long morning. They covered Manhattan, from the Park in the north, to the harbor in the south. They crossed to Brooklyn on the east side and Jersey on the west and finally, approaching 3 p.m., they came back to the center of Manhattan. To Greenwich Village. To home.

Eleanor felt nervous all over again, her skin heating up beneath her sodden clothes. It was ridiculous. She'd turned sixty this month so was surely past caring what people thought in some craven way. And this was Franklin! Next March they'd have been married for forty years and they'd been through far too much to worry about a few soft furnishings.

But it was more than that. Eleanor had decorated this flat entirely to her own taste. Val Kill had been far more hers than Springwood, but Franklin had built it on his land and to a design of his choice. Washington Square, in contrast, was exclusively hers and she felt almost as shy at showing it to him as she had been with her naked body on their wedding night. And that hadn't exactly been a roaring success.

It didn't help that security were all over the building. As they came into the lobby, Walter, the concierge, came rushing forward, ignoring the glare of Franklin's big bodyguard, and Eleanor was glad to see Franklin wave him forward and shake his hand. Protecting the president from those who might wish him harm was important, but what use was keeping him away from a few bad people if it also kept him away from the many good ones?

"You want the roof up so it's harder for people to shoot me," Franklin had accused his head guard when he'd tried again to suggest they abandon the open-top.

"No, sir," the guard had said. "This rain would spoil anyone's aim. I want it up so you don't do the assassins' job for them!"

Eleanor had laughed out loud and even Franklin had chuckled. But he still hadn't let them put up the roof. To be fair, he looked well. He had always derived more energy from people than from his body, which was handy. Even so, as he took the elevator up to 15A, she noticed he was shivering. He wasn't the only one.

"I hope you like it," she said.

He looked at her, surprised. "Of course I'll like it, Babs. It's yours."

"Ours."

"Right. Yes. Ours." He tested the word out and seemed to like it. "Let's get inside then."

Tommy was waiting at the door and Eleanor was relieved to have her there, all efficiency and kindness, as Franklin wheeled himself into the main living room. As Eleanor stood picking at her wet hem and trying to see the apartment through his eyes, Tommy put a warm towel in one of his hands and a large brandy in the other. Franklin scrubbed vigorously at his wet face and downed the brandy in a single swallow. Tommy fetched the decanter and he downed a second. That was most unusual. Franklin loved his manhattans but he was never one to gulp.

"Let's get you changed, shall we?" Eleanor suggested.

His valet rushed forward. "There's a bath run and fresh clothes waiting in your bedroom, sir."

"I have a bedroom?"

"Of course," Eleanor said, uncomfortably aware of the Greek chorus of staff watching them. "Just through here."

"Nice ramp."

"Thank you. I had them made specially for if you came."

"*When* I came, Babs. I've been busy is all." Eleanor laughed and he smiled at her. "I'll be here more often once the war is over, you wait and see."

"I hope so," Eleanor said, and found she meant it.

Blushing, she hastened into the kitchen to check on the hearty chicken casserole the cook had left on the stove. Franklin was due to give a speech at the Waldorf Astoria this evening but for now, they were alone. She could hear him splashing in his bath and for a peculiar—and not unpleasant—moment felt like a normal American housewife, pottering about her domestic tasks. But then two uniformed men arrived, asking where they should stash the boxes of gifts, and she was back to First Lady once more.

She showed them to the spare room, then retreated to hers to change her clothes, hanging her soggy suit up carefully to dry. There was a war on and clothes were precious. She had a flash memory of the WRVS clothing store she'd visited in London and shook her head sadly.

"Peace," she said to Franklin when he emerged from his room, pink-faced and cozy in soft trousers and a casual sweater.

"Peace?"

"That's what we need."

"Well, of course."

"Proper peace—a set of principles that all nations promise to uphold and a means of keeping them to those promises."

"A united nations."

"Yes!"

"Well, that's the plan, my dear."

She smiled and looked around. Franklin fitted into the apartment far more easily than she'd dared to imagine. With Tommy in her room and the staff in the spare, they were alone as she brought the casserole through and served it up.

"Do you ever find it strange, Franklin, that it's going to be up to you to make that happen?"

He chuckled. "I frequently find that strange. Every morning when I wake up in the White House I have to remind myself that I'm the President." He lifted his fork then added, "And it makes me happy every single time."

"You're not tired of it?"

He shook his head. "Tired, yes, but not tired of office. Like you say, Eleanor, we need peace and, having got us through this damned war, I'd hate to miss out on the important stuff."

"I understand that."

"Of course you do." He reached across the table, grabbing her hand. "Eleanor, if... if for any reason I don't make it to the end—"

"Franklin—"

"Please, listen. Surely we're past platitudes, you and I?"

She swallowed and nodded.

"Good, because this is important. If I don't make it to the end, you'll make sure it happens for me, won't you? You'll make them all listen? You'll make sure there's a United Nations?"

"Me? How would *I* do that?"

He laughed. "Oh Babs, you always underestimate yourself. You'll do it, I know you will."

"But—"

"And that's what makes me rest easy at night."

"It does?"

"It does. So—will you promise?"

She chased her casserole around her plate. Franklin's valet appeared in the dining room doorway, looking pointedly at his watch, but Franklin kept his eyes fixed on her. She didn't see how she could do what he'd asked and she was useless at pretending, but this was important to him and she treasured his trust.

"Then I'll do everything in my power to facilitate a United Nations," she said. "I promise."

"I'll cheer you on from up above, Babs."

"No way, Franklin D. Roosevelt. I want you right here at my side."

"I'll do everything in my power to be there."

He smiled, but it was a sad smile and she hated to see it.

"Coffee?" she suggested.

The valet coughed.

"Not enough time," Franklin said. "Sadly." And then he was gone, off to get into his dinner jacket and go to the Waldorf to tell the world why he should be the president to take them into a peace that, it seemed, he did not believe he would live to see.

She could only pray that he was wrong.

THIRTY-SEVEN
WASHINGTON, MARCH 1933

This time there was no escaping the limousine. It was inauguration day and America was watching. Even Eleanor would not have been foolish enough to walk down the street in her long white gown and pearls, with the crowds out in their thousands, and in somber mood. The country was in crisis.

Yesterday, Franklin had taken the decision to close the banks to prevent the last of the money leaching away. Hoover, the outgoing president, had raged at him as a "madman" but Franklin had simply said that there was nothing mad about protecting the people's funds.

"I'll talk to them," he'd told Hoover.

"Talk to them? To the people?"

"Why not? They're who we're here to serve."

Hoover had looked uncertain. Eleanor was pretty sure he believed he'd been in the White House to serve big business. Well, big business had let everyone down and it was time to try something different.

"But how will you talk to them?" Hoover had asked.

"On the radio. Direct into their homes."

Hoover had visibly shuddered, as if the thought of the homes of the ordinary people made him feel ill. No wonder America was in such a mess, but it didn't matter now. The limousines were swinging in front of the White House to pick up both Mr. and Mrs. Hoover—presidents in the front one, First Ladies in the second—and when they returned from the Capitol, it would be Franklin and Eleanor walking through that door. She glanced at it and felt a mix of fear and excitement tumble in her stomach.

The White House would be a different place with the Roosevelts in residence. Their children, bar seventeen-year-old John, were grown up and off running their own lives but they were here to celebrate today and they would apparently be visiting often.

"Try keeping me away," Elliott had said with a cheeky wink and the others had agreed. They had a simple delight in the White House, seeing it as a joy, an honor, and a symbol of the triumph of their father. All of them, she was sure, still felt the shadow of that terrible summer of 1921, when they'd gone to bed chattering about defeating an island fire with their newly arrived Pa and woken up to find him paralyzed. Today proved, on top of everything anyone might choose to say about political ideals, that straightforward courage could get a man a long way.

A woman too, of course. Not that any of this was about her.

The Hoovers shuffled painfully slowly down the White House steps, reluctant to surrender it to the victors. Eleanor, embarrassed, leaped out to smooth the way.

"Good morning, Herbert. Good morning, Lou."

Herbert Hoover gave her a frosty stare but silver-haired Lou shook her hand. "Shall we get this over with?" she said, falsely bright.

"Not much choice," her husband grunted and climbed stiffly into the front car, spurning Franklin's friendly overtures. Men could be such babies!

Eleanor suppressed a smile and got into the second car with Lou, suspecting she would have a far easier ride to the Capitol.

She'd been surprised by the quiet First Lady's warmth when she'd visited to discuss—or rather, not discuss—the curtains back in January and thought perhaps the country would have been better off if they'd been allowed to see more of her.

"Are you excited?" Lou asked.

"Just hoping I get through today without disgracing myself," Eleanor replied as they pulled out of the gates and into the crowd-lined streets.

"Always a worry," Lou Hoover agreed seriously. "The press love a mistake."

Eleanor thought about that. Hick was "the press" and had been uniformly helpful, though, of course, their intimate friendship might have something to do with that. Even so, she had introduced Eleanor to a number of other female journalists, who'd been very polite and interested.

"Perhaps you just have to let them in?" she suggested.

Lou shook her head vehemently. "Oh no. That would be disastrous. One needs a certain distance, a certain decorum."

Eleanor looked hastily away. If it was decorum that was needed, she was going to be useless. She focused on the crowds, smiling at those pressing forward to see them pass. Up front, she could see Franklin doing the same and hear the cheers growing in volume. The people were miserable, worried, frightened. They didn't need distance; they needed positivity. They needed to believe someone would do something for them, so she waved enthusiastically—and they waved back.

Eventually, feeling impolite, she turned back to Lou.

"What will you miss the most about the White House?" she asked conversationally.

Lou considered. "I think it will be the feeling of being cared for, you know? Never having to worry about domestic problems, or timings or travel arrangements."

Eleanor stared at her. She'd been making her own travel arrangements since she was fifteen years old and could imagine little more annoying than having someone else always telling her what to do. Help was always useful, of course. Both Missy and Tommy would have bedrooms in the White House, but they would be there to aid Franklin and Eleanor, not to run their lives for them. Why on earth would the American people vote in someone who could not do that for themself?!

They turned into the Capitol where, high up on the dome, a pair of flags flew like bright wings against the gray skies. The swearing-in ceremony would take place above the East Front steps and the presidential party was guided into the building, ready to step out, like actors on a stage, before the thousands gathered on the Capitol plaza below. Eleanor was sent out first, to take her place on one side of the rostrum, while Lou rejoined a thunder-browed Herbert on the other.

Franklin would walk the, thankfully few, steps on Jimmy's arm and as Eleanor turned to see him move toward her she felt, for a moment, peculiarly like a groom awaiting his bride at the top of the aisle. He glanced her way as he made the safety of the rostrum and she gave him an encouraging smile. Of all the grand events of today, making it out here on his own legs was the hardest one of all, though very few watching would ever know it.

He smiled back, then set his hand firmly on the three-hundred-year-old Roosevelt family bible, opened at a passage of his choice: First Corinthians 13. Eleanor glanced to the words: "If I speak in the tongues of men or of angels, but do not have love, I am only a resounding gong or a clanging cymbal." Many presidents chose the passages on which to place their hand for their inauguration oath. Most picked ones referring to law or justice or strength; Franklin was the first to pick love.

Something caught in her eye as she watched him turn to the Lord Chief Justice to swear his oath of office; perhaps one of the small snowflakes forming in the chill air, or perhaps, if she was honest, a tear of pride. Franklin's voice was strong and determined, and only she could see the shake of his hips as, with his *right hand raised, they bore his withered legs upright in their iron braces. She held her breath but, oath complete, he turned to face the crowd and could grip the rostrum with both hands once more.*

He's the President, she thought, her heart leaping. It had been a long, hard path to this point but they were here.

Here, at the beginning of a new path.

Eleanor dug her feet into the floor to save herself from swaying at the thought of all that might be ahead. America was in crisis and, over the seas, Europe was struggling too, with Adolf Hitler peddling his vicious brand of hate. Eleanor glanced to the bible, clutched beneath Franklin's hands as he addressed America. "Love is patient," she read. "Love is kind. It does not envy, it does not boast, it is not proud. It does not dishonor others, it is not self-seeking, it is not easily angered, it keeps no record of wrongs. Love does not delight in evil but rejoices with the truth. It always protects, always trusts, always hopes, always perseveres."

There was going to be a lot of perseverance needed in the coming months but, with love, she prayed they could succeed. Franklin was reaching the end of his address, kept mercifully short in the cold weather, and she focused on him once more. She knew what he was going to say. He'd run the speech by her last night and she'd smiled to hear it—their personal mantra given to the American people in a contract to move forward together.

Franklin put his head back, looked out across the vast crowd, and smiled. "Let me assert my firm belief that the only thing we have to fear, is fear itself."

The crowd went wild. Eleanor reached out and placed a quiet hand on his arm. It was what they had always said; now, they just had to hope they were right.

THIRTY-EIGHT

THE WHITE HOUSE, SUNDAY, MARCH 25, 1945

Franklin looked frail. Eleanor regarded him across a table laid for two in the Red Room and that was all she could think: Franklin looks frail.

He had looked many things throughout their life together—handsome, funny, angry, loving, guilty, sad, fevered, gray, tired, withered... But never frail. It reminded her, ominously, of that last time she'd seen Sara in Hyde Park, the time she'd had to call Franklin to come fast, before the great oak fell. She shuddered.

"How are you feeling, Franklin?"

"Beat up."

His frankness was a relief. If he'd lied to her, she would have been more concerned.

"It's been a busy few months."

He chuckled. "You can say that again!"

Elected for his fourth term, Franklin had been inaugurated in January, and insisted on having all thirteen of his grandchildren present. It had meant extra work for Eleanor finding accommodation for them and their mothers, and, indeed, stepmothers. With Anna, Jimmy and Elliott on their second marriages, it seemed, to her sorrow, that her children were no better at monogamy than their father. However, Franklin had said it was important to him for his grandchildren to see his final inauguration and, spotting dark shadows in his eyes, she'd pulled out all the stops. He was sixty-two now and no one doubted this was his last term as president. The question, perhaps, was whether he would leave in a limousine with whoever took his place, or... She shook away the thought.

It had been a grand day in the end, well worth the effort. There had been snow on the ground and the White House lawns had rung with the happy squeals of the children playing. With the country at war, Franklin had cut back the usual parade and festivities, and kept his speech—delivered very simply from the south portico of the White House—short and somber. He'd focused, to Eleanor's delight, on peace, stating that America's well-being was dependent on the well-being of nations far away and concluding that, "We have learned to be citizens of the world, members of the human community."

Two days later he had flown to Yalta to discuss that community with Churchill and Stalin, the venue again dependent, as Eleanor had pointed out bitterly, on Soviet whim.

"Stalin doesn't like airplanes," Franklin had said.

"At least he can hold himself upright in them," she'd shot back.

She had again asked to accompany her husband and again been refused. People would, apparently, have to "pay attention" to the First Lady, which was no doubt true, but seemed to Eleanor like a good thing. How were you meant to get your opinion across without attention? But perhaps that was the point. First Ladies weren't meant to have opinions and even if Franklin valued hers, it seemed he wasn't prepared to ask the rest of the world to do so too. She had only been invited to Quebec to keep Clementine Churchill busy.

Franklin had, at least, taken Anna, who'd been delighted, and the Yalta agreements seemed, on the face of it, to be largely sound. Eleanor still hated the idea of occupying Germany but she was in the minority so, as a defender of democracy, had to accept the wider view. And at least Franklin had secured official backing for a United Nations group and arranged to hold the inaugural meeting in San Francisco this April to establish the charter that would bring it into official being. That was less than a month away and the timing was opportune, for the war seemed, finally, to be approaching its end.

Last December, Germany had thrown vast resources at the American troops in the Ardennes, pushing them back and creating a wave of panic at home at this first scent of defeat. Fortunately, thanks to clever strategy and bold fighting, the Allies had got back on top within two weeks and recently the advance party had crossed the Rhine into Germany, driving for Berlin. Intelligence said Hitler had gone mad, apoplectically ordering crazy last stands and the destruction of cities to prevent them being reclaimed by their rightful nations. Many of his commanders were, thank God, disobeying him. Even the Nazis had not been able to bring themselves to destroy the Eiffel Tower and every day thousands of ordinary soldiers were surrendering to the advancing Allies on all sides.

In January the Russian troops had liberated Poland and their frontline soldiers had marched into Nazi concentration camps to scenes of unimaginable suffering. Eleanor had watched the newsreels of the skeletal Jews who'd survived what they now knew to be systematic death camps with her nails dug into her thighs. She had not tried hard enough to help those fleeing Europe back in 1939 and 1940.

"All I did was whine about the State Department suppressing visas," she'd moaned to Joe one precious night on his brief leave.

"Not true," Joe had said staunchly. "You worked with the ERC to save those on our list."

"The famous Jews, yes, the ones who needed saving for the

'good of the world,' but I didn't recognize the great mass of suffering. I didn't have the imagination to see what Hitler was capable of, despite the evidence in *Mein Kampf* and Ned Miller's brave broadcasts. I didn't have the imagination and I didn't have the courage to push through those damned rigid walls of opposition to 'immigrants.' I should have insisted on their admittance, not as a political or subversive act, but simply as one of basic human decency."

"There's no point in looking back," Joe had consoled her. "All we can get them now is justice."

"Not all," Eleanor had corrected him. "We can get them a United Nations organization to prevent this from ever, ever happening again."

She longed to discuss this with Franklin, to go over where they should have been tougher, stronger, braver... But there was little point. What was done was done and the important thing was to keep him well enough to fight for a valid, lasting peace.

But she had to face the fact that Franklin was frail. In truth, he'd been frail at the inauguration and even frailer when he got back from Yalta. Last week, when they'd gone to check up on Hyde Park together, he had asked her to drive his car. He'd never done that before. Custom-made to be operated by hand-controls, it had long been his pride and joy—his freedom. She'd taken the keys, hands shaking, and kept a frightened eye on him ever since.

"You'll be glad to get to Warm Springs," she said now, glancing out of the Red Room window to see the sun going down over the lawns. He was heading south first thing tomorrow.

"Very glad," Franklin agreed.

He was picking listlessly at his dinner and she willed him to eat. Even by Mrs. Nesbitt's low standards the meatloaf wasn't good, but the potatoes were soft and the gravy rich and he needed the nutrition. She was feeling guilty about neglecting her wifely duties. With the war surely winding to a close, Congress had suddenly started preaching to women about returning to their "true place," which was, according to them, in the kitchen, making their menfolk comfortable, and in the bedroom, making them babies. There was some pious "gratitude" for women's service and much patronizing head-patting, but it was all wrapped up in a forceful, "now get yourself back into your houses and let the men do the real work again." Even the magazines were colluding, replacing "quick and easy" recipes for harassed factory-working mothers with elaborate menus that would take a full day to prepare. Knitting was out, in favor of fancy embroidery, and the fashion pages were full of the sort of fussy dresses no one could do anything in. The billboards were at it too and you couldn't turn a corner without a giant pair of baby's eyes staring appealingly at you.

Even worse, those women who had not enjoyed the call to arms were scrambling to be heard. Yesterday Eleanor had opened the *New York Times* to find "Kelsie of Connecticut" telling the world that, "I can't wait to give up the filthy factory and do my proper job, looking after my man." Eleanor had wondered if that's how every woman felt. If "looking after my man" was what they really wanted. If so, Eleanor truly was a terribly wife. Franklin, the first man in the land, needed her to care for him more than ever, but still she champed at the role. Forever, it had seemed, she'd ridden the seesaw of public and private duty and she still didn't seem to have found the balance.

"I've got something to show you," Tommy had said, spotting Kelsie's sickly beam.

"Is it a useless wife award?" she'd asked petulantly.

"Take a look." Tommy had thrust a report under her nose and Eleanor had seen the title: "An analysis of female attitudes to working." She'd looked up at Tommy quizzically. "Read it, woman!"

So she had. The female researcher, apparently as enraged

by the domestic propaganda as Eleanor, had conducted extensive research in the factories, hospitals, shipyards and shops of America, recruiting a team to cover as many states as possible. Thousands of women had offered answers to her questions about giving up work and the conclusions were, well, conclusive: 78 percent of respondents had said they preferred working to being "stuck in the house." And why? The answers to that had come in thick and fast: The satisfaction of making something, or providing a service; the joy of taking home your own pay-packet; the camaraderie of adult colleagues; the sheer, blissful independence.

"I'm sick of pandering to those at home who don't notice the work I'm doing, let alone pay me for it," Margy of Maryland had told the researcher. "Women have brains too, you know, and it's about time you let us use them."

Eleanor had cried. She could have hugged Margy of Maryland and longed to see her in debate with Kelsie of Connecticut; she'd wipe the floor with her. Kelsie, meanwhile, would just wipe the floor. In the absence of Margy, she'd hugged Tommy and even danced her around the office, until Tommy had suggested that if she liked working so much, perhaps they should get back down to it. Eleanor had hugged her again. It had been wonderful to know that other women—many, many other women—felt the same as her, repressed, trapped even, by the domestic arena and keen to do more with their life than facilitate men.

Even so, Franklin did look terribly ill.

She bit her lip. "Maybe I should come with you to Georgia, Franklin. See you're all right."

He shook his head. "I'm always all right in Warm Springs, you know that, Babs."

She did know that. Ever since he'd first taken the glorious warm waters, he had proclaimed it a special place and had bought it lock, stock, and barrel a year later. Eleanor had fretted about the purchase, which had used up most of his inheritance from his father, but Franklin had insisted it was important and he'd been right. These days it brought relief to polio sufferers across America, some children, some adults, all looking to Franklin as their hero.

In the "little White House" on the Warm Springs site, Franklin ruled in a different way to in Washington—with the same compassion but with no restraints. In Warm Springs he went around openly in his wheelchair and was lifted into pools to do his therapy with everyone else. In Warm Springs he did not have to compromise to secure the votes of stuck-in-the-mud conservative congressmen, or appease southern racists, or mollycoddle voters into giving him time to see out the war he'd fought so bravely from the start.

"Besides," he said, patting her hand, "I'll have Daisy and Polly with me."

"Daisy will look after you," Eleanor conceded.

"And Polly will amuse me. Don't fret, Babs, a few weeks in Warm Springs and I'll be right as rain."

"What's right about rain?" she asked, remembering asking exactly the same when Sara had been dying.

"It's refreshing, renewing."

She smiled. "You always did see the bright side of things, Franklin."

"It's the prettier side, right?"

"Right, though I don't remember the streets of New York being very pretty that day we rode around it in the rain."

"The people's faces were though. And we won the election, didn't we?"

"You did, yes, though who knows if that was wise. You promise to rest?"

"I promise, Babs. The war is winding up without me and I want to get well for the United Nations meeting at the end of April. Peace is the priority now."

"Peace has always been the priority, hasn't it?"

"It's always been the *goal*. Now, it can be the priority too."

"Always the politician, Franklin!"

"Always."

She nodded. "You'll have time in Warm Springs to think over everything you want to suggest."

"I will. And I'd like you, Eleanor, to think over that too."

"Me?"

"Of course you. Do you remember our very first conversation?"

Eleanor smiled, remembering herself as a shy debutante, awkward in her flouncy dress, and Franklin had talked to her about how much money had been wasted on the American-Spanish war and how many houses it could have provided for the poor. She'd agreed with him and he'd looked at her and asked her a simple question: "Why?" It was the first time a man had bothered to do that and she'd eagerly poured out her ideas.

"'Let's talk more,' you said to me."

"And we did. A lot more. You were the most interesting woman in the room, Eleanor. The most interesting woman I'd ever met. You still are."

She flushed. "I think it's the world that's interesting, Franklin. I just seem to look at it more closely than others."

"You do," he agreed fondly. "That's why I'd like you to come to San Francisco with me."

"San Francisco?"

"To the United Nations meeting. It's your baby, Eleanor, as much as it's mine and I'd like you there with me to see it come into being."

Eleanor gaped at him. "You don't like me going to conferences with you," she stuttered.

"I don't like you going to *war* conferences, no. They're ugly and frustrating and no option is a good option. You'd hate them. This, though, this I think you'll love. So many nations are going to be attending and I've already mixed up the timetable of speakers so that the small ones are given as much precedence as the large."

"That's wonderful, Franklin."

"I thought you'd say that. Devious, but wonderful. The delegates from the Philippines and Lebanon are excellent people and will almost certainly speak better than our own men. It will be most..."

"Enlightening?" Eleanor supplied.

"Exactly! This is why you need to come. You'll make a really valuable contribution."

She was still gaping, and forced her mouth shut. "I'd love to come, Franklin. Truly."

"Good. That's very good. And then, in the summer, I'd like you to travel to England with me. Winston is keen to host us and I know Clementine would love to have you."

"England?"

"And after that, I'm thinking we might visit Arabia. There are a lot of problems in that part of the world and I'd like to... investigate them."

"As President?"

"No! No, not as President, just as..."

"A citizen of the world?"

He beamed. "Exactly."

Eleanor laughed. "When we sat down, Franklin, I thought you looked frail. But now..."

"Now?"

"Now I see you are as bursting with life as ever."

"My body is withered, Eleanor, not my brain. You know that, my dear. *You*, particularly, know that." He plucked at a loose thread on the cushion of his chair and looked around the White House drawing room. "I don't say it very often, but we wouldn't be here without you."

"Hooey!"

"It really isn't. You stood by me when I lost my legs. You stood by me even though I'd done little to deserve that. You stood by me and, even braver, you stood against my mother. I appreciated it, Babs. I don't tell you that enough but, well, here I am, telling you—I appreciated it. Still do."

"You had too much to give to be stuck in Hyde Park for the rest of your life."

"As did you."

"Perhaps. You losing the ability to walk, Franklin... I sometimes think maybe it released me to do so."

He slapped his useless legs. "Well something good came of this then. And perhaps you deserved the release." He plucked again at the thread. "I know I'm a sucker for a subservient woman, Babs. We both know that, God help us. I like to be pandered to and flirted with and made to feel important—"

"You *are* important, Franklin."

"I know, but I like to feel it too! I'm a vain man."

"No, you—"

"Don't protest. It's true. If we can't be frank at our age, when can we? I like to be pandered to. But only when I'm feeling weak. When I'm up to it, Babs, when I'm as strong as you, I like to be challenged and argued with and pushed to be more."

"That's what I do to you?"

"That's what you do *for* me. I just... forget sometimes. Sorry."

Eleanor let out a quiet laugh.

"What's that for?" he demanded.

"Simply that I think it might be what you do for me too."

"No one could push you harder than you push yourself, my Eleanor. But I hope so. Truly, I do. I hope, however complicated and tricky things have sometimes been, we've been better off in life for having the other."

"I think so," she agreed, and then, feeling awkward with the unaccustomed intimacy, added, "Let's hope America has been better off for having us too."

"Oh, I'm confident she has," he said. "It's only you I'm not so sure about. You could have been so happy with someone who loved you as you deserved, Eleanor."

She thought about it. "But would I have been as happy as I have been in the White House?"

"That was *my* dream, Eleanor. You gave everything for my dream."

She looked around. Outside the window, the light on the Washington Monument was twinkling like an old friend and she raised a hand in quiet acknowledgment. As Franklin had just said, if they couldn't be frank at their age, when could they?

"I think perhaps, my dear," she admitted, "that all along, it was very much my dream too."

THIRTY-NINE
THE WHITE HOUSE, MARCH 1933

Eleanor couldn't sleep. Her bed was comfortable and the linen was her own, delivered yesterday and fitted by the staff after the Hoovers had vacated, but it still felt alien. There were noises in the house—noises she did not recognize and noises which, even more strangely, were not her responsibility. She remembered Lou Hoover saying she'd miss being cared for and Eleanor could see what she meant, though to her, on this first night in the White House, it felt less like care and more like control.

Slipping out of bed, she pulled on her dressing gown and went to the door. Perhaps she could get a warm drink, though heavens knew how that worked. There was a bell by her bed. She should probably ring it and ask for something to be sent up, but in her experience it was as much the ritual of making a drink that soothed you as the drinking of it. Besides, she was mistress here, so she could do as she chose. Couldn't she?

She hesitated in the doorway, peering down the long corridor. She was plenty used to big houses and not intimidated by them (well, perhaps by Springwood, especially if her mother-in-law was in residence) but this one wasn't just big, it was—well, it was the White House!

"And you're very lucky to be here," she told herself firmly as she stepped out into the corridor.

A young guard leaped to attention.

"Goodness," she said, "you made me jump."

He flushed pink beneath his black skin. "Deepest apologies, ma'am."

"Not at all. You're doing your job."

"Protecting you, ma'am."

"Very kind." Eleanor had resisted protection for as long as she could remember but that wasn't his fault and now she was First Lady, she supposed it would be a matter of some import if something happened to her. Hard as it might be to believe in her heart, her head knew that if she were shot, say, or kidnapped, it would be a matter of national concern. How funny! "What's your name?" she asked the guard.

"Moses, ma'am," he stuttered.

"A fine name, Moses. Can you tell me which way to the kitchens?" She knew really. She'd paid attention when she was shown around by Lou and then again with her housekeeper, Mrs. Nesbitt, earlier today, but she felt the need to explain what she was doing wandering around in the middle of the night.

"Right down there and left to the stairs, ma'am," Moses said.

She wanted to tell him to call her Eleanor but suspected that would mortify him. "Thank you."

He tipped his hat to her, then leaned forward and said in a low voice, "Welcome to the White House, ma'am. We're very glad to have you here."

Eleanor blinked. "Thank you, Moses."

He shot her a sudden grin. "I voted for your husband. So did all my family. My pa says he's the only one that can save America."

"Goodness," Eleanor said, glancing to Franklin's door, right next to hers. "Let's hope he's getting his sleep then, hey?"

Moses nodded. "He can rest easy on my watch, ma'am. And so can you."

Eleanor looked at him. "Do you know what, I think I can. Would you like me to bring you up a drink?"

Moses flushed again, and shook his head. Eleanor brought him one anyway and, as she shut her bedroom door, heard the satisfied sigh of a man refreshed. He would go far, that lad, she was sure.

Cradling her cup—no saucer, nasty fiddly things—she went to the window and looked out. Her view was of the south lawn and, beyond it, the Washington Monument. She could just make out its silhouette, tall and proud against the milky sky, and, as she let her eyes accustom themselves to the dark, she saw that a small red light was twinkling on the top, as if saying hello.

"Hello," she whispered back. "Hello. I'm here. I'm really here."

The White House might not be her house, but at the moment she was lucky enough to make it her home. The American people had entrusted the country to Franklin and herself and she intended to repay that trust with every attempt to bring light to the current darkness.

Eleanor sipped at her tea wondering how best to do that. She wasn't good at entertaining, wasn't good at looking pretty, and certainly wasn't good at choosing curtains. But she was good at talking to people. Hick had suggested she hold a press conference for the female journalists and perhaps she was right. They got a bum deal in their newsrooms, Hick had said, always assigned to stories on fashion and food, and were keen to step up to the urgently pressing affairs of the day. Direct access to the First Lady would give them credibility. Well, wouldn't that be something!

Eleanor grabbed a pad off her desk and made a note to issue the invitations. She would ask for female journalists only and she would discuss what Franklin's New Deal was going to mean for families. If America was going to get out of this Depression, it was going to take the commitment of every single person—not only men in suits, but men in overalls and women in pinnies. Franklin was going to use the radio to talk direct to them, and Eleanor—Eleanor was going to do so too.

She set down her cup, gave the Washington Monument a small wave and turned back to her bed. She must get to sleep for there was work to be done. Much work. Eleanor smiled. She thought, strange as it was, that she might just get to like it in the White House.

PART THREE

FORTY

THE WHITE HOUSE, APRIL 12, 1945

Eleanor awoke feeling uneasy. It was a beautiful day and sunlight was pouring through the White House windows, but Eleanor had clouds in her heart. She shook the overblown fancy out of herself and looked at the clock: 7 a.m. She'd slept well but, then, she hadn't got back to Washington until late, after spending all weekend with Tommy opening up Hyde Park for the summer. Franklin had asked her to go through Sara's things for the children and it had been a gargantuan task. But it was done now.

She'd happily have stayed upstate for a couple more days. Val Kill was glorious at this time of year, but with Franklin in Warm Springs, people always seemed to need her to make decisions—not on politics of course, but on seating and menus and orders of damn precedence for the endless run of official visits that characterized White House life. Plus, she had appointments with various people today and it wouldn't be fair to let them down.

She should get up, get on. Action, she'd found from long experience, was the only thing that dragged her out of the blues, and there was plenty to be done. It was her usual bi-weekly press conference this morning and she was keen to talk to her ladies about the first meeting of the United Nations, just two weeks away. The war was dragging on, Hitler still screaming at his poor soldiers not to capitulate, but the Russians were almost within shooting range of Berlin so he would surely have to give up soon.

Yes, action was the ticket. After the press conference, she was to lunch with a lecturer for Russian War Relief, then she was meeting the Fair Employment Practices Commission to discuss the practical application of the GI Bill of Rights, before a charity piano recital at the Sulgrave Club. She really had to get up and on.

But still she sat there, pulling the covers around herself like a shield.

She thought of Franklin. She'd spoken to him from Springwood on Saturday night but had been weary and distracted after her long day. He, in contrast, had sounded well. He'd said he felt much better, and the sunshine and thermal waters were working their magic. His appetite had picked up no end and he was even having his portrait painted by some Russian artist.

"That's nice," she'd said. She hated the word "nice," but her brain had turned to mush and any more interesting words had deserted it. "Is Daisy looking after you?"

Had there been a moment's hesitation? She'd thought so, but then, her brain had been mush. He'd probably been taking a sip of his drink.

"Everyone's looking after me beautifully," he'd assured her. "I'm doing great. Looking forward to San Fran."

"The United Nations."

"Finally!"

She'd wanted to talk to him about it more but her eyes had been drooping and, really, they'd been talking about it all their lives so what more was there to say? They just had to get on and do it.

"Goodnight, Franklin."

"Goodnight, Babs."

Had he sounded wistful? Or had she been dreaming already? It had been haunting her since, but she'd been too busy to call again. She glanced at the phone, but he would still be asleep and she didn't want to disturb his rest. She twisted her wedding band and, to her surprise, it came up and over her knuckle. She'd lost weight recently—there was too much to do to sit around eating—but it was still a shock. Trying not to see anything ominous in it, she pushed the ring back down and went to her desk.

Whipping a clean sheet of writing paper out of the drawer, she grabbed her pen. It didn't need to be a long note, just something caring so he knew she was thinking of him. He would be working hard on the address he was to deliver on the radio for Jefferson Day tomorrow. He'd sent her a draft and she'd loved his focus on world responsibility and peace. One part in particular had jumped out at her: "We must go on, do all in our power to conquer the doubts and the fears, the ignorance, and the greed, which made this horror possible." He'd expanded on this later on in the speech: "The only limit to our realization of tomorrow will be our doubts of today." It was a recurrent theme —fear, doubt. He had conquered both and she with him, albeit in her own way. She wanted to tell him how good she thought it was. How proud she was of him. Did that sound foolish? She wasn't his mother, after all!

She was wasting time. Dashing off a few lines telling him how nice it had been to hear him happy, she put it an envelope and addressed it, simply, to FDR. Tommy would see it posted with his other official documents and it would hopefully reach him tomorrow morning before he had to give the address. Feeling better for having written, Eleanor marched to her wardrobe and, after a moment's consideration, selected her smartest red suit—armor for the day ahead.

The morning was predictably busy, her female journalists cheeringly interested in the United Nations and the Russian woman a fascinating lunch companion. Anna joined them and they had such a good time that Eleanor almost forgot about the Fair Employment Commission and had to squeeze in their meeting before the recital.

She was pulling on her gloves to head to the Sulgrave Club, however, when Moses coughed behind her. "Telephone call, ma'am."

Eleanor turned crossly, not needing any more delays, but, seeing his face, threw her gloves down and hastened through to the office. Tommy was holding the phone, her face grave.

"Who is it?"

"It's Polly."

"Polly?!" Eleanor's heart plummeted. Polly never telephoned her—unless it was serious. She grabbed the receiver. "Polly?"

"Eleanor! Sorry to disturb. Just thought someone should let you know that Franklin has... fainted."

"Fainted?" Polly had made it sound like a girl having a fit of the vapors at a picnic. "What do you mean, fainted?"

"Collapsed might be more accurate."

"Collapsed?!"

"He was totally fine. Sitting chatting away while Shoumie painted him and then, whoomf..."

"Whoomf?"

"He said he'd got a terrific headache and fainted."

"How is he now?"

"In bed."

"Is he conscious?"

There was a nasty pause.

"I don't know," Polly admitted. "The doctors are with him, though, so I'm sure he's fine. We're staying out of the way."

"You and Daisy?"

"Yes, and..."

"And?"

"Shoumie. Elizabeth Shoumatoff. The painter."

"I see. Thank you, Polly. I'll fly down immediately."

"Oh, no!" she cried. "I don't think you need to do that. I'm sure it's fine. You know what he's like."

Eleanor did know what he was like and, amidst his many other health troubles, he had never before "fainted." She also, however, knew that Polly liked to shock. Was she exaggerating? Taunting her with her distance from her husband?

"I'll talk to the doctors," she said. "Thank you, Polly."

She hung up and went to find Dr McIntire. He usually traveled everywhere with Franklin but there were so many medical staff at Warm Springs that only Dr Bruenn had gone down. Dr McIntire promised to get onto him immediately and came back to Eleanor, who was pacing in the hallway.

"There doesn't seem to be any immediate cause for concern," he assured her. "Franklin is stable."

"But not well?"

"No."

"I think we should go."

"I agree. I've ordered a plane for 5 p.m. and if he isn't much improved, we'll be straight down there."

"Right." She glanced at her watch, glad to have a decision. She had time to make the piano recital. It wasn't top of her list, but if she stayed here she'd just worry, so she reached once more for her gloves and headed to the car.

She knew instantly when the bad news came.

She knew the moment she saw the usher threading his way through the crowds to reach her.

She knew from his dark look, and from the way he was biting his lip.

She knew from the fact that he was daring to interrupt the matrons intent on the beautiful music.

"Telephone call for you, ma'am," he whispered.

She followed him to the hall, but she didn't need to pick up the receiver to hear the news. It was already echoing around her heart, battering at her brain, fighting to make itself not just known but understood.

He was gone. Her husband of forty exciting, challenging, stimulating years was gone.

"I'll be home as soon as I can," she said to the choked official on the other end of the line. But the White House wasn't home now, was it? Not for Franklin and not for her. Her head spun. She would have to call Harry Truman. Tell him he was president.

How could so very much end so very quickly?

"Thank you," she said to the usher, putting the receiver quietly down. "I'd better get back to the music."

It wouldn't do to alarm everyone with histrionics. Her husband was dead; there was no need to rush. Besides, she wanted two minutes to herself, two minutes to hold this terrible loss to her bosom before she had to share it with the world.

The pianist was reaching the conclusion of her first piece. Eleanor sat in the thankfully darkened auditorium and let the beautiful music roll over her. She pictured Franklin rescuing her at that very first dance, and how animatedly they'd talked. She pictured him telling Mama he was going to marry her and how furious Sara had been that he'd chosen another woman over herself. She pictured their wedding and their babies and the many happy times they'd had together.

As the piano notes built to a crescendo, she forced herself to picture the tragic loss of their little Frankie, then her mind skipped to Franklin nearly dead of Spanish flu. Her breath hitched and she skipped across the dirty, violet-scented hole in memory lane to picture him lying in bed after polio, clutching at her hand and asking her to stand up for his dream of being President. Then she pictured them walking into the White House for the first time on that cold March day in 1933—twelve years ago.

"I'm coming home," she'd said, but where was home now?

That didn't matter, she told herself sternly. There were things to be done. People to call, a funeral to arrange, a president to be sworn in. Eleanor gripped the side of her seat and prayed for strength as the music finished on a glorious run of notes. Her music too, it seemed, was finished and she must bow out as gracefully as the pianist.

Standing up with the lights, she thanked the musician loudly for her beautiful playing and apologized that she was "called back to the White House." Astonished eyes followed her, but they would know the reason soon enough.

Everyone would know. Everything would change.

It was almost midnight when Eleanor's car pulled up the long drive to Franklin's beloved Warm Springs thermal spa, to find the very building in mourning. The gate guards greeted her with eyes downcast, the lamps along the path had been draped in black fabric, and the American flag flew at half-mast over the main building.

Eleanor was shown into the sitting room of the "Little White House" to find Daisy and Polly waiting for her, dressed, like herself, all in black, even Polly's vibrant hair tucked away in a discreet scarf. They hugged, Polly with a featherlight touch, Daisy clinging to her until she politely detached herself.

"What happened?"

"He was so happy," Daisy said. "On fine form, chatting and laughing and, and... chatting."

Flirting, she meant. It was one of his favorite pastimes, after all.

"It was almost lunchtime," Daisy went on. "The staff were laying the table and he told Shoumie she had fifteen more minutes of painting and then... and then..." She burst into tears. "And then he said he had a terrible headache and slumped forward. Gone. Just like that."

"Gone?" Eleanor gasped.

Daisy wiped her nose noisily. "Not gone, sorry. But unconscious. The doctors hustled him away. He died around three o'clock, I think. He never regained consciousness, so he didn't suffer, Eleanor."

Eleanor pressed her hand. "That's good." But it was a rather more severe story than she'd heard earlier. She turned to Polly. "Fainted?"

Polly shrugged. "That's what they said. Dr Bruenn thinks it was a cerebral embolism. Swift and, as Daisy says, painless."

Eleanor forced herself to push the strange phone call aside. It would have made no difference. She could never have got to Georgia by three. She looked around.

"He's in there," Daisy said, pointing to the door of Franklin's bedroom.

Eleanor stood up, but couldn't quite bring herself to go in, to face the stark reality of his death. Back in the White House earlier, she'd spoken to the doctors, hugged Anna tight, and telegrammed her sons, all on active duty. She'd even seen Harry Truman sworn in as President. There was no denying Franklin's death, but facing it for herself was another matter. She put a hand to the door, but couldn't turn the handle.

"Has the painter gone?" she asked, stalling.

"Yes," Daisy said.

"The painter and her friend," Polly added.

"Polly!" Daisy hissed, clearly horrified.

Eleanor looked from one to the other.

"She might as well know," Polly was saying to Daisy. "It'll

come out soon enough and better if it comes from us, her friends."

Eleanor did not think Polly was her friend. She should leave whatever this was, turn the handle and walk through the door to see her dead husband. But she had always been curious—so, damned curious.

"Friend?" she asked.

Polly's lip curled upwards. "Good friend," she said silkily. "I think you used to know her. Lucy, she's called. Lucy Mercer Rutherfurd."

FORTY-ONE

THE PRESIDENTIAL TRAIN, APRIL 13, 1945

Two things she had specified to keep her marriage alive, Eleanor thought furiously to herself as the presidential train chugged at an aptly funereal pace up the line to Washington. Two things: that they never had to be intimate; and that he never again saw Lucy Mercer. Had it been so much to ask? It seemed so. For all his care of the nation, her husband had been an essentially selfish man. She knew that, of course, but it hurt that she'd had to face it so starkly at the moment of his death.

She'd finally gone in to see him, but had been reeling with Polly's gleefully imparted information and able to do nothing but stare at his empty form, so churned up by his betrayal that it had been impossible to feel the balm of grief.

Polly had been very happy to provide more details when she'd come back out. Not only, it emerged, had Lucy been with him in Warm Springs, but he had been seeing her often since her husband's death two years ago.

"Not often," Daisy had corrected, agonized by her cousin's cruelty. "Occasionally. As friends, Eleanor, old friends. And never alone."

It had been kind of her, but little help. The betrayal was not one of the body but of the heart. Franklin had been to visit widowed Lucy in her various residences, he had taken rides around the countryside with her, he had invited her to dinner at the White House—*Eleanor's* White House. Even worse, Anna had been there too. Anna, her own daughter, who had been so indignant when she'd found out about the affair at an emotional fifteen. Eleanor had known she'd forgive her father, but had not realized how far that forgiveness would go.

"We all get nostalgic as we get older," Daisy had offered.

It had not helped.

Throughout the war, while Franklin had been holding her hand and reminding her of their first meeting, of their wedding, of the path they'd trodden together to the White House, had he also been holding Lucy's and reminiscing about the happy times when his tongue had…?

"Stop!" she muttered. This was no time for torturing herself; there was enough sadness to bear already.

The presidential train was carrying Franklin's body seven hundred miles north to Washington for his official funeral. They were moving with dignified slowness so that the hundreds of people lining the track could pay their respects. The lights in the train had been dimmed, save those in Franklin's carriage so that his coffin, set high on a flag-draped podium, could be seen from far and wide. If they went around a bend, Eleanor could see it too, glowing like a beacon, the light reflected in the tears of those standing, heads bare, to watch him pass.

Eleanor could not feel grief yet, but the nation sure as hell could and that, at least, was soothing. Her light was turned low and her suit of darkest black, but sometimes people caught a glimpse of her and waved a hat or a handkerchief, or pressed their hands to their heart in a gesture of solidarity, and Eleanor loved them for it.

There had been so, so much more to her and Franklin's life together than romantic tomfoolery, she reminded herself, and the further north the train went, the more that quiet realization sank into her bruised heart. Franklin had always wanted women to flirt with, to pander to his ego. But she was the one he had asked to go to the first meeting of the United Nations with him. She was the one he had asked to ensure the vital legacy of peace was carried out.

The only problem was that she had no idea how to do that now.

She'd promised Harry Truman she would be out of the White House by the end of the week. Harry had pressed her hand very kindly and told her to take her time, but Eleanor had rarely needed to do that. She was far better getting on with things. Actions were more effective than thoughts. For tonight though, sitting through an ever-reaching parade of national grief, there was little for her *but* thoughts.

Someone coughed at the door to her carriage and she looked up gratefully to see Grace Tully, Franklin's secretary.

"Come in, Grace."

"Sorry to bother you, Mrs. Roosevelt, but the Military Department are trying to finalize the funeral plans and they want to know if Mr. Roosevelt had any specific requests."

Eleanor looked at her blankly. "I've no idea, Grace. Do you?"

She shook her head. "No, ma'am, though I did find this file in his safe in Warm Springs." She held up an envelope marked simply "burial." Eleanor thought of him sitting, alone, writing out instructions and the first tear came to her eye. How lonely that must have been.

"Shall I open it?" Grace asked gently.

Eleanor could only nod. She clasped her hands in her lap, feeling for the loose wedding ring as Grace pulled out a single sheet of paper, read it through, and then passed it to Eleanor. Eleanor read it too. Then again. The simple note asked that he be buried in the Rose Garden at Hyde Park beneath a plain white stone. It asked for no grand statue, no fancy engraving, no fund to invite public adulation. There was only one other request: "I pray that Eleanor, my dearly loved wife, will be buried with me in due time."

The tear escaped. She and Franklin had not had a perfect marriage, not at all. But they had, for sure, had an imperfect marriage together.

The train finally pulled into Union Station on the morning of April 14 and the quiet of the night was sucked up in a cacophony of respectful chaos. Eleanor had to gather herself and step out, for one last time, as Mrs. Roosevelt, First Lady of America.

President Truman (how strange that sounded) was waiting on the platform with the entire cabinet and supreme court to pay their respects. At the door, a black Army caisson, pulled by six beautiful white horses, waited to carry Franklin's coffin to the White House, and behind that a car for her. She saw Anna with Elliott, the only son able to make it here in time, standing next to the car and hugged them both. Anna looked nervous, and no wonder, but this was no time for recriminations.

"I can't believe he's gone," Anna whispered hoarsely. "And before he saw the end of the war."

Eleanor had a lump in her throat and it was Elliott who answered.

"He knew it was going to end. He knew it with absolute certainty. I remember him telling me after Yalta that 'we've got the bastard beaten.'"

Anna gave a weak smile. "That sounds like him."

It did, Eleanor thought, so much so that she could almost hear his voice and had to stop herself turning around to be sure he had not lifted the lid of the coffin and winked out at them. It would not do to look mad as well as feel it.

They got into the car and followed the caisson as it moved slowly down Constitution Avenue, onto 18th Street, and down Pennsylvania Avenue to number 1600—the White House. It had been swiftly agreed that, in this time of war, there should be no grandiose parade, but the people had felt differently and lined the streets as far back as the eye could see, many openly weeping and holding their hands up to the coffin. Eleanor envied them their abandon. She held herself stiff as they pulled up before the front door of their home for the last twelve years.

You have Val Kill, she reminded herself, but somehow she could only picture her dear cottage as it had been at the start, when everything had still been before them.

You have Washington Square, she told herself instead, but her mind instantly raced to Franklin sitting there, pink-cheeked from a morning in the New York rain. "If I don't make it to the end, you'll make sure it happens for me, won't you? You'll make them all listen? You'll make sure there's a United Nations?"

She was glad of his confidence in her but it was surely misplaced, for right now it felt like all she could do to exit the car and, alone, walk up the steps behind his coffin, half of Washington watching. At last, she was inside and the coffin was set in the East Room where an honor guard was waiting. Eleanor nodded her thanks to them and watched as the coffin was safely installed. All was as it should be but suddenly it felt so final, so stark. At Warm Springs she'd been too blindsided by Polly's revelation to even see Franklin properly, let alone say goodbye.

She could not allow that to happen.

"Could you please dispense with the guard," she asked Moses, "and open the coffin? I'd like to have a few moments alone with my husband."

"Of course, Mrs. Roosevelt, ma'am."

Was that why she had stayed as his wife, she wondered as dear Moses leaped to do her bidding, because it had given her so many privileges? So many chances in life? No. She had stayed as his wife because she had believed that he could, in some way, change the world for the better. And she had believed she could help him.

The lid was opened and there he was, Franklin, looking more peaceful in death than he had for the last hard year. Dressed in a fine suit with his hair brushed and his withered legs hidden from view, he looked years younger. There was even, she noted, a hint of a smile on his lips, as inscrutable as ever.

"I hope you're at peace, Franklin," she said softly.

She doubted he was. More likely he was raging at missing the victory party, but there was only so much one man could do. Victory would come and it would come in a large part because of his vision and courage. It would come because he had been the one in the White House. And she at his side.

"I'm glad I stayed," she whispered. "However complicated and tricky things sometimes were, we've definitely been better off in life for having the other." Eleanor bent and kissed him. "But now, Franklin, I have to go on alone. I don't know where, and I'm not sure how, but I have to go on alone." She put her fingers to her wedding band, slowly working it up and off her finger. The plain gold band shone in the light pouring through the big windows and Eleanor smiled. She'd seen her entire adult life through this pretty—and sometimes not so pretty— circle. It was time to let it go.

Bending, she placed the ring into Franklin's open palm and gently closed his fingers over it. Let the First Lady go into the ground with the president. From here on in, she would tread her own path as plain Eleanor Roosevelt.

It was terrifying.

"Nothing is so much to be feared as fear," his voice said, not from his inauguration speech but from way back in a bed in Campobello when their marriage had begun to find its new form—a form that would be beyond the wit of the Pollys of this world, but that Eleanor would forever cherish.

"I'll miss you, Franklin," she said. "I'll miss you so much." Tears threatened but she fought them back. There would be time for personal sorrow later; for now, the nation must mourn its President.

Drawing in a deep breath, Eleanor rubbed at her bare finger, stuck her chin up high and turned. "Put the lid back on please," she told Moses and, giving his arm a soft, grateful squeeze, walked from the East Room without looking back.

FORTY-TWO
THE WHITE HOUSE, APRIL 20, 1945

The red light was twinkling quietly away, as it always did. As it presumably always would. But going forward, Eleanor would not be in the White House to see it. She lifted a hand to the Washington Monument, but tonight it would not be "hello" to the great monolith that had stood as her guardian for the last twelve years. Tonight it would be goodbye.

She had spent the week in a frenzy of packing. Tommy had been wonderful, as had Mrs. Nesbitt, Moses, and their many staff. Plus, of course, most of the furnishings, paintings, and even the curtains of the White House would remain. It had never been hers. However much it had felt that way.

At last, it was quiet. Everyone else was asleep and she was free to roam. She remembered her first night here, when she'd been unsure if she was allowed to go and make herself a hot drink. Moses had been just a young guard then, now he ran the staff. He would stay, the usher's job more secure than his master's. She gave a small chuckle at the thought.

They'd arrived here in 1933, at the height of the Depression, when she and Franklin had been up to their eyes in social and economic programs to try to deliver the New Deal he'd promised the people. She thought, on the whole, they'd succeeded. Of course, it had taken a war to complete the job, which was a tragedy, but that was human beings for you—always so much quicker to fight than to love.

Or were they? Eleanor was sure that the ordinary man, and most certainly the ordinary woman, would far rather love than fight. They just wanted to do their job, bring up their families, and socialize with their neighbors. It was those at the top that created the trouble and that was why the United Nations was so important. The San Francisco meeting to establish its charter would open next week. She should be flying there with Franklin. Instead, she was emptying their things out of the White House and he—he was lying in the ground in Hyde Park. It felt as unreal as the day they'd arrived.

The funerals had been beautifully done but so very fast that they'd felt like a play. The official one had been held in the East Room barely hours after they'd arrived on the train. Franklin had been committed to God with Harry Truman sitting respectfully across the aisle as President. There had been many tears, but she'd felt too shocked to cry.

Barely had that funeral been over, than they'd been processing back to the station to take the night train up to Hyde Park for the "family funeral." That, too, had been filled with dignitaries, Anna and Elliott the only actual family as her other three children were too far away fighting the dragged-out damned war to be able to return in time.

Franklin had been carried up the hill from the riverfront on another caisson, this time led by six black-draped horses, with a hooded horse behind, the traditional symbol of a fallen leader. There had been a military band, crammed into the rose garden with everyone else, and a three volley salute. Poor little Fala, held on a lead by Daisy, had barked after each one, as if he'd been sending a personal tribute after the master to whom he'd been so devoted.

Eleanor had remained at the grave after everyone else had gone into the house to drink to Franklin's memory. She'd never been good at parties and had preferred to stay outside and stare at the fresh earth covering her husband of forty years. Had they been good years? Of course. The young people were using a new word for their other halves—"partner." It sat strangely on the tongue, but was more straightforward than the coy "companion"; more powerful too. Eleanor liked it. She and Franklin had been partners.

"You'd be sad to be leaving," she said out loud into the hushed air of the White House. "You loved it here."

"So did you," his voice said, rich and warm in her ear.

"I did. I'm glad we made it here, Franklin. I'm glad we made it here together."

"I'm sorry I'm getting you kicked out."

She chuckled. "It was only ever ours on loan."

"Yes—though we had it for a good long time, hey?" She smiled to herself. "What will you do now, Babs?"

She put up a hand to ward off the question. She had her column, of course, but goodness knows what she was going to write of interest now. She had plenty of demand for articles and books but they would shrivel up as fast as the thousands of flowers on Franklin's coffin. She would still, she hoped, be able to work for the various projects and charities she held dear, but if she wasn't the President's wife, what on earth was she?

"Stupid woman," she tutted at herself. What did it matter what she *was*? It was what she *did* that counted and there would always be plenty to do, even if it was simply serving in a soup kitchen.

The day after Franklin's internment, Ned Miller had broadcast a tragically moving story about entering Buchenwald Concentration Camp and finding the few emaciated, broken people still clinging tenaciously to life in that terrible death camp. With such suffering in the world, there would always, sadly, be plenty to do.

Eleanor raised her hand to the Washington Monument. "Goodnight," she said. "And goodbye."

Then she turned, got into bed, and went to sleep.

She was breakfasting on the sun porch next morning when Anna sidled out.

"Can I join you, Ma?"

"Of course."

Eleanor pulled out a chair and Anna slid into it, but shifted and fidgeted like she had as a teenager, cross with the world, usually for catching her out doing something she should not. Eleanor concentrated on buttering her toast. There had been no time to talk to Anna about her betrayal but now there was no escaping it. Her daughter was precious to her and it hurt that she'd colluded with Franklin to do the one thing she'd asked him not to. She didn't like that, didn't want it. The thought of him meeting that woman, laughing with her, chatting with her, smiling into her eyes, made Eleanor's guts churn in a way it had only done once before. She'd let Franklin have his closeness with Missy, his flirtations with Daisy, Polly, Princess Martha and any other giggling Lucy-prototype, but not the original. Not her.

It was so painful that all that time, while he'd been asking Eleanor to "be his full wife" again, he'd been setting up clandestine meetings with the woman who'd broken their marriage in the first place. The other day she'd caught herself wondering if, had she said yes, he wouldn't have needed to meet Lucy, but then had sternly reminded herself that this was not her fault. Franklin had had plenty of people to pander to him. He had seen Lucy out of vanity, to satisfy his constant need to be amused, and made to feel special.

As if being President of the United States was not special enough!

"Ma..."

Eleanor forced herself to look at Anna. She was her daughter. Lucy might have taken her first, true closeness with Franklin away from her; she could not let her take Anna too.

"Tell me why you did it," she said tightly.

Anna sighed. "Because he asked me to. And I didn't know how to say no." She played miserably with the edge of the tablecloth. "I could give you excuses, Ma. I could say that I felt that if I organized it, it would be under my control, which is true. I could say that it was nothing more than friendship, which is also true. But at the end of the day, none of that matters. I did it because I'm weak, Ma. I did it because I liked that he trusted me and wanted me to be part of his world. I did it because I let him charm me, as he does with everyone, and I forgot my allegiance to you and that was... that was unforgivable."

She was crying and Eleanor hated to see it.

"Nothing is unforgivable if honestly repented."

Anna looked up. "Really? Really, Ma? Because I don't want to lose you. I... I love you."

Eleanor blinked. They were not a demonstrative family, preferring to show love, like everything else, through their deeds not their words.

"I love you too," she said. "I'm just... hurting."

"I know, Ma, and I hate that I'm a part of causing that."

Eleanor looked at her dear daughter and saw pain in her eyes too. What was the point? Their relationship was good and pure and happy and she could not allow some foolish personal slight to steal it.

"I hate that too," she admitted. "But I'll recover. I've lost so much in the last week. I don't want to lose you too."

Then Anna was tumbling into her arms as if she were fifteen all over again, and Eleanor held her close and drew in her care like a balm. Love was such a complicated, messy emotion. The trick, it seemed to her, was to filter out the painful bits as best you could and cling onto the good ones with both hands. Joy, like peace, was far too scarce to waste.

They lingered together, picking at crumbs. The Trumans would be arriving this afternoon and Eleanor could hardly be sitting here like a ghost, but it still took a huge effort to force herself up and go inside to say her goodbyes. The office and domestic staff gathered in the main hall, many in tears, and Eleanor made sure she shook hands with every one. At the end of the line was Moses.

"Thank you for protecting me all these years," she said to him.

"It's been an absolute honor." He wiped a tear. "Who will protect you now, Mrs. Roosevelt?"

She smiled at him. "No one will need to protect me now, Moses. I'm of little importance any more."

"I disagree," he said stoutly.

"I'm no longer the President's wife, remember?"

He smiled. "But you are still Eleanor Roosevelt."

Eleanor stared into his soft, kind eyes and had to blink hard to keep tears at bay. There were journalists clustered outside and it would not do to look like the wreck she felt inside.

"Thank you, Moses," she said and, leaning in, dropped a soft kiss on his cheek.

Last hands shaken, she wished them all the very best, then turned and made for the car waiting at the door. The journalists called her name and she gave them a wave but did not stop and did not look back. She wanted to get to New York and the safety of Washington Square. The afternoon of the rainy parade, she'd thought perhaps, once the chaos was over, she and Franklin might be able to live in the apartment together, but the chaos had come to an abrupter ending than either of them had hoped for and that chance was gone. It was her apartment now, her life, and it was time for some peace and quiet.

To her horror, however, when she arrived at the door to the block several hours later, there were more journalists waiting, as if they'd been picked up by the scruff of their necks at the White House and dropped here. Fools.

"Welcome back to New York, Eleanor," one called.

"What's next, Eleanor?" another asked and then they were all taking up the chant: "What's next? What's next?"

Eleanor marched straight up to them.

"Nothing is next," she said crisply. "You're wasting your time here, I'm afraid. Go and find someone else to write about, my dears. This story is over."

Six months later, the phone rang.

"Eleanor!" a cheery voice said. "Harry Truman here. I have a job for you…"

FORTY-THREE

MID-ATLANTIC, DECEMBER 31, 1945

Half an hour to midnight. Half an hour to 1946—the first full year of peace in far, far too long. Eleanor should be down in the ballroom, celebrating with everyone else on board the RMS *Queen Elizabeth*, but she was far too tired. Besides, New Year without Franklin's toast felt hollow; she'd rather be asleep. What was it he had called her back on the cusp of 1943: "The person who makes it possible for the President to carry on." Well, it turned out she'd failed at that, but perhaps she could at least make it possible for his influence to carry on.

That was why she'd accepted this job, but it was terribly daunting. It had been very kind of Harry Truman to think of her but perhaps she should have stuck with her first instinct and told him she wasn't the right person. This was far too important to mess up.

"I want you to be one of the U.S. delegation to the first United Nations General Assembly," he'd said to her.

Just like that, straight out, as if it was something she might have been expecting, which she most certainly had not. She'd been delighted when Congress had ratified American participation in the UN and keen to hear more, but to be involved herself...!

"That's very kind of you, Harry," she'd replied. "But I've got no experience of foreign affairs whatsoever."

"Neither had I when I went to Potsdam, but I coped."

"You did admirably."

"As will you."

He'd got her there. Even so, she would have resisted far harder if Frank had not been staying with her at the time and urged her to accept. Then he'd got onto his siblings and they'd all said she'd be "perfect" for it, which had been very kind of them and, as it turned out, impossible to resist. She'd agreed to let the appointment go to Congress for approval, assuming it would be turned down, but in the event only one old southerner had voted against her. So here she was, heading across the Atlantic to London with four other delegates and a team of State Department secretaries, to try and carve out a route to actually uniting nations beneath the self-created banner.

"Why me?" she'd asked Harry Truman when she'd seen him before departure.

"Because you know more about basic human rights than anyone. And, more importantly, because you care about them."

Well, that much was true, she thought as she changed into her nightdress and washed her face, and she was starting to fear she was the only one of the U.S. delegation to do so. She'd arrived at the docks in her own car yesterday evening to find out from the steward that the rest of the delegation had been driven from the station in Army limousines, motorbike outriders blaring horns as if they were the very saviors of the human race.

As far as she could see, if these were its saviors, the human race was in bother. They were pumped full of their own importance and had come with all manner of sycophantic assistants. She, meanwhile, had been told Tommy was not invited and she'd be provided with a secretary. Fools—her Tommy would do more work than ten of this lot. Edward Stettinius was only here because he wasn't ready to retire yet, James Byrnes was a man obsessed by his own prestige, and the two senators, Tom Connally and Arthur Vandenberg, were her least favorite sort of politicians—in it to tell everyone else how to conform to their opinions. The alternatives were no better, and already she feared the Americans would get a reputation for arrogance.

Mind you, her opinion of them could not be any poorer than theirs of her. It had been perfectly clear after only twenty-four hours in their company that they thought her a foolish woman, only chosen as Franklin's widow. They would have happily had their first meeting without her, save that Durward Sandifer, her bright young State Department adviser (not a patch on Tommy but definitely the best of the delegation) had tipped her off and she'd been able to walk in as if invited. They'd looked amusingly put out and had tried to ignore and talk over her for the next two hours. She was used to that though. They forgot she'd chaired meetings with trade union officials. She'd locked horns with southern fools at race conferences. She'd argued for childcare centers with business chiefs who apparently thought children were looked after by fairies. She knew all their tricks and had simply repeated what she had to say again and again until they'd been forced to acknowledge it—and Durward quick to minute it.

This Assembly was not, she thought crossly as she brushed her teeth, your average conference. Delegates were not coming from far and wide simply to sit at the free bar, but to fight for a new way of living—a way that was utterly vital to the survival of mankind. The war was ended, and the issue before them was how to create a new world order that ensured every nation got on with their neighbors. She'd said that in articles, she'd said it in her column, now she must be prepared to say it in the Assembly where it could actually count. The war had been ended with a weapon so destructive that it brought with it an imperative for a new world order.

Eleanor had hated the atomic bomb, but she had not stood against its use. The Japanese had shown no sign of surrendering and it had felt like the only way to stop the endless killing. When she'd seen the pictures of the suffering people of Hiroshima and Nagasaki, however, she had been devastated. She'd remembered Irving Lowen coming to see her in 1943, asking her to urge Franklin to greater speed on the project and had supposed it would have been worse if Hitler had got hold of that merciless weapon. Then they might all be gone.

She had longed to pick up the telephone and ask Franklin his opinion, for he'd always been so wonderfully clear in his thinking, but Franklin was not at the end of any line now and the bombs had been dropped.

Fifteen minutes to midnight. Eleanor applied moisturizer and clambered gratefully into bed. The room was relatively stark as the ship had not yet been converted back from its wartime role as a troop carrier, but that suited her fine. The men had complained at breakfast that their beds were hard, but she'd told them at least they weren't on the way to face the Nazi guns on Omaha and they'd shut up. For herself, she hated sailing as much as ever, but she refused to let it stop her being part of creating a lasting peace.

She lay down and closed her eyes and, as so often since his death, Franklin insinuated his way into her thoughts. They'd lived such separate lives that she'd wondered if she'd miss him, but she hadn't realized how much they'd talked. Passing conversations, phone calls, telegrams, little notes... They may not have laid down side by side every night but they'd managed the pillow talk all the same. And now... Now she had to talk to herself.

"You can do this, Babs," she said out loud, but it didn't

sound the same as it had in Franklin's warm, gently teasing tones.

It had been the same on VE day, less than a month after his death. She'd listened to the announcements by Winston, Stalin, and Truman, and heard Franklin between their lines. She'd found it hard to celebrate liberation without him and done little in the way of partying on either VE or VJ Day. But, then, she'd never been good at parties. That very first debutante ball had been agony—until Franklin had come along and she'd been able to talk instead of dance.

"Plenty of talking ahead, Eleanor," she told herself. "And plenty of *doing* too."

"You'll make sure it happens for me, won't you?" Franklin had said. "You'll make sure there's a United Nations, I know you will. That's what makes me rest easy at night."

"Rest easy, Franklin," she whispered as she snuggled beneath her covers. "I'll do my best, I promise."

Five minutes later, a cheer went up from the ballroom as the delegates toasted the arrival of 1946 with the finest champagne the country could afford, but Eleanor did not hear it for she was fast asleep.

The Methodist Central Hall in Westminster was an ideal place to launch a bid for world peace. Built of beautiful white stone, with a towering dome, it was a temple to humanitarian virtues and Eleanor felt a huge thrill as she stepped into the central hall to a buzz of myriad languages from the 850 delegates, representing fifty-one nations. She looked up to the podium and saw, behind it, a giant map of the world in the blue and gold colors adopted by the UN, with two olive branches curved beneath. This peaceful future world was theirs to shape, and she was here to be a part of it.

She'd promised Franklin she would make sure this

happened, but she was here for herself too. She was here for the principles of freedom, equality and decency that she'd held for so long. She was still scared, but in this vast hall, that fear felt right—one *should* be scared, for the responsibility was enormous. But surely with so many people here to work together, it would be possible?

She'd been assigned to Committee Three, the social, humanitarian and cultural committee. "Invited," Senator Vandenberg had called it when he'd stopped her in the middle of her morning walk around the deck, but it had been clear her "fellow" delegates had been meeting without her—doubtless around midnight brandies—and had decided this was the sort of fuzzy, "do-gooding" committee on which a woman could do least harm. She might have argued, save that in her opinion it was exactly the sort of committee on which a woman—or indeed a man—could do the most good. Who wanted to be stuck with boring finance, legals or admin, when you could wrestle with the key issues of what it was to be human? She'd thanked him prettily and sent a private cheer to the seagulls.

The assembly was called to order and Eleanor slid into her seat, finding herself maneuvered to the end of the American section and thus right next to the Russians. They were staring suspiciously around the settling delegates, sizing up allegiances, and little wonder given they were led by Andrei Vyshinsky, Stalin's chief prosecutor at his despicable show trials in the 1930s. The Soviet delegation was clearly here to defend their own rights rather than fight for anyone else's, but the only way to meet that was head on. Eleanor leaned over to say a smiling hello and, startled, the Russians nodded politely and shook her hand.

Turning back to the rest of the hall, she noted the representatives of the many smaller nations, remembering how Franklin had re-ordered the speeches in San Francisco to give them equal precedence. She hoped that would happen here too, for how could this Assembly fight for equality among the peoples of the world if they did not recognize it in their own ranks?

She was pleased to note plenty of people of color among the delegates, though strikingly few women. The British delegation, to their credit, had three females, including Ellen Wilkinson, a Member of Parliament and militant fighter for workers' rights. There was a woman with both the Danish and Norwegian groups, as well as with New Zealand and China, plus one apiece among the Poles and Belorussians. Eleanor made a note to seek them out, for if there were going to be battles with the Soviets, they might be useful.

Scanning the dark-suited ranks, she was delighted to spot Minerva Bernardino, a beautifully dressed Caribbean woman in a striking, flower-decked hat, whom she'd met on the Inter-American Commission of Women in Washington in the thirties. Minerva had been exiled from the Dominican Republic at the time for opposing the then-dictator. Eleanor had sent her a letter of congratulation when she'd been allowed home and successfully fought for female suffrage. She looked forward to working with her.

Further along, she saw Hansa Mehta with the Indian delegation, also standing out from the somber crowd in a beautiful sari. This inspirational woman had fought for the educational rights of girls in her home country before being voted onto the Bombay legislative council in the first provincial elections of 1937. The female delegates here in London might be few, Eleanor thought, but they were strong.

They'd need to be.

The first few days were a whirlwind of plenary work, with endless speeches and ballots as core officials were put in place. Many of the speakers expressed profound desire for a truly united nations, which warmed her, though most of them could have said it in half the time. The men seemed obsessed with rules and points of order, and were able to talk about them at great length, which Eleanor found excruciating, especially as speeches had to be translated into both English and French. She missed having her knitting to occupy her fidgeting hands in the tedious debates (not even debates, more showcasing of opinions), but when she'd asked the rest of her delegation if she could bring it along they'd looked at her utterly mystified, so she'd decided it was best to leave it in the hotel.

She tried to seek out the other women in the breaks but with 832 men to eighteen women, it could be hard to find your way through the masses. Eventually, infuriated, she asked Durward to issue an invitation to them all to take tea with her in Claridge's on the next afternoon off. Perhaps, that way, they could find the time and space to converse without the deafening noise of the men.

The afternoon came and Eleanor paced her suite. The staff had provided a delicious tea-trolley with a spread of sandwiches and cakes that made her feel guilty, as the British were still under heavy rationing. She'd seen the shortages first-hand when, between UN sessions, she'd met friends and visited American organizations who'd pressed invitations upon her. It was hard to find the time with so many briefings and notes to catch up on, but people were more important than words and she was getting better at speed-reading the papers last thing at night over a nice cup of British tea.

As the clock ticked around to 4 p.m., Eleanor began to feel foolish. She desperately wished Tommy were here to keep her calm and, if necessary, eat up the unwanted cakes with her. Why would all these busy delegates want to visit her on their afternoon off? She felt a twist of nerves in her stomach that reminded her of damned debutante balls. Franklin had saved her from those but he wasn't here, and Tommy wasn't here, and who would want to come along to meet plain old Eleanor?

There was a sharp rap on the door and she raced to open it. Standing there, in another glorious hat, was Minerva

Bernardino, accompanied by elegant Marie-Hélène Lefaucheux of France. Coming down the corridor were the three British women in sensible suits, then the two Indian ones in flowing saris. Behind them were an assortment of others, all right on time and all chattering away in a tumble of languages—a happy sound that filled Eleanor's heart right up to the top.

"You came!" she cried, standing back to usher them inside.

"Of course we came," Minerva said, grabbing her in a very welcome hug. "Who'd say no to Eleanor Roosevelt? You're an icon, woman!"

Eleanor blushed furiously. "Hooey!" she said. "I'm just a person trying to get a job done, as are we all."

"And we'll get it done far better than the men," Minerva said, winking at her, "especially now we're together. Thank you so much for this."

And then the other women were squeezing in and suddenly Eleanor's big suite felt rather cramped, and the fancy sandwiches and cakes looked as if they weren't quite enough, and she was happier than she'd been since arriving in London. Happier, perhaps, than she'd been since Franklin's death. At last, they could cut through the formalities and actually get something done.

The conversation flowed and Eleanor was instantly rapt. Frieda Dalen of Norway and the impressive Evdokia Uralova of Belorussia urged the importance of insisting on equality not only of races, nationalities or religions, but of genders.

Hansa nodded urgent agreement. "We must avoid the use of 'man' in the language of the UN documentation," she said, putting down her tea cup with force.

"But surely," Eleanor protested, "everyone understands that in this context 'man' is simply short for human and not a designation of gender."

Hansa laughed bitterly. "In my country, Mrs. Roosevelt, if you are not very specific in your terminology, they will use it against you. We must say 'men and women' or simply 'people' or 'human beings.'"

Others rushed to agree with her. Eleanor found it most enlightening and quizzed them further as the teapot was replenished time and again. She became guiltily aware that her life in the White House, with the freedom it had offered her to get involved in so many interesting events and movements, had blinded her to the restrictions on women across the world. But this, surely, was the whole point of a united nations—to come together, share experiences, and learn about different cultures and understandings. Certainly the female delegates all felt so.

After the tea, they took to sharing a table at breaks and five days later, after a second, more official meeting, the women of the first United Nations General Assembly issued an open letter calling on "the governments of the world to encourage women everywhere to take a more conscious part in national and international affairs, and on women to come forward and share in the work of peace and reconstruction as they did in the war and resistance."

Eleanor was proud to be a part of it and hoped it sent out a strong message to the 78 percent of American woman who'd said they derived satisfaction from working. It seemed there was more than just peace to fight for here and she was delighted to discover that many of her fellow females would be on Committee Three when that more specific work, thank God, started next week. The dignity of man—and of course woman—was at the heart of the work that would be done here, and she could not wait to get going.

FORTY-FOUR

LONDON, FEBRUARY 1946

"With all due respect, Mr. Mates, I think it is time we listened to another point of view."

Eleanor sent a heartfelt look of thanks in the direction of Peter Fraser, Prime Minister of New Zealand and currently Chairman of Committee Three. Leo Mates, the Yugoslav, had been talking for some time, at increasing volume and ferocity, and it was getting them nowhere. Beyond their doors, they could hear the happy sounds of the other committee members lunching in the big dining area, but they were still locked in bitter debate. Eleanor's stomach rumbled, but she put a hand down to quieten it. This was an issue far more important than her empty tummy.

Contrary to the placid expectations of the U.S. delegation, the humanitarian committee into which they had safely tucked their females had turned up the hottest potato of the entire General Assembly—the right of political asylum. All across Europe, around a million poor souls were stuck far from their homes. They were labeled "displaced persons" by the authorities which, to Eleanor's mind, made them sound far too impersonal. They were not "displaced," they were lost, destitute, miserable. Many of them had no homes to return to, many of them didn't even have families left. That was bad enough but it had emerged in discussion that many of them were terrified that returning home would cost them their life—and they were all from the Soviet bloc.

Mates glared at Fraser. "There can be no other point of view. Refugees should return to their homeland and it is foolish to think otherwise."

Eleanor bristled. She'd had quite enough of this. "What is foolish, Mr. Mates," she said, "is calling any of the esteemed delegates at this Assembly foolish."

There was a smattering of applause and Mates colored but did not sit down.

"The 'esteemed delegate' from the USA can know nothing of this, for there are no American refugees."

"That is true," Eleanor agreed. "But surely the very fact of me being here, in London, to meet with the representatives of the fifty other countries on this wonderful organization, shows that I wish to understand their needs."

"So, let me explain them to you. Refugees need to return home."

"But what if home is dangerous to them? What if the regimes in their homelands will punish them for their beliefs?"

Eleanor could feel the room holding its breath. Few dared to challenge the Soviets face to face and she had avoided it so far, but this was getting ridiculous. The Russians were earnest, interesting men but had absolutely no sense of compromise and, sometimes, you had to stand up for what you believed was right.

"Anyone who does not wish to return home must, by sheer definition, be a traitor or a quisling," Mates shouted.

"You think so?" Eleanor asked. "Do you believe, then, that the brave communist soldiers currently in exile from Franco's fascist Spain should be returned there?" Mates stared at her.

"Do you?" she pressed. "Because if they are, they will certainly be executed for holding communist beliefs."

"No one should be executed for holding communist beliefs. Communism is the purest, fairest form of government."

"I see." Eleanor looked into his eyes. "And the purest, fairest form of government would never persecute anyone for holding opposite opinions to itself?"

"*Wrong* opinions."

"As the fascist government in Spain would believe communist ones to be."

"But—"

"If the Soviet government is prepared to guarantee freedom of political opinion to all its subjects, alongside freedom of speech and freedom of religion, then of course its subjects should return home. But, also, of course, if they did so, their subjects would return home of their own accord and not need rules to demand it."

Mates slammed his hand down on the table. "Governments must be allowed to prosecute criminals."

"I agree. But holding a different political opinion to the current regime is not a crime."

Mates looked as if he might explode, but all around the table people were nodding and murmuring agreement and, for now at least, he was silenced. He sat down muttering furiously about "corrupt Western ideologies" and Eleanor knew this would not be the last they heard of the issue, but at least they might be able to get some lunch. Her stomach rumbled again and she stood up and headed for the door.

"You told him!" Minerva said, catching up.

"I told him," Eleanor agreed ruefully, "but I doubt he was listening."

So it turned out. When Peter Fraser pushed the committee to come to a consensus, both Mates and his Russian backer, Amazasp Arutiunian, folded their arms and refused to agree on the right of political asylum. With an answer due to the plenary that evening, Fraser was forced to take a "majority vote" instead. That meant a debate on the main floor, which would mean a late session. Eleanor groaned. She had hundreds of letters to get through. She'd thought that leaving the White House would mean a drop-off in correspondence, but people still seemed to think she had influence and, with her presence here regularly reported in the papers and on the BBC, many of them were writing to her care of Claridge's.

Some were sweet, some were angry, most were heartbreaking. Refugees, desperate to find their families, somehow believed she might be able to pull strings they could not reach, and she would dearly love to, but the strings all across Europe had been severed by the Nazis and there was nothing left to pull. With their homes bombed out and their relatives shot or gassed in the death camps, people were more alone than Eleanor could imagine it possible to be. Add the fear of being shot if they returned to their country and it was a picture of misery. A home was meant to be where you felt safe and if it took until dawn tomorrow to argue that, then Eleanor was happy to stay. She had failed to help them during the war; she mustn't fail them again now.

Over dinner, it emerged that the Russians were sending in the big guns. Their lead delegate, Andrei Vyshinsky, would take to the podium to argue the Soviet position to the General Assembly. It was bad news. He was fiercely clever and utterly ruthless and whichever poor person had to go up against him would be like a slave thrown into the lion pen.

Eleanor was very impressed when one of the British delegates volunteered to provide the view of the majority of Committee Three, but as the session prepared to convene, it became apparent that an American voice was expected too. Eleanor was busy asking Evdokia Uralova for a way into the Soviet mentality, so did not notice the rest of her delegation huddled together, brows creased. It was only when John Foster Dulles sidled up to her, that she realized what was coming.

"Mrs. Roosevelt," he said, more placatory than she'd ever heard him, "the United States must speak in the debate, and since you are the one who has represented us in committee, do you think you could say a few words to the Assembly?"

"Tonight?" she asked. "Now?"

"If you would," he said. "I'm afraid nobody else is familiar with the subject."

Eleanor stared at him, finding it hard not to relish this. The men who had routinely ignored and sidelined her throughout both the preparatory work and the Assembly itself, were coming, cap in hand, to ask her to take to the main stage on a key issue?

"Why Mr. Dulles," she replied, all meekness, "in that case, I will do my best."

Her triumph did not last long. Andrei Vyshinsky made a highly polished speech, driving home the subtle point that if governments were expected to care for their people, then their people must return to be cared for. Eleanor sat watching him command the full auditorium with smooth, clever rhetoric and felt increasingly terrified that she was expected to counter this hugely authoritative man.

She had not done too badly at the United Nations so far, but if she failed here, she would be proving the low opinions of her fellow delegates about the capabilities of women. Worse still, she would damage the cause of all women struggling to make themselves heard in political and business arenas, indeed in all walks of life. It was a heavy charge and suddenly, more than at any point in the month of the Assembly so far, Eleanor wished Franklin were here. He would stand up and wipe the floor with this man. His voice would ring with conviction as he stood up for liberty, individual rights and tolerance. Yet again she missed Tommy at her side, to order her jumbled notes and soothe her nerves, and was thankful when Minerva winked confidently at her. She nodded her thanks. The women were behind her; she could do this.

Vyshinsky was reaching the climax of his speech and, almost as if he'd heard her thoughts, his voice rang out proclaiming that man had paid too much for a tolerance which "is known in history by the name of Munich." A gasp rang around the auditorium. So many of the European nations in this room had felt betrayed by Chamberlain's Munich accords. And every single person had seen them collapse beneath the weight of Hitler's greed and ambition. But that had not been about tolerance.

Somewhere ringing in her head, Eleanor heard Winston Churchill raging about how the Munich accord had been drawn up from cowardice and a selfish desire to stay out of other people's fights. It was exactly the attitude she and Franklin had fought for years in America—the idea that as long as something wasn't in your own back yard, it wasn't your concern. But the whole world was everyone's back yard these days. The war had proved that and the atomic bomb had confirmed it. Tolerance was not making meek agreements to keep trouble at bay, tolerance was being brave enough to live alongside people with different views to your own—something the Soviets stubbornly refused to recognize, let alone attempt.

Oh, she was angry now. Vyshinsky was nothing but a bully and she couldn't wait to get to the podium and speak the truth to counter his silky lies. But he was playing a politician's game, talking on and on, clearly hoping that some of those not yoked to the Soviet plow would grow bored and go home, skewing the ballot in their favor. Eleanor rose to her feet and the Chair, taking his cue, called order.

She was on.

Eleanor walked steadily up the steps to the podium and faced the Assembly. It looked like an awful lot of people from here, most of them gray-haired men who would not be keen on being "harried" by a woman, but tough luck. She'd been asked to speak and she had plenty to say. She placed the single sheet of quick notes she'd made with Durward on the podium and gathered her thoughts. If Vyshinsky could evoke Munich, she could evoke Spain. She had done it in the committee and she would do it again here. She repeated her argument that Spain would execute returning communists and insisted political beliefs were not a crime. The comparison clearly confused a few of the Soviets in the hall but drew approving nods from many others. Eleanor paused to draw in a breath. She could do this. Thinking of all the important work she'd been party to in the last weeks, she cited the human rights guaranteed in the UN Charter, so freshly drawn in San Francisco that the ink might yet be wet.

"Are we so weak in the UN that we are going to forbid human beings the right to hear what their friends believe?" she demanded.

People looked at each other, nodded perhaps. Eleanor scanned the hall and, noting the large South American party fidgeting at the back, knew she had to keep them there and get them onside. Principles were one thing, but what people needed was stories—human moments that could engage their emotions as well as their rational thoughts.

Drawing on the history Franklin had told her as he'd shared his various new stamps over the years, she spoke of Simón Bolívar, the "Great Liberator" of South America, who'd fought for the freedom not simply of nations but of individuals. The South Americans began nodding too and her confidence grew. She didn't have Vyshinsky's smooth tongue or his clever turn of phrase, but she meant everything she said. Those refugees were not representatives of any state, they were simply people trying to live their lives unmolested, and one of the duties of the United Nations was to allow that to happen.

She looked around and saw Durward nodding eagerly at her from the side of the stage. It was late. She had made her point and must trust the wise people in front of her to understand it. "I only ask," she concluded, "that this Assembly will consider what makes man more free: not governments, but man. Thank you."

She picked up her tiny sheet of notes and, swallowing hard, left the podium. To her huge surprise, someone started clapping, then someone else, and suddenly the auditorium was filled with applause. She paused at the top of the steps, bemused. Was that for her? Of course not, she berated herself, it was for the point she had made, the principle she had outlined. Well, all she could hope was that those clapping her would vote as she had urged. It was down to the ballot and, though that terrified her, it was democracy and she had to let it take its course or she was more of a tyrant than the Soviets.

Even so, she felt sick as the votes were cast. People kept congratulating her on what she'd said, but only those who agreed with you did that, and there were plenty more who did not approach. She was almost faint with relief, therefore, when the results of the ballot were announced past midnight, resoundingly in favor of allowing refugees the right of political asylum. Eleanor felt that she had, finally, done something to atone for failing so many persecuted people in the midst of the war. It would mean a whole deal of continued trouble for the Western agencies trying to help them find homes, but it would also mean thousands of people, guilty of nothing more than disagreeing with their ruling power, would not die. That, frankly, was worth all the trouble in the world.

The hall emptied fast as people went gratefully to their beds, but Eleanor lingered, adrenaline rushing around her veins. She looked to the olive branches beneath the blue-and-gold map, and felt a small glow of pride. No doubt the Assembly would have voted that way anyway as they were all decent people (even the Soviets, they were just deluded), but it felt good to have had a part in the decision. It felt good to have done something.

"I think you'd have been proud of me, Franklin," she whispered to the air.

"You know I would," she thought she heard him say.

Goodness, she was getting fanciful! She put a hand onto the back of a chair to steady herself and thought back to their first ever conversation.

"We need to unite nations, not divide them," she'd said to him.

"Yes!" he'd agreed eagerly, then he'd reached out and taken her hand and it had felt as natural as if he'd always been doing it. "Yes, exactly! Come and sit down, Eleanor. Let's talk more."

"Let's talk more," she muttered.

She jumped as someone at her side said, "My thoughts precisely."

Embarrassed at being caught jabbering like a fool, she spun around to find Arcot Ramasamy Mudaliar, distinguished Indian politician and head of the newly formed Economic and Social Council, smiling at her.

"You must be tired, Mrs. Roosevelt," he said in his soft, cultured voice, "but do you have time for one last question?"

"Always," she told him.

His smiled widened. "Excellent. You see, we'd like to ask you if you would be part of a new commission to draft a Declaration of Human Rights."

The words chimed in her ears like music. "Declaration of Human Rights?"

"Exactly that. In fact, what we'd really like to ask is if you will chair it."

Eleanor looked from the blue-and-gold map, back to the hall, almost empty of delegates but ready to be filled again tomorrow, and the day after, and as long as it took to pin down a new way forward for the world. It was a way that would be difficult to find, a way that would take the best minds to work out the laws, finance and administration, but at heart, it would be a way that would define and defend human rights. She had come to this Assembly terrified about her abilities, but now she was here, all she could truly see was the vital nature of the task before them. She was not ready for this to end.

"Mr. Mudaliar," she said, sticking out her hand to shake his, "just tell me where to sign."

EPILOGUE
SPRINGWOOD, DECEMBER 1948

Eleanor's hands shook as she drew from her bag a small, rolled document and held it up. It was not the cold sending shivers through her body, though a bitter, ice-laced wind was blowing off the Hudson, but awe. Here, in her hands, was the living evidence of three years of the hardest work of her life: The Declaration of Human Rights.

She untied the ribbon and unrolled the single sheet, scanning the brief text. It contained a preamble and thirty straightforward articles, though they had not been straightforward to establish. Never had Eleanor's patience (not her strongest quality at the best of times) been stretched as far as it had in chairing the committee charged with drafting this precious document.

To Eleanor, the piece of paper before her was a commonsense statement of the most basic human rights: the right to life, to liberty, to security; the right to work and marry and raise a family; the right to leave your country and return to it; the right to seek asylum or fair trial. She could have written it in ten minutes at the start of 1946 when Mr. Mudaliar had first asked her to be involved, but that was not the point. The point was that to other nations and cultures and, indeed, to many within her own, it had not been nearly as clear-cut.

Every single one of the 1300 words within the Declaration had been wrangled over. Eleanor had heard more fine points of law and philosophy in the run of committee rooms that had defined her life since the London Assembly than she ever had before—or ever wanted to again. She'd been hugely grateful to be able to involve Tommy, her capable secretary throwing herself into UN work with the same enthusiasm with which she'd approached government, charity and press work. She'd been a marvel and kept Eleanor sane and often amused throughout the whole process. But it had been hard.

Even Article One, stating simply that, "All human beings are born free and equal in dignity and rights" had been subject to so much dispute that she had almost despaired. Hansa had led the fight to use the words "human beings" instead of "men" and it had taken far longer to win than it should have done. Women, however, had not been the greatest issue for so many countries, her own included. Despite the horrific lessons of the holocaust of the Jewish people by Hitler, many still believed some human beings were worth less than others. The South Africans had been loudest and fiercest in their refusal to accept racial equality, but Eleanor had come under several attacks over continued segregation in the USA and had had little defense. Earlier this year, thank God, Harry Truman had signed an executive order ending segregation in the U.S. armed forces, but in the south most public places were still separated by color. It was not good enough and pained her personally but, as she had forcefully argued on more than one occasion, the ratifying of the Declaration would provide a standard to work to, then they must all do their part to meet it.

The presentation of the Declaration had been the culmination of the third UN Session, held in the suitably grand Palais de Chaillot in Paris for the last three exhausting months. Eleanor had feared, despite the many passionate speeches in its support, that it would not pass the vote. The Soviets would find a way to block it, she'd been sure. Their combative obstructionism of 1946 had hardened into a darker opposition to all things "Western," for the Russians had gathered Eastern Europe under its metal wing and shut it behind what Winston Churchill had, oh so aptly, called an Iron Curtain.

Eleanor had been horribly aware of the paradox of discussing an article on "freedom to leave your country" with nations who had closed their borders to their own people and were treating anyone who attempted to cross them as criminals. Even while the speeches had rung around the Palais de Chaillot, a mere 650 miles away, West Berlin—an island of Western occupation within Soviet-controlled lands—had been blockaded by Russia. Its people were only surviving thanks to American and British planes flying daily supplies in to them and yet in this grand palace, Russian representatives were straight-facedly discussing human liberty.

Winston, Eleanor remembered, had told them never to trust the Russians and he'd been right, but poor Winston was out of power, voted into obscurity by a country hungry for change. Eleanor understood it, but felt sorry for the man who had given so much. Fighting the war had nearly killed Winston; it *had* killed Franklin. Stalin, however—never truly an "ally"—lived on, carving out his own victory from their efforts. Eleanor might have won the battle over keeping frightened refugees from having to return to Russia, but Russia had countered by refusing to let any more out. These days, it felt a hollow victory and she had truly believed they would find a way to block the ratification of the Declaration.

They had not. The Declaration had been approved by

forty-eight of the fifty-eight nations now making up the UN, with eight abstentions from the Soviet bloc and two absentees. Not one person had dared to vote against it and that had made her wild with joy. It might be a long, hard road to turn the fundamental principles of human dignity into enforceable law, but those principles were agreed.

Finally, those principles were agreed.

"We did it," she said into the cold air. She set the Declaration on the simple block of white marble before her, weighting it down with four pebbles washed smooth by the ever-flowing Hudson. "We did it," she said, louder this time. "We did it, Franklin."

"You did it, Babs," his voice said, as warming as his favorite manhattan. "I knew you would."

Had he?

Eleanor thought back to the dread days of 1918 when, celebrating rescuing her husband from Spanish flu, she'd found the letters that had broken her marriage. The pain of that time had smashed her into tiny pieces but, when she'd finally put them back together, they had taken a new form. Not as pretty, perhaps, not as soft or yielding or trusting, but far stronger, far more independent, far more satisfying. She'd made wonderful friends and learned to widen out her expectation of what was possible in life. And throughout all that, in a way that no one save themselves would ever understand, had stood one person—Franklin.

"You're the most interesting woman I know," he'd said to her, time and again.

At the end of the day, who could want more than that?

Eleanor kissed her fingertips and pressed them to the stone, hoping that, with this vital step to a new world in place, her dear husband could rest in peace. She stepped back to look at the inscription: plain and simple, as he'd wanted: FRANKLIN DELANO ROOSEVELT 1882–1945. And beneath that a space big enough for a second name. For *her* name. One day she would lie in the rich Hyde Park soil with him, together for eternity.

But not yet.

No, not yet—there was still far, far too much to be done.

A LETTER FROM ANNA

Dear reader,

I want to say a huge thank you for choosing to read *The President's Wife*. Throughout my research into Eleanor Roosevelt I kept coming up with one thought—I can't believe how amazing this woman was. She was so open in her thinking, so genuine in her compassion for her fellow human beings, and so inspirationally hard-working in the pursuit of fairness and justice. It's been my absolute honor to write about her and I hope that you enjoyed this novel and might be interested in some of my others. Your email address will never be shared and you can unsubscribe at any time.

www.bookouture.com/anna-stuart

Eleanor Roosevelt was a woman ahead of her time. She stood up publicly against racial segregation, fought for refugees and those suffering persecution, and had many friends in the LGBTQ+ community. She was inspired by individuals—by listening to and dealing with the direct problems of the people she met, rather than grouping and judging them based on bias and fear. Despite coming from a very privileged background, she was deeply interested in people from all walks of life, always keen to help those suffering, and tormented by the inevitable frustrations of the political system that, as she saw it, got in the way of common sense and compassion. And she did all this whilst dealing with heartbreaking personal problems of her own. *The President's Wife* has barely scratched the surface of this astonishing woman but I hope you've enjoyed getting to know her, and would encourage you to read more about her life and actions and to visit the excellent Eleanor Roosevelt Center if you're ever in Upstate New York.

If you've enjoyed this novel, I'd be very grateful if you could write a review. I'd love to hear what you think, and it makes such a difference helping new readers to discover one of my books for the first time. I also love hearing from my readers—you can get in touch on my Facebook page, through Instagram or via my website.

Thanks,

Anna

www.annastuartbooks.com

 facebook.com/annastuartauthor
 x.com/annastuartbooks
 instagram.com/annastuartauthor

HISTORICAL NOTES

Eleanor Roosevelt was a truly remarkable woman and it has been my honor to learn and write about her. My only concern has been not having the scope to do her many achievements justice, but that would have taken five books, so I had to limit myself largely to World War II. Sadly that also means that many vital people and key events and achievements had to be left out so I would like to mention them here.

KEY PEOPLE

Lorena Hickok

I mention "Hick" several times in this novel but come no way close to describing what she meant to Eleanor at one point in her life. Lorena Hickok was gay, as were a number of Eleanor's close friends, and Eleanor undoubtedly had a very intense relationship with her. There has been – and will always be – much speculation about whether that relationship was sexual. Certainly the letters between them were passionate, although several studies of letters of this period prove that to be not unusual between close female friends. Even so, they make it clear that the two women shared a bed and kissed each other but no more explicit details are available.

Personally, I don't think this matters. They were, it seems to me, in love with each other for a period and what physical shape that relationship took is no one's business but their own. Hick gave Eleanor a sapphire ring and they sent valentines to each other but, more importantly, she gave her confidence, security and happiness at a very difficult period in her life. The intensity of their relationship ultimately ran its course, but they stayed very good friends. Maybe, as I suggest here, Eleanor had been too burned by Franklin's betrayal with Lucy Mercer to ever throw herself fully into a long-term relationship again. Maybe she was too preoccupied by her work to have time for one. Maybe she was too intrinsically linked to Franklin to break free enough to fully commit to someone else, or maybe she didn't feel she could "indulge" herself that far, for she was ever a woman who lived to make life easier for others. We will never truly know but certainly Hick was vital to Eleanor and she loved her dearly, so I am sorry there was not more space for her in my book.

Joe Lash

Joe Lash also features in this novel, but perhaps not as much as he could have done given how very close Eleanor was to him. The going away party she threw him when he went into the army was peculiarly lavish – far more so than she gave any of her own sons – and she broke several official engagements (most unusual for her) to rush to see him when he was on leave. There is documented evidence of them lying on a bed together, with her stroking his hair, though this seems to have been in a maternal way, and she was instrumental in helping him and Trude be together and, ultimately, marry. When I realized that

Joe had been born barely a month after Eleanor lost her third baby, the first Franklin Junior (Frankie), I felt that might have something to do with it, but that speculation is purely my own.

Eleanor, despite (as she told her daughter Anna later in life) never really liking sex, was a woman given to passions. This was possibly rooted in her childhood adoration of her father. He was largely absent due to chronic alcoholism but courted her devotion with very loving letters and occasional visits where he would take her out to eat or riding around the park. Around the age of ten, Eleanor's future dreams were that she and her father would live together forever, just the two of them. When he died, she held onto that fantasy and perhaps carried those feelings into later life. She was endearingly naive in how freely she gave her love and attention, but must also have chosen wisely as none of her intimates betrayed her, and most of them stayed as friends throughout her life.

Louis Howe and Harry Hopkins

Franklin had two hugely influential advisers in his career. Louis Howe was a hard-boiled ex-journalist who became Franklin's political aide in the twenties. It was he, in part, who spotted Eleanor's political nous and encouraged her to join groups and campaign for her husband. The pair were very good friends and, between them, kept the Roosevelt name alive until Franklin was recovered enough to re-enter the fray. Sadly, Louis was asthmatic and suffered ill health and he died of bronchitis in 1936. Introducing him to this story would have complicated it too far so I had to leave him out.

Harry Hopkins was introduced to Franklin by Eleanor and was originally her ally on their complex team, but shifted over to Franklin when he became President and became his chief adviser during the war. A widower, he moved into the White House in May 1940 with his daughter, Diana, who Eleanor took on as her godchild and looked after with some devotion for years. He didn't move out again until December 1943 when his new wife insisted (fairly!) on getting a home of their own. This added to Franklin's loneliness in the latter war years, after his mother's death, and Missy's stroke, so I was sorry to leave him out but there is only so much room in a novel. Apologies, Harry!

Hall Roosevelt

Hall was Eleanor's younger brother to whom she was devoted. They were an isolated pair, their mother dying of diphtheria in December 1892, their middle brother Elliott of the same in May 1893 (aged just three), and their father, falling out of a window on a binge, in August 1894. As a result, they were close and Eleanor, seven years his senior, brought him up almost like a mother. She took him to school, visited him and had him to live with her and Franklin in the holidays. Sadly Hall, like their father, became an alcoholic and died of a failing liver, in agony, just a month after Sara passed away in 1941. Eleanor spent ten days at his bedside and Franklin was a big comfort to her once he was gone, so I did want to show this important part of her life, but it just didn't fit into the wider narrative so I had to leave Hall's tragic place in her life to these notes.

Marguerite LeHand

'Missy' (so christened by young Anna, who also turned Malvina Thompson into 'Tommy') is a fascinating woman. Recruited to help out with Franklin's vice-presidential campaign in 1920, she showed herself to be a skilled secretary and swiftly – especially after polio struck – became his most trusted day-to-day assistant and close companion. How close is, as with Eleanor and Hick, a matter of continued speculation. She travelled everywhere with him, occupying a room next to his, and tending him at any point in the day and, quite possibly, night. Once the Roosevelts moved to the White House, she became, in effect, his Chief of Staff (though, as a woman, she was never granted that title, nor the pay that should have gone with it!). She was utterly devoted to him and definitely imagined living out life after the presidency as just the two of them. Whether the relationship was consummated or not cannot be known and, as with Eleanor, does not actually matter very much. She had other relationships, with both Earl Miller and William Bullitt, Ambassador to France, but they did not last. She certainly held the position of Franklin's emotional wife for many years, although he was always capable of detachment and remained close to and reliant on Eleanor at all times.

Missy's health was always weak, probably the result of the serious rheumatic fever she had at fifteen. She had a suspected heart attack in summer 1927, and then a breakdown followed by a serious stroke in summer 1941. (Both linked by some historians to her possibly finding out Franklin was back in communication with Lucy Mercer, but I did not have space to explore that here.) When it became clear she was not going to recover, Franklin changed his will to settle half of his estate on her. It was only for life, reverting to Eleanor and the children at her death, but it does show how important Missy was to him.

Lucy Mercer Rutherfurd

Lucy was, by all accounts, a lovely woman – attractive but also kind, lively and good fun. She was a key part of the Roosevelt household when working as Eleanor's secretary from 1913 and the children loved her. Her affair with Franklin probably started in the summer of 1916 when Eleanor was in Campobello with the children and Franklin stayed in Washington to "work." Discovering it through her letters devastated Eleanor. In Franklin she'd thought she'd found someone she could truly trust and love without obstacle, and I believe finding out he'd turned his affections elsewhere nearly broke her.

What it meant to Franklin, we cannot know, but there seems little doubt his relationship with Lucy was more naturally physical than his relationship with Eleanor and that must have been heady. Would he have left Eleanor and his children to marry her? Possibly. Would she have denied her Catholic faith to marry him? Probably. In the end, the insistence of Sara Roosevelt, a formidable matriarch who also held the purse-strings, counted for a great deal, as did the suggestion that the public would never vote for a divorced president.

Amidst all that, where did Franklin's love for his wife – undoubtedly very real in the first decade of their marriage – come into it? We won't know that either, but they certainly had a very strong bond that pulled them back to each other time and again. It was more cerebral than physical, but no less vital for that, and I hope this novel explores their unusual and hugely influential marriage in an interesting and honest way.

I was astonished, and saddened, to find out that Franklin had been seeing Lucy in the three years leading up to his death. It's possible, in fact, that they never lost contact, as he seems to have arranged for her to view his first inauguration from a secret car and there is evidence of a few letters over the years so there may be more that were destroyed. Lucy first seems to have visited the White House for dinner on August 1 1941, entered in the guest book under the codename "Mrs. Paul Johnson," probably following her contacting Franklin to ask for help with securing treatment for her dying husband, Winthrop Rutherfurd (with whom she seems to have had a genuinely loving marriage). She is recorded as dining there several times in 1942, and after Winthrop died in March 1944, the meetings stepped up. In summer 1944 Franklin approached Anna about helping with arranging further visits. She was torn but her father was an ill – indeed dying – man by then and she couldn't resist his plea for a little nostalgic comfort. Lucy was in Washington for a period that July, also meeting with Anna and her husband, and again around the weekend of Franklin and Eleanor's fortieth wedding anniversary, visiting him either side of the party for that big milestone, which I found very painful on Eleanor's behalf.

Lucy spent time with Franklin in Warm Springs in November 1944 and was obviously there during the fatal stay in April 1945 when he collapsed and died. This was not one or two brief meetings but a sustained liaison, probably just emotional, but a betrayal all the same and catty Polly could not resist telling poor Eleanor at the very moment of Franklin's dying. Some researchers believe Polly had always been sweet on Franklin and never forgave Eleanor for "taking him" from her, though that doesn't explain why she tolerated him having Lucy around. At one point I considered making more of Franklin's final betrayal of his wife in the novel but, in the end, I concluded that seeing Lucy again was the egotistical, and perhaps fond, act of a dying man, rather than any grand love affair, and did not want to give it too much precedence in Eleanor and Franklin's rich and long-ranging story.

ELEANOR'S WORK

The United Nations

Eleanor said later in life that she considered the Declaration of Human Rights to be her defining achievement and it certainly took all her incredible skills as a negotiator to get it drafted and ratified by so many different nations and cultures. It is not a binding document, carrying no force of law, but it is a shining statement of ideals and has stood the test of time.

Eleanor's time with the UN deserves a book of its own, but its importance to me in this one was as a confirmation of all her and Franklin's truly-held beliefs about how nations should work together to promote a lasting peace. I did not have space for the many fascinating twists and turns of the early work of the UN but I hope the epilogue shows readers the vital, core success of her work.

Eleanor was also passionately sure that women should be involved as far as possible, believing them to be more naturally peaceable. The other female delegates, briefly mentioned here, all deserve to have their own stories told. Maybe one day... What I do know is that if all women – and men – were a tiny bit more like Eleanor Roosevelt, global peace would be more than achievable. Sadly, as current events are proving, war continues to lure humans into its destructive net. That the United Nations still exists and operates is excellent but it needs – as do we all – to do more to bring harmony back to the world.

Other achievements

Eleanor's key skill seems to me, in my wide study of her, to have been her ability to listen to other people. She was naturally humble, astonishingly unconcerned about other people's opinions of her, and hugely interested in everyone else. She had her prejudices when younger. Her early, casual dismissal of both Jews and people of color were embarrassing to her later but were a product of her age and she soon abandoned them when she started talking to individuals. From early on, she stood for equality and fairness, speaking out clearly and unashamedly in books and articles, in her astonishing daily columns (that make wonderful reading online for interested readers – https://erpapers.columbian.gwu.edu/my-day), and in her many lectures and talks.

Eleanor was instrumental in a project called Arthurdale to rehouse the poor in a self-sustaining community. It wasn't entirely a success, but the concept was brilliant and only the frailties of the humans involved let it down – something that Eleanor was to hit up against time and again.

As mentioned in the novel, she sat in the aisle of a segregated meeting to stand against the practice. She also left a women's club for refusing to allow her Jewish friend, Elinor Morgenthau to join, and resigned from a key group for refusing to allow Marian Anderson, a talented black singer, to perform at their event. Better than that, she went on, with Louis Howe, to organize for Marian to sing in the 'Freedom Concert' on the steps of the Lincoln Memorial for some seventy thousand spectators. She also invited her to perform in the White House on a number of occasions, including when the King and Queen of England visited.

Eleanor felt injustices against the ordinary people very strongly and one of her great regrets of the war was that she could not save more refugees. The State Department was criminally isolationist and paranoidly certain that anyone trying to get into the USA could be a Nazi spy, and did everything possible to hold up any immigration with red tape. In 1943, for example, immigration to the USA was only 10 percent of its stated quota, and this in a time when people were desperately fleeing persecution! They played on the fact that much of America was antisemitic and had little sympathy and little taste for any reports of what were later to be proved as the terrible atrocities of the Holocaust. Eleanor did her best to push their interests, but Franklin, a consummate politician, refused to wade into the trickier areas of federal legislation and, to her lasting regret, most of her efforts were in vain.

A NOTE ON TIMINGS

There are a few places in this novel where I have taken liberties with the exact timeline of historical events, in order to better show its emotional lines without clogging the narrative. Apologies for the historical purists (of which I am normally one myself) but there is history and then there is story and I have worked hard, in this novel, to combine both.

47/49 East Sixty-fifth Street

Sara promised Eleanor and Franklin a house of their own as a wedding present, then, without consulting them, bought a plot and commissioned an architect to design and build it – complete with second half for herself! In the novel, I show her revealing the plans to them in January 1908 but in reality it was probably earlier than that as they moved into the completed residence the following December. I chose to write the scene in the January to show Eleanor at the start of the endless "baby" stage of her life and draw out the excitement she must have felt at gaining a home all of her own for her growing family, only to find out it would barely be her own at all.

Franklin's "full wife" request

Franklin apparently did ask Eleanor to be his "full wife" once more on the trip south to inspect the factories and bases, though exactly what he meant by that can only be speculated. In reality, he gave Eleanor some days to consider his request and she delivered her decision at a separate dinner, but for the sake of narrative pace, I kept the conversation all to that one night on the train.

Eleanor's chair of the Declaration committee

I show Eleanor being asked to chair a Human Rights committee at the end of the novel whilst she is still in London. In truth, she was invited onto the committee shortly after her return to the USA and appointed chairman by unanimous vote at its first meeting in Hunter College, New York, in May 1946. I hope readers will forgive me "jumping the gun" but the spirit of the appointment is, I hope, clearly shown.

Anna and Lucy

Eleanor was exceptionally hurt by Anna's involvement in helping Franklin to see Lucy in 1944–5. Relations between them were tense for some time – far longer than I show here – but they did reconcile and remained close throughout their lives so I felt justified in showing their reunion before Eleanor left the White House.

ACKNOWLEDGMENTS

Much has been written about Eleanor Roosevelt, so I have had a wealth of scholarship and personal testimony on which to base this novel, which has been a huge help. I also had a wonderful research trip to the USA last autumn and owe an especial debt of gratitude to the wonderful staff at the Eleanor Roosevelt Center. Anna Fierst, Eleanor's great-granddaughter, was kind enough to respond to my queries. As chair of the center and vice-chair of the National Women's Foundation, she is an impressive woman in her great-grandmother's excellent mold, and I was very grateful she devoted her valuable time to putting me in touch with the park rangers on site.

Then, despite me inconveniently visiting in the week of Thanksgiving when the cottage was closed for decorating, Franceska Macsali Urbin, the Supervisory Park Ranger, welcomed me very warmly to Val Kill and showed me around, answering my many questions with patience and knowledge. It made all the difference seeing the space Eleanor loved to call her own, helping me to envisage her life and personality, and I am hugely grateful. The center is not just a brilliant monument to vital history, but also an active, engaged movement to improve life in the present day and I was delighted to work with them and hope they feel I have honored Eleanor with my novel.

I also found the FDR Presidential Library and Museum an excellent resource for my research, as well as the White House Visitor Center in Washington, DC. And I must offer a big thank you to my two excellent 'research assistants', Stuart and

Mum. They patiently trekked around New York and Washington, helping me find Eleanor's apartments, exploring graveyards, and, memorably, eating Chinese takeaway in the car outside Val Kill so we'd have the energy to make the walk up to Top Cottage! It was lovely having them both with me on a fabulous trip we'll all remember very fondly.

This book is dedicated to the memory of my grandma, Courtney Swiggett, an American who grew up in Boston and Long Island, then bravely swapped them for drizzly England and even drizzlier Scotland when she met my British grandpa who was over in Washington on government war work. She was a reverse GI bride and one day I would love to write their story as a novel. Grandma's father, Howard Swiggett, was a well-known thriller writer in the USA in the fifties and I hope Grandma would have been proud to see me follow in his footsteps. I was gutted when we lost her to breast cancer just before I turned sixteen and my heart turned over seeing some of the pictures of Eleanor, as they really reminded me of her. So, Grandma, this one's for you, as well as for the still-thriving American branch of my family.

There are many very good books about Eleanor—as there should be—but ones I found particularly helpful were Blanche Wiesen Cook's comprehensive three-part biography, *Eleanor and Franklin* by Joseph P. Lash, and *A World Made New* by Mary Ann Glendon. Eleanor's own books, the very aptly titled *You Learn by Living* and *Tomorrow is Now* are fascinating reads and show her simple, human philosophy directly. I'd also recommend visiting the full online collection of Eleanor's *My Day* columns, which can be found here: https://erpapers.columbian.gwu.edu/browse-my-day-columns

My aim, with this novel, was to concentrate on the war years, but I was sad not to have more space to cover earlier times and, in particular, Eleanor's intimate relationships, especially the one with Lorena Hickok, who was hugely important to her.

I would strongly recommend both *Eleanor and Hick* by Susan Quinn and the novel *White Houses* by Amy Bloom for anyone with a particular interest in this.

As always, bringing this book to the shelves has been very much a collective effort and I'd like to thank all the wonderful team at Bookouture, especially Natasha, Alba, Mandy, Sarah, Melissa and Kim, for their enthusiasm, expertise and all-round wonderfulness. You're the best! A big shout-out to my fabulous agent Kate Shaw, and, of course, to my home team—Stuart, Emily, Rory, Hannah and Alec. You're the best too!!

Finally, as always, a huge thank you to my readers. It's my mission as a historical fiction writer to release women from the shadows of history and, although Eleanor Roosevelt is probably the most well-known person I've written about, I hope this novel reveals the deeply human woman behind the public façade. Thank you for choosing to share her story.

PUBLISHING TEAM

Turning a manuscript into a book requires the efforts of many people. The publishing team at Bookouture would like to acknowledge everyone who contributed to this publication.

Audio
Alba Proko
Melissa Tran
Sinead O'Connor

Commercial
Lauren Morrissette
Hannah Richmond
Imogen Allport

Contracts
Peta Nightingale

Cover design
Lisa Horton

Data and analysis
Mark Alder
Mohamed Bussuri

Editorial
Natasha Harding
Melissa Tran

Copyeditor
Anne O'Brien

Proofreader
Liz Hatherell

Marketing
Alex Crow
Melanie Price
Occy Carr
Cíara Rosney
Martyna Młynarska

Operations and distribution
Marina Valles
Stephanie Straub
Joe Morris

Production
Hannah Snetsinger
Mandy Kullar
Ria Clare
Nadia Michael

Publicity
Kim Nash
Noelle Holten
Jess Readett
Sarah Hardy

RAISING READERS
Books Build Bright Futures

Dear Reader,

We'd love your attention for one more page to tell you about the crisis in children's reading, and what we can all do.

Studies have shown that reading for fun is the **single biggest predictor of a child's future life chances** – more than family circumstance, parents' educational background or income. It improves academic results, mental health, wealth, communication skills, ambition and happiness.

The number of children reading for fun is in rapid decline. Young people have a lot of competition for their time, and a worryingly high number do not have a single book at home.

Hachette works extensively with schools, libraries and literacy charities, but here are some ways we can all raise more readers:

- Reading to children for just 10 minutes a day makes a difference
- Don't give up if children aren't regular readers – there will be books for them!

- Visit bookshops and libraries to get recommendations
- Encourage them to listen to audiobooks
- Support school libraries
- Give books as gifts

There's a lot more information about how to encourage children to read on our websites: **www.RaisingReaders.co.uk** and **www.JoinRaisingReaders.com**.

Thank you for reading.

Printed in Dunstable, United Kingdom